roughing it

ALBANY ARCHER

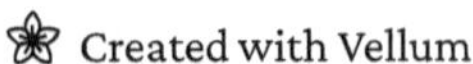 Created with Vellum

Image from Anna Fury

to everyone who loves the tension of two beautiful strangers having to share one bed

introduction

Blakely

I'm a city girl through and through—or at least I play one on social media. When a comment from an internet troll hits too close to home, I decide to show everyone what I'm made of. If this foray into the wilderness boosts my brand and gets me away from the oppressive loneliness of my life, well, even better. My guide is grumpy. Brash. A total assh...jerk. And the best-looking man I've ever seen.

It's thirty days. With one bed and one sexy country boy. No problem, right?

Hudson

I'm all about the outdoors—give me nature over people any day of the week. My focus is on my family business and my brothers. I don't have time for anything else, especially not a frivolous, spoiled social media princess who doesn't belong in my woods. But the promise of growing Peak Adventures is too good to pass up, and that's how I find myself stuck in a one-room cabin with the most infuriating—and beautiful—woman I've ever met.

It's thirty days. With one bed and one gorgeous city girl. What's the worst that could happen?

content note

This book is an open-door romance, meaning there will be on-page, explicit sexual content. Strong, descriptive language is used throughout, including during intimate encounters between the MCs.

Additionally, the book contains on-page drinking, feelings of self-doubt and loneliness, an emotionally abusive parent, parental estrangement, discussions of difficult childhood experiences including a brief mention of inappropriate behavior toward a minor, on-page near drowning, and on-page car accident with injury.

Expect instalust and love and a medium-ish burn. If these aren't your thing, you probably won't enjoy this book. But, with that said, these two go through a lot of growth. All spicy scenes are full of consent and eager enthusiasm. If you're interested in which chapters bring the heat, you can check out the dick-tionary in the back!

I've done my best to identify potential triggers, but if you see others, please let me know. Take care of your brain, your heart, and yourself!

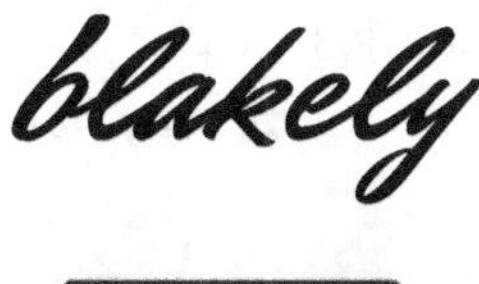

I am so totally screwed.

Wrapping my arms around myself, I stare at the flickering fireplace. *Shit.* How did this happen?

Of all the things I expected and hoped for when I started this adventure, love wasn't anywhere on the list. So how did I fall head over heels for a man like Hudson Brooks, a man built for small towns and a quiet life? A man who's everything I'm not.

My trek into the northern New Mexico mountains was supposed to show the internet trolls I'm more than a pretty face.

No. That's a lie.

It was my chance to escape the oppressive loneliness of the city and the toxic faux-friendships around me.

But love—I never saw it coming. My brain spirals, thinking of all the ways Hudson and I differ. All the reasons I should go. All the reasons I should stay.

Then my handsome outdoorsman steps up behind me— the heat from the fireplace nothing compared to that of his body—and I melt into his touch. He draws me closer, large hands brushing over my back and side, thumbs glancing the underside of my breasts before settling on my hips.

His gruff voice rumbles in my ear. "It's your last night. Tomorrow you leave. No more tiny one-room cabin for you, Princess. Unless—"

Spinning, I press my fingertips to his lips, shivering when he nips them. I don't want to talk. Think. Instead, I want to relish his calloused touch, his weight on top of me, his scent. I need to imprint this, *him*, in my mind. If I can't be brave, at least I can take the beautiful memories of the last thirty days with me to Austin.

I'll need them.

Hudson frowns, his lips turning down behind my fingers, the faint wrinkles in his brow becoming more prominent. He's waiting for me to say something. Anything. I open my mouth, then shut it because, for the first time in my life, words fail me.

"I've tried to figure out how to get you to stop talking for the last month, and now you go silent on me?" His voice is playfully grumpy but tinged with sadness. He doesn't want this to end any more than I do.

Giving him a small smile, I press my forehead against his chest and sigh. "Don't call me Princess." Then, without another word, I unbutton his shirt, relishing the sensation of the flannel as I tug it off his broad shoulders. My lips trail over his warm skin, stopping at his heart. I rest my ear there, the steady, strong beat of his pulse thumping in my head, matched only by the growing throb between my legs. It's ridiculous, the effect this man has on me.

I reach lower, unbuttoning his pants. Sliding them down his hips, skimming his powerful thighs. Then I ghost over his thick cock, and the hunger in me sharpens. I long to take him into my mouth, my body.

Hudson takes his time undressing me, stopping as he removes an item of clothing to kiss me, caress me, stare at me as if he's committing each curve to memory.

"Stay." He whispers the word against my neck between well-placed kisses.

My eyelids flutter, and I swallow hard, a lump tightening in my throat. "It's not fair to say that while your lips are on my body, Bear."

He chuckles, his warm breath against my skin igniting every nerve. The urge to erase any distance between us takes hold, and I lead him to the bed we've made ours over the last twenty-nine days.

Hudson drapes himself over me, his weight a comfort I never expected to crave. A comfort I didn't know I was missing.

The significance of our last night together hangs over us, but then Hudson kisses me, a deep, bruising kiss that curls my toes, and my worries cease. I part my lips, letting the taste of him wash over me. With a soft curse, he pulls away, blazing a trail down my jaw to my neck, the rough edges of his teeth grazing against my skin, making me shudder.

His molten mouth moves lower, taking one of my sensitive nipples, worrying it with his tongue and teeth until I'm arching on the bed. At the moment I need it most, he switches to the other side and repeats his sensual onslaught.

"Fuck me, Blakely, you have the best tits." He cups my breasts in his calloused hands and pushes them together, nuzzling his face against my already hardened peaks. While he toys with my breasts, he pushes his knee against me, and I work myself against him, chasing the friction I yearn for.

A gentle *tsk* is the only warning Hudson gives me before pulling his knee back, and the high I'm pursuing slips away.

"So eager. We have all night. Need you to be patient."

Like a petulant child, I shake my head and pout.

"My bratty Blakely, you better watch that lip, or someone's gonna bite it."

At his words, I push my bottom lip out further and stomp my foot into the mattress for good measure.

With a laughing huff, he nips my lip and gives my inner thigh a sharp spank. The little sparks of pain send a surge of lust coursing through my body.

"Hudson... I need you."

"And I told you to be patient. If you're a bad girl, I'll keep you right on the edge, aching to come, dripping and desperate until the sun comes up."

Do I want that? Yes. No. Maybe?

His lips trail down my body, leaving no room to focus on anything but his mouth and its journey. He breathes against my stomach and kisses his way lower, lower. Cruelly skipping over where I want him and nibbling the back of my knee instead. His fingers inch up my legs, their path languorous. I wriggle—a fruitless attempt to get him where I need him—but all he grants me for my effort is the barest brushing over my pussy.

Can he hear the throbbing radiating from within me?

"I plan on savoring you." He looks up from between my thighs. "Especially if this is our last night together."

His words stab my heart. I want the pain gone; I want him. Only him.

"Please, Bear." The voice whispering in the dark belongs to a woman on edge, and I startle, realizing it's my own.

The power he has over me should be disturbing. We're still strangers in so many ways. Losing myself so easily to anyone should have me clamping my legs shut and running for the hills, but for him, I burn from the inside out. A wanton fire consumes me, one water can't tame. No, the only way to extinguish it is more fuel. I have to be consumed and turn to ash in his arms.

Blessedly, he slips a finger inside me, and I squeeze my thighs together to keep him there.

"Open your legs, Spitfire. I promise I'll give you what you want. Let me take care of you."

His sexy voice curls around my ears and down my spine. I relax my hips and let my legs splay out to the sides, and he rewards me by adding a second finger. I purr, happy to have something, anything, in me, stoking the fire. When his tongue sweeps against me in a wide, flat stroke, time loses all meaning; sensation is all that remains—his fingers, tongue, and teeth. The fire rages.

He lifts his head, forest green eyes glittering, beard and mouth damp. "I'd bathe in this pussy forever if you let me. You gonna make a mess, baby? Give me a shower?"

A wildfire of desire courses through me. "Hudson, wh-when you say things like that... oh, fuck me. Pl-please keep going." I ache for more. For release. For him to douse the flames. But he keeps adding tinder. A third finger slips into me, the stretch pushing to the delicious line where pain and passion dance. His mouth locks onto my clit, alternating between swirling circles and sucking pulses.

"Moan for me, Blakely. Give me those noises."

Beholden to his command, I cry out. Thick, rough fingers search and scissor in me; his tongue tickles and teases me. The pleasure he's giving me reaches its peak.

I am aflame.

It's too much and not enough. I whimper, my over-sensitive clit needing a break but the rest of me screaming for more. I squirm in his grip, and he relents, pulling his fingers out of my quivering pussy. He places one last chaste kiss below my belly button, leaving goosebumps on my skin as he licks his way back up my body.

He positions himself at my entrance, but I hold a hand up. With a smirk, I swirl my finger in the air, losing myself in the look he gives me. With a hungry growl, he flips us, guiding my spread legs over his hips.

A queen on my throne, I gaze at the delicious man beneath me, drinking him in. Everything about Hudson calls to me. Like one of his snares, he's the perfect bait to lure me into his depths.

He watches me as though I'm precious and rare. There's awe in his eyes. And something else. Something deep, primal, ancient—a song sung for millennia.

Love.

"Fuck. You're a thing of wonder. I need in you. Now."

Tingles of anticipation shoot through me, every nerve primed and wanting. The fire inside me roars back to a blazing inferno, demanding to be burned out. There's no more room for patience in either of us, and, in one fluid snap of his hips, I take every inch he has to offer.

"God, Hudson, you feel so good."

"You were made for me, Blakely. This hungry pussy is where I belong. I have to stuff my dirty girl. Isn't that right? Your greedy cunt needs my cock."

"Y-yes!"

"Tell me. Say you need my cock."

"I need it!"

Hudson slams me down as he thrusts upward. "I said, say you need my cock. Word for word, Blakely. Say your greedy cunt needs my cock."

Pink rises from my sternum to my cheeks. It isn't embarrassment at his filthy words—it's pure heat. "My greedy c-cunt needs your cock. Give it to me, Bear!"

I tighten my walls around him and rotate my hips, the rhythm between us rapid and reckless. Hudson's thumbs brush my nipples before wandering lower to my hips and guiding my thrusts, forcing himself deeper and deeper into me. I let out a gasp when his teeth latch onto the sensitive spot where my shoulder and neck meet. Euphoria floods my system, and it's all I can do not to float away as he pants against my neck. I claw at his back, his shoulders, his hair, searching for any purchase I can find.

His nimble fingers flick my clit, and the first thrums of my orgasm blossom. A soft pinch and the pure pounding of his wide cock hitting the perfect place inside me plunge me deep into the cooling waters of release.

Burning. Ash. Relief.

My plaintive sob echoes in the dark. The swirling endorphins of my emotional release battle my panic at the thought of leaving him. The desire to tell him. The need to stay. My head falls forward, and tears drop onto his skin as he drives into me.

"Fuck, Blakely, are you okay?"

"Yes, don't stop," I stutter through my tears. In this moment, we're as close as two people can be, but I want more. I grasp his dark brown hair, as though this will allow me to pull him tighter to my body. Tether his soul to mine.

Reading the signs of his impending release, I squeeze my innermost muscles and roll my body in tandem with his faltering thrusts. One more tight clench of my pussy around him, and he spills inside me. The warmth spreads from between my legs to my heart.

Lifting my face, he thumbs away the tears on my cheeks and brushes delicate, sweet kisses over my forehead, nose, and lips. For all his gentleness, he still steals my breath.

"What happened?"

"I-I'm embarrassed." I try to hide, but he tightens his grip on my chin, lifting my face so I can't look away.

"What do you mean? After everything we've been through and learned about each other? We've seen each other in ways neither of us expected." His voice drops, growing husky. "I've touched every inch of you, licked every inch of you. Seen you vom—"

I cut him off with a glare and a kiss.

Chuckling, he continues, "Why are you embarrassed?"

"I..." Refusing to let the words die in my throat the way they have so many times over the past few days, I whisper, "*Iloveyou.*" Then I squeeze my eyes shut, childishly hoping it means he can't see me either.

"Open your fucking gorgeous eyes and look at me." The command in his tone, the same command that riles my feathers and curls my toes, has my gaze snapping to his. "I love you too, you beautifully infuriating creature."

Just like he has from the beginning, Hudson sees me.

Crushing his mouth to mine, my stomach flutters at his admission. He lifts me ever so slightly, our shared releases dripping down my thighs, then Hudson rolls us so he's on top. Somehow he's hard again. Still hard? Whatever the case, he slowly pushes back into me.

This time, there's no rush or urgency. The pace is unhurried. Purposeful. His lips skim along my jaw before moving to my ear and down my neck. Everywhere he touches prickles. Another orgasm crashes over me, but it isn't a fire—instead, it's a cooling, calming balm. A soft, sweet release sealed with murmured I love yous and promises I fear we can't keep.

We lay in each other's arms, my cheek resting against his sweaty chest. I trace lazy swirls in the smattering of hair there. The cabin is quiet, the air filled with our commingled scents.

The man I've grown to love over the past month guides my face upward and presses his forehead to mine. "Stay."

The single word holds more power than any other we've shared. Heavy. Loaded with expectations and fears and dreams. *Stay.* How can four letters weigh so much?

New tears form. How many times did he try to have this conversation, only for me to avoid it? But now, time is up, and once again, words fail me.

How can I leave? How can I stay?

"Hudson, I..."

He's everything I never expected to find: a partner to share my life with, to love, whose strength and spirit keep me from being so alone. With him, I can just be. The good, bad, and ugly of me on display, yet he wants it all. The choice should be easy, right?

Hudson holds me tighter without saying anything, trailing his fingers up and down my back and making soothing shushing noises against my hair before climbing out of bed. He's back in a flash, a rag in his hand. He takes the time to kiss away my tears and clean me up, then gathers a pile of blankets and wordlessly leads me to the front porch.

Together, we cuddle on the swing in the crisp night air—fall doing its best to fight off winter's will. I snuggle in, the warmth of his hard body putting the blankets to shame. We sit, wound in each other, taking in the rustling of the trees, the chirps and croaks of the nocturnal wildlife, and the twinkling of the stars. So different from the noisy, bustling city I once thought of as home.

Now, the idea of leaving this behind makes me ache for fresh air, sunsets that make you cry, a tiny cabin in the middle of nowhere, and the man who challenges me, frustrates me, and loves me.

Can I give up everything—my career, my cushy life, the city, being *Blakely Bradshaw*—and stay here with him?

"Rest." Hudson's lips brush against my ear.

The gentle rocking of the swing, the heat of Hudson's body, and the way he caresses my hair—all on the heels of my mind-melting orgasms—has my brain surrendering its fight. Sleep weighs me down, and I sink into my Bear's arms, hoping against hope tomorrow won't find us.

blakely

FORTY DAYS EARLIER

"Don't forget my BBs; today only, you can use code BBHairCare for twenty percent off your purchase of a custom shampoo and conditioner set from Stellar Strands."

I toss my expertly colored honey-blonde locks, ensuring the light hits them at the best angle to emphasize the shine. "And as always, thanks for joining me in today's live! You guys are amazing. Remember, if you can't make it to a live, they are available in my stories after they end!" I give the camera a picture-perfect smile and inflect my voice to maximize engagement and convey sincerity. I'm a master in the art of connecting with people I've never met.

With a wink and a kiss, I sign off, hearts, likes, and comments flowing in, propelling the serotonin boost only social media can give my needy brain. It floods my veins, and like an addict, I chase the high daily. But it never lasts.

Already, the buzz is slipping away. As I pack away my ring light and stand, the quiet inside my apartment surrounds me. Of course, there are ambient noises. Downtown Austin is never truly silent. I tilt my head, soaking in the sounds—the endless symphony of car engines, tires on roads, the never-ending construction, university students and workers making their way home—the nameless hum of a place alive and vibrant all hours of the day. Usually, I love it and the welcome distraction it brings me. Tonight, though, it isn't enough.

Lately, I've been questioning everything about my life, which is ridiculous. On paper, I'm goals. Money comes in a steady stream. I have a manager who keeps me booked with local events and online companies, connections with cosmetic and clothing stores, and over a million followers across my various social media channels. I'm living the new American Dream.

So what's missing?

Someone to share my life with. That's what, or rather *who*, is missing. While I excel at connecting with people through a screen, I can't do the same with the ones I see every day.

My ex made our lack of connection crystal clear when he publicly dumped me for another local social media ingenue—one with a fast-rising star—on the eve of my thirty-third birthday. Turns out he'd been sleeping with her pretty much the entire time we were together. Months later, I'm still recovering from the sting of that fiasco.

I put on a brave mask, of course. Made jokes about not falling into the standard post-breakup blues. No drunk dialing, no cutting bangs, no sex relapses. I actually did a whole series on it. It did killer numbers.

But what do I have to show at the end of the day? A perfectly lonely apartment with a stunning view of downtown Austin. Each room is carefully curated for peak return on investment, not because I like the color scheme or uncomfortable designer furniture. Those same rooms sit unused by anyone besides the woman who cleans twice a month.

Ugh, I need to snap out of this pity party, stat. This isn't who I am. I'm Blakely Bradshaw. Influencer. South by Southwest darling. Living my best life in the eyes of the public.

Squaring my shoulders, I scroll through my contacts, passing by friends' names, not texting any of them. If I'm totally honest, *friends* is too kind a word for ninety percent of the names in my phone. What's less than an acquaintance but more than a stranger? Most see me as one of two things: a free ride or a way to boost their fledgling social media careers.

Still, a hanger-on who pretends to listen is better than being alone in my too-empty apartment with my too-loud thoughts, right?

I pause on Mia's contact info. She's the best of the worst. I can always count on her for a fun night, at the very least.

> Hey! Free tonight?

MIA
> Depends.

Typical.

> How about dancing and drinking?

MIA
> Always. Folklore at ten.

Plans for the evening set, I scrounge up a pre-made meal from the fridge and pop it in the microwave. As I ponder my existence and wait for my keto lasagna, a notification interrupts my thoughts. A peek at my phone screen causes instant regret.

It's one of *those* notifications. Do I maybe have a few

keywords set up for immediate notification? Yes. Are they specifically focused on negative things? Also yes. Am I financing my therapist's beach house? Triple yes.

Bracing myself, I read the snippet visible on the screen.

UR such a spoiled little rich girl who can't do anything

Sliding my thumb along the lock screen, I pull up the full message.

UR such a spoiled little rich girl who can't do anything. Getting by on your looks. It's not like you have any actual talent. Must be nice to be a drain on society.

I waste no timing in deleting it. This one is mild. Worse comments come in on a regular basis. While I definitely give too much power to the way others view me, there are some comments I'm numb to. Being called spoiled and talentless are two of them.

When I first started, the comments from nameless, faceless trolls telling me how wretched and awful I am hurt. I took them personally. Cried.

A lot.

Now, I manage to ignore all but the worst. I like to say I'm coping by forcing myself to grow thicker skin. My therapist disagrees with me. She says I have a negativity bias and a tendency towards rumination. I say coping is coping.

Though it's possible the paid professional is right.

Hours later, I slip past the line and enter the crowded club. All I want is a night of dancing and drinking. If I happen to flirt with a gorgeous specimen, so be it. I'm not taking anyone home, but it's always nice to be appreciated.

Mia sidles up to me, her glossy black hair piled in messy ringlets on her head, a gold dress clinging to her curves. Her phone is already out, one platform open and livestreaming. She pulls me into the frame, and immediately, I'm on.

I curl the tail of my ponytail around my finger and grin into the camera, tilting my chin to let the overhead disco lights bring out the blue in my eyes. I do a little shimmy, the sparkles in my wide-leg jumpsuit setting off my tan. Squishing my face to Mia's, I giggle. "Hey, y'all! My girl, Moments With Mia, and I are painting the town red tonight! Hit us up if you're out and about."

Giving the camera my signature wink and kiss, I slip out of the frame and visibly relax, my posture dropping, no longer worried about playing up my angles for the camera.

Flagging down the bartender, I bat my lashes. "Margarita on the rocks, no salt." The heady combination of lime, tequila, and triple sec burns so good. Each sip mixes with the heavy pulse of the electronic music. Together, they drum out any lingering negative thoughts, and I fall into the steady beat until my worries and loneliness fade away.

I'm not lonely. I'm surrounded by people.

Right. Me and my two hundred closest friends.

No, brain, we are not going there tonight. Fresh drink in hand, I make my way onto the dance floor and let the music drive my body. It doesn't take long for a handsome college-age boy to slink up next to me. Oh, the confidence of youth. Whatever. He can dance, and that's what I'm looking for tonight.

Several songs and another margarita later, I wriggle a finger at College Boy. "Any chance you're headed to the bar? I'd love a bottle of water." My vowels are getting long. My West Texas slips out when I've had a couple of drinks.

College Boy doesn't seem to mind my accent. He nods eagerly and races to the bar.

See? Totally not alone. Or lonely. I've got College Boy. Though I'd prefer it if he took two steps back.

Mia nudges me, dancing into my space. "Find a puppy to do your bidding?"

I shrug. "He's sweet. I figure he's probably thirsty, anyway."

"Oh, he's thirsty." She pops her hip. "Taking him home?"

"No, he's too young. Have to throw him back."

Mia's loud laugh draws attention to us. As if on cue, we both smile. You never know when your picture could end up online.

Leaning in, I raise my voice enough to be heard over the music. "Do you ever get tired of it?"

"What?"

"This. The attention and having to always be picture ready when you're out, even though we really aren't anyone worth mentioning. Being alone when you're surrounded by people."

Her sour look throws me. "Speak for yourself. I am absolutely worth mentioning. Don't drag me down just because you have self-esteem issues now that you're firmly in your thirties."

Before I can reply to her catty remarks, she glances behind me with a smug grin. "Your puppy is back."

Well, hell.

Another hour of sweaty dancing and strong margaritas has me feeling no pain. No doubt. No fear of being alone. Nothing but the music and the booze.

And College Boy's hands in places they should not be. Nope. Not happening.

Slipping out of his octopi-esque hold, I give him what I hope is a non-annoyed smile. "Hey, um..." Crap, what's his name? "Thanks for the dances, but I'm calling it a night."

"Cool, let's get out of here."

"No, sorry if I wasn't clear. I'm going home alone."

He frowns. "Seriously? You're bailing on me?"

"I'm not sure what you think is happening." He stares at me like I owe him something. I am so not in the mood for this. "It's been a long day. Enjoy your night." I spin on my heels and make my way to the exit, but a hard tug on my arm stops me in my tracks.

"Don't be such a tease. With the way you killed those drinks and how you were dancing on me, I figure you're more than down." College Boy is close enough for me to smell the beer on his breath.

"Excuse me?"

"Your friend told me you play hard to get and like an aggressive alpha-male type. She said that's what older women are into." He tilts his head towards Mia, who smirks and gives me a wave. "So let's go to my place, and I'll show you how much of a man I am."

I can't help it. I bust out a loud cackle. He's got to be shitting me.

College Boy's face darkens, and his hold on my arm tightens. But for the life of me, I can't stop laughing. If this twenty-two-year-old man-child thinks he's showing me anything else tonight, he's got another thing coming.

With my free hand, I snag my phone from my jumpsuit pocket and text the bouncer, Glenn. Pro tip: it pays to know who's mixing your drinks and working the door. Seconds later, the reassuring shadow cast by Glenn's massive frame melts my tension away.

"This kid bothering you, BB?"

Jerking out of the butt munch's grasp, I turn big eyes on Glenn. "Yes. He doesn't understand that no means no, and you guys have a zero-tolerance policy."

"Damn straight we do." Glenn grabs College Boy by the

collar, and in a blink, I'm back to being alone. Only this time, I don't mind it so much.

Mia bolts over, faux worry playing on her pretty face. "BB! Babe! Are you okay? I can't believe the puppy put his hands on you!"

I don't even pretend to believe her. Instead, I scowl without speaking until she squirms.

"Whatever the kid told you, I had your best interest in mind."

Putting on my sweetest smile, I step closer to Mia. "Telling a random guy in a bar I like aggressive men, that's in my best interest?"

She waves dismissively. "Please. He was harmless. Friend to friend, you need a good dicking. You've been off ever since Ryan dumped you. Maybe you should try to get him back."

"He cheated on me."

Mia shrugs. "Yeah, but he's so good for your brand."

So much for sisterly solidarity. I beeline straight to the exit. I need out of here. The club, yes, but maybe the town, too.

The early October air cools my skin, and I let the background noise of the city calm me. Twenty minutes and one chatty rideshare later, I'm home, scrubbed of makeup and College Boy's touch, curled up in the one room in my showplace apartment that is truly me. It's also the only one I never film in. No, this space is all mine.

Pulling my plush purple comforter to my chin, I scroll through my socials. I thumb through my feed, ignoring the snarky comments and hearting the kind ones. I'm about to close out the app, ready to be done with the day, when a tagged post catches my attention. It's me at the club, dancing with College Boy. Great. I have a margarita and a far off expression as I sway to the music. The caption says *Blakely Bradshaw is a bitch and a tease. Left me high and dry tonight after acting like she wanted it all night.*

That little punk. Expecting sex from a partner because they danced together, or for any reason, is dangerous. I'd like for someone to teach him a lesson. With their fist.

My damn cat-killing curiosity gets the best of me, and I open the comments. The most liked ones are at the top, my attention instantly drawn to them.

urMomisafour: That's bullshit, man. Girls like that are always cock teases. Think they're too good for us regular guys. Love to see her try and live without her team of stylists and sycophants for a week. Doubt she'd even make it twenty-four hours.

InsrtScr33nHere: Right? Bet she's ugly as shit without all that makeup and filtering.

OverIt: Naw, she's still a fox. With a personality like that, she'd have to be.

GeekGuad: Someone should drop her spoiled ass in the middle of nowhere, Naked and Afraid style. I'd tune in to that train wreck.

Maybe it's the lingering effects of the alcohol or the adrenaline from the drama on the dance floor, but these random comments spark an idea. One that will get me away from this place while affording me guaranteed content. It's perfect.

For the first time in days, a real smile pulls at my lips. I can't wait to spring this on my manager.

"Dammit, Kirk! This is a great idea!" I spring up, my chair falling over with my sudden rise.

Kirk raises his slim shoulders. "Blakely, it's a fantastic idea, but also dangerous. An unknown guide, the wilderness. Maybe we should pitch this idea to Ryan?"

I squeak at the sound of my ex's name. "Ryan? Are you shitting me right now, Kirk? No way. One, he'd never be willing to leave town for a month. Two, he's never lived anywhere besides Austin. Three, he's a douche canoe."

Kirk fights off a grin. "I'm not sure your third reason is valid to the discussion. And to your second point, despite how you grew up—"

"I can't believe we're having this conversation."

Holding his hands out placatingly, Kirk motions me to sit. "Calm down. I'm not saying no."

At my glare, he stops talking. "It's my idea, and it makes more sense for me to go! Besides…" I inhale slowly and flip personalities, pushing down my anger to draw on my social media darling voice, the voice I perfected as I became *Blakely Bradshaw*, social media influencer extraordinaire. "The buzz will be amazing; I'm the ultimate city girl. The draw of me spending a month roughing it in the country practically writes itself. Documenting my experiences—hiking, communing with nature, shooting a bow, or whatever you do in the wilderness." I play dumb and wave my hand as I continue, not giving Kirk a chance to stop me before I've said my full share. "People love a fish out of water story, and there's no cuter fish than me. Admit it. I'm right."

Anxious pangs flutter in my stomach when Kirk doesn't respond right away. His sharp brown eyes take on a far-off look. The one that means he's running through potential liabilities, pros, and cons. He's the best at his job; there's no question about it. He's taken his roster of social media clientele to entirely new levels in the few years he's managed us, picking up several musicians and artists along the way. International investors are knocking at the door, looking to buy into his management firm and expand it.

"Blakely, we can make this work, and it's a fantastic idea. But, and don't take this the wrong way, look at yourself." Kirk grabs me and walks me down the hall to one of the many full-length mirrors mounted around KJ Media Management headquarters.

I wink at my reflection, my face fully made up, my nails recently manicured, my blonde hair perfectly styled. Then it hits me—Kirk's point. Can I make it thirty days without all this?

Straightening, I meet his gaze in the reflection. I've never been one to back down from a challenge, and I'm not about to now. I drop the *Blakely Bradshaw* shield and let Kirk see me— the real me.

"I need the break away from," the words are thick in my throat, "my lonely apartment. Away from having to be on all the time."

He gently squeezes my bruised arm. Concern floods his features at my flinch. "BB, what happened?"

"Nothing I couldn't handle. Honestly." I slip off my cardigan and show him the light bruises on my skin. Before he can say anything, I cover the marks. "Last night, some kid at Folklore didn't get it when I told him I wasn't interested. Coupled with Mia's reaction and some feelings I've been fighting for a while now, I... I need this, Kirk."

Desperate for a change in subject I flash a bright smile, thankful when Kirk lets me play pretend. "Plus, I'm no fool. I didn't make it this far without knowing a good shtick when I see one. This is a career-changing move."

I face my manager and friend, shoulders back, head high. "People will tune in just to watch me fail—I won't," I say with a toss of my hair, "but it'll draw tons of fans and haters alike."

"Fine. Fine. I'll take care of the arrangements. I'll ensure you have Wi-Fi at the cabin to upload stills and large recorded videos. Depending on where you end up for this, the unlimited data on your phone will hopefully work for live spots."

Kirk paces around me as he works through the logistics of the things I wouldn't have considered. "A week should be plenty of time to find a guide, get your things in order, buy gear, map out a few stock posts, and reach out to sponsors. We'll need transportation—flights possibly—and a car service to drive us; that way, I can at least see you off before leaving you alone for a month."

In a teasing tone, Kirk adds, "You'll have electricity and indoor plumbing, but the idea is to see you in the country. The untamed wild. Maybe leave the beauty queen look and designer threads at home?"

Tapping my chin, I hum. I'll have to really streamline my morning routine.

"So, assuming I can find someone willing to agree to this, what's their plus?"

"It's a ton of free publicity for their business, plus a month with me in a cabin. Who wouldn't want that?" My stomach rolls when I think of College Boy's grabby hands.

As if reading my mind, Kirk bumps my shoulder. "Yes, you're right, of course. But I mean it, Blakely. If you're doing this, I expect daily lives, stills, and check-ins, if for no other reason than to make sure you don't get chopped into pieces during a livestream. God, can you imagine the press?"

In a deadpan voice, I say, "Yeah, my getting turned into a wind chime would devastate your bottom line." Kirk blanches at me. "What? You missed that episode of *Criminal Minds*? All kidding aside, if you don't want me to get killed, don't pick a weirdo!" I can't help but smile. I trust Kirk to thoroughly vet whoever he picks. He'd never send me into any sort of danger.

Kirk rubs his forehead. "If you weren't so damn good—"

"We both know you're going to give in. Stop fighting it."

He purses his lips, and I know I've won. Fist pumping in triumph, I crow, "You won't regret this, Kirk. This will be massive!" With a giddy grin, I kiss his cheek, laughing at the blush heating his skin.

"Get out of here. I need to call my husband and tell him I'll be late." He dismisses me, his words softened by the friendly tone. "Finding someone who can handle you won't be easy."

The high I get from social media, the buoyant lightness that only comes with likes and comments, fills me now. This time, though, it's even better. I created this happiness for myself. I made this happen.

As I bounce out the door, I call back, "I don't know what you mean. I'm a dream, and you know it."

hudson

I adjust the bill of the stiff baseball cap harder than necessary. I can't get the damn crease right. Of course, this wouldn't be an issue if my jackass middle brother hadn't pilfered my favorite hat before leaving on a ten-day wilderness retreat.

Asshole.

I reread the sticky note he left me, then crumple it and toss it away. *Needed one that's already broken in* with a goddamn smiley face as if that makes up for it. Fucking Gray.

Our business phone rings. I ignore it. The same number's been calling off and on for the last couple of days, but seeing as I don't know anyone in Austin, I let it ring. If it's someone wanting to book a guided hunt or excursion, they'll leave a message. Is it bad business to not answer? Too fucking bad. I have a shit ton of paperwork to do.

And a hat to break in.

In the fifteen years since my family moved to Trail Creek from the Panhandle, we've owned and operated a jack-of-all-outdoor-trades business. Fly-fishing, guided hunts, hikes, rafting—even skiing and snowboarding lessons in the winter—Peak Adventures does it all.

We've done well for ourselves, so much so that our parents took early retirement, leaving the business for my brothers and me—mostly me—to run five years ago. Since then, we've added ATV tours, cabin rentals, corporate wilderness retreats, and survival training.

Gray's out on a combo corporate retreat and survival training with the bigwigs of some tech company from Albuquerque. Lucky bastard. I'd trade places with him in a heartbeat. Give me the quiet and beauty of the northern New Mexico landscape over spreadsheets and invoices any day of the week, but someone has to keep us in the black. And technically speaking, they requested anyone but me.

Apparently, I came off as *rude* while booking them. I'm not rude. I just don't have time or patience for wishy-washy weekend warriors who can't decide what to book. Yeah, I can be direct, but give me a straight shooter over a bullshitter. If I ruffle a few delicate feathers, so be it. No sweat off my sack.

With a grunt, I refocus on the blue-light glow of my multiple screens. Fucking paperwork. Did the font shrink when I wasn't looking? I'm squinting at the tiny numbers when my youngest brother's voice startles me, and I delete an entire row of data. *Shit.*

"Looking for your readers, old man?"

"Ha, you're real funny asshole. I'm thirty-five, not seventy. Why are you here, anyway? Thought you took that bachelor party from Santa Fe fly-fishing."

Bo shrugs and plops into the chair next to my desk, kicking his feet up. "Already met our limit."

"And where are the paying clients now?" I can't help but notice the twitch behind my eyelid coincides with Bo's arrival.

He grins at me, the same one that gets him out of trouble

with our parents and into trouble with the single women in Trail Creek and the surrounding areas. "Dropped 'em off at Ava's and told them to order the stuffed sopapillas. I'll pick them up after I clean and bag their catches."

"And then?"

"I'm taking them to the hot springs. It's like a strip club without the cover charge." He waggles his dark eyebrows at me.

I lean back in my chair and cross my arms. "That's not true. It's gonna be you and twelve other dicks in a giant pool of hot water."

Bo's easy laugh has my lips curving up in spite of myself. "You're not lying, brother. It'll be a sausage fest, but hell, they paid for two full days. Gotta keep our ratings up."

Ratings. Reviews. Fucking social media. Another aspect of this job I hate. I stay as far away from all that as possible. Gray and Bo have better temperaments for it, anyway. They are the ones who reply to customers and post "thirst traps" with our brand in the shot. Hell, I didn't know what a thirst trap was until I stumbled onto one of our socials and got a full view of my baby brother's bare ass.

If I had my way, I'd do nothing but guide work, and the rest would sort itself out. Despite the entire world revolving around social media, you sure as shit won't catch me on camera cheesing it up or bro-ing it out. What could you hope to gain from strangers on the internet fawning over you? Seems like a waste of time and energy and a vapid void for people who need their egos stroked.

I'll leave that to the younger Brooks brothers. Of course, the town eats it up, too. Saul, Trail Creek's daddy figure, scolds Bo and Gray for being "salacious," but the old man loves the attention it brings. Their most recent post supposedly went viral. Peak Adventures collaborated with several other Trail

Creek businesses, including the Great Dane, Flora and Fauna, and Davis Designs, for a cross-promotional series.

What a bar, a tattoo parlor, a custom home builder, and our company have in common besides being in Trail Creek and guys in their thirties willing to take their shirts off on camera is a mystery to me. Still, Bo and Gray assure me the post is business-minded and garnering positive attention. They also pointed out it wasn't just men; the Davis women were involved as well—as if that makes it better.

My gut says my brothers use that crap to score dates rather than drive up business. But so long as they keep me out of it, they can do what they want. The socials are their domain.

The phone rings again—same Austin number. Again. Bo jerks his head towards the phone. "You gonna get that?"

"No."

With a sigh, Bo snags the phone from its cradle. "Peak Adventures, the wild is waiting. Bo Brooks speaking."

I'm at a disadvantage, only catching Bo's side of the conversation, but my hackles rise when he cuts his eyes to me with a shit-eating grin.

"Yeah, man, I remember you. How goes it?... You saw that? What'd you think?... Ha, no, he's usually not. And strictly speaking, he doesn't know he's in it."

The twitch in my eye kicks up to double time. I frown at Bo, who has the sense to look away. I swear if he used me in that video without my permission, I'll knock the laughter clean off his ugly mug. Bo knows damn well how I feel about that nonsense.

"He's stubborn... Oh, trust me, I know who she is... Now that's interesting... No, I agree. It's a fan-fucking-tastic idea... You've called how many times?... Shit, I'm sorry... Yep. He's standing right here giving me the evil eye."

Pure mischief colors Bo's features as he thrusts the phone into my hands. "It's for you."

Shit.

"Hudson Brooks. Who's this?"

People aren't my forte. But they especially aren't my forte when I've overheard half a conversation that has my blood pressure doubling.

"Kirk James from KJ Media Management in Austin, Texas."

"I don't know what a media manager is, much less why you'd be so desperate to get ahold of me. Care to clear things up?"

When he doesn't answer, I huff. "I'm a busy man. You want something. So lay it out or hang up." Shit or get off the pot, buddy.

"Of course. How inconsiderate of me. I've attempted to contact you over the past few days."

I snort. That's an understatement. Seven calls in two days, not counting this one.

"Look Curt—"

"It's Kirk, actually."

My eyes drift to the ceiling as if the recessed lights can grant me patience. "Kirk, let's cut to the point. Why have you been chasing me like you're a dog and I'm the tail?"

The mystery man, Kirk from Austin, laughs. "I spoke to both of your brothers. They were incredibly helpful and mentioned yesterday and today would be my best opportunities to get a hold of you as you'd be working alone in the office."

What the hell? I grunt, the only indication I'm still on the line.

"If you don't mind, let me start over. I'm Kirk James, and I manage Blakely Bradshaw."

He pauses. Like those words should mean something to me.

When I stay silent, he gets the hint. "If you aren't familiar with her, Ms. Bradshaw is a well-known and popular social media infl—"

"Let me stop you right there, Kirk. I'm not interested."

"You don't even know what I'm going to say."

"Don't need to. I have zero interest in anything to do with some city girl who makes her living off social media."

Bo nudges me and mouths, *"Hear him out."*

I glare at him. Covering the mouth of the phone, I say, "I'm not doing this shit."

"Listen to him, Hudson. You need—"

"You're lecturing me on what I need? When's the last time you went to the dentist?"

My little brother waves my words away. "You need to get out of your rut, man. You've been stuck for six years. Plus, it'll help the business." Bo grins, knowing he's said the magic words.

Blowing a breath out of my nose, I count to ten. Through gritted teeth, I say, "My brother thinks I should let this ridiculous conversation continue. Enlighten me, Kirk."

"My thanks to Bo, then." He chuckles, clearly not intimidated or put off by my tone. Have to admit it earns him a point in my book.

"As I was saying, I manage Blakely Bradshaw, a social media influencer based out of Austin. She's looking for a new adventure, one that would be lucrative for her but also for the person who's at her side during this little experiment."

"Experiment? Speak plainly. What are you asking for?"

"I want you to spend thirty days with Blakely in one of your most secluded cabins. Take her on hikes, teach her to fish—all the things you'd do with one of your wilderness or survival retreats, but on a one-on-one basis. And I want you to let her film portions of it for use on her social media channels."

I sit without speaking, trying to process the layers of bullshit wrapped around this request. "One more time?"

"You and Blakely. One month. One cabin. You teach her survival skills and show her out in nature without the trappings and conveniences of the city around her. She films it."

Damn. That's a lot to take in.

"Why are you asking me to do this? Both my brothers would be more than happy to play lapdog for some socialite or whatever the hell this woman is. Me? I have no interest in this."

"Which makes you perfect."

Not the answer I expect.

Kirk somehow interprets my grunt of confusion. "Blakely has a reputation. It's not bad, but she's known for being this perfectly put-together pretty girl. She's ready to shake things up. And she has some personal things to gain from an experience like this."

"I'm supposed to take her on some kumbaya spiritual journey? Let her reconvene in nature? That's not what I do. If I agree to this, and it's a big fucking if, I'll treat her the same way I would any other Joe off the streets. No special treatment."

"That's what she's looking for. And if I may speak bluntly, it's exactly what she needs."

His words intrigue me more than I care to admit.

"Again, not saying yes, but bottom line, how does this ridiculous publicity stunt benefit me and my business?"

"Daily live spots and posts, plus sponsored posts along the way, will go out to her followers. She promotes Peak Adventures and you. Mr. Brooks—Hudson—I can all but guarantee your business will double from being connected to her."

I glance over at my brother, who holds up a sticky note that says, "*Say yes!*" If I roll my eyes any harder, they might fall out of my head, but the idea of our business doubling intrigues me. Maybe I should cut back on the caffeine. Or get laid. Something's gotta be affecting my ability to think rationally.

"And if this goes to hell in a handbasket?"

"If this doesn't bring in the numbers I'm expecting, you'll be fully compensated for your time. But I can already tell this is going to be huge."

The words are out before I can stop them. "So, what's the expected timeline?"

And with that, I find myself the reluctant leader of a one-on-one wilderness encounter with some social media princess. What the fuck am I thinking? The last time a city girl swept into Trail Creek, I ended up with a broken heart. Now I'm putting myself in close quarters with another one?

Fucking hell.

As we work out the details, Bo dances around the office. He's already texted Gray, who is blowing up my phone, too. Fuckers. They've known this was coming for days.

Kirk clears his throat, catching my attention. "Good luck, man."

I can't stop my scoff. "Luck? I don't need luck. I'm an experienced outdoorsman and she's staying with me. If anyone needs luck, it's the spoiled city girl. She has no idea what she's in for. Like I said, no special treatment. This isn't a day spa."

He chokes back a laugh. "I wouldn't lead with calling her spoiled." He pauses, his voice thoughtful, when he finally speaks again. "She may surprise you. The moment I read the reviews on your business, and you in particular, I knew the two of you would make for a fascinating dynamic."

"What is that supposed to mean?"

"You'll see. I've got a good feeling about you two, though. And my gut is rarely wrong."

Kirk hangs up, leaving me staring at the phone and wondering what in the name of Johnnie Walker Blue I've gotten myself into.

CHAPTER FOUR

Heavy pounding on my front door wakes me from a deep sleep. I bolt upright and shove the sleep mask up my forehead. A second round of knocking has me checking my phone screen for the time. Who on earth is here at seven-thirty?

"BB! Come on!" Kirk's muffled voice snaps me out of my sleep hangover.

Shit. Today is day one of my Austin exodus. Kirk told me—a few times—he'd be here early. We have a long day ahead of us to wherever he's taking me.

At another hard knock and Kirk's mumbled threat to pick the lock, I stumble out of my bed and scramble for the door, my colorful curses melding with the steady knocking.

Wrapping my robe around me, I fling the door open, and Kirk gives me a knowing look. "You overslept."

"I swear, I set an alarm! Just give me—"

He kisses my cheek. "I knew you'd be late. The good news is, I'm here thirty minutes early. This isn't my first Blakely Bradshaw rodeo."

I bump his shoulder in mock anger and jut my lower lip out

in a pout. "Then the least you can do is make coffee while I get ready."

Like magic, Kirk pulls one arm from behind his back, revealing a travel mug. He waggles the cup out of my reach. I make grabby hands, desperate for the nectar of life the tumbler holds.

The first sip of coffee, rich and creamy with the perfect amount of caramel, helps push the haze of sleep from my mind. I whisper to the lid, "Ah, my beloved. How I've missed you."

Kirk snorts. "I hope for your sake, and his, you have access to a coffee maker."

I freeze. "Wait. Is there a chance it won't?"

"You're going from here," he gestures around my apartment, "a luxury high-rise with all the amenities you could ever want, to a one-bedroom, one-bathroom cabin in the woods. Yeah, BB, there's a chance there won't be a coffee maker."

"That doesn't work for me." I trail off, trying to figure out if I can cram my Nespresso into one of my overstuffed suitcases. "The place surely has a percolator, at least. No one's that savage."

Under his breath, he mutters, "Seriously, Mr. Brooks, I wish you the best of luck."

Thirty minutes later—exactly as Kirk predicted, the clever bastard—I'm ready. As I fasten oversized hoops in my ears, I say, "My bags are in here."

Kirk stares at me for a beat.

"What? Do I have a stain or something?"

"Remember when I said today would be a long day of travel?"

"Yes."

"And remember how we talked about leaving the full Blakely Bradshaw look here in Austin?"

"Yes." I smooth my palms over my belly-baring top and high-waisted wide-leg jeans.

He gestures to my heeled boots. "You're a little over-dressed. You look fantastic, don't get me wrong." He ducks his head at my scowl. "We have a flight to Albuquerque and then a three-hour car ride. Are you sure you don't want to wear something a little more casual? Maybe tennis shoes? Those boots cannot be comfortable."

Shit. He's right. I dressed the way I usually do. This is fine. No biggie. Not a massive setback and a sign I'm destined to fail at this whole *back-to-basics* experiment. "Give me five."

He nods, and I scramble to my closet, searching for a cute but comfortable travel outfit. When I rejoin him, I'm confident I've nailed it. How can you go wrong with athleisure wear?

"Come on, Kirk. Be a gentleman and help me with these bags. Marcus will kill you if he finds out you didn't offer to help." I bite my lip to keep the smile off my face. He loves me.

Kirk grabs the first bag with a huff, almost falling over at its weight. "What did you pack in this thing? Rocks?"

"No! Only the necessities, like you said."

"Four suitcases are the necessities? Oh, my bad. I meant four suitcases packed to the brim and weighing in at a metric ton each are just the necessities?"

"I may have overdone it a little, but I don't know what I'm walking into! You haven't told me where I'm spending the month, so I have warm clothes, cool clothes, a variety of shoes and accessories, my makeup, my skincare routine, my hair straightener and curler."

Kirk's raised eyebrows stop me mid-list.

"Okay, I may see your point. You said we are flying into Albuquerque? At least tell me which direction we're going from there. Fall in New Mexico could be comfortable, like here, or cold if we're higher in the mountains."

"We're heading Northeast from there. I recommend warmer clothing." He shoots my thin yoga pants and cropped high-neck tank a critical once over.

"I was planning to wear a cardigan."

He points to my platform sneakers. "So along with warm, I also suggest some of the more practical items you have."

"Fine." My eyes bounce from suitcase to suitcase, something suspiciously similar to failure flitting around my chest. "I need more time."

"I figured. I was actually an hour early. Let's see if we can narrow this down." His calm smile has some of my nasty doubts melting.

He's such a sneaky little shit. And I couldn't be more thankful for it. Or him. Even if I do help fund his lifestyle, he's still the most trustworthy and nicest person in my life.

Jeez, that's depressing.

"Earth to BB. You there?"

Kirk's teasing and the waft of coffee beneath my nose pull me back from my mini spiral. "Oh, yeah. I'm ready to make the hard cuts." Opening the nearest suitcase, I pull out items. "My custom shampoo and conditioner? Necessity. My custom perfume? Not a necessity. See? Easy."

A blush heats my cheeks when Kirk fixes his gaze on the fluffy blankets and extra pillows. When did I become this person? I survived for much longer with much, much less. Thirty days is a walk in the park. I've grown accustomed to things a certain way, but my determination and pride are riding on this, too. I'm not just a spoiled social media star.

With renewed determination, I dump out the entire bag and then do it again three more times.

"Get the ring light, Kirk. If I have to pack all over, we may as well film it."

Kirk grins. "This is pure gold already."

The tiny town of Trail Creek is picturesque. Hell, it's adorable. Its pristine downtown square, four stop lights, and mom-and-pop shops are giving me major flashbacks. I grew up in a place like this—a tiny West Texas town straight off the set of a made-for-TV romcom, at least on the surface—but the shiny, happy facade of my childhood hometown hid a hideous inside. One full of people who love to judge and gossip but never do a damn thing when you actually need them.

Panic claws at my throat. What am I doing? I ran at seventeen and never looked back. Swore I'd never end up in a one-horse town where people think they know everything and look down on you for it again.

People still think they know everything about me and judge me, but at least as Blakely Bradshaw, I control the narrative. Plain ol' Blake Lee Shaw never had that luxury.

"BB, you okay?"

I force a smile to my lips. My *on-air* voice slips out. "Of course! I mean, look at this little hamlet. People will eat it up. I can already picture the Stars Hollow comparisons in the comments. Can you grab some rolling shots through town for me?"

"For sure. And you're right; it's charming."

Swallowing back a sour retort, I point out the window. "Is that a bakery? Let's grab a snack."

As soon as Kirk and I step inside, the rich aroma of coffee roasting perks up my mood and attention.

"Hi, welcome to The Bee and The Bean." A young girl in her mid to late teens greets me while the pretty woman beside her goes wide-eyed.

"Blakely Bradshaw? Oh my gosh, I follow you! You're really here." The tall woman comes around the counter and extends her hand. "I'm Clairy Davis, welcome to Trail Creek."

I silently curse myself for suggesting we stop. I don't look awful, but I do look like I've been traveling for six hours. And thanks to the whole *only packing necessities* thing, I don't have my travel bag of emergency makeup. I smooth my high ponytail and turn my smile up to eleven.

"Hi, it's nice to meet you. What is this magical place?" I'm laying it on a little thick, but being extra nice will offset how I look. Plus, this might be the cutest place I've ever been that serves pastries and coffee.

The younger girl answers, "This is my aunt's place, The Bee and The Bean. Why are you here?"

Clairy scolds, "Waverly, mind your manners, or I'll call your mom." To me, she says, "What Wavey means is, how can we help you? Coffee? Baked goodies?"

I fixate on the pastry display, indecision and regret running through my mind. What am I doing? It's day one, and I already wish I was back in Austin.

In my lonely apartment.

With my lonely life.

No. Nope. I need this. And carbs. One more perk of this adventure? Leaving the packaged meal lifestyle behind.

"If you're torn, I recommend the sea-salt croissant with a drizzle of honey. It's one of our most popular items."

"Sounds fantastic." I surprise myself by meaning it and answering in my normal voice.

Waverly studies me. "You sound different. Less *Alexis Rose-y*; it's better."

"Uh, thanks. Do you and your aunt want to grab a selfie?"

The cute gray-eyed teen shrugs.

Clearly, she's not my target demographic.

Clairy bustles around packing my pastry and a coffee to go before slipping into frame with her niece and me. Once we finish taking pictures, Clairy thrusts a massive bag into my arms.

"What's this? Not one croissant." The heft alone tells me there's way more than a single treat.

"I figure anyone willing to spend a month alone with Hudson Brooks deserves all the carbs she can eat."

At my bewilderment, Clairy lays a warm hand on my arm. "Sorry, I didn't mean anything by that. Hudson is great, really. Everyone in town loves all three Brooks brothers. Bo and Gray, Hudson's younger brothers, have been talking about you for over a week. They're excited about what this could mean for their business."

Bo and Gray are excited, but surviving Hudson requires pastry. Interesting. I flick my eyes to Kirk and find him pink-cheeked and looking anywhere but at me. Yeah, that's not suspicious. What have I gotten myself into?

Fixing my face, I beam back at her. "Oh, no. It's fine! I only have the company's name. Peak Adventures. Kirk here forbade me from doing any Googling. He's a real taskmaster."

Kirk's snort lessens some of the tension in my shoulders. Clairy grins at him. "Yeah, he looks like it."

I wave at both Clairy and Waverly. "Bye, ladies. It was nice meeting you. Thank you for the bonus pastries! DM me so I can tag you in our picture."

With that, Kirk and I slip back into the quiet of the rented car.

As we pull away, I glare at him. "What's wrong with him?"

Hands up, Kirk gives me his best puppy dog eyes.

"Nuh-uh. Spill it."

"You trust me, right?"

"You know I do."

"Then believe me when I say he's nothing you can't handle."

Of course, I can handle the mystery man. I can handle anything life throws at me.

We pull up in front of a cute, westward-facing A-frame office. The Peak Adventures sign displayed front and center is bathed in a mixture of oranges, purples, and reds as the sun sinks behind the not-so-distant mountains. Like everything in this quaint town, it's picture-perfect, which suits my needs.

As Kirk unloads my bags—two, thank you very much—I position myself in front of the building and take advantage of the lighting. Angling my camera so the Peak Adventures sign is visible, while also granting myself a flattering angle, I snap a variety of shots. I thumb through the pics, deleting the obvious nopes until I narrow it down to the top two. Slap on a filter, add a caption, and voila, post done. The second I post, the number of likes jumps.

Seeing those hearts gives me my fix of serotonin. This is going to work. I'll spend thirty days away from the drama of fake friends, creepy college boys, and my lonely apartment. When I return to Austin, it will be with scores of new followers and a clear head, ready to tackle what the future holds.

Stretching my neck and back, I ask, "So, where is this guy?"

Kirk gives me a slight frown. "He's in the office. He texted me saying he'll be out shortly to greet you, but I have to get back on the road, or I'll miss my flight."

My nose wrinkles. I thought he'd be here out front. It's kind of rude, but oh well. Whatever.

"Yeah, you get going. Don't leave Marcus waiting too long; you know how anxious he gets when you travel without him."

A dreamy smile lights up Kirk's face at the mention of his husband. I'm not jealous at all. Totally happy for them. I don't wish someone missed me enough to worry when I travel.

Sure, Jan. Keep telling yourself that.

"You've got this, BB." Kirk wraps me in a hug. "It's going to be life-changing. Beyond ratings or followers, I hope this brings you whatever you're really searching for."

His words stay with me long after the car disappears into a speck in the distance. What *am* I searching for?

When the universe doesn't answer me—that bitch—I sigh and spin, crashing nose-first into a solid wall of muscle. Two large hands reach out to steady me before dropping away. The warmth of their grip, even for that brief moment, sends tingles down my spine.

Righting myself, I say, "Thanks, sorry about that. I didn't see you..." My words trail off as I catch sight of who I ran into.

Holy shit. My walking wall is gorgeous.

Drop your jaw, melt your panties, please have my babies gorgeous. His tousled dark brown hair is perfect for tugging. And no man this rugged should have such full, kissable lips. Mix that with his square jaw, almost hidden by his dark, trimmed beard and strong brow, and my ovaries are dancing a conga.

But the real kicker? In a startling beautiful contrast only the human face can hold, this brawny, burly, built by the outdoors man has a smattering of freckles across the bridge of his straight nose and cheeks. Cute wouldn't be the first, second, or tenth thing to spring to mind when describing a man like this, but damn if those freckles don't scream the word. They give a boyish charm to what would otherwise be a brutally handsome face.

He's delicious.

The sound of his throat clearing pulls me from my perusal. My cheeks burn as I meet his gaze, and what I see there knocks the air from my lungs. The pine trees surrounding us have nothing on the green of his eyes, but it's the intelligence, curiosity, and—if I'm not mistaken—annoyance shining out of them that locks me in place.

The next thirty days will either be the best thing I've ever done or the worst mistake I've ever made.

Extending my hand, I introduce myself. "Blakely Bradshaw, but I'm sure you already know that. You must be Hudson Brooks?"

He doesn't take my hand. Which... awkward. He studies me, starting at my roots and ending at my toes. I shift from foot to foot, uncharacteristically squirmy just from his presence.

"Can't say I've ever heard of you."

Ouch. That'll leave a bruise on the ego.

Already chafing under his stare, I snap, "Do I pass inspection?" If I'm a teensy bit bitchy, I don't think that can be held against me. He still hasn't taken my damn hand.

A smirk—as if this sex god incarnate needs anything else to push him into the *do me now* category—tugs at his lips. "Load your bags. We've got an hour on the road and need to get there before full dark."

"Load my bags? You aren't going to help?" I glance around, hoping Kirk will miraculously reappear.

"Nope. You're on my time and turf now, Princess."

My mouth drops open at the nickname.

I'm set to give him a proper tongue-lashing, but he continues. "And rule one is you schlep your own shit. If you can't load it, you can't bring it." He spins on his heel and climbs into the waiting Jeep.

Well, hell. Mistake takes the lead.

hudson

I watch as the most beautiful woman I've ever seen tries and fails to load her suitcases into my Jeep.

Once my hands brushed Blakely Bradshaw's smooth skin, I knew I was in trouble. Does it justify my being an asshole and hiding in my car? Probably not, but I need space before I do something stupid like ask her if she'll wrap her thighs around my head and let me wear her like a pair of earmuffs.

What the hell am I doing? Besides holing up in my Jeep, hoping she didn't spot the outline of my cock against my zipper.

I haven't reacted to a woman like this ever. Not even with Paige, and I thought she was the one. I snort. *The one.* More like the gone.

There's a loud thump behind me, and I twist in my seat so I can enjoy the show. Blakely stands with her fists on her hips, glowering at one of her rose-gold suitcases, which now lies in the dirt.

This has disaster written all over it. What's this city siren doing out here? Does she think she can hang with me, learn from me, for thirty days? She can't even lift her goddamn suitcase. When she stamps her tiny foot before kicking the immobile luggage, I let out a bark of laughter.

That gets her attention.

Blue-green eyes, ocean eyes—and not the murky shores off Galveston, I'm talking somewhere exotic—stare at me wide and glistening with unshed tears. Her cute button nose scrunches, and she's honest to god pouting, her puffy, biteable as fuck lip pooched out. What I wouldn't give to run my teeth over it.

"I need help. Can you please put my bags in the car?"

Every word ends in *uh* and is sweet enough to give you a mouth full of fucking cavities. It's also fake as hell.

"Sorry. No can do. I told you, Princess, if you can't carry it, you can't bring it."

The pout and big doe-eyes disappear, leaving a spitfire in their place. "Don't call me Princess. My name's Blakely, which you'd know if you'd bothered to introduce yourself after plowing me over outside."

Yep. Knew it. Her natural voice is much more mellow, the vowels a little longer, and no more of that annoying vocal fry bullshit. She almost sounds like she grew up in the Panhandle or West Texas. Interesting.

I rest one arm on the steering wheel and raise an eyebrow. "I plowed into you? If memory serves, you slammed that pretty face into me."

"Yeah, well, you're still a jerk who didn't introduce himself or shake my hand. And who won't help me load my bags!"

"Good counterpoint," I say, my voice dry as a bone.

"Ugh, you're the worst!"

"No, you're just a spoiled city girl used to getting her way."

Blakely's mouth opens, but she snaps it shut and makes

another feeble attempt to lift her suitcase into the back. She gets it halfway in before losing her grip.

"What am I supposed to do?"

"Figure it out, or leave it behind. Either way, do something quick. I'm hitting the road in five minutes, whether you're loaded or not."

"You won't leave me here. I'm the customer!"

"I absolutely will leave you here. When I agreed to this shitshow of a circus you've brought to my door, it was with the understanding you'd follow my rules. Or didn't your boss tell you?"

A little *hmph* sound pierces the air. "Kirk is not my boss. If anything, he works for me." Her arms cross, pushing her more-than-a-handful tits together. My cock would look fantastic sliding between those while bumping into her pouty pink mouth.

Fuck. I've got to get a grip on my hormones. I'm thirty-five, not fucking fifteen.

"Tomato, tamato, Princess. Still doesn't get your bags in the car."

If looks could kill, the daggers Blakely shoots my way would be my demise. The next thing I know, the driver's side half-door swings open, and a small finger pokes me.

"Listen here. You and I will spend the next thirty days together and have a grand old time doing it. I've got goals. Plans. Things I want to learn about myself. Things I want you to teach me while I'm out here. So put those muscles to good use, you bear of a man, and help me load my bags so we can get to the great motherfucking outdoors."

The boner from earlier roars back to life at her fiery outburst, and my chest tingles where she poked me. A steady stream of thoughts runs through my head, none of them related to being outdoors—apart from a single highly detailed one where I chase this gorgeous creature through the pines until I catch her and fuck the sass out of her. The image of the supple skin of her back, red and raw from being pressed into the bark of a tree, my lips soothing the sting away while she slumps in my arms a pliant, sweaty mess, has me adjusting myself once again. If I don't stop this train, I'm gonna come in my pants.

Shaking my head and forcing that last image out of my mind, I crane my head. "Did you call me a bear of a man?"

"Yes! I mean, look at you all massive, with that sexy dark beard." She gestures at me before her mouth drops open. "I didn't mean sexy. I mean scruffy. Your scruffy beard. Like a shaggy bear."

"Scruffy. Whatever you say, Princess."

"Do. Not. Call. Me. Princess."

"Spoiled? Diva? City Mouse? Pick your poison."

Another flash of anger has her tight little body tensing. "You can call me Blakely. Ms. Bradshaw, if you're lucky."

My lip tugs up in one corner. Fuck if that isn't sexy.

She smiles at her own joke before it falls. "My *friends* call me BB. But most, with the exception of Kirk, don't like me, so I guess BB would fit for you, too."

I frown at her, pondering her words. "I don't dislike you."

"You've got a funny way of showing it." Her muttered words are barely audible.

Dammit. Rubbing my hand down my face, I swing my legs out of the Jeep and jerk one of her bags off the ground. "Come on. I'll load this one, then help you with the other."

She blinks once. Twice. "You're breaking your rule?"

"Guess I'm in a giving mood."

Blakely squeals and jumps to hug me, knocking the suitcase from my grasp when her arms wrap around me, and her legs come off the ground, trusting I'll catch her.

"Thank you! I swear, I only brought the essentials. If you follow me, you'd know I started with four bags this size before we left Austin. I pared it down to these two."

She says it with so much pride, like she deserves a goddamn gold star for bringing fifty pounds of crap instead of a hundred.

And damn if I don't want to give her one.

Her chest presses against mine, and the sweet scent of her hair tickles my nose. She smells like summer. As if realizing where she is, she stiffens and wriggles out of my grasp.

Clearing her throat, she says, "Now that we've settled baggate, care to do a quick live with me?" She snags her phone and waves it at me.

"Hard pass, Princess."

"I told you not to call me that. It's a super short check-in. It doesn't have to be live; we can do a recording, and I'll upload it while you drive."

Before I can turn her down again, the camera is on, and her entire disposition changes. She's back to using that fake affectation when she speaks, her smile tugging at her lips but failing to meet her eyes.

"Hey, BBs! I finally made it to Trail Creek, New Mexico. You won't believe how quaint and quiet it is. When you book your trip here, whether for winter snow fun or summer swimming, make sure you check out The Bee and The Bean; the coffee and bakery items are amazing."

I watch in disbelief as she stretches the word *amazing* into an orgasmic sound.

"Um, also, I met my guide, the capable and climbable Hudson Brooks of Peak Adventures." She gives the camera a conspiratorial wink and playfully tugs at my arm. When I scowl, a quick flash of annoyance flickers across her face.

Pouting into the lens with a dramatic whisper, she says,

"He's a little camera shy, BBs, but I promise you, he's a snack! Scratch that; he's the whole meal."

The overwhelming urge to grab her and shake her until the camera falls to the ground is a powerful temptation I'm hard-pressed to resist. I can picture it. Her pink lips parting to tell me off before my tongue slips between them and explores her mouth. The sweet taste of her filling my senses. Her lush body pressed against mine, my hands gliding up her legs, cupping her rounded ass...

I shake my head, clearing out the vivid images. Focus on the annoyance, not the breathtaking beauty.

She gives one more giggle and signs off. Once the camera is out of sight, Blakely rotates her shoulders and cracks her neck, then spins toward me. The twin pink spots high on her cheeks hint at her anger. The words out of her mouth confirm it.

"You couldn't even wave? What is wrong with you, Hudson? Kirk explained how this works. Part of the arrangement is you being on camera!"

"I will be, but only when I want. I'm not your puppet."

I leave her standing there, mouth open, eyes blazing. I grab both bags, toss them into the back of the Jeep, and climb in. Sixty seconds pass, and she still isn't in the goddamn passenger seat. After another thirty, my patience cracks, and I lay on the horn.

"Get in now, Spitfire, or I'm leaving you here."

"Jeez, you're a jerk!"

She purposefully takes small, slow steps, dragging her feet before finally getting in. As if she can't help herself, she stands, popping her head out of the uncovered roof, fucking phone in her hand.

I shouldn't do it, but the draw to mess with her is too strong to ignore. Without saying a word, I slam on the gas, tires screeching as we peel out of the parking lot.

Blakely jerks forward from the momentum, then scrambles to sit. "Are you trying to kill me?"

"Nope, getting us on the road. We've got a way to go, and it's hard enough in daylight."

"You could have asked me to sit."

"I asked. You must not've heard."

"You did not, you liar. You're pissy because I didn't jump when you said get in the car. In case you can't tell, you're not the only one with a strong will."

I'm certain of that. This woman is made of will and fire and spunk and sass. I clench the steering wheel so hard my knuckles turn white.

Blakely leans in and brushes her lips against the shell of my ear. "That's a tight grip you have there, Bear. Do you have lots of practice?" She flutters those long lashes. "Gripping things, I mean."

A growl slips out of my throat, and I look at her, our faces dangerously close. One inch and I can have the kiss I imagined. Her ocean eyes run over me like a physical caress. She moves a millimeter closer, the scent of cherries on her lips.

"Eyes on the road, Hudson," she whispers as she sinks back into her seat.

The way I want to thread my fingers in her hair and pull her back, kiss that sassy mouth until I know it better than my own. Drawing a steadying breath, I remind myself she's a client—an annoying client who's already driving me up the wall.

We don't make it five miles before the questions begin. For the eighty-sixth time since waking this morning, I ask myself what the fuck I'm doing.

"So what's the cabin like?"

"You'll see when we get there."

She rubs her temples as if I'm the exhausting one. "Do you live out here full time?"

"No."

"Does anyone live out here?"

"No."

"What do you normally use the cabin for, then?"

"What is this? Twenty damn questions? How about you enjoy the scenery, the fresh air, and the goddamn peace and quiet. Isn't that why you're here?"

Her glare bores into the side of my head. Am I too harsh? Fuck, yes. But what's with the interrogation?

"Why did you agree to this? You seem absolutely miserable." The hurt in her voice makes me angrier at myself for snapping.

The steering wheel creaks beneath my clenched fists. "My brothers and your boss—" at her raised eyebrow, I amend my word choice, "your manager—were very convincing. Apparently, you're a big fucking deal. Once word you were coming got out, people in town kept dropping by to tell me how amazing you are."

"Good to know some of the people in Trail Creek have taste."

I smirk. "Now that I've met you, though, I think less of them." I hope she can tell I'm joking. Mostly.

Her tiny fist bumps against my bicep. "Ha ha, you're hilarious."

Thirty seconds of glorious silence pass. Hopefully we're done with the Q&A portion of the night.

"What about you?"

Nope. More questions. Sighing, I ask, "What about me?"

"Does your wife or girlfriend follow me?"

My laugh is harsh. "I'm single. Have been for a long ass time."

"I'd love to say that's surprising, but having met you..." Her laughter takes the sting out of her words.

The bright light of her screen pierces the growing dark around us. "I'm starting to think Kirk didn't vet you at all. Have you read your reviews?"

"What reviews?"

"On your socials and the regular places like *Yelp*. Here's one. 'Peak Adventures is amazing! Will book with them for summers to come!'"

"That's a great review."

"Yeah, but that's only part of it. Here's the rest. 'Everything except Hudson Brooks was top tier. While the man clearly knows his stuff, he's abrasive.'"

"Who said that?"

A little wrinkle forms between Blakely's eyebrows. "What? I don't know. It's an anonymous review."

"Then it's irrelevant."

"No, it's not! These reviews impact people's perceptions of you. Don't you care?"

I consider her words. Do I care what people, strangers on the internet, think of me? "Nope. Not one bit."

Her incredulous expression tells me she can't relate. She goes back to reading reviews, laughing now and then at the ones calling me rude or harsh.

"Enjoying telling me how much people hate me?"

The giggles vanish. "No. Shit, Hudson, I'm sorry. I didn't... I'm out of line."

The serious tone of her voice has me reaching over the console to squeeze her thigh. "Hey, I'm teasing. Seriously, that shit doesn't bother me. I ignore it. Some fuckhead on the internet who has enough time to write about me being a hardass is no one who matters."

Blakely tilts her head. "That's a healthy outlook on it. My

therapist would approve." Her shoulders droop. "I struggle with not reading what's written about me. Not buying into the hate."

"Who could hate you? You're so charming." I lay on the sarcasm but shoot her a wink.

When she doesn't answer, I let out a sigh and try to get her to talk the only way I know how. "Any of those reviews say I'm not good at what I do?"

"Not a single one. In fact, for every person who mentions you being... difficult, there are two more shouting your praises. And even the ones who seem annoyed by you have to admit you're excellent at what you do."

"See. Even if they don't like me, they can't deny my expertise. Their shitty opinion doesn't matter. All I'm taking from these reviews is that I'm the best."

"That's what you got from them?"

"Hell yeah, and don't you feel safe knowing you're in such experienced hands?"

Blakely's brilliant smile shows her straight white teeth. "Experienced hands, huh? I teased you about that earlier. That firm grip of yours."

I groan but play along. "I spend a fair amount of time alone. It's important to have a strong grip."

She snorts. "I bet it is."

We settle into a comfortable silence, and I use the opportunity to study her. I'm transfixed by her beguiling features, scarcely visible but for the dying rays of the sun and the beginning twinkle of the moon filtering through the heavy treeline.

"It's beautiful out here."

"Yeah. Beautiful." She catches me staring before I jerk my attention to the road.

If Blakely's uncomfortable, she doesn't show it, and the tension in my back lessens with each mile closer we get to the cabin. The cool air whips her long ponytail, her summer scent mixing with the pine.

Shit. Where did this gorgeous woman come from? And what the hell is she doing in Trail Creek with me?

I'm about to ask her when she gasps.

"I saw a deer!" Her excitement is palatable.

"There were five back there."

She stares at me, mouth open in disbelief. "Five? No way. I was looking and saw one. You're teasing me."

"Don't believe me?"

"Nope. There's no way you saw five."

"Fine. Look to your right... now."

Blakely does as I ask and squeals as two mule deer dart into the dark.

"And over my shoulder now."

Again, she follows my directions in time to catch sight of a young buck staring at the car. She spins in her seat, propping herself up on her knees to watch until we travel too far away for her to see.

"How did you do that? Are these like tame animals you feed? You know where to expect them?"

"Are they tame? That might be the most..." I stare at her for a beat, trying to wrap my head around her thinking. "No, they aren't pets. I've spent fifteen years in the forests near Trail Creek and the years before that outdoors in other places. It's my job to see them."

"Color me impressed. I mean, you're a total jackass, but at least you're a competent jackass."

That pulls an unexpected laugh from me. "I should put that on my business cards."

Her responding laugh, a real one, not a simpering giggle or curated chuckle, makes my chest ache.

I am so fucked.

CHAPTER SIX

To say I'm surprised by the cabin is an understatement. Set in a clearing surrounded by a mix of aspen, pine, and spruce trees, it melts perfectly into the scenery. It's rustic and charming, with a covered porch and swing.

But it's also small. Really, *really* small. Kirk said one bed, one bath, but I imagined a layout similar to an apartment. The reality is very different.

It's one *room*—not one bedroom, just one room. The kitchen, living space, bed, and even the large clawfoot shower/tub combo are out in the open. It's a gorgeous bath, deep and long, perfect for soaking. It even has space for two. But with only a shower curtain for modesty, I can't help but think of how exposed I'll be while using it. The only place with a door is the water closet housing the toilet and sink.

A flash of a too-small trailer, the width hardly more than my wingspan, with dingy smoke-stained walls zips through my mind.

"I'd give you a tour, but…" Hudson's gravelly voice pulls me back to the present.

Snapping on an overly bright smile, I clear my throat. At least the ceilings are high—and charming with their exposed beams. "It's lovely. I didn't think it would be so... cozy."

He chokes on a raspy chuckle like it's an unused muscle. "Cozy. That's one way to describe it." He drops his single duffle bag onto the bed and pulls out clothes, placing them into the two-drawer dresser against one wall.

"So, what's this cabin for?"

"You asked me that on the ride up."

"And you didn't answer me, so I'm asking again. If this is some sort of sex-torture cabin, it needs an update. You've gone way too homey on the vibe." This earns me a lop-sided, almost grin from him. "Really, what do you guys do with this cabin if you don't live here?"

"We rent it out."

"You have clients renting out a secluded sex-torture cabin?"

"No, we have clients renting a regular cabin." His irritation is clear, but a tiny part of me enjoys irking him way too much.

As I explore the open room, I pick up a gorgeous quilt lying on the back of the couch. "If no one lives here, why do you have such nice things? This quilt is heirloom quality."

He huffs through his nose but doesn't answer. I can imagine him pawing the ground in exasperation like a gloriously frustrated bull.

Because I can't help myself, I ask, "Are you bringing my bags in?"

He stops mid-fold—one eyebrow cocked, mouth agape—then shakes his head.

"Was that a no head shake or an I'm-disgusted-with-you-but-will-bring-your-luggage-in head shake?"

This time, he snorts. Progress.

"So, what's the game plan?"

Sighing, Hudson turns his back to me. "Unpack and sleep."

That's a more short-sighted plan than I expect, but at least he answers me. "Unpack and sleep. Sure. You know what would make unpacking easier? If you'd bring in my bags." I flutter my lashes at him.

He bites off each word. "Tell you what, Princess—"

"Blakely," I snap back.

"Tell you what, Spitfire." I don't correct him this time. Don't ask me why. "I'll bring them to the porch, but not an inch further."

I narrow my eyes. "Why? What does it hurt to bring them in?"

"It doesn't hurt me a damn bit, but it's already more than I'd do for anyone else, and I swore to your boss—"

"Manager."

"—I wouldn't give you any special treatment."

"That's so dumb."

"And bringing them in *would* be special treatment. Like I said, if you—"

I wave. "Yeah, yeah, if you can't carry it, you can't bring it."

He stands there looking at me, all cocksure and sexy. His broad shoulders fixed, his stance obstinate. If Hudson Brooks thinks he can out stubborn me, he's in for a shock. Without saying anything else, I stomp out to the Jeep. His smug smirk falls away when I stride back minutes later, clutching a sleep shirt, shorts, and a small bag with my toothbrush and other toiletries. But no suitcase.

"You left them in the Jeep?" he asks, disbelief in his voice.

"Yep."

"I give it two hours."

"I'll leave them out there the entire thirty days. If *you* decide to bring them in, I'll gratefully accept them and unpack, but otherwise, those suitcases are staying out there."

"It's dangerous here at night; you can't be running to the Jeep at all hours for your shit."

"Then. Bring. Them. In."

Hudson's jaw tenses, and his jaw tics. "Do what you want."

I push past him, beelining for the water closet, desperate for space from his handsome, frustrating, won't-bring-in-a-lady's-suitcase face.

When I step out with my teeth brushed and no makeup, Hudson's green eyes take me in.

"You look different."

My hand flies to my cheek. He's seeing Blake Lee. Her nose is wider, less of an adorable button, her face rounder, less sculpted, and her eyes smaller. What does he think of her?

Is he like everyone else? Overlooking her until she's forced to transform into Blakely, a supernova who demands your attention?

I brush my hair forward, using it as a shield. "So, one bed. Is this where those gentleman genes finally kick in, and you offer it to me?"

Hudson's full lips flatten into a hard line, then he takes two steps, eating up the space between us. With a surprisingly tender touch, he pulls the soft scrunchie from my wrist and gathers my hair into a low ponytail, pulling it away from my face.

"Why'd you hide? I said different, not bad."

My cheeks warm, and I look away, only giving him a *hmph* in reply.

He grips my chin, tilting my head back. He inches closer. Closer. And just when I expect him to zag, he zigs.

"If you think I'm giving you the bed, you've got another thing coming."

The certainty in his words sparks annoyance. And desire. Damn him.

I square my shoulders. "Oh, I'm taking the bed."

"Over my six-foot body, Spitfire."

"We'll have to settle this the hard way."

"As if there's any other option?" His smirk transforms into a full-on grin, and I melt a little. Double damn him!

Swallowing, I give him a saucy smile. "On three?"

"One, two, three. Shoot!"

DAY ONE

Hudson's lips brush against my stomach, his gaze on me as he whispers into my navel. "What do you want me to do, little Spitfire?"

I wake with a start, the deep rumble of a man's voice in my ears and an unfamiliar ceiling over my head.

"Morning, Princess. Sleep well?"

Hudson.

The cabin.

"It's Blakely, you bear." I groan and flop to my side on the couch, pulling the blanket over my head.

"Not a morning person?"

"You try sleeping on the first sofa ever made and see how you feel." The ache in my back has me gritting my teeth. I am not spending twenty-nine more nights on this couch. That much is damn sure. "What time is it, anyway?"

"Five fifteen."

I sit up, the blanket pooling around my waist. "Five fifteen! In the morning?"

"Of course, in the morning. The day waits for no one. Haul your suitcases in from the Jeep since you refused to do it last night. Then you and I are going on a hike."

"My luggage is fine where it is, but let's focus on the real mystery. Why are you waking *me* up at five fifteen in the stupid morning? Won't the hike still be there at eleven?"

"Of course, the hike will still be there. The land isn't going anywhere; what kind of question is that?"

"Ugh, you are seriously rude. I mean, why so early? What does it matter if we go now or later?"

"If we're out as the sun rises, we'll see more animals. Plus, it'll…" He pauses as if searching for the right words. "Make for compelling imagery."

"Oh, so it's prettier now? Why didn't you say that?" I eye my taciturn roommate, turning away when he catches me.

"Get your stuff and get dressed. We're leaving in ten minutes."

"Ten minutes?"

"That a problem?"

"Yes, I can't be ready that quick!"

"Sure you can. Brush your teeth, slip on some layers and hiking boots, and you're good to go."

"What about hair and makeup? You don't understand."

"Hair's easy; pull it up in a ponytail. And you don't need makeup. You're beautiful as is."

Something wild flutters in my chest. "You think I'm beautiful?"

Hudson's ears turn pink. "No."

"So you don't think I'm beautiful?"

At my frown, he stammers. "No, yes. Fuck." His hands run over his face. "I mean, you look better without all that crap. I told you last night."

"No, last night you said *different.* Which definitely doesn't mean better."

"Just get your shit and get ready. You've got nine minutes, Spitfire."

Spitfire. A shiver courses through me as the lingering memory of my dream creeps to the forefront of my mind. When Hudson lumbers into the kitchen, mere feet away from the couch, banging around cabinets, I'm pulled back to reality.

With a sigh, I make the quick trip to the Jeep and rummage around. Despite Hudson's semi-compliment about not needing makeup, if I'm going to be on camera, I have to at least do the key points. Slim my cheeks and nose and plump my lips. If I can dress in three minutes, that leaves six minutes but zero to do anything to my hair.

Okay, if I leave my hair alone and only contour my nose, I can always use a filter for any pictures to slim my cheeks, but that doesn't solve the issue of a video or live. Ugh, I need a physics degree to figure this out.

"Eight minutes." Hudson's warning snaps me to action. I scramble, my arms full, as I sprint to the small bathroom. A delicious aroma hits my nose as I throw on clothes and do a half-assed speed job on my makeup.

Coffee.

Thank goodness. At least one thing about this morning is coming up Blakely.

Eight minutes later—seriously, what's up with this man's internal timer—Hudson knocks on the bathroom door.

"Time to go."

I barely have time to check the charge and signal on my phone before he thrusts a tumbler of coffee and one of the pastries from The Bee and The Bean into my hands.

At my unasked question, he shrugs. "The pale blue bag gives it away, and it's the only thing besides what you slept in last night and are wearing now you bothered to bring in. I figured Clairy must've loaded you up. You seem like the type who needs carbs and caffeine to be tolerable."

What. A. Jerk.

I snatch the coffee and croissant and stomp past him. This better be the best sunrise in the history of sunrises.

Together, we set off, me doing my best to keep pace with Hudson's longer stride. The coffee is delicious, and the day-old croissant tastes as buttery and chewy as the one from yesterday. This isn't terrible. It's still dark out and a little chilly, but not unpleasantly so. I can totally hike.

It's clear after way too much silence, Hudson isn't going to strike up a conversation, so I do what I do best. I talk.

"What are you?"

He pauses and cants his head to the side. "What?"

"Rancher, cowboy, lumberjack?"

"Do you see a Stetson? Or any cows or horses? And lumberjack? Why on earth would you think... No. I'm not a lumberjack." He mumbles something about ridiculous city women as he shakes his head and walks away.

"So, if you aren't any of those, what are you?"

"Not sure there's a term. I guess outdoorsman?"

Outdoorsman. I test the word on my tongue and weigh it against the man who stomps ahead of me. The surety in his steps, the way he smells like a forest in the fall—yeah outdoorsman suits him.

In my live, I called Hudson a meal, but even that isn't enough. He's a buffet. Everything about him aside from the adorable freckles—Seriously. So. Fucking. Cute—says *rawr daddy.* The sunkissed skin, the messy hair hidden beneath a ball cap, the faint wrinkles on his brow and around his piney eyes. The impudent tilt of his lips when he smirks, the work-honed body...

Yeah, I'm not going down that road before the sun's up.

Another ten minutes of hiking—all uphill, I swear—and the first twinge of pain starts in my feet. I swallow around the discomfort and speed up to catch Hudson. It's less of a hike and more of a power walk.

"Do we have a particular destination in mind?"

A grunt is my answer. Loquacious he isn't.

"Some cliff, a clearing?" No answer. "You must have something in mind." Nada. "The air here is so crisp; it's almost too clean, you know?" Zilch.

My feet scream for me to stop, and I swear the path gets steeper. "I have a surprisingly strong signal up here. I worried it would be a massive dead spot."

Silence. The power of this man's selective hearing is astounding. I chatter mindlessly, doing anything to keep my mind off the steadily growing ache in my boots, the way my toes throb, and my heels slip. It's still too dark to see much, so I can't even enjoy the scenery. The only noises are my prattling and heavy breathing.

No animals. No sunrise.

Each step transforms into needles pressing into my soles. I bought highly recommended socks and boots. I did the research. What the hell is happening?

It's been hours. Okay, that's not technically true, but my feet burn like they're being roasted over blazing coals. Quality hiking boots, my ass.

"Hudson, how much further? We've been walking forever. Where are we even going?" I'm being whiney, but my feet are killing me. And I'm betting we aren't making a loop, which means doubling at least this distance to get back to the cabin.

I shudder.

"We still have a ways to go."

"A ways? What does that mean in regular measurements? And why haven't we seen a single animal? You said we had to come this early because the animals would be active."

He stops, his aggravation with me clear. "Maybe if you stopped complaining, we'd see something. No animal will come within fifty feet of us with the way you've been squawking."

"Why didn't you tell me to stop talking earlier?"

"I thought you had enough common sense to figure it out when I stopped answering your questions."

"Listen up, asshat, my feet hurt! I'm sorry I'm not used to traipsing through the mud and muck on a daily basis. Some of us live in actual civilization."

"Isn't the whole point of your little wilderness excursion to experience life in the outdoors?" Hudson's lips twist. "Where's your camera now, Princess? Don't want your fans to see the real you? A spoiled brat."

I suck in a sharp gasp at his words and fight back the prickle of tears. He's not the first one to call me spoiled, and I'm acting awful right now, but it's worse coming from him for some reason. Plus, my feet hurt, and it's barely six, and I've only had one cup of coffee, and that stupid couch was uncomfortable.

God, I really am a spoiled brat.

But he doesn't get to be mean about it.

Anger combusts, scorching away any lingering tears. "Don't call me Princess. How many times do I have to say it? You are the most insufferable, arrogant prick I've ever met. I'm going to the cabin. Fuck you, fuck these boots, fuck the wildlife, and fuck the fucking sunrise!"

Holding my head high, I spin and walk—limp—away from him, not caring if he follows or not. Five steps. Then ten. My heart clenches when I don't hear him. Okay, I care a little. I really thought he'd follow me. Which is silly. He can't stand me; he's made that abundantly clear.

A solid, warm hand on my lower back startles me. "Dammit, Spitfire. Sit. Let me check your feet." He guides me to a nearby stump. When I stubbornly stand, he growls, "Sit."

Lower lip trembling, I plop onto the stump with the grace of a cow on ice. My entire body aches. Hudson's movements are no-nonsense, quick and efficient as he pulls off my boots and socks, then lifts my feet. But they still knock loose the hibernating butterflies in my stomach.

"Shit, you've already got blisters forming."

The urge to smooth out the crease between his brows rides me hard, but I keep my hands firmly in my lap.

Like I'm made of glass, Hudson carefully slips my socks and boots back on, then helps me to my feet. "Let's get you back. A better guide would've checked your gear before we set out. I'm sorry." He hooks one arm around my waist and arranges one of mine around his back, supporting my weight.

Surprise has me freezing up. Even in the short amount of time we've spent together, I know he's not the kind of man prone to apologizing. The heat of his body against mine stirs up a yearning, the need for touch and love, for someone to care for me and about me. I fight to keep from resting my head in the crook of his arm.

"Don't look so shocked. I made a mistake. It's only right I own up to it." He smirks. "Besides, if checking your gear and getting you properly outfitted keeps you from complaining about your feet for the entire month, it's worth it."

And there he is.

When we finally arrive at the cabin, I can hardly move. The sun has fully risen now, but any potential appeal is lost to me. Even with Hudson's sturdy frame supporting me, my feet sting like someone branded them.

I kick off the hiking boots from hell, drop to the floor, and gingerly peel off my socks. My heels and toes are red and raw. And worst of all, my pedicure is completely ruined.

Hudson studies me and then, without a word, sinks to the floor and carefully takes one foot in his large, calloused hand.

"What are you—*ohhhh*." I fight off a moan when his strong fingers press into the pressure points of my arch.

I study his handsome, serious face as he works his way to my ankles and then my calves. He's close enough for me to count every single adorable freckle. If I had a lifetime, would I run out of patterns to trace?

Who is this man? His mood is indeterminable. One minute, he's scolding me; the next, he's being nice.

"Thank you."

He grunts in reply and drops my foot, my words breaking the spell between us. "Show me what you packed."

The idea of going out to the Jeep and lugging in my suitcases sends phantom pains slicing through the nerves in my feet. Biting my lip, I go to rise from the floor, but Hudson's heavy hand on my shoulder halts my momentum.

"Sit. I'll be right back." A few painful throbs from my feet later, he returns, slinging down my suitcases and squatting in front of me. "Open 'em up."

In another life, Hudson commanding me to *open 'em up* while he kneels between my legs would be prime fantasy material. It is in this life, too. That's the only explanation I have for why my answer comes out breathy. "What do you want to see?"

"Any gear you brought."

His words have the same effect as a bucket of cold water. Right. Professional.

I rummage through my bags until there's a decent pile next to Hudson. He wordlessly sorts through it and then disappears without saying anything. AS quick as he left, he's back with a small first aid kit.

"Pop your feet in my lap." I don't move, and he frowns. "Let me take care of you."

Those words send a flutter through me, dumping me right back into horny on main territory. Biting my lip to keep from saying something I'll regret, like *kiss it all better, Daddy,* I lean back into the couch cushion as he settles my feet in his lap.

"Soak in Epsom salt tonight. It'll help any muscle soreness from overcompensating for your feet." Hudson's touch is gentle as he rubs in ointment and wraps the blistered areas in moleskin. He gives each foot one last squeeze before slipping on a fresh pair of thick socks. "Your gear is good quality."

I love how surprised he sounds. "I did my research."

"It shows. The problem is leather boots like yours have to be broken in over days or even weeks. Again, that's on me. If I'd checked your gear first, I'd have noticed they're brand new out of the box."

As he talks, he grabs the demon boots, bending them and working the soles back and forth.

"Slip on some shoes that won't kill your feet and load up. We're running back to town and grab you a pair of light hikers. They'll do while we break in these sturdier ones. Ruined feet won't do you any good out here. You also need a warmer coat, gloves, and some rain gear."

"Wait, you're taking me shopping?" I raise one eyebrow. "Is this a trick?"

He rolls his eyes at me. "We leave in five. Be ready, or I'll—"

"Yeah, yeah, I know the drill. You'll leave without me."

Hudson keeps up his silent treatment the entire drive to Trail Creek and back, breaking it once to get my shoe size and once more to veto the only cute rain jacket in the entire store. Apparently, it wasn't "functional" enough for the king of the outdoors.

Back at the cabin, I once again attempt to pass the time by making small talk with him, but after my tenth unanswered question, I give up and decide to do a quick live.

I definitely don't mention the failure of the hike. Instead, I focus on the cabin itself. My BBs love the tour of the comfy cottage—and the quick flashes I give them of an oblivious Hudson in a fitted t-shirt and dark joggers. The flood of comments and reactions pump pleasure into my brain, and by the time I wrap up, I'm fizzy with the dopamine dose. It's almost enough to make me forget about my aching feet and the grumpy bear who won't speak to me eighty percent of the time. And why it bothers me so much.

I rise from my makeshift command center and shuffle to the couch, stretching my stiff body. Like a weight, Hudson's eyes drag over me, wandering my curves as I arch my back.

"See something you like?"

He freezes, his shoulders tensing. "No."

I can't resist teasing him. "I'm down to share the bed."

A blush spreads to his ears. His *I'm embarrassed* tell.

"I'm not sleeping on this couch again. You can suck it up and share the bed with me, or *you* can take the couch."

He opens and shuts his mouth before muttering, "I don't sleep with clients."

A tendril of disappointment curls in my heart. "Is that another of your rules?"

He nods, arms crossed over his strapping chest.

"Look, Bear, I'm sure you're aware of how attractive you are, but you must also be aware of your awful attitude. Trust me. When I say I'm willing to share the bed with you, the only thing I intend to do is sleep."

He grunts but doesn't say anything else. Instead, he retreats the handful of steps to the kitchen.

"Aw, you aren't afraid of little old me, are you?"

"That doesn't deserve an answer."

"What a shocker," I say to myself before speaking up. "I'll build a pillow wall between us, keep my cooties on my side. But seriously, please don't make me sleep on this medieval torture device of a couch again."

"It's not that bad."

"For an hour or two at a time, you're right. But for an entire night? No. It's worse than bad."

"Fine."

"Fine?"

He drops a plate with a sandwich and chips in my lap. "I said fine."

Wiggling my expertly bandaged feet, I collapse onto the couch among the contents of my unpacked luggage. I can't ignore that Hudson Brooks is breaking more and more of his rules for me. Or the giddy way that makes me feel.

CHAPTER SEVEN

Dropping the sandwich I made in Blakely's lap, I bolt for the porch. What am I doing? Bringing her luggage in, agreeing to share a bed. What's next? Taking her on a romantic picnic? This woman's got me disregarding every rule, crossing every boundary I've put in place over the years.

Keep the relationship clear. Client and guide. Keep the walls up. The rules serve me well. You carry your own shit. You leave when I say it's time. You sleep on the couch, or your bedroll, or tent, or wherever I tell you to.

Clients balk from time to time, but they always fall in line. Not Blakely Bradshaw. She pushes and pushes, and while it drives me batty, I also can't get enough of it. I want her to push me. Push me to my breaking point, so when I snap and kiss the breath out of her, I can have an excuse for my actions.

Plead temporary insanity. It's not my fault, officer; the bewitching goddess drove me to it.

These feelings must be guilt over not checking her boots before we went on that clusterfuck of a hike. That's all. I screwed up. What guide worth their salt doesn't check the client's gear? Those turquoise eyes filling with tears had my gut twisting and my chest aching.

I may be direct, but I never want to be the reason a woman cries—even when that woman drives me up the fucking wall with her never-ending questions, stubbornness, and sexy little body.

The faint sound of water running draws my attention. She's taking a bath. Is she using the Epson salt like I told her? Did she remove the moleskin? Is she able to situate herself? Is she wet and soapy? Does she need someone to wash her back?

My cock strains against my pants, the image of Blakely covered in suds and nothing else sending all the blood in my body below my belt. With a growl, I launch myself from the swing and stomp towards the forest line. I need to burn off some excess energy before I make a terrible, wonderful mistake.

I can't let this woman get to me. This isn't me. I'm the responsible one. The clear-headed, rational one. Not like my brothers, who follow their whims wherever they may take them. No. I'm practical. There's no room in my life for a woman like Blakely, a spoiled social media starlet who plays pretend all day. I live in the real world, where things aren't handed to you because of your name. You have to work for them.

The real world, where when you let someone in, they stomp all over your heart and throw it back at you like it's chicken shit. Where the bright lights of the city draw in women like Blakely Bradshaw like a rooster to the dawn.

Focus, Hudson. This is nothing more than an opportunity to grow the business. Help spread Peak Adventures' name. Nothing else.

Pine trees and the October air fill my lungs. Each deep inhale settles me. The quiet cleanses the desire and irritation lingering in my system—except not really, because somehow in less than forty-eight hours, Blakely Bradshaw has wormed her bratty way under my skin.

I can't pinpoint why. She's a client like any other.

Liar. My mind taunts me with flashes of blue-green eyes and honey-blonde hair. Curves that put the winding mountain roads to shame. And a fiery mouth I want to fuck so goddamn bad.

Groaning, I run my hand through my hair and force myself to focus on why this woman is wrong for me. Starting with her pampered ass complaining about the couch. I'll show her how much she's overreacting—typical princess behavior. Of course, a couch isn't good enough for her. She needs eight thousand thread count sheets and baby goose feathers or some shit.

With righteous indignation on my side, I trek to the cabin. I have enough sense to peek my head in before storming inside in case she's still soaked and slippery. Instead, I find her on the bed, my grandma's quilt tucked around her, like it's where she fucking belongs.

"Welcome back."

Instead of answering, I grab the first aid kit and work on properly drying her feet and tending the sore spots with ointment. I may have dropped the ball once today, but I won't do it again. It's my job to make sure she's safe.

"Enjoy your walk? Or whatever you were doing in the dark, alone in the forest." She grins. "I'm not saying you're giving off serial killer vibes, but..."

Fuck if she doesn't have the cutest little toes. I bet she'd giggle if I sucked them... and like a startled deer, I jerk away, dropping her foot onto the bed.

"Hey, careful." She wiggles those pink-tipped toes at me, and I retreat to the safety of the bathroom, taking my time cleaning up before stomping to the couch and flopping down. The lumpy cushions give beneath my weight, causing the springs to jab into my back. Gritting my teeth, I toss until I find a semi-comfortable spot.

"I can hear your back aching from here."

I don't say anything; instead, I tuck my arms behind my head and close my eyes.

Unbothered by my lack of response, Blakely keeps talking. "I'm so glad I brought toilet paper. Did you know you only have one-ply? It's barbaric."

"What?" Her words catch me off-guard, and I forget my resolve to ignore her.

"Toilet paper. Two-ply versus one-ply. Kirk laughed at me when I packed a twenty-four pack of the good stuff, but there are some things you can't compromise on."

I huff out a laugh and mutter, "Couch, hike, toilet paper, me. Is anything about this place good enough for you, Princess?"

"Don't call me that."

Shit, I was louder than I thought.

The lamp clicks off, and Blakely clears her throat. "I'm mostly joking about the toilet paper, though chaffing is a real concern. Thank you. For taking care of my feet, for making me a sandwich, for agreeing to this even though you hate me. This place is lovely."

"I don't hate you, Blakely." I hate she thinks that.

"It's a pretty brave thing, me being alone with you in this cabin, miles and miles away from another person. Leaving my entire world behind for a month to spend it with a stranger. It may not seem that way to you, but for me, it is. I'm trusting you, Hudson."

My heart jumps in my throat, her last words ringing in my ears. I wait for her to say more, to say anything else, but for once, she's silent.

As I drift off to sleep, she whispers, "So you know for next time, I prefer mustard on my sandwiches."

And I lay there in the dark, grinning like an idiot.

Two hours later, my grin is long gone. This couch fucking sucks. I've sat on it here and there, but I lean more towards the single recliner or the barstools. Damn if Blakely isn't right.

I toss and turn, hunting for a comfortable spot, but it doesn't exist. I'm too long for the stupid thing, too, so it's either let my feet hang off or curl up, but I'm too fucking wide to curl.

From across the room, Blakely's steady breathing stirs the still air. She's passed out cold. I don't blame her. That bed is fucking comfortable. I replaced the old one when I started staying out here on my own a couple of weekends a month.

Guess I should replace the couch, too. But you can bet your sweet ass it won't be until my Spitfire's back in the city where she belongs. Shit. Not my Spitfire. Not my anything. Just a client.

I stifle my thoughts because if I don't sleep, I really will be a fucking bear tomorrow. Yanking my pillow off the couch, I pad to the bed. We are two adults sharing a sleeping space. Nothing more.

Careful not to wake her, I slip between the sheets. She stirs a bit, and I hold my breath, hoping she'll settle. Instead, in the slivers of moonlight, I see a knowing smile.

Without opening her eyes, she whispers, "Told you the couch sucks."

Little brat.

"Need me to build that pillow wall?" When I don't answer her, she murmurs, "G'night, Hudson."

Damn, if her sleep-filled voice doesn't do something to me. In an out-of-body moment, my hand moves of its own accord and smooths a stray tendril of gold hair behind her ear.

When my roughened hand brushes her smooth skin, Blakely nuzzles into my touch but shows no other signs of being awake. She follows the heat of my palm, searching for more—like a touch-starved kitten. As gentle as I've ever been, I cradle her cheek. A soft mewl falling from her full, pouty lips is my reward.

No. I can't read into it. Her reaction is some sort of involuntary response. She'd act this way if anyone caressed her beautiful face. And what the fuck am I doing touching her while she's asleep, anyway?

Don't be a fucking creep, idiot.

I roll to the edge of the bed, angry with myself for touching her without consent and for thinking her sweet little sigh is anything more than a reflex. And for wishing it is.

She's a client. Nothing more. She'll never fit in here, never settle for someone like me. She's another Paige. A city girl playing at the country life. The refrain plays in my head until exhaustion pulls me under.

DAY TWO

Something warm and soft snuggles against me, and a waft of floral and citrus fills my nose. Blakely.

Shit. My face is buried in her hair, while her cute little nose presses to my neck and her arms wrap around my waist. One of her legs rests between mine. The only way we'd be closer is if I was inside her. My dick jumps at the thought, and I groan, willing my blood to flow to other, more needy parts of my body, like my fucking brain.

She wriggles and stretches, and just as I untangle myself from her grasp, she cracks open one eye. "Hudson?"

I grunt out a sound that could be *mornin'* if you squint real hard.

"What are you doing?" We're still wound together, and she studies me warily.

I'm painfully aware of the hard-on pressing against her hip. Fucking morning wood. And city sirens.

"Your arms are around me." And mine are still around her, but I don't point that out.

"What are you implying?" she asks but makes no move away.

We're locked in a fucked up game of chicken, neither of us willing to give in first.

"You're on my part of the bed."

"So you think we're all snuggled up because of me? If I remember correctly, and I do, you're the one who crawled into the bed last night." When I don't answer her, waves crash in her ocean eyes. "You're holding me just as much."

I pull my arms away—losing the battle—and put an inch of space between us. "It's not like I grabbed your leg in the middle of the night and put it between my thighs."

"I don't know, Hudson, maybe you did."

Her indignant huff puts a burr under my saddle. "I don't make it a habit of cuddling with city women with more shoes than sense." As I say it, I roll to my side and shift, giving her my back.

"And I don't make it a habit of talking to jerks who sleep-hug people without their knowledge."

Her words drive me to my feet, angry at my body's reaction to her, frustrated with her for curling into me, annoyed at the universe for wanting so much more. My fingers flex, and I fight the desire to cup her chin and shut her sassy fucking mouth with mine. I fold my arms. Better than accidentally giving in. "So does this mean I get a reprieve from your constant nattering?"

"Who even says nattering anymore? Who are you, Davy Crockett?"

I grunt and stomp to the bathroom, leaving her on the bed, sulky and deliciously sleep-rumpled.

To my retreating back, she hollers, "You better not take too long in there!"

The way my dick tries to jump out of my pants, it won't be long at all. In the relative safety of the only doored room in the cabin, I let out a groan and shoot daggers at my cock. Fucking traitor.

How the hell did Blakely and I end up with our arms and legs around each other? And why did it feel so fucking good? It's been years since I've wanted someone the way I want her. I swear she was safely on her side of the bed when I crawled in a little after midnight. It's nearly seven now. Did we spend the entire night that way?

I'm not a heavy sleeper, but I'll be damned if I stirred even once. Not until the scent of flowers and fruit flooded my senses. My hand drifts to my cock, giving it a tight squeeze. I dig in the medicine cabinet before uncapping the lid on a familiar clear bottle.

I work myself, using the lube to ease the rough friction from my touch, but before long, it isn't my work-worn, over-sized paw sliding down the length of my dick; no, it's a smaller, softer hand. One with pale pink polish that can't quite close around it. The fantasy takes on a life of its own, transforming to Blakely on her knees, that pouty, petulant, perfect mouth licking my cock. I grit my teeth and drop my head, my heavy pants bouncing off the walls.

Her glowing skin against my larger body, writhing, sweating, panting. Her puffy lips stretched and swollen around me. Fuck. With a groan, I come, my head falling forward, torn between satisfaction and defeat.

I've got to get a grip. Well, the other kind of grip. I flush and wash away the evidence, giving myself a stern talking-to while I brush my teeth. She's a city woman. She's not staying, and she's not interested. I'm making a fool of myself, falling into a trap I swore I never would again. After another round of reminders, I'm ready to tackle whatever the fuck today brings my way.

But as soon as I'm back in her presence, Blakely surprises me.

"Hey. Peace offering?" She has two cups of coffee and a smile. So fucking pretty. She hasn't added the armor she calls makeup yet. She's beautiful then, too, but I prefer her this way, effortlessly perfect in her imperfection.

I freeze, thinking about what I did behind the bathroom door. Fuck, I hope she wasn't there the whole time.

Her grin dims. "This morning was awkward, and we both said some things. Anyway, I don't want to spend the entire month fighting. So we spooned a little in our sleep; it's no biggie."

Our fingers brush when I take the coffee, and I swear she shivers.

I clear my throat and say, "Seeing how you aren't up to hiking, we'll get a baseline of your wilderness experience and survival skills." Something else I should've done yesterday before taking her on the hike.

"Fine. I need to get ready."

She raises a single arched eyebrow at me as if to say, *move the fuck out of my way, asshole.* So I do.

And thus begins day motherfucking two.

"No one needs to know North, South, East, and West! GPS exists for a reason. And if you don't have GPS, you give location-based directions."

I don't answer.

"You know, go past the Sonic. When you see Target, turn left."

The snort is out before I can stop it. "Do you see a Target out here? Me saying turn left at the tree won't help you."

Her lips press into a thin line.

"As far as GPS, you can't count on always having your phone with you, having service or battery. If you can orient yourself, you can get to where you need to go, no matter where you are."

She huffs. "And knots? Why do I need to know how to tie a trillion different knots?"

A flash of Blakely tied to my headboard, knots around her delicate wrists, has me reaching to adjust myself as subtly as possible. Clearing my throat, I say, "They each have a different purpose. A taut-line hitch and trucker's hitch are good for securing shelter. A figure-eight knot can help secure a harness. A—"

"Okay, Professor Knothead, I get it. Knots are everything." She throws the rope she's been fiddling with on the ground.

I try to suppress my annoyance, but I fail. We haven't even talked about fire starting, plant identification, situational awareness, or shelter building with natural materials. And it isn't happening today. We've been out here for hours—most of that spent orienting her to the cardinal directions. She's a surprisingly accurate shot with the BB gun, though.

"Can we call it a day, please? This is stupid. I'll never need to know any of this."

"So it's all for show." There's more anger in my tone than I mean for her to hear.

She has the good grace to look contrite, her shoulders rising. "No. I mean, yes. Maybe? Would I like to learn these things? Yes. Will I use them down the road? No."

"Tell you what, Princess." Heat flares on her face at the nickname she hates, but it's fucking fitting in this moment. "We'll call it a day." My lips tip into a smirk. "If you can navigate us home without using your phone."

Her pretty mouth drops open before she snaps it shut. She scans the thick band of trees and rocky trails around us. We're a fifteen-minute walk from the clearing, but I can tell by her demeanor she's lost.

Crossing her arms, plumping those perfect tits of hers, she says, "I hope you're prepared to sleep outdoors because I have no idea where we are. The asshole who is supposed to teach me to navigate by the sun and moon or whatever sucks."

"Only one of us will have a problem sleeping outdoors, and it sure as shit isn't me."

With a huff that could knock a pig's house down, she spits, "At least point me in the right direction."

It takes forty minutes—forty minutes in which she only speaks to gripe at me. But she's so damn pleased with herself I don't have the heart to tell her how badly she did.

There's another rule broken.

I sip a glass of whiskey and watch Blakely at her makeshift command center talking to Kirk while dinner cooks in the oven. I don't mean to eavesdrop, but it's a small fucking cabin. Besides, I only understand half of what they say; the rest sounds like code—stills, trending, streams, sponsorships, branded posts.

Once she finishes, she glances around. I mirror her actions, chuckling to myself. How she demolished the space is beyond me. She's been here two days, and it looks like a bomb went off in her suitcases—the clothing, shoes, and toiletries scattered like shrapnel.

I'm not such an asshole that I didn't offer her a drawer in the dresser, but she refuses to use them, opting instead to dig through her bags. Taking another long pull from my glass, I shrug. Her shit, her business. Even if it makes me twitchy.

The little slips of lace especially.

Blakely's voice pulls me from my panty-laden fantasies. "I'm doing today's live spot on the porch swing. Want to join me?"

"What, don't want your adoring fans finding out how much of a slob you are without someone to pick up after you?"

I can just make out her blush under the makeup she's wearing, but it's there. *Ding, ding, ding.* Hit the nail on the head.

"No," she sniffs. "The porch swing is a more interesting location. They've already seen all the inside has to offer."

"Whatever you say." I follow her to the porch and plop down on the swing. She's close enough that I can feel goosebumps arise on her skin when our knees brush. Blakely grabs my bicep, using it as leverage while making herself comfortable. My arm tingles where she touches me, and I keep checking to make sure it isn't actually trembling.

The swing starts with a soothing sway. For a moment, I pretend this is my real life. Sitting on this porch in the twilight with a gorgeous woman at my side.

Then she turns the goddamn camera on and opens her mouth.

"Hey there, BBs!"

I cringe at her too-high voice, her vapid giggle, her mask, but if Blakely notices, she doesn't show it.

"Today, I'm coming to you from the porch swing. I know, right? A real-life cabin porch swing. Can you believe it?" She giggles into the lens before panning the open clearing. "Look at this view."

The way she flips back and forth between herself and the clearing is seamless. It'd be impressive if it weren't so ridiculous.

"The cabin is amazing—*sooo* rustic and cozy—but the best part is this porch! Hudson and I have spent hours out here communing with nature and enjoying the fresh air. Say hi to my BBs, Hudson!"

Blakely angles the camera to catch us both, but my face hardens in a frown. As quick as the camera is on me, it's gone.

"Okay, now that you've seen him live, I know you're drooling. He's the total package: handsome, good with his hands," she says, winking into the lens, "and a fantastic teacher. I've learned so much from him already. By the end of the month, I'll probably be able to lead my own wilderness training. And don't forget, you too can book your next adventure with Peak Adventures when you visit Trail Creek, New Mexico. Keep tuning in for more pictures and updates! Take care, my BBs!"

The livestream ends, and Blakely tosses her phone beside

her. I watch as her mask slips away. It's oddly fascinating, like a snake molting its skin.

"Lead your own training? I'm an amazing teacher? You called me an asshole and said I sucked a couple of hours ago." I raise both eyebrows and look at where she's slumped.

She wiggles a bit, then shrugs. "I'm not going to make you look bad."

"Why not be yourself?"

The confusion and hurt on her face make me wish I could swallow the words. But one thing I've gleaned since meeting Blakely, she doesn't stay sad for long. Her irritation overpowers all other emotions, and I find myself on the wrong end of her tiny pointed finger. Again.

"I *am* myself. You don't know me, Hudson. You've spent two days with me."

"Spitfire, I know more than you think. A key part of my job is the ability to observe."

She scoffs, but I barrel ahead.

"You raise the timbre of your voice and put on this superficial affectation when the camera comes out. You titter like a schoolgirl, and let your IQ drop ten points. You don't want your so-called fans to see you fail. You don't want them to see your mess, but that's the real you. I've learned all that in two days."

Despite the warning bells, I lean in and whisper, "If you drop the armor, what will I know about you in thirty?"

"You want to learn more about me?" Her words are faint, to the point they sweep away with the wind.

I tuck a piece of hair behind her ear. "You're the most frustrating—"

She opens her mouth, no doubt ready to verbally smack me, but my hand is there, cupping her chin.

"And fascinating person I've ever encountered."

Her eyes lock on mine, but now they hold a different heat. I curve into her, our lips within inches.

We are close enough for little puffs of her air to slip into my lungs when she speaks. "Do you have any idea how long it's been since someone wanted to know me? The real me?"

She shuts her eyes and angles her head. Those petal pink lips part. Half an inch more, and I could taste them. My nose brushes hers and...

With a jolt, I slam my feet onto the porch, bringing the swing to a dead stop and bolt into the cabin, leaving a stunned Blakely in my wake.

CHAPTER EIGHT

Things that suck about sleeping in a one-room cabin? There's only one room. Want to take a bath? I hope you don't mind clingy shower curtains because that's all that separates you from the open air. Need to use the bathroom? There's a door, but you know exactly who was in there before you. And when. And for how long.

Not to mention, when you almost kiss someone, and they reject you, there's nowhere to run. Oh, and you have to sleep next to them. Because in addition to only having one room, you only have one bed.

I always loved the one-bed trope, but it's clear to me now —all those authors are snake-oil peddlers who sold me a lie. It's not cute. It's not romantic. It's. The. Worst.

Now I have to sleep on this cloud of a bed under the family heirloom quilt his grandma made and act like our near kiss didn't happen. It's a good thing I have excellent denial skills— on the outside, anyway. Internally, I look like *The Scream* come to life.

I'm actually reconsidering the devil's couch at this point.

But that would mean going inside, and right now, I'm glued to the porch swing spiraling from Hudson's dismissal. A litany of past humiliations—a mental playlist I like to call Blake Lee's Epic Fails—starts as if cued by a director.

Young me, sitting on the rotten front porch of our trailer house while my mother combs nits out of my hair, crying and begging her not to do this outside where people can see. Getting my period at a sleepover and not knowing what to do, so I stash the stained blanket in a closet and run all the way across town to get home. An evening spent with an older guy at the lake, and he has to explain what sixty-nine is because when he asks me to turn, I think he means my back to his chest.

Eesh. And these aren't even *bad* memories, just embarrassing ones.

While I'm frolicking down shitty memory lane, the sun sets, and the temperature drops. It's October in the mountains, and the difference between Austin and Trail Creek is apparent. But I can't bring myself to go inside. Partly because of the smarting slap of rejection, but also because I didn't lie in my livestream when I said I love it out here. It really is the best part of the cabin. The stars and moon are out, casting the clearing in a soft, ethereal glow. In the distance, the faint gurgle of running water sounds, along with the subtle bristle of the leaves and the rustling of animals. It's peaceful; the flotsam left from my brain-o-shame journey fades away more quickly than usual.

I take a deep breath, filling my lungs with the crisp, clean air—the heady scent of pine and earth. Goosebumps prickle on my arms and legs, and I fight off a shudder, wishing I had on more than leggings and a thin long-sleeve shirt.

The quiet snick of the door and creak of the porch draw my attention. "Brought you a blanket. It gets cold out here."

Damn this man. I can't take him being nice to me right now. I'd much prefer he call me spoiled or stubborn. Anything but standing in the glow of the moon, worried about me catching cold. When I don't say anything, he drapes the blanket over my shoulders before disappearing into the cabin.

For a moment, I think about not using it. Leaving it abandoned on the porch. Sitting out here freezing for the rest of the night to prove a point.

But considering I'm out here alone, I'd only be proving the point to myself. So I wrap up in the blanket the grumpy, infuriating, ruggedly handsome man I almost kissed left me.

I don't know how long I sit, but when I come inside, Hudson lies on his back, staring at the ceiling. Without a word, I climb into bed as well, hugging the edge, curling my body as far away from his as possible.

"Goodnight, Spitfire," he whispers.

DAY THREE

Despite my plan to cling to my half of the bed, Hudson and I wake up wrapped around each other again. His arms band around my waist, his hard cock pressing against my ass. I resist the urge to wriggle, despite how good, how right his touch feels.

A part of me wonders if it isn't a sign, an endorsement from the cosmos—or at least our subconsciousness—to go for it. But Hudson wordlessly pulls away, acting as though it's nothing.

Which is fine. Totally fine. Lesson learned, remember Blakely? He doesn't want you. Or he does want you and can't admit it, but also, it's a terrible idea and has shitstorm written all over it.

The sound of running water catches my attention, and I

shift to my side, the silhouette of Hudson's thick frame visible behind the thin shower curtain. Not wanting to be a voyeur, I stumble into the kitchen and pour myself a cup of daily motivation.

With each boosting sip, my senses come online. And that's when I smell it: orange blossom, gardenia, and honeysuckle.

My shampoo.

I can't say it's my most rational moment, but I stomp to where Hudson is showering. And in some sort of out-of-body experience, I yank back the shower curtain. There may be a snarl involved.

"Are you using my sham—" The words die on my tongue as my brain finally processes what's in front of me.

Hudson's large hands massage his scalp into a sudsy lather as water drips down his broad chest. My eyes follow the droplets as they journey through the slightly more than a smattering of dark hair all while a litany of naughty, naughty thoughts fills my mind.

I swear I do my best to keep my eyes on his face in the few seconds I have the curtain open. But...

Have I been wondering what Hudson Brooks has between his legs since the moment we met? Yes. Did I make a calculated guess based on the outline pressing against the front of his pants and my hip in the morning? Also yes. But seeing it live and in person? There's no comparison.

Then, the realization of what I'm doing hits me. I'm perving. On Hudson. In the shower. I'm violating his personal space and being a total creep. I shut the curtain with a jerk, but it's too late to unsee.

Behind the safety of the thin barrier between us, I press my fingers to my temples and groan. "I'm so sorry."

His gruff chuckle sends chills down my spine. "I get there's no door, but you could at least start with hello."

"Right. Good morning."

"Need something?"

"It's stupid, but in for a penny, in for a penis. Wait, no! Pound. In for a pound." *Ohmyfuckinggodwhatiswrongwithme.* I bump my fist against my forehead and mumble, "You're using my shampoo."

"Sorry. Grabbed whatever was closest."

A flash of annoyance tempers some of my shamebarassment. "Seriously? I only brought one bottle, and it isn't even a full bottle, and what if I run out? I can't use whatever three-in-one store-brand garbage you have! Plus, it's seventy dollars a bottle."

The curtain snaps back. "Seventy dollars? Princess, you got ripped off."

"It's specially made for me. Customized for my hair and with scents I selected."

Hudson's face is torn between amusement and horror. "Are you shitting me? It doesn't smell that good."

"You are such an asshole. And you're wrong. It smells amazing. I smell amazing."

With that brilliant parting shot, I stomp away, muttering. "Stupid jerk, using *my* shampoo. And has the audacity to say it doesn't smell good. What a... a... ugh! I can't even think of a word to call him."

"You seem fond of asshole."

I spin, a thousand lashes on the tip of my tongue, but they shrivel to dust at the sight of him clad in a towel. He's still damp and too damn beautiful. It isn't fair.

Scrambling for my phone, I drop onto the couch. I need to talk to literally *anyone* who isn't Hudson Brooks. And there's one person who always answers my call.

Kirk's smiling face greets me. "Blakely! How's my favorite social media maven doing today?"

"You picked the biggest asshole on the entire planet, possibly the entire universe, for this! You did it on purpose. Admit it."

"BB, calm down. What happened? You were fine the last time we talked."

"Things change, buddy."

The back of the couch shifts as Hudson leans against it. "The princess is upset I used her fancy-ass city girl shampoo."

"Don't call me Princess!"

"Apologies, Spitfire. Or should I call you Peeping Tina?"

Kirk cocks his head. "I might be missing some information here. Hudson, where's your shirt? Blakely, are you still in your pajamas? What exactly is going on out there?"

We both mumble, "*Nothing*," in perfect unison.

My manager holds his hands up. "Okay, my bad. Let's take a calming breath."

Hudson plops down next to me, his bare leg burning against mine. The towel strains to keep his thick thighs contained. "It's all good. Just a misunderstanding."

If I had the power to shoot eye daggers, Hudson's body would be pinned to the wooden walls right now. "Don't speak for me, jackass."

Our eyes lock, and I'm caught in his orbit, the crushing weight of his gravity pulling me closer and closer. Chests heaving. Bodies ready to collide.

"I know I'm on the outside looking in here, but you two should kiss and get it over with."

Kirk's tease snaps the tension between us, and I slam the phone on the table without saying another word.

One awkward moment of silence later, Hudson asks, "You called your boss to tattle on me?"

"He's my manager, and no. I wanted to talk to anyone who isn't you."

Hudson slumps back into the cushions, and for a second, I worry I offended him. Add it to my karmic tab, I guess.

"Hudson, I'm sor—"

"Sorry about using your shampoo and shit. It, um, smells pretty good."

From the table, muffled words that sound suspiciously like *did you two kiss yet* have me diving for the phone.

"Hang up, Kirk!"

A husky chuckle pulls my attention. "How about we start today over?"

Taking a deep breath, I swallow my pride. "I'm sorry. I overreacted to the shampoo, peeped on you in the shower, and called and told on you to Kirk."

The panty-dropping smirk he gives me has me squirming on the couch. "I knew you called to tattle."

Waving his words away and rising from the couch, I say, "Can I make you a cup of apology coffee?"

"My second apology coffee in three days. At this rate, you'll be making my coffee the rest of your time here."

I roll my eyes and pour us each a cup, his black like his soul, mine sweet and creamy. Carrying the drinks to the couch, I say, "Yeah, right. Don't get used to it." As he takes his cup, an electric zing snaps through my fingertips where our skin meets. I suck in a gasp of air and stare as his Adam's apple bobs in his throat. He feels it, too.

"Hud—"

With a grunt, he's on his feet. "We're hiking today. Your feet are in better shape, and you've got lighter hiking shoes. Be ready in ten."

And once again, my Bear runs.

Hike 2.0 is much more in line with what I expected on day one. The path is a gentle slope, covered in pine needles and brush, not feet killing rocks of death. It's later, so the sun is up, its rays casting shadows on the forest floor around us. Having lived the first half of my life in the plains of west Texas and the second half in the Texas Hill Country, I'm not used to the majesty and overwhelming height of the surrounding trees. Or the altitude.

Let's be real, a Texas hill has nothing on a northern New Mexico mountain.

So, while my feet are fine, my lungs aren't, and it isn't long until I'm begging Hudson to stop.

"Please? I can't breathe."

"If you can talk, you can breathe."

"You have the worst bedside manner in the world, Hudson. Has anyone ever told you that?"

"Seeing as I'm not a nurse or doctor, no."

"R-U-D-E. That's what I mean."

"Oh, then yes. One bratty princess said I'm rude after reading a bunch of bad reviews about me."

Guilt pings in my chest. That was shitty of me. I would cry in the fetal position if someone sat down and started reading the crappy things people say about me aloud. What was I thinking?

And more than that, what am I doing? I'm failing at the tasks Hudson has set out for me, failing at finding myself, failing at everything. So far, all I've discovered is I suck at navigation, and Hudson has the power to make me feel completely out of control.

"Luckily for her, I don't give a shit what people think." I

raise my head to find Hudson watching me. "Come on, Spitfire, a little farther, and we'll be there."

We step out of the treeline and into a small clearing overlooking the edge of a cliff. Below us is a glassy lake; in the distance, clouds float like cotton candy wisps around mountain peaks. The trees below us are glorious shades of green, rust, and gold.

It's flipping amazing. The peace that's proven so elusive for so long settles over me, and for a moment, I forget about my struggles. It's just me, the sky, the breeze, and the trees.

A rough finger brushes an errant strand of hair from my cheek and tucks it behind my ear.

Me, the sky, the breeze, the trees, and Hudson.

My skin prickles where he touches me, and I slip closer to his warmth on instinct. Hudson has about seven inches on me, but I know I'd fit perfectly into the cradle of his arms.

"Wild hare."

I shrug. "Yeah, those damn little front pieces never grow like the rest."

"What?"

Lifting my chin, I'm met with confusion. "What do you mean what?"

He doesn't answer, simply shakes his head and points. And holy shit, there's a family of rabbits a handful of feet away. I grip his arm and whisper-yell, "Bunnies!"

"Not recording this?"

"No." I drop my hand down the length of his arm, tangling our fingers together. "I want this one for myself. Thank you for bringing me here. It's amazing."

We stand in silence, enjoying the quiet, the warmth, the wind.

"Usually, people hold hands before seeing each other naked."

Hudson's words have me dropping his hand from mine and heat rushing to my cheeks. With a glare, I stomp back toward the cabin.

I get ten feet.

"Hey, Spitfire? You're going the wrong way. Cabin's *southeast*."

In. Suffer. Able.

DAY FOUR

I'm at my slapdash vanity, applying mascara. Turning my head side to side, I check that everything is as close to perfect as possible. It's time to go live.

Hudson is already at the small kitchen table eating breakfast—eggs, bacon, and steaming biscuits. I set up my phone and put everything in place so I can easily make myself a plate while talking. Once I have it all just so, I fix on my best social media smile and hit record.

"Good morning, BBs! Being out here in the wilderness works up my appetite!" I pause and make a show of adding food to my plate. "I'm so lucky my roomie is also a fantastic cook. He prepared this tasty breakfast for us."

I nibble the edge of a piece of bacon and moan like it's the best thing I've ever put in my mouth. Across the table, Hudson snorts. I keep my smile in place, though I once again wish for eye-daggers.

With a sugar-sweet flutter of my lashes, I switch the camera to Hudson. "Tell my BBs what you have planned for us today?"

He doesn't answer, and I consider kicking him under the table. He sighs in time to save his shins. Barely.

"We're finishing baseline survival basics testing. Knowing

your strengths and weaknesses helps a guide determine which skills to focus on."

Moving around the table so we are side by side and both in frame, I nod sagely. Then I give the camera a coy grin. I can't help myself. "What are my strengths?"

"And weaknesses?" He raises a dark eyebrow in challenge.

Gritting my teeth, I say, "And areas where I can grow."

"Blakely's weaknesses—"

"We just agreed to call them areas for growth, Bear." I cut my eyes to the camera lens, wondering how many people caught me calling him Bear.

"Blakely's 'areas for growth'"—he actually uses air quotes, the bastard—"are numerous." His scowl slips into a smirk. "Cardinal directions, for example."

"That's not true!" I pout.

Hudson makes a *hmph*. "It is true." He isn't looking into the camera. No, the full force of his attention is on me. "You also need to work on your knot tying, situational awareness, and the other skills we didn't get to."

I'm about to snap back at him when he says, "But your greatest strength is your ability to adapt." His eyes lock on mine. "Throw you in an unknown situation, and you acclimate."

For a precious few seconds, I forget I'm live. Forget there's an audience. Forget anything exists except for those green eyes and me. Is this a compliment? Or is he saying I'm a chameleon? Changing myself to fit the situation? Another dig on the persona he says I wear?

"Huds—" Before I get his name out, he jerks his head toward my phone. I plaster on a smile, and with a high-pitched giggle, I say. "Okay, that's it for now, BBs. Don't forget to like, share, and save!"

When I end the live, I dump the eggs and bacon back onto the communal plate, picking at the fluffy biscuit.

"There you go again."

"What are you growling about now, Bear?"

"You didn't eat any of the food you raved about."

"It's not like I wasted it. You already made it. I wouldn't have eaten it even if I didn't do the live. What's the big deal?"

"The big deal is you put on this ridiculous show. You made a pretend plate of food. You sat over there for half an hour putting all that shit on, changing the way you look. When the way you look is beau—" He shakes his head. "For what? For strangers to fawn over you? To feel good about yourself? You that needy, Princess? Mom and Dad could only afford state school, so now you have to get your ego stroked online?"

Anger and hurt battle for hold. In the end, though, anger wins. I push back from the table, my chair clattering to the floor. "You don't know anything about my mo—" I stop myself from saying the word *mom*. "My childhood. And this show, as you call it, is my job, asshole! I'm sorry if it offends you, but this is how I make my living. It seems shallow and vapid to you, Mr. Salt-of-the-Goddamn-Earth, but we can't all be jerks who push people away every chance we get."

Hudson glares but doesn't answer. Instead, he strides toward the door.

"Oh no, you don't. I'm not done!"

He makes it to the porch before I catch him, grabbing his shoulder. "You don't have any room to talk. The Hudson who rubbed my feet, tucked my hair behind my ear, and brought me a blanket—who is he? Is he the real you? Or is the real you the guy who yells and calls me a brat and a liar and is too scared to kiss me? Which is it?"

Suddenly, his mouth is on mine, stealing the air from my lungs. He grips my hips, and I stretch to wrap my arms around his back. His tongue prods my mouth, begging for entrance, which I happily grant.

When his fingers tangle in my hair, I can't help it, a small moan escapes from the back of my throat while my hands wander his wonder of a body. Then, as quickly as it begins, it's over. And I'm left alone on the porch, fingertips pressed to my trembling lips.

There may as well be a Hudson-shaped puff of air for how quickly he ran away.

No survival skills testing happens. Instead, Hudson vanishes for hours. I'd worry if his Jeep wasn't still parked in the clearing—freaking man-baby.

He kisses me and pushes me away like it's nothing. Like I'm nothing.

What's the saying? Fool me once, shame on you; fool me twice, can't fool me again. Being shown twice in quick succession I'm not wanted is enough of a lesson for me.

Surely.

I'm tossing stuff into random piles, hunting for headache medicine when he returns.

"We need to talk."

"Really? You tell me how pathetic I am, kiss me, storm off for hours, and now you want to talk? Whatever could we possibly have to discuss?" I say in the driest tone possible.

"I'm sorry."

"You're sorry? For what?"

"For what I said about your job. I was out of line." His jaw clenches. "And..."

"And?"

"For kissing you. It shouldn't have happened."

Ouch. That stings. "Because you aren't attracted to me?" Why that's my question, I wish I knew.

"It doesn't matter."

"Why doesn't it matter?"

His fingers flex, and he sways, as if he's keeping himself from moving toward me. "This can't happen. You and me can't happen."

The weight of his words crushes me. The kiss between us was a tiny taste, a nibble from a feast I long to gorge myself on. But something is holding him back. So, with a sharp laugh, I gift him the chance to back out of the emotional tangle this conversation is weaving. "Okay. So what? The kiss was to shut me up?"

I silently plead for him to pick up the small olive branch I'm offering. *Spar with me, Bear. Push back.*

The uncertainty and sadness disappear, replaced by the grumpy frown. "You were yammering on. Seemed like the quickest way to make you stop."

Grinning at him, I say, "So I didn't eat any breakfast, and my guide abandoned me without lunch. Any chance you've got dinner planned?"

When he stomps into the kitchen, I know we'll be okay. I study the lines of his broad back, and the memory of our kiss sears me. I want more. But Hudson can have it his way.

No more kissing—for now.

hudson

I watch Blakely eat the dinner I made for us. She keeps stealing glances at me, but since I can't stop staring at her, I catch her each time.

What the hell was going through my mind when I kissed her like that? And why do I want to throw all the dishes on the ground, lay her out on the table, and do it again?

I hadn't expected her to follow me when I ran, but I should have. Something I've learned about Blakely Bradshaw? She's not one to back down.

When she called me out, eyes ablaze, cheeks flushed, it was too much to resist. I wasn't lying when I said it seemed like the best way to get her to shut up, but I would be if I said I wasn't dying to taste her fire. I have no business getting involved with this pampered, spoiled, superficial, beautiful, fiery, clever, sharp-tongued woman. But for the first time in years, I wish that wasn't the case.

It's been six years since Paige left me, and my engagement ring, high and dry for the glitz and glamor of a town with more than two stoplights. Her parting shots—how I'll never be more than a small-town mountain man—play in my head like a broken record.

But then the song changes, and all memories of Paige drift away like smoke. I'm left with Blakely's real laugh, her bright, toothy smile, the glossy shine of her hair. The way her eyes trailed over my body when she pulled back the shower curtain. The way she bit her lip, as if she needed a physical barrier to keep from putting her mouth on me. The press of lips to mine, her soft moan in my ear, the crush of her lush body against my firm one.

Fuck.

How the hell am I supposed to stay away from her? She's everything I shouldn't want—a city girl more at home in shops and fancy restaurants than in the forest—but I can't ignore the pull between us.

And she feels it, too. The kiss we shared said more than words ever could.

"Earth to Hudson!" Blakely waves her hand in front of my face.

I grunt and shake my head. "Huh?"

"Eloquent as always. I complimented you on dinner and asked what we have on the docket for tomorrow."

"Need to make up for today. Get those last baseline assessments done."

Her snort makes me smile in spite of myself. "Please. I'm the lowest of the low in all the things."

"You did pretty good with the BB gun."

"I showed those paper men who's boss, didn't I?"

When she flexes her thin arm, I fight a chuckle. "Do you have a lot of practice with guns? I can't imagine there are many places to shoot a BB gun in the city."

She frowns. "No, there aren't."

I wait for her to say more, but she doesn't. Instead, she gets up from the table and dumps her leftover food into the trash and her dish into the sink.

"I'm going to sit on the porch for a bit and reply to comments. Have to keep the BBs happy." She smiles, but there's a tightness to it.

Whether it's because of the turn our conversation took or because she thinks I'll judge her for the social media shit, I can't say. I'd ask, but she's already gone.

I last twenty minutes.

"Want a blanket?"

Blakely looks up from the glow of her phone screen, and this time, the smile she gives me is real. "Thank you. I'm still not used to how cold it gets once the sun sets." She reaches out a hand, but I plop onto the swing next to her, draping the blanket over her lap and gently tucking it beneath her legs.

Her breath catches when my hand brushes her knee, and despite the layers between our skin, I swear sparks tingle along my palm.

Clearing my throat, I ask, "So, how's it going? The, uh, commenting stuff?"

She giggles. "The *commenting stuff* is going fine. Have you looked at Peak Adventures' account lately? You've gained close to a thousand new followers already."

"No, I don't mess with that shit."

Her pointy elbow digs into my side. "Oh right, I forget you're above all this." Thankfully, there's no bite to her words.

"Some of us have to make a living the old-fashioned way." I give her cute little nose a quick flick.

The porch goes dark when she closes her phone. Twisting so her back rests against the side and drawing her legs up beneath her, she cocks her head and asks, "How did you learn all this?"

"All what?"

"How to be a, what did you call yourself? An outdoorsman?"

"Oh, uh, my dad's former military."

She gestures for me to keep going. I lean back against the swing and enjoy the sway. "He learned wilderness survival during his time in the army. When he was home from deployments, he took me and my two younger brothers camping and trekking." I glance at her to see if I'm boring her, but I swear, in the dim light, she looks interested. "He'd drop us off and make us navigate to the campsite or make it so we had to earn the tent by catching dinner. When he didn't re-up, it turned to almost every weekend and any breaks we had from school."

She pokes my thigh with one of those adorable toes. "I bet it had less to do with training you on the great outdoors and more about giving your poor mom a breather from all the testosterone for a couple of days a week."

I chuckle. "You're probably right."

We sit quietly until Blakely asks, "When he dropped you off, was it you and your brothers or just you?" There's curiosity in her voice, but also something more. Concern maybe?

"Me and them." I scratch the back of my neck.

"So you were in charge of two younger boys while learning to navigate?"

I grunt. Where's she going with this?

Thankfully, she doesn't make me stew too long. "When did it go from weekends to a job?"

"We'd been to Trail Creek on vacation, and Mom and Dad fell in love with the place. Next thing I knew, they declared they were moving, and I was welcome to stay and finish school where I was, or I could pick up and come with them."

"School?"

"College. I was twenty. Gray had just graduated, and Bo

was starting high school. I transferred and finished my business degree while helping Dad get Peak Adventures going."

"Business degree?"

The question is clear in her voice, and immediately, I'm on the defense. Paige's voice echoes in my mind. *"Is this really all you want to be? Some small-town nobody?"*

I laugh, but there's a sharp edge to it. "Yep. Surprised? Have my MBA too. I'm more than a dumb-ass country boy."

"I didn't... of course you are. That's not what—"

Blakely reaches for me, but I push her hand away. "Don't worry about it, Princess. I'm sure all us hicks come off the same to you." Without giving her a chance to say anything else, I jerk from the porch swing and retreat into the cabin and a glass of whiskey.

The first sip is more of a gulp, and I relish the burn in my throat. It helps counter the burn in my heart. This is why I can't think about kissing her. She's just like Paige. I'll never be good enough for a woman like Blakely Bradshaw, and I'd do well to remember it.

DAY FIVE

I wake first, my internal alarm clock going off, and damn if I'm not pressed firmly against Blakely's back. I'm her big spoon, my face buried in her hair while I hold tight to her slim waist.

As carefully as I can, I unhook my arm and roll to my cold side of the bed. In another world where she isn't everything I don't need, a world where she isn't leaving in less than a month—instead of rolling away, I'd pull her closer.

But then I remember her surprise about my degree. The way she made the same assumption as so many others—that I'm nothing but a dumb mountain man. Happy in the forest, clicking rocks and tracking animals.

And I am. But I'm more than that. I run the business. I keep us in the black. I do the taxes and the finances and the scheduling. I'm the one who suggested adding corporate retreats and girls-only weekends.

When she climbed into bed last night, I expected her to strike up a conversation, but instead, she turned her back and pulled the blanket up to her chin like she had the right to be upset. Typical princess behavior.

When I step out of the bathroom, Blakely is curled up in the recliner, sipping a cup of coffee.

I scoff. "No apology cup this morning?"

"Nope."

My hackles rise. "You don't think you owe me one?"

"Nope."

"Is that all you're gonna say?"

"Yep."

"Get ready to go," I snap, before crossing over to my dresser. She doesn't answer. What the fuck?

Eight minutes later, Blakely stands at the door, arms crossed, waiting. Without saying anything, I push past her, out into the open air, and stomp over into the clearing on the east side of the cabin. With a grunt, I point to the small ring of rocks. "Sit." Then I gather up the supplies to get today's shit done and over.

I'm doing my job and then drinking the afternoon away.

I toss a flint and steel at Blakely's feet. "Build a fire." Then I stand and watch. If she thinks she's getting any other information from me, she's sorely mistaken.

She holds the pieces like they may bite her before striking them against each other. Her eyes cut to me at the first sparks, but I'm a statue. Blank-faced and stony-eyed. She huffs and tries again. Another shower of sparks, but since she hasn't set any tinder, nothing's ever gonna happen.

"Fail. Next." Before she can argue, I look at the list and say, "Since you can't start a fire, you can't boil water, so that's a fail. You never mastered knots, so building a shelter is a fail. I'm not bothering with foraging. If it doesn't come with a Michelin star, I'm betting you aren't interested in eating it. And as far as first aid, given that you needed me to bandage your feet, I'm marking that as a fail, too. Congrats, Princess. You have zero survival skills."

With every word, Blakely's face grows redder and redder. I'm being an asshole.

"It's really shitty that the most words you've said to me in five days is the crap you just spewed at me." She rises to her feet and stands before me, her ocean eyes blazing. "I didn't ask you to bandage my feet! You did that all on your own. And as far as this bullshit skills assessment, you can kiss my ass."

"I'm sure you're used to having people kiss your ass, but that isn't me, sweetheart."

"No, you're just a judgmental jerkwad who uses the guise of teaching to make himself feel better." Her voice changes into what I assume is a terrible impersonation of me. "Oh, I'm Hudson Brooks, the god of the wilderness, and anyone who can't live like the Swiss Family Robinson is an idiot."

My lips twitch. "Swiss Family Robinson?"

"Robinson Crusoe."

"Are all your examples fictional?"

"Bear Grylls. What the fuck ever. And that's not the point! The point is, you're standing here telling me how much I suck, like I don't already know, rubbing it in. You're a prick, and I wish I hadn't come out here."

A stream of tears starts while she's yelling, and her voice cracks. My stomach twists. I take one step toward her, but she immediately moves back.

"Don't you dare touch me. Not after the way you treated me last night and this morning."

The twist in my gut curls tighter, anger and resentment mixing with regret into a vile mixture. So, of course, bile is what comes out. "Are you shitting me? You're complaining about how I treated you? You, who thinks I'm too stupid to go to college? You, who has done nothing but turn your nose up and complain since you got here? You wish you weren't here? Then go the fuck home."

As soon as I say it, I wish I could take it back. My throat is thick, and no matter how much I swallow, I can't get rid of the lump there. "Blakely, I didn't—"

"No. Shut up," she snarls, tears still running down her cheeks, eyes snapping with fire. "I am sorry, sorry you didn't give me the chance to speak last night. Sorry you made a judgment about me. Sorry you're still pissy and taking it out on me this morning. That's the only apology you're getting. If you don't like it, too bad."

She's a hurricane of fury and frustration, and it's no less than I deserve.

"It's interesting you have a business degree. Interesting but not surprising. It's bullshit for anyone to think you aren't smart. I never once even implied that. You're clearly brilliant. You know more about survival and the land than I could ever hope to understand. And you obviously have a savvy business mind despite agreeing to this," she gestures her hand between us, "clusterfuck."

I want to pull her into my arms and whisper my apologies into her ear. Demand she hear me. But I'm struck silent. Caught in the storm of her wrath.

Blakely plows ahead, chin high, teeth bared. "Incidentally, for all that you claim I've judged you, you've judged me plenty. And made a shit ton of assumptions. You're the only one with a college degree, and not because my parents could 'only afford state school,' as you so rudely said a few days ago. I mov—"

She stops, cutting off whatever she plans to say next. I watch her chest rise and fall, fury brilliant on her face.

"You don't know nearly as much about me as you think you do. You said I was fascinating. And you'd know me so well if I only dropped my shields. How about you take your own advice. Whatever chip's on your shoulder, I'm not the one who put it there." She throws the flint and steel at me. "Since you've marked me as a complete and total failure, I'm done for the day. If you need me, I'll be drinking."

Blakely takes three steps, then turns back. "And don't call me Princess!"

DAY SEVEN

It's been two days since our fight in the clearing. To say it's been awkward as fuck is an understatement. Neither Blakely nor I have spoken more than a couple of words to each other. She still makes a shit ton of noise, talking to Kirk, doing lives, and walking around the cabin singing—terribly—but unless we're bickering over stupid shit, she doesn't have anything to say to me. The only smile she's given me is that fake ass one she uses on her socials. I hate that smile.

On the plus side, we kept our lips to ourselves, so I guess that's a win.

Yeah, huge fucking win.

Blakely sighs softly in her sleep, her face peaceful and relaxed. I think about her accusations. That I've judged her, made assumptions, put words into her mouth. And fuck if she isn't right. Her admission that she doesn't have a degree surprised me. I figured a woman like her had some fancy-ass and useless degree that cost more than a starter home. I also think about our conversation when I told her about how Peak Adventures got its start. Up until I blew everything to pieces, she'd been listening eagerly.

Fucking shit hell. I'm an asshole.

I grab my phone and fire off a text to the group chat I have with my brothers.

I fucked up.

GRAY

What'd u do

BO

Not surprised

Made some assumptions and yelled at her

GRAY

Ur an idiot

Got that. Thanks.

BO

You've gotta get Paige out of your head man

Who said anything about her?

BO

Whatever. Advice?

GRAY

Unfuck it!

BO

Why are you worried about it?

Why am I worried about it? She's just a client, right? No different from anyone else who hires me for guide work.

But that's not true. From the moment I met her, Blakely Bradshaw wormed her way under my skin—fast and deep.

Wish I knew.

Picturing the hurt on her face leaves an ache in my chest. I hate that I put it there. God, I was a judgmental asshole. I don't know her as well as I thought, but fuck, I want to. And heaven help me, I miss her endless prattling and teasing.

BO

Oh shit. You like her!

GRAY

Time to eat crow brother

Guess it's my turn to make apology coffee.

BO

One word: hotspring

That's two words, dumbass.

BO

I close out the chat and stare at Blakely. They're right. I do like her. But she scares the hell out of me, all while pulling me closer and closer. I'm like a goddamn bug drawn to car headlights on the highway. I'm gonna end up smashed, but I can't stop myself from flying headlong towards her.

Despite this likely ending in pain, I reach out and give her a gentle shake. "Spitfire, wake up."

"No."

I chuckle at her pouty lips and voice. "Come on. I have a surprise for you."

She opens one eye. "Are you going to give me a test with no

instructions and then make fun of me when I fail? Oh, I know, you're going to accuse me of being judgmental while you make up facts about my life. Or maybe you're going to take me back to that scenic cliff and shove me off it? Thanks, but no thanks."

I rub my chest, each word a barb that latches onto my heart. "I deserve that. Did you bring a swimsuit?"

Her eyebrows jump. "What?"

"A swimsuit," I grunt.

Blakely glares at me. "Yes. Why?"

"Trust me?"

"Trust you? I want to. I really do. But then you almost kissed me, did kiss me, yelled at me, told me to leave...Hudson, what do you want from me?"

"Right now, I want you to put on your swimsuit and trust me." I hold my breath. "Please." *Give me another chance.*

She stares at me and blinks twice before grumbling. "Swimsuit? It's October. You're lucky I brought one. Asshole. This better be worth it."

blakely

Hudson Brooks is going to be the death of me. Cause of death? Emotional whiplash. I seriously can't keep up with him.

The past few days have been awful. I've put on a happy face for the camera, but as soon as I finish recording, silence falls over the cabin, and I hate it. But Hudson pissed me off and hurt me. So I keep all my witty thoughts to myself, even if I have to grit my teeth to do it. I'm a little stubborn. It's the Taurus in me.

The divide between us hasn't kept me from drifting to Hudson while asleep, and honestly, wrapped in that grumpy bear's arms, I've never slept better. But then the sun rises, and so does my frustration—along with the desire to punch him in his adorably freckled face. *Or kiss it.*

The presumptive bastard said I was judging him. Ha! If he knew how I grew up... I shake my head, shutting down that line of thinking as I adjust my bikini top. Kirk thought I was silly for packing a swimsuit, so I snap a quick selfie with a single-finger salute to show him how wrong he was.

I have no idea why I need my swimsuit, just that Hudson

asked me to trust him. *Idiot, party of one.* Didn't I tell myself I wouldn't let him fool me again?

But for some stupid reason—one that is more sexually motivated than I should admit—I do trust him, at least with pieces of myself. I'm safe with him. He won't physically hurt me.

Emotionally, though? Jury's out.

I twist my hair to get it off my neck, then give myself a once over in the mirror. I'm makeup-free, and I don't hate it. Things like his insistence that I don't need to contour and shade my face into someone else's lure me back in. Every time Hudson shows me who he could be—a hair-tucking, foot-rubbing, dream-kissing wonder of a man—I want more. Who is he beyond the gruff nature-expert persona? What material built the walls around his heart? Because judging by our fight, that shit is durable.

Like I have any room to talk. I didn't just build walls; I built a whole new *me* to get away from my past.

Hudson knocks on the bathroom door. "You ready?"

I'm vain enough to admit I love how his mouth falls open and his eyes heat when he sees me. With his hand still in the air, he stutters over his words. "You, uh, that color, looks... wow."

Gesturing to my turquoise swimsuit, I say, "This color looks wow?" When his ears turn pink, I nudge him in the ribs. "Thank you, I think. Your color also looks wow."

And it does. Muscular arms peek out from the fitted white t-shirt, and gray sweatpants hug his thighs—and other parts. I've always loved a thicker man, and Hudson Brooks is *thick*.

"But," I wrinkle my brow, "where is your swimsuit?"

"Under." As he answers, he tosses a pair of sweats and an oversized shirt at me. I stand there, holding both items, until he huffs. "Didn't figure you had any ratty clothes."

The memory of opening a drawer and finding a family of mice living in my favorite Barbie pajama dress makes my stomach knot. Fighting a shudder, I push the image and the word *ratty* from my mind and slip the clothes—his clothes—over my swimsuit.

They drown my smaller frame and engulf me in his scent. If he wasn't watching me, I'd pull the collar to my nose and use it like a scuba mask.

"Here." He thrusts coffee into my hands. "Owed you one."

I stand there with my eyebrows quirked, a question on my face despite knowing what he means. Am I a little evil? Maybe. But I'm okay with it.

Another huff. "Apology coffee. It was, uh, my turn." He rubs the back of his head.

Hiding my grin behind the warm tumbler of go-go juice, I extend my hand in an *after you* motion. But rather than leaving, Hudson goes to the kitchen and throws fruit, cheese, bread, and other snacks into a pack.

"Are you taking me on a romantic picnic?" I ask, hiking the too-long sweats up, Urkle style, in a futile attempt to get them off the ground.

He freezes and gives me a look of complete and utter bewilderment. "A picnic?"

"A *romantic* picnic," I correct, not bothering to hide my smile now. Having Hudson Brooks on the ropes may be a better high than social media.

"No. It makes sense to bring food."

"Should I bring a blanket for our picnic date?"

"It isn't a picnic. Or a date."

"Hmmm, a handsome man, a beautiful woman, a mystery destination, tasty food... put all that together, and it can only mean one thing—picnic date."

"It's not a picnic." Hudson slings the bag over his shoulder and then, like it's habit, places his hand on my lower back. The shivers are instantaneous. This is what his touch does to me.

In the spirit of impish mischief and a smidge in the spirit of wanting to keep the upper hand, I say, "Ah, but you didn't deny it's a date." When he stops walking, I crack up. God, I love teasing him.

Shaking his head, he catches up to me, his wide, warm hand guiding me to his Jeep. Now, I really am curious.

"Where are you taking me in your sweats, with a pic—" At his frown, I laugh and amend my words. "With snacks that we need the Jeep?"

He opens the door and stands, arms crossed and foot tapping, until I roll my eyes and climb in. It isn't until we're both buckled and the Jeep is creeping down something that in no way resembles a road does Hudson answer me.

"Hot spring."

I squeal. Full on piglet style. "There are hot springs out here? Why am I just now learning this?"

"It isn't something on the regular itinerary. But I thought…" It takes him a beat to find his words. "I thought it would be a relaxing place to talk."

"You, Hudson Bear Brooks—the man who spent the last eight days speaking in monosyllabic grunts and, I'm pretty sure, a few growls—want to talk?"

"Yeah."

"You're off to a fantastic start."

The steering wheel creaks beneath his grip. "Can we wait?"

"Till we get to the springs?"

A nod is my only answer.

"Are these healing waters going to grant you the ability to speak for more than thirty seconds?"

This earns me a sigh. "No. I'd rather wait till I can give you my full attention."

Oh. Well. I don't have an answer to that.

He glances at me. "Okay?"

"Okay."

It's twenty more minutes of driving down the mountain, filled with my singing and Hudson's occasional muttering, before the Jeep stops in a small clearing.

He clicks the locks on the door, so I can't get out.

"If you brought me all this way to kill me, jokes on you. You could have done it at the cabin and saved on gas."

Judging by the thin line of his lips, my joke doesn't land. "Which direction did we travel?"

"What?"

"If something happened to me, and you had to walk to the cabin right now, which direction would you go?"

"Um, up?"

"Up?"

I point back the way we came.

He sighs like I've greatly insulted him, then unlocks the Jeep. "We'll work on it later. Let's go."

Making a very mature face at his back, I climb out. And once again, I'm blown away by the beauty surrounding me. To our right lies the first of a series of small pools rimmed in natural stone. The framing backdrop—dipping valleys thick with pines and aspens and rising cliffs carved in oranges, reds, and browns—is beyond amazing.

I scramble for my phone because as much as I want to hoard this moment, I know clickbait when I see it. Hudson only huffs twice while I take stills for a post. The hot springs are already working their magic. Wonder if I can convince him to let me get a shot of him shirtless. Hmm, better not press it.

His patience wanes, and he jerks his head toward the water. I go to argue, but the little wrinkle between his eyes has me closing my mouth. Instead, I hold my hand out and follow the path he picks down the rocky trail. I'm thankful for his strong grip when I hit more than one slippery spot the closer we get.

While Hudson stands to the side, I quickly strip off my borrowed sweats and sink into the balmy water. Every bone in my body, every muscle, every nerve melts into malleable goo. The only thing holding me together is my skin.

I'm almost too relaxed to drink in the glory of Hudson's shirtless chest when he grips the back of his t-shirt and pulls it over his head.

Almost.

This is my third chance viewing Hudson sans shirt, and it's no less divine this time. He doesn't have a six-pack, but he's solid—the kind of fit that comes from hard work, not a gym. I sink a little lower and stare at all the golden skin on display.

Yep. Stare.

The gray sweats drop to the forest floor, and those thighs are what I'll dream about tonight. *Please crush me like a watermelon, sir.*

He slides into the warm water, my floating toes brushing his legs as he settles across from me. The spring is smaller than the bath back at the cabin and more round, sort of like a two-person hot tub, with natural seats formed in the stone over eons. It's highly intimate, and my body, heart, and brain are all hyper-aware of it.

I cut my eyes to Hudson's face, and he's watching me. Then, one of those long fingers reaches out and strokes the arch of my foot. "I was trying to say earlier... you look nice today."

"Thanks, I'm not even wearing any makeup. Someone keeps saying I don't need it."

"Sounds like a smart person."

"He has his moments. But so far, they've proven to be few and far between."

Silence falls back over us, and I let Hudson's lack of complete sentences go for now. It's not like he can get away from me. The rustle of the trees, the chirping of birds, and the bubbling of the warm water soothe me into a moment of Zen. This is actually really nice. Maybe I could get used to small-town life again if it includes hot springs.

If I had a nice fruity pink drink and more direct sunlight, this would be a pretty perfect moment.

Out of nowhere, Hudson blurts, "Alexander."

"Huh?" I say, both because I'm lost in the casual way he pulls my feet into his lap and caresses my ankles, and by the random word.

"My middle name. It's not Bear. It's Alexander."

"Hudson Alexander Brooks. What a distinguished name. I like it; it suits you. But you're still Bear as far as I'm concerned." I lean forward and tickle his jaw, forcing my hand steady despite the current tingling through the places we are skin to skin. "My grumpy, grouchy, grizzly Bear."

Crap. Not my Bear. Not my anything. I drop my hand and slump back against the rock ledge. "So, Bear," he squeezes my feet at the nickname, "you brought me out here to talk. Yes?"

"Yes."

This man. It's like pulling teeth. "You have my attention. My phone is with our clothes, and my muscles and mind are relaxed. Now's the time."

He swallows, and I'm struck with the sudden desire to lick his Adam's apple. But I refrain.

"I owe you more than an apology coffee, Blakely." He sighs and drops his head back. "Something about you…"

"Dazzles you? Awes you? Mesmerizes you?"

His gruff laugh makes my chest flutter. "Honestly? Yeah.

But also frustrates me, makes me stupid, makes me... an asshole."

"Oh? I hadn't noticed," I say with a snort and a flick of water in his direction.

A ghost of a smile flits across his lips before disappearing. "You asked me who put the chip on my shoulder?"

I nod.

"Six years ago, I was engaged."

I blink. Then blink again. That is not what I was expecting. "Engaged?"

"Yeah."

"Are you divor—"

"No, never married. She hoofed it outta here a month after accepting my ring. Paige grew up in Albuquerque. We met while I was finishing up my master's."

I wait, giving him a chance to say more. His grip on my ankles tightens. "I had a class that met once a month in person at UNM, and she asked me out for coffee after the first one. Five post-class dates and suddenly she was talking about moving to Trail Creek with me after graduation."

"After five dates?" I can't help but compare their situation to ours.

"Yeah." He pauses again, his hands moving from my ankles to my calves. "It just sort of happened, but I spent three years thinking she was the one. She spent three years thinking she could turn me into something I'm not."

Something closely resembling jealousy slithers through me.

"When you asked about my degree, it was her voice I heard. Telling me Trail Creek wasn't enough. I wasn't enough. How she deserved more than to be stuck in some podunk town with a hick like me." He pauses. "And I lumped you in with her."

"What do you mean?"

"Shit. I'm trying to explain, but I'm fucking it up." He runs his hand down his face. "When you came here, all pink luggage, fancy-ass shampoo, and big city attitude... well, I wasn't fair to you. And you were right when you said I judged you. I'm sorry."

"I know what people think when they first meet me. And I admit I lean into that persona. So I don't blame you for thinking I would be like Paige." I wrinkle my nose and spit her name out like it's a green sour candy. "I probably am in some ways. But I want to be clear. I don't think you're some small-town nobody. You're a businessman. A teacher. Someone your brothers look up to."

"How do you figure?"

"There's no way they don't idolize the older brother who guided them to shelter and safety on multiple camping trips."

"You make it sound like a big deal."

"Hudson, you were what? Thirteen? Guiding an eleven-year-old and a seven-year-old through wild terrain with only your skills and smarts?"

His small frown has me wanting to back off the topic. "I'd been doing it for five years at that point. Three of those with Gray. My dad... he knew he could trust them with me."

"That's a big ask for a kid, though." I brush his dark hair off his forehead. "But I'm sure he did."

"Will you tell me something else I got wrong about you?" Hudson's question is quiet, but there's no mistaking it.

Memories twist and twirl. Ugly ones leap forward, vying for the honor of clouding my mind. The day my mother's boyfriend made a pass at me, and when I told, the story flipped, painting me as the problem. Coming home after school that same day to a locked trailer and everything I owned packed in my little hatchback. Working multiple jobs as

I remade myself from Blake Lee Shaw, sad, shunned, and scared into Blakely Bradshaw, confident, cool, and carefree. The evening of my thirty-third birthday, finding out what so many others knew: my ex was a cheating bastard. The aching loneliness of my apartment...

"I could use a snack. How about you bust out the picnic?" I wriggle, putting a little distance between us, but Hudson is undeterred. He simply pulls my feet back into his lap, tracing the same soothing circles as earlier.

"Come on, Spitfire."

Not meeting his eyes, I swirl my hands in the warm water, staring at the little eddies my movements make. "I already told you this in a roundabout way, but I didn't go to college. That's why I'm so impressed by you having your business degree. I wanted to go to school, but it didn't work out for me."

"Your parents didn't help you pay your way? Or support you?"

A harsh laugh bursts out of my mouth. "No. I'm really not a princess. Or if I am, I'm a self-made one." Inhaling for five counts and then exhaling for six, I rein in the anger I still feel towards my mother. "I, um, my dad wasn't around, and when I was seventeen, my mother and I... we had a..." I nibble on my thumbnail, "falling out. So, no, there was no one to help pay for college or offer support."

"Shit, Blakely—" Hudson pulls me into his lap, wiping my little vortexes away. I'm straddling him now. My ankles hook around his wide hips, and my hands flutter before settling on his shoulders.

Heat surrounds me—the water and Hudson work like dueling furnaces, but I still shake in his arms. I bite back the urge to kiss him, instead leaning into the comfort of our teasing banter. "If you start pitying me, I'm liable to drown you in this hot spring. Got it, Bear?"

He chuckles. "Yeah. Got it. Can I still apologize for my fuck up?"

"That I'll allow."

"So gracious, aren't you?" His deep voice and breath skim over my ear, raising prickles of anticipation along my over-heated skin. "I'm sorry for the way I acted during your skills assessment. It was unprofessional. If you wanted, you could blast me six ways to Sunday on your social media platforms."

"Is that what you think I would do?"

"I thought I knew, but lately I'm thinking I don't know shit." His hands grip my hips. "Including how to do this."

"How to do what?" My words come out as a whisper, and my stomach flutters when my chest brushes against his.

"Not want you." Then he tugs me forward and presses his lips to mine in a breath-stealing repeat of the kiss we shared four days ago.

hudson

Kissing Blakely is as effortless as breathing. It's also the best bad idea I've ever had. There's no way this ends in anything other than heartache and disaster. But dammit, she fits against me like she was cut to be mine.

Blakely's lips part, and I have to hold myself back from fucking her mouth with my tongue. With a groan, I break the kiss. She steals a few more small kisses, pecks really, but they make me want to own her mouth with mine.

"Fuck, Spitfire." I hold her arms, bracing her away from my chest. "I swear I didn't bring you out here to make out. I wanted to talk."

She leans in again, eyes heavy-lidded. "We talked. This is better."

I nip her lip and chuckle. "Let's get out and enjoy the picnic." As soon as I say the p-word, I sigh because I know what's coming—

"It is a picnic! I knew it! You big softie." She shifts from my lap and I immediately miss the press of her body, the slight weight of her against me.

The air is brisk now that we're out of the hot spring, and I fight a grin when the towel I toss to Blakely hits her in the face.

"Rude." She huffs as she wraps it around herself.

She dries off and slips into my clothes, and damn if that doesn't call up something primal from deep within me. As she struts towards the food, I see her in a new light.

A self-made princess—so much more than the spoiled brat I assumed she was.

And she's enjoying being outdoors. With me. It's in the way her eyes soak up the majesty around us, the way she lifts her face to follow the calls of the birds.

Questions rest on the tip of my tongue, but before I can ask them, a grape bounces off my forehead.

"Tell me more about your family." Blakely stretches out on a large rock, her hair shining like spun gold.

"There isn't much to tell."

Another grape hits me in the chest. "Just tell me about them."

"Stop throwing fruit."

"Start talking, and I'll stop throwing."

"What do you want to know?" I plop onto the rock next to her, sitting up straighter when she scoots closer.

She nibbles a piece of cheese. "How is it working together? I could never work with anyone related to me. Do you ever wonder why your dad taught you your wilderness skills the way he did? What did your mom think of his methods?"

I stiffen. "My parents are great. What's wrong with the way I learned?"

Blakely shrugs. "You spent a good chunk of your life literally guiding your brothers through the wilderness. Teaching them how to survive after learning it on your own. That's a lot of pressure for anyone."

"I told you, my dad trusted me. It was a privilege to be responsible for them."

"And now?"

I stare at her.

"Are you still responsible for them?"

"It's my job. I'm the oldest; I have an obligation to the family business and to them." My muscles tense. She's pushing buttons I didn't know I had.

The cool touch of Blakely's hand on my cheek soothes my temper. "I'm trying to understand you and them. That's a heavy weight to put on a kid's shoulders, but you, no pun intended, bear it well."

"I wouldn't be who I am today without those experiences."

"And is who you are now who you want to be?" she asks, studying my face.

My initial reaction is to lash out. That's a bold question coming from her. What with the social media persona she built. But I'm not trying to dig my current hole deeper.

When I stay silent, she sighs, and her features soften. "I'm sorry I pushed the topic about your family stuff. Tell me about your brothers."

Her apology makes me feel worse. I brought her out here to apologize. To explain about Paige. To learn more about her. Not to shut down. And for sure not to kiss, though the guilt of that isn't as potent as it was.

Before I can say anything, my phone rings with a video call —as if mentioning their names summoned them. Bo's number is on my screen, and if Bo is calling, Gray is right there with him.

"I need to take this. Something could be wrong."

Her smile is gentle. "Always the responsible one."

My brow creases with my frown. Why do her words feel more like an accusation than an observation?

"Yeah?" I bark as I hit the answer button.

Bo's grinning face fills the screen. "How's it going? You unfuck things yet?"

Blakely covers her mouth but can't stifle her giggle. "Yeah, Bear, did you unfuck things?"

"Bear?" Gray asks as he shoves his way into the video frame.

I glare at my brothers, a warning in my scowl.

"Fuck yeah," Bo says, "I'm totally calling you that from now on."

"No," I grunt. "Only one person gets to call me that." The evil gleam in my brothers' eyes tells me I haven't heard the last of it.

But Blakely, being Blakely, takes this as her cue. She elbows me over and grins into the camera. "Hi! I'm the one who gets to call him Bear. You must be Bo and Gray?"

Bo's mouth drops open. "You're pretty."

I not-so-subtly guide Blakely out of frame. "Did you two need something? Everything okay?"

"Hey, put Blakely back on. We have to look at your ugly mug all the time," Gray says, smirking.

The familiar throb I associate with my brothers starts ticking behind my eye. "Gray," I snap, "is everything okay?"

"Yeah, man. We called to check on you, that's all. You need to relax, Hudson. We're not kids anymore. Shit, Baby Bo will be thirty this year. We aren't gonna bankrupt the business in a month without you there to triple-check everything."

My jaw aches, and it isn't until Blakely snakes the phone out of my hands that I realize how tightly I'm clenching my teeth.

She slips into her social media voice and dives into conversation with practiced ease. "Have you seen an uptick in bookings yet?"

Gray nods. "Yeah, we're booked out through the spring with more requests coming in daily. It's fucking unbelievable. We've had to push some a ways out because, with just the three of us and Dad as reserve, we don't have the staff to take them all on. It's the best problem we could have."

Blakely preens and gives me a smug smile before turning to the phone. "Hudson told me about how you guys used to go camping with your dad when you were young."

Bo's face lights up. "Yeah, it was awesome. Hudson taught Gray and me everything we know."

"He sounds like a great big brother."

"He is. He looked out for us growing up. Kept us out of trouble."

Gray snorts. "He still does, even though we're grown."

My throat tightens at their words. Do they think I don't trust them? I'm supposed to teach them, lead them, not make them think I don't have confidence in their abilities or place in the business. Is my overprotectiveness holding them back?

Clearing my throat, I turn to Blakely. "Hop back in the hot spring. I need a minute with these two."

"Sure, Bear. No problem. I could use more time to soak." She gives Bo and Gray a friendly wave. "Nice to meet you two."

I wait until she's in the water before focusing on my brothers.

"The least you could do is let us see her in her swimsuit."

If a snarl could throttle a person, Bo would be blue in the face right now.

"Woah, woah. Just teasing, Bear. Damn."

"Fucking hell, Bo. Don't call me that."

"Oh, so the pretty woman can, but your own brother can't?"

"Yes."

"Shit, you really like her, huh?" my youngest brother asks, the teasing tone melting from his voice.

I glance over at Blakely, and when I see her staring out over the valleys and cliffs, I nod.

Gray's words are careful. "Hudson, she's here for a month, and you aren't built for casual. Don't get me wrong, I think she'd be good for you, but what happens when it's time for her to go?"

My chest aches, and I rub a clenched fist over my heart. Gray's right. It's all too easy to imagine Blakely coming home to me every day, putting on one of my t-shirts to sleep in, curling up at my side. For the next three weeks, I could have the fantasy future I thought I lost when Paige left.

But the ending is already written.

Bo shoves his way back onto the screen. "Don't listen to Gray. This is a once-in-a-lifetime chance. You like her. And she's a captive audience. I'd say turn on the charm, but we both know you don't have any."

I roll my eyes as he continues. "She's the first person you've had an inkling of interest in since Paige. You'd be stupid to pass this up. She could fall in love with Trail Creek. And you. If Hallmark movies have taught me anything, it's that the city slicker is never actually happy with their busy, lonely life."

"Hallmark, huh?"

"Hey, don't knock it."

"So, look," I swallow, "I'm sorry if I made you two feel like I don't trust you. You've proven yourselves time and time again. I'm, um, proud of you both."

Gray groans. "Oh shit, Hudson, don't go getting all sappy on us. We know we're awesome. We learned from the best." He winks. "Now get the fuck off the phone and get back to the beautiful woman wearing a swimsuit and sitting in a hot spring."

Bo gives me a salacious grin. "Yeah, time to finish unfucking things."

The call disconnects, and I stand there for a moment, gathering my thoughts. That conversation was like being the ball in a fucking pinball machine, but a small weight lifts from my shoulders. I told my brothers I'm proud of them. It's something I should say more often.

Sure, Bo and Gray are jokesters, and they drive me up the wall, but they're good men. And they want what's best for Peak Adventures as much as I do. It's time I show them I believe that.

Blakely's voice draws my attention to her. "Did you have a good talk with them?"

I shrug, but then I see the top of Blakely's turquoise bikini sitting next to the hot spring and choke on my tongue. Her back is to me, but knowing she's topless has all the blood in my body rushing to my cock, leaving none for my brain.

"What are you doing?"

She peeks at me over her shoulder, a suggestive look on her face. "Enjoying the view and the water."

"Why is your top off?" My voice is ragged and rasping. Without thinking, I close the space between us, yanking my t-shirt off before slipping it over her head.

Her surprised squeak pulls me back to reality, and I huff out a laugh.

Blakely wriggles her arms through the sleeves and presses her lips into a thin line. "You could have asked me to put my top back on."

"Wasn't thinking clearly."

Blakely grins. "Did the idea of me topless short-circuit your brain?"

"Everything about you short circuits my brain." I extend a hand and pull her from the water. I realize my mistake once she steps out of the hot spring. The brilliant idea I had to cover her up is now see-through. Fuck. Me.

She arches one delicate eyebrow at me, and I spin, giving her my back. "Trying to be a gentleman here, Blakely."

The rustling of clothing calls to me like a lure to a fish, but I stand firm. It isn't until she laughs and gives me the all-clear that I turn back to her. It's not that I don't want to see her; I do, but...

"We need to finish our talk."

"About your parents? Your apology? Kissing?"

"Yes." She holds her hands out in exasperation.

"Your family. Why you're here."

Blakely makes a sour face. "Talking about my past requires something stronger than a hot spring."

"How do you feel about whiskey?"

"I'm usually more of a wine girlie. But when in the wilderness." She shrugs.

I brush my lips against hers, pack up our picnic—*fuck, she's got me calling it a goddamn picnic now*—and guide her to the Jeep.

The ride back to the cabin is quiet but comfortable. I figure we're both lost in our thoughts. Two factions war in my mind. Side one shouts that I'm an idiot setting myself up for a Paige redux. I'm endangering my business. My reputation.

The other side isn't screaming. No. It's a quiet, steady beat. Encouraging me to be brave and do what I want for once.

And fuck it. What I want is Blakely Bradshaw in her annoying, bold, infuriating, and bewitching glory.

When I pull into the familiar clearing, I say, "Why don't you shower, and I'll make us some dinner."

Blakely nods, and I take my time unpacking the Jeep to give her a semblance of privacy. Once we've showered and eaten, I grab two lowball glasses, drop ice in each, and pour generous servings for us.

"Sip it."

My laugh when she takes a drink and sputters earns me a glare. Rubbing her back, I croon, "Breathe through it. It'll grow on you."

"So…" She coughs and glares at the whiskey. "Which awkward topic do you want to tackle first? My childhood trauma? Your repressed emotions? Breaking the no kissing rule?"

I shake my head. Leave it to her to lay it all out. Drawing a long drink from my glass, I weigh the pros and cons of each topic. "Let's move to the couch."

Blakely curls up beside me while I study the amber liquid like it'll tell me what to say. Scratching my beard, I mumble, "Why do you think I have issues with my family?"

Her soft hand pulls my face so we are eye to eye. "I said repressed emotions." At my wan smile, she gives me a sweet kiss. "From what I can tell, you have a wonderful family, better than most. But I also think you carry an unnecessary amount of pressure. How much of that is because of the way you learned your trade? How much of that is who you are? It's not a bad thing, Bear. I just wonder what you'd be like without the weight of expectations around your neck."

Her words swirl in my head. When I don't answer, she presses on. "What about Paige? You admitted she still colors your perspective."

I stiffen at the mention of my ex. "I apologized for that."

"You did. I'm not saying it's a bad thing." Blakely gives me a small smile. "How about we change gears for a bit?"

"Tell me something about you."

The ice clinks in her glass as she slams what's left of her whiskey back. "Refill?" she asks with a gasp.

"I told you to sip it."

Blakely waves her hand. "Yeah, yeah."

I top off both our glasses and wait.

"So Kirk is the only person who knows this, but I grew up in a small town west of Abilene. Dirt poor." She shivers, and I automatically pull her closer, wrapping an arm around her. "Like, trailer on blocks, bugs and worse in the walls, no food on the weekends, poor."

Her long lashes rest against her cheeks as she closes her eyes. "All I wanted was to get out of that place. The town, the trailer. My senior year, I got my wish."

The way she spits the words tells me there's more to the story.

She sighs. "Anyway. I started a new life in Austin and never looked back. I'm here to grow my brand. To prove people wrong."

I brush my thumb over her supple bottom lip. "Is that the only reason?"

"Looks like I was wrong about you being emotionally stunted." Setting our glasses to the side, she shoots me a half smile. "I was lonely as hell. I thought coming out here might give me a chance to figure out what I want. But I wasn't expecting to want you."

Maybe it's the whiskey or the vulnerability of her words, but with a growl, I capture Blakely's lips. All the bickering, the tension, the flirting crash over me, and before I know it, I have her pinned between my body and the couch.

Our mouths collide, her tongue slipping between my lips. Can she taste my loneliness, my lust, my need?

I should stop. I'm ignoring every rule I've ever set. Instead, I rock against her, and with each press of my hips, her shirt rides a little higher. The soft material of the fuzzy pink sweater is no competition for the silk of her skin.

The dip of her waist, the flare of her hips—every curve of her body is a winding road I long to travel. It would be so easy to lose myself in this moment. Where nothing exists outside this cabin. No responsibilities, no work. Just Blakely and me.

Breaking the kiss, her lips puffy and pink, Blakely whispers, "This is going to end badly, isn't it?"

I trail open-mouth kisses down her throat until I reach the crook of her neck. Here I bury my face and inhale her sweet scent.

She lifts my head, those fathomless eyes searching my face. "If we stop now..."

I swallow. If we stop now, we can walk away, mostly unscathed. Instead of answering her, I seize her in another bruising kiss and let her lips push away all my doubts.

blakely

DAY NINE

Thwack! Thwack!

Grumbling, I rub my sleep-swollen eyes. "Hudson, what's that noise?"

When he doesn't answer, I stretch my toes in search of his thigh to poke. I reach as far as my five-five frame will go, but find nothing except cold sheets. What the hell?

Thwack!

This time, the mystery sound makes me jump. It's rhythmic and harsh, but I can't place it. Hudson isn't here or fussing about the racket, so he must be involved, which means I for sure need to figure out what's going on.

Thwack!

With more of my wits about me, I pad to a window and scan the treeline. Nothing on this side of the house stands out. So I try again, nudging the front door open and peering over the clearing.

And there, like some sort of pagan lumberjack god, stands Hudson Brooks, chopping wood.

I scramble from the door and dash to get my phone. My spidey senses are tingling. Hudson plus an axe is top-notch material. But I screech to a halt because I am in no way, shape, or form camera-ready.

So, like a multitasking fool, I yank a brush through my wavy hair and pull on leggings and a tank top. I shove my hiking boots on with no regard for my feet, and one of Hudson's discarded flannels tops off my outfit. It'll do; after all, this live isn't about me.

Without even pointing the camera at myself, I start talking. "Hey, y'all! I'm coming to you live from my adorable cabin in the woods. And BBs, you are in for a treat today." I train the phone—and my greedy eyes—on Hudson. I'm rapt with attention as he wipes a gloved hand across his forehead. Tiny beads of sweat glimmer on his skin, and despite the chilly weather, he's shirtless.

I want nothing more than to trace his skin with my tongue, gathering those drops of salty-sweet sweat. But I'm once again a paragon of restraint. I deserve a cookie for all the damn restraint I've shown. With a pout, I settle for zooming in closer than necessary.

"BBs, are you seeing this?" I whisper, not bothering to look at the screen. They are eating this up. Who wouldn't?

Hudson's dark hair is disheveled and windswept. He hasn't trimmed his beard, but it only enhances his rugged looks. He turns his face to the sun for a moment, the rays casting his golden skin in their light.

Another urge strikes me, and I have to ball my free hand into a fist to keep from stalking across the clearing, digging my fingers into his scalp, and kissing the dickens out of him.

My mouth drops open as he swings the axe , splitting a large piece of wood in two.

"Holy shit," I whisper before catching myself and turning the camera so I'm on screen. With a purr and a giggle, I say, "Daddy's swinging big today." From the corner of my eye, I see Hudson's head shoot up, a hint of pink tinting his bronze skin. He glares at me, so I wink and wave.

"Hudson, say hi to my BBs! They're very impressed by your *big axe.*" I make sure to place a heavy emphasis on the words, knowing they will fluster him more and drive my fans wild. Plus, I know first-hand how big that axe really is.

Well, not first *hand* given that we haven't done more than kiss since the hot springs. It's like I'm living in my very own closed-door romance.

Whenever I think we might move ahead a step, Hudson pulls back. It's been two days of tooth-achingly sweet kisses and chaste touches and nothing else. I'm practically throwing up the bat signal, trying to move us forward, but Hudson holds firm. When I ask him why, he gives me a hug or soft kiss and steers the conversation to other things, or makes me do more terrible knot tying, fire making, or navigation practice—which I'm somehow getting worse at.

The sight of Hudson, so masculine and just *rawr,* has me squeezing my thighs together. I imagine those rough hands exploring my body, pinching my nipples until they ache—the warm, sweaty scent of him enveloping me.

Yeah... those kisses need to give way to more ASAP.

"Hudson! I said say hi!"

All I get is a frown before he sets another large piece of wood on the block and, again, in a single swing, cleaves it cleanly in half.

"This may be the hottest thing I've ever seen. Send a heart

if you agree!" My phone screen fills with hundreds of hearts. This is so going viral.

I step closer to where Hudson works, my heart and the pulse between my legs pounding in tandem. "Can you teach me how to do that?"

His eyes run over my outfit, a flicker of appreciation shining when he sees I'm wearing his shirt. "Technically, I can, but this isn't a toy. The blade is sharp." His eyes narrow before nodding at the cabin. "Go get the gloves we bought; your hands are too delicate to do this without protection."

I squeal, then whisper into the camera, "BBs, hold tight. Enjoy the show while I go get my gear." Setting my phone on a nearby cord of wood, I angle it so Hudson is in view. For his part, he turns his attention back to chopping wood, and by the time I return with my gloves, the stack has grown considerably.

"I'm ready to try my hand at chopping wood." I flex my bicep in the general direction of my phone. We should both be perfectly in frame. When I reach for the enormous axe, though, he stops me.

"Need you to do a little legwork first."

Narrowing my eyes, I ask, "What do you mean?"

"Take all the split pieces and stack them by the door."

The pile at his feet is massive. "Are you serious?"

"Yep."

"How about you show me how to do it first, then I'll help pick up?"

"Nope. Stack first."

My nose wrinkles in distaste, but with a sullen sigh, I pick up a couple of pieces of wood and carry them to the porch. I do this a handful of times until the stack next to the door is knee high.

"Can I be done yet?"

Hudson grumbles but extends his hand, encouraging me to step closer. With a gentleness that belies his size, he snags the hair tie off my wrist and carefully pulls my hair into a messy bun, making sure all the long strands are up and off my neck and back.

"Wouldn't want your pretty hair to get in the way," he murmurs.

Sparks dance along the sensitive skin beneath my ear, where his lips graze as he speaks.

"Ready?"

With a resolute nod, I hold out my hand, nearly falling forward from the weight when he places the axe in my grip. Over my shoulder, I call out toward my phone. "Damn, y'all. This axe is heavy! Which makes what we saw this morning even more impressive." I wiggle my eyebrows and grin.

"Who are you talking to? Me? Because I know it's heavy."

Bless his heart. I point my thumb at my phone.

Annoyance tightens his features. "You're still filming? I thought you ended it when you went inside."

I screw on a smile and, through clenched teeth, say, "Of course, I'm still filming. Now show me what to do." Louder so the audience can hear me, I giggle. "Hudson, you big goof, the BBs are waiting!"

When he doesn't do anything, I widen my eyes in a silent plea of *please-move-you-giant-handsome-asshole*.

His sigh tells me he's giving in, but also that I'm going to catch hell for this later. Oh well. Worth it.

Glancing over his shoulder, he pulls us out of the phone's aim. Then he leans in and nips my ear before whispering, "Don't think we won't talk about this."

Guiding me back into the frame—all while ignoring my little whimper—he places his large hands over mine, showing me how to grip the handle properly. He guides my arms up and over my head, then down, and in a smooth swing, the axe cuts through the air with a *whoosh*. He repeats the action three more times.

I should pay attention to my actions, but all I can focus on are his arms around my body, the heat of his chest against my back, and the subtle scent of my shampoo mixing with his natural one. I can't be held responsible when my body reacts, my back arching so I can press my ass against his hips.

"Blakely." His voice is a low warning, but it doesn't stop him from rocking his hips. "It's a good fucking thing this releases a lot of tension." Then louder, he says, "Ready to try on your own with an actual piece of wood?"

Hudson takes a step back, and I feel empty without the weight of his body against mine. But it also helps clear my head.

Flashing a brilliant smile at my phone, I say, "Okay, BBs! Here I go!"

With a Herculean effort, I swing the axe up and let the weight carry it downward. A third of the wood splits away and falls to the side. I did it.

Dropping the axe, I crash into Hudson, jumping and grabbing his shoulders. "I did it! I chopped wood!"

"Sure did, Spitfire." His fingers brush against my jaw, and for a second, I think he might kiss me. Despite the phone filming us. Despite the thousands of people watching him with hearts in their eyes. But he just smirks.

Taking a calming breath, I walk over to my phone and smile into the camera. "BBs, I hope you saw that. I'm practically a wilderness expert now." With a quick goodbye, I sign off and take a couple of steps toward the porch.

"Hold up. Where do you think you're going?"

"Um, inside."

"Nope. You said you wanted to learn how to chop wood."

"And I did." I give him my best *duh* face.

"You cut one piece of kindling. Now get over here and let me show you again. This time without an audience."

Like a scolded child, I drag my feet over to him. But when he grips my hips and hauls me into position, there's nothing childish about the feelings he ignites. Hudson's large fingers walk a path upward, skating over my rib cage, then skating over my shoulders and down the length of my arms until our fingers curl together. He guides my hands, positioning them on the handle.

I swear my heart is pounding loud enough for the people back in Trail Creek to hear it.

He swallows, the sound faint but audible. Then, he steers my swing and helps me put more force into it, so this time, the axe head strikes in the middle and splits the log evenly. Before I can do a celebratory dance, a new uncut piece is on the stump we're using as the base.

We repeat that same sensual slow dance. His hands skimming my body until our hands clasp together. I'm sweaty and tingling, but the only release comes from the crack of the wood.

When his hands once again follow the path up my back, his hips buck forward, and on instinct, I press back, grinding against him.

"Fucking hell, Blakely." The axe falls to the ground, and Hudson's lips are on mine. My kiss is desperate, full of longing and need. I beg for entrance to his mouth, and when he grants it, I run my tongue along his teeth and shiver at the slight prick of his canines.

Hudson lifts me so I can anchor my legs around his waist. His calloused palms slide along the bare skin of my back, and I can't help but rock against him. The kissing. The touching. The glorious grinding lasts another handful of minutes. If I could just get a little more pressure...

A pained groan leads to my feet landing back on the ground. Hudson's chest rises and falls at a rapid pace, the black of his blown pupils eating up the green of his eyes. I want him.

Resting his chin on my head, he hugs me before giving me a small nip to my lower lip. "Leave it to me. Cold front's coming in tonight. Need to make sure we have enough wood." Then he's right back to it, the now familiar *thwack* sound filling the air.

Dazed from his touch, I stumble to the cabin. When the door snicks shut behind me, I lean against the wood to cool off my overheated body. I'm all worked up. The hot and heavy make-out session, combined with the forty-eight hours of teasing kisses and nothing more, has me needing relief.

Now.

My eyes land on the clawfoot tub. In the eleven days I've been here, I've taken way too many rushed showers. A nice long soak is exactly what I need. Decision made, I turn on the water and set the temperature to my liking. I leave a trail of clothes strewn in my path while I go to grab bath oil from my belongings. Cursing when I trip over my freaking hiking boots, I briefly consider picking up the mess on my side of the cabin, but veto that idea. I do kick my boot for good measure, though.

I add several drops of the fragrant oil into the warm water, inhaling the soft floral scent before stepping into the deep tub.

It's so quiet, with only the unwavering crack of splintering wood breaking the silence. Grabbing my phone from where it rests on a bundle of towels, I pick my *Spicy Night* playlist and set it to random. Hozier's seductive lyrics and voice draw me in, and I let my mind go where it wants—and it wants Hudson.

Hudson chopping wood, shirtless, sweat running down his body. Hudson naked in the shower, his thick cock straining with need. Hudson tasting me, his surprisingly soft lips parting mine. Hudson on top of me, spreading my legs, pushing into me, filling me. Hudson whispering filthy things in my ear while I come on his... axe.

My hands roam my slick body, skimming the valley between my breasts. I toy with my nipples until they bead, then give them a teasing twist before moving lower. Raising one leg, I rest it over the lip of the tub and circle my clit, my hips twitching with each pass. Slipping a single finger in my warmth, I slowly work it in... then out. In. Out. In. Swirl. Out.

Then, I add another.

I continue my daydream, my sexy Bear pinning me to the wall, his rough hands charting the curves of my body, claiming my pussy in his name. The thrilling visual of Hudson's broad shoulders splitting my thighs, my heels digging into the powerful muscles of his back, has me bucking against my hand, trying to go deeper. My fingers aren't thick enough, not long enough to give me what I'm searching for. I'm so close, but I can't quite get there. Frustration threatens to pull me away from the edge. I need more.

Spying the faucet from my half-shut eyes, I wriggle and turn the water back on. I position myself under the steady stream with both legs splayed wide over the sides. Then, I use one hand to spread myself open. The continuous cascade of warm liquid falls onto my clit and couples with my fingers inside me. All it takes is the addition of the images of a certain sweaty, bronzed god's face buried in my pussy to push me over the edge. I call out Hudson's name far louder than I intend, but I'm basking in my boneless afterglow, so I can't be concerned.

"Blakely, are you okay? I heard you scream my name."

Hudson peers down at me, my hair floating around me in wild tendrils, legs spread eagle. With a yelp, I sit up, splashing water over the edge of the tub and onto his feet.

Frozen in a silent stand-off, we inspect each other—me sitting in lukewarm water looking at him. Him staring at me like he's seen me naked, which now he has. I lick my lips. Will this be the tipping point for him? Are my wet body, my hardened nipples, the spread of my thighs just hidden from his view enough to make him snap and give me what I want?

Despite his pink-tinged cheeks, he doesn't hesitate to drink me in, staring at my face and moving lower to what's hidden beneath the water. I enjoy the heat of his gaze on me until he grabs a towel and wraps it around my shoulders, effectively shielding me from view.

The flimsy weight of the towel feels like a piano settling on my chest. With a nervous laugh, I wave a hand. "Sorry, um, I thought I saw a mouse."

"Yeah." Hudson blushes and looks away from me. "A mouse. Sure." Without another word, he strides out the door. Then I hear the familiar sound of wood being demolished in a single swing.

As Hudson predicted, a cold front comes through—and not just outside. With each passing hour, the temps drop, and by the time the sun sets, it's in the low teens. Meanwhile, in the cabin we're sitting at a frosty negative ten, best I can tell. Whether this is because Hudson's upset about the live spot or embarrassed about my afternoon self-delight, I can't say.

"Gonna shower."

"Okay, enjoy." I smile at him from where I'm curled up on the couch. An unintelligible grunt is his reply. Remind me what

I see in him again? Then he pads through the cabin in his boxers, restoring my memory.

While Hudson showers, I take the initiative to make dinner. Growing up the way I did, I counted on free breakfast and lunch at school. Weekends and long breaks I existed on peanut butter and jelly sandwiches or dry cereal. Things that were easy to get from the local food bank and didn't require me to cook. Half the time, the stove and oven didn't work. So making dinner is way outside my comfort zone, but a peace offering can't hurt, and it's too late in the day for apology coffee. I'm hoping we can talk about things—all the things—and maybe move on from kissing to something more.

Or at least get back to kissing.

I stir the lumpy sauce. Some of it's bubbling, and some isn't. The noodles aren't boiling, but they've been in the water for ages, so I figure they're fine.

The shower turning off acts as my timer, and I plate the food. Hudson joins me in the kitchen in a considerably better mood. How can I tell? Well, he says three words to me rather than just grunting.

"Want a drink?"

I nod and take the offered water before sitting. With a deep breath, I say, "So, this afternoon—"

"What is this?" He's frowning at his plate while twirling his fork through the noodles.

"It's spaghetti. Quit changing the subject."

"No."

I wrinkle my nose. "No? What do you mean, no?"

"No, this is not spaghetti. This is undercooked noodles with a can of tomato sauce poured over the top. Do you not cook at home?"

"Um, no, actually I don't. I use a meal service; they deliver all my meals for the week, and I nuke them when I have time or am hungry. But also, we still need to talk about—"

Hudson cuts me off again. "Give me your plate; I'll make us something edible."

Irritation has me narrowing my eyes. He's clearly refusing to address the masturbating elephant in the room, and he's insulting the dinner I made. I follow him and watch him dump the food in the trash.

"Hey! I'm sure it tastes fine!"

"Did you try it?"

"No, I didn't get a chance before you scooped up my plate!"

"I did you a favor."

"You know what, Bear? I'm not even hungry," I grumble with my hands in the air. "Make whatever you want."

I spin and sulk my way to the couch, sinking down with a dramatic sigh. *Smug, sexy, know-it-all bastard.*

Stretched out on the uncomfortable cushions, I do my best to ignore the delicious aromas. Eventually, though, my curiosity gets the better of me, and I peer over the back of the sofa. Hudson moves around the kitchen with practiced ease, chopping vegetables, mixing something in a bowl, coating some kind of meat in a breading. When he turns around, I dive below the couch back so he can't see me spying.

"Food's ready."

"I'm not hungry." My traitorous stomach picks that moment to growl.

"Liar."

Grumbling a few choice words, I peek back over the couch. "I'll eat, but only if you agree to talk about what happened today."

"Fine."

"Fine." I make my way to the table and take a tentative bite of the sweet and spicy chicken. Dammit, it's delicious. "Thank you. This is great," I say, shooting him a half smile.

"Hot honey chicken."

When I raise my eyebrows in question, he huffs and points at my plate. "Hot honey chicken. The meal."

"Where did you learn to cook?"

He shrugs. "YouTube."

"Okay, let me be more specific. I want a longer-than-one-word answer. What made you decide to learn about cooking?"

The eye roll he sends my direction is epic. "Mom did most of the cooking while we were growing up, but when we were camping with Dad, we had to fend for ourselves. I spent the first few years fumbling my way through shitty meals, so I figured it was worth it to figure out how to make something that tastes good."

Once again, things come back to his childhood spent fending for himself and his brothers.

Before I can push the topic any further, Hudson asks, "Want to tell me why you were filming me this morning?"

I snort. "Because I'm a genius."

Hudson is unimpressed with my answer. "When I whispered in your ear, kissed your neck... those moments were for you and me. Not them." His eyes linger on me; the same hungry gaze I witnessed this afternoon evident in his expression now. But it's colored with something else. Anger? Frustration?

"I doubt they saw anything. The way we were standing, your back was to them."

He sighs. "Not the point."

"It's not a big deal."

"Princess, it's a very big deal."

I frown at the use of *that* nickname. He only calls me princess when he's upset with me.

"Do you ever think about anyone but yourself and your numbers?" The harsh words have me sitting up straighter, itching to defend myself.

"Of course I do! I was thinking of you when I was jilling off in the bathtub!" Lifting my chin, I stare him down.

A possessive growl rumbles from his throat. "That's not what I'm talking about, and you know it."

"All *I know* is *you know* exactly what I was doing when I called out your name. Sorry, not sorry. I'm a healthy young woman. It's natural. I'm also not apologizing for filming you today."

I glide my foot up his leg, enjoying the way he shifts as I graze his calf. "It was the sexiest thing I've ever seen." I pause, a smile dancing on my lips. "It's why I needed to take matters into my own hands."

"Fuck, Blakely."

My foot snakes a little higher, and I grin. "You do the same thing when you disappear into the bathroom."

He makes a slight noise of protest, but I press on. "We're both adults here, Bear. Admit it. You think about me when you..." I wiggle my eyebrows at him.

Hudson makes a non-committal grunt and tears his eyes away from me, suddenly paying extra attention to his plate.

"Admit it!" I chirp in a sing-song voice, my foot traveling higher, inching up his inner thigh, where I brush against something significantly harder.

"Blakely," he groans, a warning tone to his voice.

"Hudson," I purr, ignoring his warning. Before I move my foot again, he grasps my ankle, featherlight at first, then firmer. His hand is warm and dry and the right amount of rough. I wish he'd touch me anywhere else. Everywhere else.

"You should put socks on, Spitfire; your feet are like ice." He drops my ankle and rises from the table as if he didn't dump a bucket of water on me.

I pout at him but follow suit, taking my dish to the sink. He steps to the side, leaning against the counter, watching me as I rinse off my plate. "You just going to stare?"

"No."

In a flash, he's behind me. Hudson's hand ghosts down my back before settling on my hip. His heated breath against my neck sends a wave of longing through me. Then his lips skim across the tops of my shoulders.

A nibble, a quick swipe of his tongue, a gentle suck. I'm shaking and squirming, and in a desperate attempt to keep his mouth on my skin, I lace my fingers in his hair, gripping tightly. My hips rock back into the cradle of his pelvis, and a ragged moan slips from my throat. The world is a haze of sensation and Hudson's hot, wet, teasing kisses.

Every nerve in my body tingles with each lap of his tongue, each press of his lips.

Then his teeth graze my ear, murmured words dripping down my spine like honey. "So you think I'm fantasizing about you during my private time? That's what you wanted to talk about?"

"Yes, that's it." The words feel like glue in my throat.

With a smirk, Hudson steps away, leaving me aching with need. He silently makes his way to the bathroom, eyes on mine as he closes the door.

hudson

I add more logs to the already roaring fire, hoping it will keep the cabin warm overnight. Blakely is already in bed, huddled under the blanket, shivering.

"The fire is great, but now that I'm further away and in my pajamas, I'm freezing. I'm so used to central heat and air and cranking the thermostat up when the temps are this low."

The mention of Blakely's "pajamas" has me adjusting myself. It's no wonder she's cold, considering the slip of silk and equally tiny shorts she's wearing. "Once you fall asleep, you'll be fine."

"Thanks for the helpful advice, asshole."

I chuckle and climb into bed. Making myself comfortable, I rest my arms behind my head and consider the best way to explain how her filming me without my knowing makes me feel. However, my body has other plans, and my eyes droop. The hours spent chopping wood to get Blakely out of my system were reset by her blatant admission and flirting tonight. Thankfully, my solo time took care of the lingering tension, but now I'm tired.

Fighting off the fatigue, I clear my throat, ready to talk, but a noise I can't place sounds in the dark. An animal? No. The fire? No.

Blakely.

"Spitfire, what're you doing?"

"It's m-my te-teeth."

I run my hand over my face, a gesture I often do when dealing with my city mouse roommate. "You're dramatic."

"N-no. I'm n-not. I'm just c-cold."

"Scoot closer, but don't you dare put your icy feet on me."

Without hesitation, Blakely snuggles up next to me, and the chattering of her teeth stops. Mere seconds later, her cold toes press into my calves. Little brat.

I whisper, "I might think this was a ploy to get closer to me."

"We always end up like this anyway, may as well start this way, too. Now, shhh, time to sleep, Bear," she whispers back, her eyes already closed.

"Before you fall asleep, we need to talk."

Blakely presses her body to mine. "Can it wait till tomorrow? You're so warm. I want to cuddle." She skims her lips against my jaw. "Unless there's something else—besides talking—you want to do."

Fuck. Do I want to do more than talk? Of course. I want to ravage her gorgeous body. Leave marks all over her skin. Taste every inch of her, bite and bruise her in the best way. Despite a fuck-ton of kisses, I haven't been able to take the next step. Despite craving her like nothing before.

There's enough lingering doubt to keep me from taking things to the next level. Each kiss pulls me deeper, and if I go beyond that, I'll end up hopelessly lost in the whirlwind that is Blakely Bradshaw.

I may have crossed the kissing line, but I'm holding firm

against anything more—or at least trying to. Today's show for the camera tells me it's the right call. Don't get me wrong. Blakely getting so worked up over me swinging my axe that she had to get a little release didn't hurt my ego. *Fuck, that was hot.*

But she filmed us without talking to me. Her focus was on her viewers and her account. I was already wary of getting hurt like I did with Paige, but now I wonder if Blakely wants this or if it's a ploy to grow her account. I need to sleep on this.

I need to know this is real.

My cock adamantly disagrees with me, though, and is aching to slide into her. I grab her wandering hand before it has the chance to slip beneath the waist of my joggers and press a chaste kiss to her knuckles.

"We can wait until tomorrow to talk. But don't think you're getting out of it." My mouth captures hers before moving to her forehead. "Get some sleep, brat."

She huffs but doesn't argue with me, which I take as a win. Blakely is going to be my undoing.

But part of me welcomes it.

DAY TEN

From behind me, Blakely stirs. I stoke the fire and glance at her over my shoulder. She looks so cute, rubbing her eyes, hair all rumpled, pillow lines on her cheeks.

"What time is it?"

"It's three. Go back to sleep. I'm adding more wood to the fire. Don't want it to go out."

"Did the temperature drop again?"

"No, it's holding steady."

She pulls her knees to her chest, watching me. The flicker

of the flames bathe her in their orange glow, like some sort of fire goddess.

Setting one last large piece in the flames, I crawl back into bed and pull Blakely to me, spooning her from behind. I drape one arm over her stomach, the other under her pillow. Her body melts against mine, and I hide my face in her hair, taking a greedy inhale of her sweet floral scent. *And that damn fancy ass shampoo.*

She squirms, trying to turn to face me. "Stop all that wiggling," I grumble and hold her tighter, relishing the sensation of her ass against my cock.

Blakely huffs, "Spoilsport," and shifts against me once more.

It takes every ounce of willpower I possess to keep from rutting her right here and now. Gripping her hip, I nudge her ear with my nose. "Sleep."

It isn't long before she's snoring in my arms, adorable little snuffles and sniffs. I kiss her neck twice, then let exhaustion pull me under.

A handful of hours later, I wake with Blakely wrapped around me like vines on a trellis. Unwinding myself from her grabby hands, I take in the pout of her lips, the small lines around her eyes, the turned-up tip of her nose. Her blonde hair has gone from silky waves to messy snarls, but it only makes me want to tangle my hands in the mussed strands.

Fuck, Hudson, you big sap. Get a grip. I scold myself as I take a leak. Blakely's got me waxing poetic in my head. I blame Bo and his Hallmark movie mentions. And her pillowy lips. And hourglass curves. And maddening mouth.

I curse myself on the way to the kitchen, but I make two cups of coffee—one black, one with two sugars and more cream than could ever be right.

A soft yawn precedes thin arms wrapping around my waist. Blakely buries her face in my back. "Good morning."

Turning, I steal a quick peck and hand her the mug.

"For me?"

"For you."

After the first sip, she smacks her lips like I've made her some gourmet creation. "Mmm. Liquid gold." Then she smiles. "Thanks for keeping me warm last night."

"Turns out sleeping next to you isn't the worst thing."

She laughs. "Careful, that almost sounded like a compliment."

"Don't let it go to your head."

"Oh, don't worry. You keep me humble."

"There are many words I could use to describe you, but humble isn't one."

She rolls her eyes, hands me her half-finished coffee, and strolls to the bathroom.

"It's too cold for what I had planned. How about a cabin day?" I ask, placing our mugs on the counter.

Her eyes study me, narrowing for a moment. "This feels like a trick. You aren't going to make me weave a blanket from roots and build a windproof shelter out of my hair or something equally terrible?"

So fucking dramatic. I don't bother answering her. She blows a raspberry at me and disappears behind the bathroom door. While she's in there, her phone buzzes. And buzzes. And fucking buzzes.

When the damn thing goes off for a fifth time, I snap, storming to the bed and answering the video call. "What?" I growl in greeting.

"Um, Hudson? It's me, Kirk James. Blakely's manager?"

I settle on the mattress and kick my feet up. "Is something wrong? Why're you calling?"

He holds his hands up in a placating manner. "No. No. Everything's good. Better than good, even. Is Blakely available?"

"She's in the bathroom."

"Oh." His eyes flit rapidly.

My lips press into a thin line. "You squeamish about women using the restroom, Kirk?"

"No! I'm not sure how Blakely—"

"Everybody shits."

The slim man turns pink all the way to the top of his bald head. Crap. I probably offended him.

Then I hear a scandalized screech and the sound of small feet stomping across hardwood. "I wasn't doing that!"

I glare at Kirk like this is his fault. "It's okay. You don't have to be embarrassed."

"I was washing my face and brushing my teeth." Each word sounds like a dog snarling. I'm in so much trouble. May as well dig the hole a little deeper.

The heat of Blakely's eyes bore into my forehead, but I fight off the prickles on my scalp. "She snores. Did you know?"

Kirk shakes his head, mouth still open.

"Yeah. Louder than my fucking father. You should've warned me."

His nervous laughter filters over the video. "Sorry, man, I had no idea she snores."

"I don't snore!" Blakely flings herself onto the bed next to me, finger out, ready to poke me. I snatch her hand before she has the chance and gather her into an angry bundle in my lap.

"You do. Loudly. And talk in your sleep. It's a wonder I've gotten any rest at all."

"You're making that up. No one has ever complained about sleeping next to me, thank you very much."

"They were probably all scared you'd yell at them," Kirk chimes in.

"It's a good thing I'm not scared of you. Isn't it? This way, you get to hear the truth." Her mouth drops open, but before she can tell me off, I press my lips to her cheek and hand her the phone.

The tension in her jaw and shoulders disappears, and she relaxes against me.

I'm considering kissing her again when Kirk interrupts. "Blakely, glad you are up. Let's talk numbers. The livestream yesterday was massive."

Blakely tilts her head back and beams at me before turning to Kirk. "Really? I knew it would be huge. I haven't looked at it since posting!"

"You should; people are eating it up. They are big fans of Mr. Brooks there and the idea of the two of you as more than roommates." Kirk's eyebrows wiggle up and down, and he gives us a knowing grin. "I knew you two would make a compelling couple."

With a wave of her hand, Blakely refocuses the conversation, and while she's perfectly at ease, my agitation triples. "Get serious. Let's talk numbers. What are you seeing?"

"Your biggest post to date. 'Blakely Bradshaw and her Sexy Lumberjack' is trending."

Blakely elbows me in the ribs. "I knew it."

"You need to read through the comments. I recommend you do it together." Again, he shoots us a shrewd look. "So, you two finally kissed."

"There have been a few errant kisses, some heavy flirting, and a touch of mutual masturba—"

As I snarl, "Blakely!" Kirk yells, "Stop right there! I love you, BB, but nope. Please don't finish that sentence."

She giggles and shrugs. "Fine. I expected Hudson's reaction, but I never pegged you for a prude, Kirk." She leans into the lens and, in a dramatic stage whisper, adds, "Marcus tells me things."

Kirk covers his face. "This is so inappropriate."

With another laugh, Blakely ends the call and immediately opens one of her many apps. I watch her scroll until the screen is nothing but a blur. Every now and then, she laughs or groans, but then she goes stock-still in my arms.

The picture on her phone makes my breath catch. It's the two of us—my arms around her waist, my mouth grazing her ear. She's angled toward me with a dreamy look on her face.

If I didn't know better, I'd swear we were a couple. Blakely saves the image to her camera roll, a pink flush on her cheeks.

She ducks her head. "What? It's a great picture of me." She wriggles in my lap until we face each other, her legs on either side of my hips. "Want to hear some of the comments?"

"Um..."

"Listen to this one! *'I swore I'd never follow Blakely Bradshaw, but if she keeps sharing that delicious hunk, I'll be a follower for life.'* You're helping me convert the haters."

When I don't say anything, she continues reading. Many of the comments mention me or speculate on Blakely and me as a couple.

"They love you, Hudson! You could start your own account and have thousands of followers within a month."

I listen, frozen in confusion and frustration. This is everything I've avoided. There's a reason I don't deal with this shit for the business. I don't want or need a bunch of random assholes talking about me and my love life. Or whatever the fuck this thing is between us.

Minutes pass before she realizes I haven't spoken. She tips her head to the side. "What's up?"

"Nothing. I'm gonna check on the fire." Shifting her off my

lap without speaking, I skulk to the fireplace. I'm wrong for walking away without talking to her, but I'm liable to say something I'll regret—something about her only thinking of herself again.

After stabbing the logs with the poker, I hunker on the couch, losing myself in the flickering flames and my thoughts. I signed up for this, but I never planned on people seeing something so intimate. When I brushed my lips against her neck and whispered in her ear, I thought it was just us. Not Blakely, me, and thousands of internet shit stirrers.

The weight of the couch cushions shifts as Blakely perches next to me. She's close. Very close. For a second, I consider putting some space between us, but then she settles a hand on my thigh and starts talking.

"Hey, you okay? You kind of ran off there at the end of the conversation. I thought we were having fun."

I keep my eyes on the fire. "I don't know what to think about all this. It's fucking invasive."

"I thought you didn't care what a bunch of strangers on the internet think of you?"

"This is different. It's not about me as a guide. This is about what I thought was a private moment between us." I pause and rub my beard. "I feel a little used. "

Blakely sucks in a gasp of air at my words. "Used?"

"Being played to boost your numbers, or whatever it is that matters to you and Kirk. Is any of this real to you? Or is it all a show for your job, your persona? It's so easy for you to flip the switch and become *Blakely Bradshaw* social media star."

She climbs into my lap, looping her arms around my neck. "It's no show. I mean, it's kind of a show, but I'm not using you. It's a symbiotic relationship. Each time I post something, your business grows, too. I thought you understood how this works. Do you want me to take the post down? I will. It won't stop the reposts or the trending, but—"

"No. I... fuck." My head falls forward into her chest. "I don't know, Blakely. They aren't even using my name. I'm Blakely Bradshaw's lumberjack or hunk."

"Hudson, I promise, you're so much more than either of those things. I've also been pretty damn honest and obvious about the fact that I'm attracted to you." She lifts my chin and caresses my jaw. "If you think this is me trying to butter you up to get you on camera, or worse, some kind of long con for viewers, you don't know me at all. You asked me to trust you; can you do the same? Trust that I have our best interest at heart, but also that I want you. With the cameras and without."

Her words are what I've been wanting to hear: that I can trust her, that whatever this mutual attraction is between us, it isn't some fake romance to get viewers.

As I open my mouth to tell her this, she says, "We're still learning about each other. How about we play twenty questions? I have so much I'm dying to know about you. And you can do the same." She waves her hand like she's shooing a fly. "But in a way less tense way." She trails off and raises her eyebrows at me. "What do you say, Bear?"

I have a thousand questions I want her to answer, but I can start with twenty. "Fine, but I get to go first."

"Deal. How about some more whiskey?"

"It grew on you?"

"If you mean can I choke it down? Then yes." She grins. "It's a lot like you."

The idea of Blakely choking me down makes my dick ache, but to cover it up, I give her a teasing push. When she slides out of my lap, I stride to the kitchen and grab the bottle.

When I return, Blakely snags the whiskey before curling up next to me, resting her head on my shoulder and throwing her legs over mine. Like it's what I was born to do, I trace lazy circles on her arm while my other hand settles on her knee.

"Alright, Spitfire, question one: how the hell did you end up a social media star?"

She gives me a wry grin before sipping the dark amber liquid. Her little cough is so fucking cute. "I thought we were easing into this." When I don't offer her a reprieve, she sighs. "It was honestly an accident. I'd been in Austin for ten years, eking out a living. Then Covid happened, and everything went tits up. I was lucky to keep busy with freelance jobs and work remotely, and thankfully, I had enough saved to keep paying my bills. But I had way too much extra time, so like everyone else during the pandemic year, I started vlogging."

"Vlogging?" I open my mouth, and she tips the bottle to my lips.

Her laugh dances in my ear along with the pops of the fire. "I had a stupid rant about how much my roots had grown out go viral, and overnight, I had an influx of followers. I never looked back." She pauses to take another drink. "I curated my following into a niche market focusing on Austin style and popular places to be seen. And suddenly, I was someone."

I squeeze her knee. "You were always someone."

"Trust me, I really wasn't. And I'm still not. But it's nice to pretend."

She goes quiet before snorting. "Boy, that was way more answer than I was expecting to give. My turn. Question one: if you didn't work for Peak Adventures, what would you do?"

"There's nothing else." We pass the bottle back and forth; each sip warms me from the inside out, as does the easy conversation between Blakely and me.

"Nothing? You never dreamed of being an astronaut or fireman or circus clown?"

"Circus clown?" I chuckle and give her neck a quick peck.

"I don't know! I just mean you couldn't have always wanted to be a guide and wilderness expert."

Did I ever want anything else? Did I ever have the option? Rather than answering, I ask my next question. "How old are you?"

"Um, wow. What a deflection. That's rude to ask, by the way. I'm thirty-three, if you must know. What about you?"

I smirk. "Thought it was rude to ask?"

"Well." She hiccups; her pretty eyes glassy. "You already did, so I figure we're past being polite."

"Thirty-five. Easy one, what's your favorite ice cream flavor?"

"Strawberry, hands down. Was Paige your last serious relationship?"

I raise my eyebrows at her question. Ballsy. "Yeah."

"Have you dated since then?"

"You asked two questions in a row. And yeah, I've dated, but nothing long-term." I eye her. "Same question to you."

"I dated another Austin influencer, Ryan, for too long. Turns out he's a cheating cheater." This time, she tilts the bottle up for more than a shot.

"When did it end?"

"The day before I turned thirty-three. He was the gift that kept on giving."

I snort at her deadpan tone and pull her in for a kiss. The desire to stamp the mention of another man out of her mouth has me stealing the nearly empty bottle and moving it out of the way, not caring if it spills. Flipping us so Blakely is underneath me on the couch, I seize her lips with mine. I flash back to a couple of days ago when I first crossed this line.

Our kiss is fervent, needy. Her tongue slips between my lips, and her lithe body presses up against mine. She's so warm, so alive. I pull her closer, loving how she tastes like whiskey and melts at my touch.

The ragged moan she lets out has my balls tightening and my cock throbbing. With a curse, I break the kiss.

"Why do you keep pulling away from me?" There's a note of hurt in her words.

I sweep a stray strand of hair off her face, then rest my forehead against hers. "I'm sending you mixed messages, and that's not like me. But, Spitfire—" I lift my head so she can see the sincerity in my eyes. "I want to believe this attraction is more than just for show."

"It's more. I promise." She punctuates her words with soft kisses. "I want you, Bear. So much."

I snag a few more greedy kisses, savoring the whiskey on her tongue. Denying myself everything I want, I gently push up and put space between us and say, "When it happens, and it *will* happen, it won't be on this shitty couch after we've been drinking."

Blakely licks her swollen lips, all flushed like a displaced goddess.

And I'm the mortal fool denying her.

Soon, there will be no more hesitation or holding back. No more worrying about what might happen, and I'll praise her like she deserves.

I just hope I'm not left holding a shredded heart when Blakely's time here comes to an end.

CHAPTER FOURTEEN

DAY ELEVEN

I wake up in our bed with a pounding head and a fuzzy brain. Stupid whiskey.

Hudson and I kissed. A lot. More than all the past few days combined, but then he pulled back. Again. And I finished what was left in the bottle.

This song and dance—one step forward, two steps back—is getting old.

Despite my mental haze, I clearly remember Hudson's concerns. It stings thinking he doesn't trust my motives, but I guess I can't blame him. I haven't given him a ton of reasons to believe me.

"How're you feeling?" Hudson asks, coffee already in hand.

"Shhh. Why are you yelling?"

He smirks. "I'm talking in a normal voice. You're hungover."

"Ugh, why aren't you?"

His low, rumbly chuckle makes my stomach flip. "Some of

us can handle our whiskey," he says. His handsome face grows serious. "If you're worried we did more than kiss, you shouldn't be. I wouldn't take advantage of a situation like that."

"I trust you, Bear." I pause and swallow. "And you can trust me, too."

Hudson kisses my temple. "I believe you, Spitfire. Now get dressed while I make you a coffee."

I wrinkle my nose. "Why? Isn't it still too cold to do anything?"

"Nope. Cold front moved out. It's a balmy forty-seven out there."

Groaning, I pull the blanket up over my head. "And what does this mean for me?"

He yanks the cover down. "We're going fishing."

One brisk shower, two cups of coffee, a dry piece of toast, and a tiny disagreement about what to wear while fishing later, Hudson and I are on our way. His arms overflow with a small styrofoam cooler, his backpack, fishing rods, and a trowel.

"What's the little shovel for?"

He shakes the cooler at me. "Bait."

My feet come to a stop. "What?"

"Fish won't bite an empty line."

"Don't you have those fake ones?" My words squeak out.

"Sure, but digging for worms builds character." He raises his eyebrows at me.

I blanch. "I am *not* touching a worm."

"You're too good to do some digging, Princess?"

"Yes?"

"Are you asking?" Shaking his head, he peels open the lid on the cooler, showing me some sodas, water bottles, and snacks. "Worms work better, but we're using spinners today."

"You're such a shit." With a toss of my hair, I power ahead of him, not stopping until I reach the water's edge. He only has to adjust my direction three times during the twenty-minute hike from the cabin to the lake, so I'm claiming it as a victory.

Hudson steps onto the bow of his small speedboat and before I can run away, he's got me onboard. The purr of the motor and the splashing of the water against the stern echo in the eerie quiet of the large body of water. Hudson navigates us away from the shore, the clearing long out of sight, hidden in swathes of trees and the distance we've put between it and us.

"How deep is this water?" I ask.

"Maxes out around ninety feet."

I shake my head and mutter as I stare out over the dark, choppy water. I prefer my water clear, like pools, hot tubs and springs, the Caribbean. This is the perfect setting for a scary movie about a water ghost rising from the cryptic depths and taking its revenge on the living. AKA us.

It doesn't help that the sun is hiding behind clouds. And while Hudson wasn't lying when he said it's warmer than yesterday, it's still cold, especially with the occasional wind bursts. Out here in the open water, there's no buffer, and it rips through my sweatshirt.

I'm ready to tell Hudson that we should go back to the cabin when my raincoat hits me in the face.

"What the hell?"

"I figured you'd forget your jacket, so I grabbed it. I can't stand listening to you whine about being cold all day. Put it on."

Hudson's going to owe my dentist for all the teeth grinding he provokes. "Nice to know making out didn't change your personality. Still an asshole, I see."

He laughs—an honest to god laugh. The unexpected noise evaporates all my annoyance and makes me tingle. It's magnificent. Rough, loud, authentic. I've heard him chuckle, bark, even snort, but this is special.

Hudson snags one of the fishing poles, places the lure on the line, and hands it to me.

"If I catch a fish, do I have to touch it?"

"You eat fish, right?" He raises one eyebrow at me.

"This is so not the same as eating already dead, prepared, cooked fish." I bat my lashes at him and pooch my lower lip.

"Fine," he sighs. "If you catch anything, I'll help you remove it from the hook. Happy?"

"Yes, very." I give him a quick kiss.

After what feels like ages of quiet, I scoot closer and nudge him with my knee. "We should have stayed in bed and gotten to know each other more. Instead of this." I gesture toward my tangled fishing line and the gloomy water.

"I can't believe I am saying this, but don't you need content for your socials?"

"Sure, but this is so…" My nose wrinkles.

"That explains it perfectly." He chuffs, then grows silent. His eyes cut to me once, then twice.

"What?"

Hudson jiggles his fishing pool, his eyes fastened on the tiny red and white bobber dancing in the water. "It goes without saying, but I don't want any more personal moments filmed."

"Hey." I lean in and nuzzle my face against his. "You don't need to worry about that. I'd still like to have you in my lives and stills, but only these types of things." I wave around us. "Anything else is ours, Bear. I promise." As I speak, I skim my fingers over his thigh, inching ever higher until he snatches my wrist.

"Fishing now, fun later," he says.

"Boo. How about fun now, fishing never?"

"Blakely..."

"Fine," I huff.

Hudson helps me unknot my line and shows me how to cast, telling me to wiggle it, let it sink, then slowly reel it in and repeat. He models it for me, and while I don't care about fishing, I care that he cares. He's so detailed and thorough as he explains what to do, and that level of expertise is damn sexy.

Within the first hour, Hudson catches four fish, and I catch zero. To say I'm thoroughly unimpressed by fishing is an understatement. I shoot him a dirty look whenever he reels one in. After the fourth unanswered catch, it's time for a distraction.

"This is boring."

"Spoken like someone who hasn't caught a fish."

I level him with a glare and toss my hair. "No, spoken like someone bored out of her mind. We're sitting here with a stick and string." I tilt my face back, hoping for even a flicker of sunshine to warm me. "In summer, with the heat of the sun and a bikini, I could enjoy fishing, but right now? *Blech.*"

Hudson doesn't answer, but I'm used to it at this point.

"Oh!" I perk up. "How about we continue our twenty questions game? We didn't finish last night."

He grunts. "Fine. It's my turn."

"Fire away, Bear."

"Do you have any siblings?"

My voice is tight when I answer. "I have a half-sister."

Hudson wrinkles his brow. "Care to elaborate?"

Nibbling my bottom lip, I shift in my seat. "She was a couple of grades ahead of me in school, but we had very different childhood experiences."

He sets his rod in the holder and turns. "How so?"

I fiddle with my pole, willing a fish to bite. "We have the same dad. It's one of those small-town secrets that everyone knows. Her life was night and day from mine. She grew up in a big house with her mom, her grandparents, and eventually a nice stepdad. She was popular and well-liked. Meanwhile, I was living on the outskirts of town, hoping the water wouldn't get turned off and trying my best to be invisible at school. It's not her fault, but it made it hard to be around her, wondering if, with a small ripple in fate, that could have been me."

Hudson secures my reel and wraps me in a warm hug. "For what it's worth, I'm glad you're you." He pulls back, a smirk on his full lips. "Even if you're a brat."

With a laugh, I say, "Okay, enough emotions. Let's get to the good stuff. Plus, you asked two in a row, so I'm cashing in a big one. Do you use condoms and get tested regularly?"

"Shit." He gapes at me, his mouth open. "That's a personal question."

"Yeah, but if we're going to progress in our... relationship, we need to talk about it, right? So why not tie it to a game." I wink at him.

Hudson's back is ramrod straight, and his ears are pink. "I last tested two months ago and haven't been with anyone since. My bloodwork was negative for anything. I always use condoms with casual partners. What about you?"

"I have a birth control implant but have only gone without a condom with one prior partner." I pause, thinking of my last relationship. "Ryan and I always used condoms. I never felt right going without one with him, which given how much he was sleeping around, turned out to be a good thing. I got tested when we broke up. It came back negative, and I haven't hooked up with anyone since."

I watch Hudson's face. He's taking in everything I shared. It's a blunt way to find these things out, but it's a conversation that has to happen.

His Adam's apple bobs, and a mixture of emotions flicker

across his freckled face. Anger, heat, hunger. "You deserve someone who thinks enough of you not to cheat."

Smiling at him, I say, "I agree. Know anyone up for the job?"

He doesn't answer, opting instead to thread his fingers into my hair and pull my face to his. "What would your preference be with me?"

"With you?"

His nose brushes mine before his lips graze against my mouth. "Uh-huh."

"I would want to feel all of you. *Nothing* in between us." I lean in, ready to claim him, when his line jerks, snapping us out of the moment.

Hudson: five. Blakely: zero.

Another eternity passes, and I still haven't caught a single stupid fish. However, I do manage to snag some candids and even convince Hudson to pose for a selfie with me after swearing I won't post it anywhere.

Balancing my phone in one hand, fishing pole in the other, I lean against the railing, mindlessly scrolling and hearting comments.

"Be careful, Blakely, wouldn't want your lifeline—I mean your phone—to fall in the water, now would you?"

"For your information, I have excellent balance, and I'm a pro multitasker. I can hold my phone and fish, no problem. Not like I'm catching anything, anyway." I stick my tongue out at him, then roll my shoulders, put on my best *Blakely Bradshaw* smile, and with a steadying breath, go live.

"Hello, BBs! I'm coming to you from the middle of Lake Pika—which is named for a local animal. You need to search for this adorable little critter! It's so cute!" I giggle and then pan to Hudson. "And here's my amazing guide and cabin mate, Hudson Brooks of Peak Adventures in lovely Trail Creek, New Mexico. He's taking me fishing. Can you believe it?" I scan the lake and the surrounding trees with my camera, then turn it back on myself and continue. "Ever the chivalrous one, Mr. Brooks did not make me use live bait, though I have to say I'm getting slightly suspicious. We have been fishing for a hundred years—"

"Two hours," he snorts from behind me.

I grin and roll my eyes at the camera. "Fine, two hours. The point is, I've yet to catch a single fish! Meanwhile, my virile outdoorsman here has managed to catch seven. What do you think, BBs? Did he give me the bad luck pole? Or maybe all the fish have crushes on him?" I give a conspiratorial wink into the lens. "From the comments on my last livestream, all y'all do!"

Hudson huffs and goes back to his rod and reel. Shit. Was that too far? Keeping my smile on my face is no easy feat, given the anxiety cartwheeling in my stomach. Did I make him mad? I'm about to cut the live and check with him when an unexpected weight tugs on my line.

Faster than I can scream, my phone flies from my hand, and I tumble over the side into the icy water.

Stinging liquid rushes into my nose, and the shock of the freezing temperature steals precious seconds before my brain and body agree on what needs to happen. Kicking my feet, I claw for the surface.

I'm a strong swimmer, but I'm wearing heavy boots and multiple layers and have no idea which way is up. The frigid water locks my muscles, and I'm on the verge of panic. Dread claws my throat with each bubble of air that escapes from my lungs, but light filters through the murky water. Surely, I'm close.

I am *so* not dying while fucking fishing. Or before I get to sleep with Hudson Brooks.

Something grasps my arm and hauls me in the opposite direction I'm swimming. With a glorious burst, I'm free from the depths, sputtering out lake water while sucking in fresh air. My entire body shakes, and despite trying to speak, no words will come out.

Like he's talking through a wall, I hear Hudson. "Blakely, baby, you're okay. I've got you."

My first muddled thought is *get me out of this fucking water*. The second is *he called me baby*. Third? *Holy shit, he's naked.*

"Blakely!" his voice snaps louder.

I turn wide eyes on him.

"I'm climbing the ladder, then I'll pull you in. You're okay."

All I can do is blink.

"Fuck. Taking that as a sign you understand."

He heaves himself onto the back of the boat. I get a quick flash of his toned ass and bare thighs before he wrenches me out of the water and into his arms.

"Blakely, can you hear me? ... Blakely!" Hudson's voice is sharp and thundering. "Fucking say something!"

Am I not answering him?

"N-naked?"

He muffles a snort against my hair. "Yeah, baby. I'm naked. Had to dive in after you." His mouth is warm against my forehead. "I'm so fucking sorry. Gotta get you out of these wet clothes. Okay?"

"S'okay."

I'm sitting on the cooler, swaddled in a blanket. My feet are bare, and my clothes are in a pile next to me while a half-dressed Hudson rubs my arms up and down. Up and down. It hurts. Like when your leg falls asleep.

"P-pins."

"Yeah, goddamn pins and needles. It stings, but we've gotta get your blood flowing."

My eyes narrow. *Now* he understands me?

Wind whips my wet hair and slices through the blanket. Trembling, I inch as close to Hudson as possible while he steers us back to shore. My muscles ache, and my throat and nose burn—how much water went up it anyway—but my mind clears.

As the fog lifts, I realize I wasn't in the water more than a minute before Hudson fished—*ha*—me out, but it felt like a lifetime. The boat glides toward the shoreline, but it can't go fast enough. I want back on land. Now.

"I d–d-don't like f-fishing."

Hudson tucks me closer, pressing kisses to my lake-soaked head. We dock, and he grabs me and crushes his lips to mine. Then he breaks away, throwing my blanket-clad body over his shoulder. "Gotta get you warmed up ASAP."

"Hudson, p-put me down!" I may be in shock, but I still have my dignity. Or at least what remains after falling into a lake in the middle of a live.

Shit.

"No, it's faster this way."

"I n-need my phone."

His steps falter. "Are you seriously worried about your phone?"

My tongue is like a dead slug and won't cooperate. "Livestream. When I fell. Th-thousands of people. I need to l-let them know I'm okay."

"Fuck." He spins around, me still slung over his shoulder like a sack of flour, and runs to the boat.

When he grabs my phone, the stream is still going.

"Tell them. P-please?"

I can't see what he's doing, but I hear him growl, "She's fine." Then nothing.

"W-way with words," I grouse from my skewed vantage point.

"Yeah, I'm a real fucking wordsmith." He squeezes me. "Stay with me, Spitfire."

The next time I blink, Hudson's anxious face hovers over mine. "You back with me, Blakely? You passed out for a sec there."

I nod or do some sort of wobble while I place where I am—curled up on something soft and warm. I go to sit up, but firm pressure keeps me in place.

"You need rest."

Again, I imitate a dashboard bobblehead. "Okay."

My nose and throat sting, and my head pounds; maybe the nodding is too intense. What am I lying on? It's so fluffy and cozy. I could fa—

"Nope. Resting, not sleeping. Need you to stay awake."

My eyes are like two bricks. "I'm tired," I pout.

"That's the adrenaline fade."

The fireplace crackles to my left, close enough for me to enjoy the heat. My brain tries to puzzle everything out like the world's worst word problem: *If the bed is fifteen feet from the fire, but Springy the evil sofa isn't stabbing Blakely in the back, how many gallons of water did she drink from the lake?*

There's a breath passing as a laugh. "Moved it."

"Huh?"

"The mattress. You needed to be closer to the fire."

"Oh." I blink at Hudson. Twice. "Thank you." It's then I realize soft sheets graze every bit of my body. I peel the blankets back, and yep... I'm naked.

"Sorry." Hudson chokes out the word, then sits by my feet, head in his hands. "I asked if it was okay, but you were out of it. I had to get those wet clothes off you, and you weren't—" He swallows. "You probably think I'm fucking incompetent."

I take in his defeated posture. This stoic, beautiful man. He thinks he failed me.

"Hudson."

He lifts his face, and the worry I see there stabs me in the chest. "Yeah?"

"Were you naked, or did I imagine that?"

I smile at his pink ears. "Where was your underwear?"

"I was going commando. I don't think I've ever undressed that fast in my life."

Warmth that has nothing to do with the fire or blankets speeds through me. I crook a finger and say, "Shut up and get under this blanket with me right now."

He stares at me like I've grown a third eye. Or like he had to tow me out of a lake deathtrap, carry my waterlogged body home, and find a way to keep me safe when I passed out. Oh, wait...

"Not asking, Bear. Get your ass over here and warm me up. We both know the fastest way to get me hot is for you to touch me." I giggle at my double entendre. I'm funny. Or maybe I'm really out of it.

Crawling up the length of the bed, Hudson climbs under the covers and wraps his burly frame around mine. The brush of cotton against my bare back raises goosebumps over my flesh.

I bring his hand to my lips and press a soft kiss against it. "Hudson, you dove into Lake Doom, naked."

"Blakely, I—"

"Hush, this is the best part. As I was saying, you dove into Lake Doom naked and pulled me to the surface. You carried me home and made me a pallet on the floor. You watched over me, making sure I was okay. You don't need to apologize. You didn't fuck up."

"It's my job to keep you safe. And so far, I've taken you on a hike that led to blisters and fishing that ended in disaster."

Rolling over so we're face to face, I give him a small smile. "Don't forget about tormenting me with knot tying and navigation."

He huffs. "Those are actual skills, not punishments." His lips press to my forehead, and his voice drops. "Scared the shit out of me when you went over, Spitfire."

The fire pops, and I shiver. "Me too." Swallowing, I thread one of my legs between his, stealing as much of his precious warmth as I can.

Things could have gone very differently today.

Hudson draws symbols I don't recognize on my skin, his fingers walking the expanse of my back. I shiver again, but this time it isn't from the cold.

I need Hudson.

Is it rational to want him right now? No, probably not. But fuck it.

I kiss him. Kiss him like he saved my life. Like I've wanted to since I saw his cocky ass outside Peak Adventures. Like he set my nerves on fire with that first kiss days ago and has been denying me what I want since.

Like he's what I'm searching for.

The kiss grows, morphing into something hungrier. When his tongue slides along the seam of my mouth, I open to him. His breath becomes mine, and for the first time since falling into the water, I can breathe.

I inhale him, every brush of his tongue, every nip, every scorching press of our lips. And then, like always, Hudson breaks the kiss.

He murmurs against my neck, "Blakely, easy. You had a big scare, and we need to get your temperature stabilized."

"I want you to warm me, Bear."

Hudson's fingers skim my neck, tilting my face. "Take a shower. It'll help. Rinse off the lake water. I'll make some tea."

Tears spring to my eyes at his rejection. *Fucking post-terrible-experience emotions.*

"No, don't cry. That's not... I'm not turning you away."

"Feels like it."

"Shit." Gently gripping my trembling chin, Hudson kisses his way from my jaw to my ear and whispers. "Shower first. Then we'll see what else we can do to keep you warm."

hudson

I pace the cabin floor, snarling at my stupidity and the fishing gods. I've never felt so helpless as when I watched Blakely fall into the icy cold water while I stood there like a bump on a log. The time it took me to shed my clothes could have been—I shake the thought from my head. She's safe. That's what matters.

It isn't until Blakely emerges from the shower in a cloud of steam and sweet smells that the tension melts from my muscles. Rushing forward, I bundle her up in an oversized towel and carry her to the makeshift pallet I created while she was out of it. I should make her some tea or cocoa, but I'm not ready to let go of her yet.

The minute or so she was underwater, and I couldn't find her, was one of the scariest of my life. Between her disappearing over the side of the boat and then going loose limbed and silent on me during my desperate power hike to the cabin, I aged ten years.

"Hey, Bear?"

"Yeah."

"Are you planning on letting me go?" She's smiling at me, her eyes shining with mischief and thankfully clear of the haze from before.

No, not if I can help it. I reluctantly place her on the mattress. "Stay here. I'll be right back."

Small, dainty hands grab my forearms, pulling me into her space. "I'm not going anywhere. You and I have unfinished business," she says, dropping a quick peck on my lips.

A relieved sigh slips from my mouth; someone's feeling more like herself. She's making it so damn hard to walk away, but I need to get sugar, caffeine, and warmth into her.

And grab her some pajamas. I wonder if I have any spare small thermals...

I dig through the armoire and find a couple of worn but thick long johns and toss a pair to her. "Put those on while I make you some tea."

Thankfully, Blakely wasn't out too long at a single point. About halfway through my frantic journey to get her to safety, I realized holding her upside down while running wasn't the best way to transport her. But it was the fastest. Still, I swear this woman makes my IQ plummet. I'm a complete and total idiot when she's around.

"Hudson, are you making a four-course meal over there?"

Huffing a silent laugh, I ignore her even if I'm fucking delighted she's back to her bratty self.

"Thank you."

I stiffen. She's thanking me? This whole thing is my fault.

"It couldn't have been easy, carrying me all the way back here."

"I made better time than we did hiking together." She scoffs like I've offended her, and I smile as I sample the hot tea I made. Blakely Bradshaw has the navigational sense of a box of hair. She was even swimming the wrong dadgum direction in the lake.

Grabbing the mug, I return to our pallet. Blakely rises, the ignored thermals still lying where I threw them. She clutches the towel to her chest, the firelight flickering over her bare shoulders and legs, casting her in a golden glow. My breath catches. She's so beautiful.

"The pajamas I gave you not work?"

She grins at me, a coy smile that hints at deeper things. Things people do in the dark. "It's silly to put clothes on just to take them off."

This woman. I clench my jaw. "Baby, I'll hold you all night."

"That's not what I want."

I swallow. "Today—"

Cupping my face, she kisses the sprinkling of freckles on my nose and cheeks. "Today was a total disaster, but it wasn't your fault. You saved my life."

"I don't want you thinking you need to—"

"Don't you dare finish that sentence. I've been trying to get in your pants for days now."

She winks at me, but her face softens when, in a hushed tone, I say, "Tell me one more time. It's not an act."

God, the way I hope she says what I need to hear.

"It's not an act. I want you. I have since you yelled at me over luggage and threatened to leave me in Trail Creek." Stretching on her tiptoes, she nips my earlobe and mutters, "Asshole."

Then her towel falls to the floor in a crumpled heap, and my brain, heart, and lungs all stop working. My Spitfire stands before me in all her glory, a masterclass in curves and indulgence.

"No more waiting, Bear."

My gaze burns down her body, gathering every intimate detail I can. The line of her slender neck and elegant collarbone. The heavy sway of her ripe tits. The flow of her trim waist to the swell of her hips. The neat strip of hair between her quivering thighs.

Fuck.

The way I need her, want her, is written on my face and rapidly straining the cotton of my sleep pants. Today was a tipping point. I was already two steps over the fence when Blakely fell into the lake, but hearing her say this is real eradicates any remaining barriers between us.

And now I'm going to show her. The invisible line I tried to draw is long crossed, and I don't plan on looking back.

I set the tea on the small side table and drop to my knees before her—putting us face to pussy. "You're gorgeous," I rasp as I give in to the itch to touch her like she's mine. My hands glide up the back of her legs, curling to grip her inner thighs. Then I brush my mouth against the skin below her navel. Her breath hitches, and her thighs clench when I pepper kisses lower. There's power in knowing she's as affected as I am.

Jerking my head at the mug, I say, "Tea first." She goes to argue, but I silence her by blowing a stream of air close enough to ruffle her trimmed curls. "Sip it while I sip you."

Her gasp sounds over the crackle of the fire. "W-what do you mean?"

Grinning like the devil from my sinner's throne, I growl, "I mean, I'm gonna lick your juicy cunt until you're so warm inside and out you'll forget every second of being in that fucking lake."

Blakely's eyes go wide, pupils blown. She says, "Thank you." Then groans and mutters, "Thank you? Cool. Totally cool, Blakely."

I hide my smile in that sexy crease between her hip and

thigh. "Now drink." The command is clear, but so is the plea. I need to make her come on my tongue. As sure as I need to eat, breathe, and sh—

The hushed sound of her slurping tells me she's following my order. To reward her, I ghost my hands over her hips and my lips over her thighs.

"When I touch you, how wet will you be for me?"

She doesn't answer. That won't work. I rise so we're eye to eye. Blakely stares at me, surprise written on her pretty face, the mug still at her mouth.

"I want answers when I ask a question, and if you *don't* answer, you might find yourself on the wrong end of a spanking." She shifts, rubbing her thighs together.

Leaning in, I whisper what I hope she knows but have to confirm. "If you don't like this kind of play, or aren't up to it, tell me now, and it stops. I'll spread you out and eat you like I promised, but without the dirty talk, the pussy slaps, or bringing you to the edge until you're ready to explode."

"No." Her throat bobs. "I like to play." Then she grins and takes a sip of her tea. "For someone I've spent days begging to speak, you suddenly have a lot to say."

My teeth graze against her jaw. "I save my words for what's important." I straighten to my full height so I tower over her, slip my fingers into her hair and tug, drawing a whimper from her. "If you want to stop, all you have to do is say it. No matter where we are or what we're doing. Understand?"

"Yes."

"Anything I should know?"

"Biting, spanking, edging are all good." Her eyes dip to my lips, and she licks her own, "And your hand on my neck—"

I slide my hand to her pulse point and give it a gentle squeeze. "Like this?"

Her throat constricts as she swallows. "Yes."

My thumb skims the column of her neck, lingering on her hammering pulse. I give it another squeeze, loving how her eyes flutter. "You wear that necklace so well, baby. But it'll have to wait for another time." With that, I drop to my knees and bring my thumb to her clit, skating around it, teasing her.

Her sharp gasp has me cutting my eyes upward. The cup is at her lips. My tongue darts out, licking along her pussy but not breaching her. Not yet. It's hardly a scrap, but even the barest hint of her salty-sweet musk blows out my sense of taste, ruining all future flavors.

"Need more, baby. Spread your legs wider for me; let me see you." I split her lips with my pointer and middle fingers, burying my nose in the soft spot above her clit and inhaling. How does she smell like goddamn flowers everywhere?

Blakely's words wobble, and she bucks forward. "You've seen me."

"No, I need to see all of you. From the inside out." I glide one hand down the length of her leg and grip her ankle, tracing the delicate bones. Then I lift it and hook her knee over my shoulder. "Keep one hand on that tea; use the other to hold your balance."

"So bossy."

Even when I'm face deep in her, she has to sass. "You're gonna love how bossy I can be." With her body where I want, I stare at her glistening pussy. "Fuck, Blakely, you're beautiful everywhere. Every inch of you is perfect." My hot breath raises goosebumps over her skin.

She gifts me a needy whimper when I sweep a finger along her slit, then move higher, teasing her in lazy, slow circles. "Look how wet you are. Let me have a real taste now." In one long, broad stroke of my tongue, I lave her from opening to clit, savoring the mewls and moans my touches pull from her.

Groaning at the first true burst of her flavor, I become a

man possessed, desperate to explore each delicious inch of her. My tongue loops her clit before parting her folds and searching out every bit of her sweetness I can find. Fucking Blakely is overstimulating in every way possible. My hips jerk forward, and I grip myself, squeezing my throbbing cock in the hopes I can stop myself from coming.

Blakely gasps, and when I look up, she's watching me, mouth agape.

"Spitfire, I'm gonna drink this cunt dry, but if you stop, so do I." I huff a laugh on her sensitive bundle of nerves when she yanks the tea to her mouth.

Ignoring my own needs, I spread her open again and dive in. The more I lick, the wetter she gets until she's dousing my beard. And it only fuels the intensity of my craving for her.

"Shit, baby, I'm bathing in you."

Her back arches as I slip my tongue inside her, thrusting in and out, fucking her like it's my cock. When her walls clench, I wrap my lips around her clit, my teeth grazing over it. Her hand tightens in my hair almost to the point of stinging, and I soak it in.

I love that she's as lost in me as I am in her.

"Blakely, how much tea do you have left?" She doesn't answer me, so I follow through on my earlier threat. Lifting my face from her molten core, I bring my open palm down on her pussy, the sharp smack ringing out.

"Hudson!" she moans, and her knee buckles. But I don't let her fall. I'll never let her fall again.

I bite the inside of her thigh, not hard enough to leave a mark, just enough to gauge her reaction. The gush of sticky wetness that drips from between her legs tells me everything. My girl likes a hint of pain with her pleasure.

"Answer me, Blakely, or you'll get another spanking." I

soothe my lips over her rosy ones, the heat of her pussy radiating like a furnace.

"I drank it all."

"Atta fucking girl." With renewed effort, I work her to the edge, licking and sucking. It's sloppy and messy and perfect. I point my tongue and use it like a missile, seeking all the ways to make her crumble. Just as her body tells me how close she is, I stop. Then I repeat it all again, adding pressure to her clit that has her babbling my name mixed with praise and pleas.

"Hudson! It f-feels so good. Don't stop! Pl-please!"

"Please what?"

"Please, l-let me come!"

Setting her leg back on the ground, I rise to my feet. Blakely whimpers in frustration, tears watering in her eyes.

I cover her mouth with mine, silencing her desperate whines. Plunging my tongue between her lips, I share her own exquisite honey with her.

Breaking the kiss, I snag the cup from her hand and lay her on the pallet. Her hair fans out behind her, and her tits bounce as she giggles. She's an abundance of beauty I can't wait to devour.

"I won't leave you wanting." Smirking at her, I say, "For long."

Settling my body over hers, I start at her jaw, kissing my way down her neck, licking her collarbone, lapping at her sternum, skating my teeth against her shoulder blades. Everywhere I touch is aflame. As sure as she was freezing before, she's burning now.

I reverently cup her breasts, brushing my thumbs against her pert nipples. Lowering my mouth, I whisper against her flushed skin, "Your tits are so fucking perfect. I imagined my cock sliding in between them the first day we met. And ever since you flashed me, I've dreamed of running my hands over them, sucking and biting them until you come from that alone.”

Blakely snorts out a small laugh that shifts to a needy moan when I roll her sensitive tips between my fingers. “I th-think you mean ever since you w-walked in on me getting off to a—shit, Hudson, that feels so good—fantasy of you.”

Chuckling, I wrap my hot mouth around one of her nipples. My rough hands—hands that have no business touching such silky skin—trace over her chest, pinching and twisting the pebbled flesh until she arches off the mattress. I suck and lick and nibble, and Blakely’s stuttered breathing tells me it’s exactly what she needs. My teeth skim over the sensitive nubs, and at her encouragement, the grazing becomes tugging. I split my attention between her hardened peaks, leaving them bright pink and shining with my saliva.

As my mouth blazes lower, I ask, “Is this what you want?”

“Yes,” she whispers.

“I didn’t hear you.” Placing my hands beneath her legs, I spread her wide, then reinforce how much I want her words by giving her pussy another love tap. “If you want me to keep going, you need to be louder.” I lift my head, locking my eyes on hers.

“Yes, keep going, please,” she says, her words ringing out in the dim cabin.

“Good girl.” I lower my mouth back to the promised land that lies before me. My weight presses Blakely into the pallet, but it doesn’t keep her from bucking against me. Or me from rocking into the mattress. I’m two thrusts away from coming in my pants like a goddamn teenager.

“More, Hudson,” she whimpers.

“You’re so wet. My dirty, bratty Spitfire and her spoiled, greedy cunt.” I tease her with a mix of licking and kissing. Then I fasten my mouth on her clit, humming against her. Blakely writhes beneath me as if she's torn between pulling me closer or pushing me away.

She's desperate to come; I can feel it. Smell it. Between the edging earlier and what I'm doing now, she's almost there. My cock is hard to the point of pain, but nothing is going to draw my attention away from Blakely Bradshaw on the cusp of coming.

"I need..."

"What do you need?"

"Fingers, put your fingers in me."

A single finger caresses her clit before slipping inside her. I dip in and out, celebrating each wriggle, each desperate shimmy.

"More."

A second finger follows her desperate demand. I pump them in and out, circle them. Bury them as deep as they'll go, knowing they aren't anywhere near as filling as my cock will be. At that thought—the lush heat of her wrapped around me —I groan, and Blakely jerks as the sound pulses against her clit.

I crook my fingers, using the rough pads to apply pressure, aiming to hit the magic spot inside her that will fracture her into thousands of boneless pieces. And if I'm lucky, drench me even more.

"Are you a squirter, baby? Will you rain down a flood?"

Blakely's muscles tense, drawing my fingers deeper. "Give me that sweetness, Blakely. It's mine." I thrust my tongue into her core alongside the two fingers already buried deep. There's no way I'm not tasting this gift.

Beholden to my words, she falls apart. And it's as fucking breathtaking as I thought it would be. She tears at my hair, and if I'm bald when this is over, fuck it. Her hips thrust upward, and I drink down every glorious drop.

I don't let up until she pushes my head away and tries to draw her hips from my hold. Today will live in my mind until I'm old and gray as one of the worst and best days of my life. I almost lost this infuriating woman while gaining more of her than I ever expected.

"Fuck, you taste like a goddamn dream," I say as I shift so my head rests against her lower stomach, rising and falling with her panting breaths.

"No one has ever said that to me. Or made me come like that."

"Idiots." I nuzzle against the soft curve of her stomach. "You should stay here with me. I'll do that every day."

"I might die of dehydration if you do that every day."

My barked laugh echoes around us, and I kiss my way up her body, worshiping her breasts again before continuing to her mouth. Gathering her in my arms, I smell the crown of her head as her hands wander my body. With each scratch of her nails down my back, my dick twitches. But I meant it when I said I'd hold her all night.

"Bear?"

"Spitfire?"

"I want more."

"You want more what?"

"More of you. I want you inside me."

I sit up and search her face. "Blakely, this was about you."

She narrows her eyes. "Want to make this about me? Put. That. Big. Thick. Cock. In. Me." She snags my bottom lip with her teeth and pulls me on top of her, locking her legs around my hips. "Now, lose the pants."

I may be a decent guy, but I'm no fucking martyr. If she wants me to fuck her, who am I to argue? Wasting no time, I sit back and tug my pants down, my cock springing from its cotton prison.

Blakely licks her lips and reaches for me. The slide of her delicate hand up and down my shaft has me wishing I could pause time because this is gonna be over way too fast.

Using my dick like a leash, she guides me to her, lining me up at her entrance. But I snag her grabby hand and bring it above her head. Her wrists are so slim I can pin both with one hand. This frees the other to rub the head of my cock against her clit. Only when she's begging do I glide my length between her pussy lips—letting her arousal coat me—and press into her wet warmth.

And fuck me. Blakely Bradshaw's pussy is a goddamn miracle. Nothing. Abso-fucking-lutely nothing has ever felt this good, and I'm only an inch in.

"I need you, Hudson. All of you."

"You're a needy little thing, aren't you?"

"Yes. So needy." She bites her lip and looks at me with hooded eyes. Tonight, the waves in the depths of her blue-green irises are wild. Untamed. Hungry.

With a relief that's on the verge of pain, I sink my entire length into her until I'm fully seated. I groan at the exquisite pressure of her walls hugging my cock.

"You're so fucking tight."

She kisses me and gently bucks her hips, cueing me with her body.

"Want me to move, Blakely? Want me to stretch you and make you come apart beneath me?"

Her breakneck nod nearly headbutts me. I pull all the way out, then push in, this time in one fluid movement.

"Oh god, faster. Please," she begs.

I consider edging her again, but I don't have it in me to hold out. So I set a steady pace, thrusting in and out, relishing the moans she pants in my ear as I withdraw then surge forward. When she clamps her pussy around me, gripping my cock like a vice, I almost spill right then.

Gritting my teeth, I summon every ounce of control I have. "Fuck, if you do that again, I'll lose it."

"Maybe that's what I want."

I bury my face in her neck before freeing her hands so I can grip her hips. Lifting her grants me a deeper angle. I tilt my pelvis, bumping against her clit as I thrust. Each snap of my hips pounds Blakely deeper into the mattress. My grunts and her groans mix with the rhythmic slap of skin on skin and the crackle of the fire.

Her body trembles, and in a gasping pant, Blakely calls out, "Don't stop!"

Leaving me no choice but to obey, I drive into her. Tension coils in my stomach, and heat prickles at the base of my spine. I'm close, but I won't go without her.

"Surrender for me. Come on my cock. I need to see you dripping with my cum."

Blakely's pussy quivers and tightens, and heat washes over me. Her orgasm pulls me in its wake, and I spill myself inside her while her name tumbles from my lips.

I collapse on top of her, as mindful of my weight as I can be. The aftershocks of her release clench my softening cock, and I never want to leave the paradise between her thighs. But I need to take care of her, so I ease out, hating to break the connection between us. Rolling to my side, I walk my fingers over her sweat-coated skin. A strand of damp hair clings to her forehead, and I coil it around my pinky before kissing her.

"Do you have any idea how good you feel?" I ask. And I don't just mean being inside her. I mean all of it. The sparks, the banter, the annoyance, the passion.

She curls into my arms and rubs her face against mine. "Do you?"

I let myself believe she means beyond what we just did, too, even though it's a dangerous game.

We linger together, and once our breathing slows, I untangle myself and carefully pick her up and bring her to the bathroom, dropping her on the toilet while I wet a washcloth.

"You don't actually expect me to pee in front of you, right?"

"Yep." Every muscle in my body is relaxed, and I'm ready to crawl into bed and cuddle my girl.

"Back to one-word answers?" She grins at me from where she sits, her cheeks and chest an appealing shade of pink.

"Yep." I cross my arms and lean on the sink, raising my eyebrows at her.

Blakely squirms before sighing. "I can't go with you watching. At least wait outside the door."

"Fine."

Moments later, I hear the telltale signs that she got over her unnecessary shyness, followed by running water. When she opens the door, I scoop her up and carry her to our rumpled pallet.

Lying her down, I gently widen her legs, then clean up the remnants of our time together. She's quiet and pliant, her eyes heavy and soft. A sex-drunk smile plays on her lips, and she's a fucking sight. Tousled hair, beard rash on her chin and other more sensitive places, red marks on her hips and neck. Gorgeous. *And mine*, a greedy voice deep in the back of my mind whispers.

Snuggling her, I sprinkle her shoulders with chaste kisses, enjoying the peace. Then, like a silent alarm goes off in her head, Blakely bolts upright and searches through the blankets and pillows.

"What're you doing?" I ask.

"Where's my phone?"

"You need it now?" There's an undercurrent of frustration in my tone.

She's looking around like it might drop from the sky. "Yes. No? I don't know! But—"

With a sigh, I pull it out from my side of the mattress.

"Thank you." Her eyes widen, and she looks at me. "Holy shit! I have a ton of missed calls from Kirk. I'm guessing your 'She's fine' sign-off didn't sit well with him."

Pulling her back into my arms, I kiss her neck, her jaw. "How about instead of worrying over Kirk, we eat something, and I hold you like I promised I would?"

Without another word, she melts into my touch, her quickly forgotten phone clattering to the floor.

CHAPTER SIXTEEN

blakely

DAY TWELVE

Bzzzzz. Bzzzzz.

More than half asleep, I swat away the gnat buzzing around me. It's too damn early, and I'm too deliciously sore after spending last night with Hudson Brooks between my legs to deal with annoying bugs.

My heart skips a beat. I can't believe we slept together. Or how good it was.

Bzzzzz. Bzzzzz.

The persistent sound drones again. I grit my teeth and ignore it, confident it will fade away. Instead of worrying, I opt to snuggle closer to my bedmate. Yesterday was as amazing as it was awful. I shudder at the foggy memory of the icy water, sighing when Hudson pulls me tighter into his warmth.

Bzzzzz. Bzzzzz.

Okay. This is getting out of hand. Is it an army of flies?

Next to me, Hudson growls, his face hidden beneath a pillow. "Make it stop."

I stretch my hands out, trying to pinpoint where it's coming from. Groping around the bed, I come up empty, so I force myself into a sitting position. Eyes only partly open, I search the dark cabin. Nothing.

Bzzzzz. Bzzzzz.

The noise is close. I peek over the side of the mattress and —aha. It's my phone. Not bugs. I yawn and squint at the faint glow of the screen as it vibrates against the cabin floor.

With an annoyed huff, I snatch the phone and hit ignore. A quick glance shows that I have close to twenty missed calls from Kirk and hundreds of notifications from my socials.

"Who is it, and what the hell do they want?" I don't fight the smile Hudson's crabby words bring to my lips.

"It must be about me falling overboard. Who would've thought that'd be such a draw? I probably made some sort of *influencer fail* reel."

Tossing his pillow off his face, Hudson pulls me against him. The unspoken message that my phone isn't welcome is heard and received. I run my fingers and lips over his sleep-warm skin.

He presses a kiss to my forehead. "How'd you sleep, baby?"

"I like it when you call me baby."

"How'd you sleep, Spitfire?"

"I like it when you call me that, too."

"How'd you sleep, Pri—"

Pinching his nipple, I say, "*Don't* call me that. And I slept well. Surprisingly. I thought I'd have nightmares. Must've been all the TLC you showed me."

A soft sigh sounds as I place featherlight touches over his broad chest, across his solid stomach, and just as I reach the trail of dark brown hair leading lower—

Bzzzzz. Bzzzzz.

"Fuck. Answer it."

"Ugh." I yank the sheet over my bare chest and smooth my hair. Opening the video call, I don't bother with a proper greeting. "Kirk, it's six thirty in the morning."

"Hi to you too, Blakely. Nice of you to answer."

"I'm sleeping."

"I've been calling you since yesterday afternoon and evening trying to check on you. I even called Hudson."

"I fell in freezing water; I need to rest and recuperate," I say, making my best sad puppy face at him.

"Oh, is that what you're calling it? Try again, BB. Have you looked at your socials? Or have you been too busy?"

Hudson grumbles, "What's going on?"

Kirk grins. "Glad to see you too, Hudson."

"Not that I care, but why?"

Rolling his eyes, Kirk asks, "Do you have any idea what's going on right now?"

"No," we say in unison.

"Blakely, I expect Hudson not to know, but you, of all people." He scolds me as if I'm a disappointing child. "Have you really not been online since yesterday?" When I shrug, he shakes his head. "Go look at your account, and once you have, call me. Got it?"

I nod and hit End.

Hudson sits up and rests his head on my shoulder. "Explain."

"You know as much as I do."

When I open one of my social apps, the first thing I see is shaky video of Hudson and me. It takes me a couple of beats to figure out what's happening because the angle is strange, like the camera is moving around and filming us from below.

There in the blurry frame is Hudson tugging jeans over wet skin while I huddle in a blanket. The video goes black before catching the gloomy sky. Then it cuts to us, proof of our heated, post-lake kiss caught for everyone to see.

Hudson grabs the phone. "Shit." He turns his green eyes on me, anger and hurt swirling to darken them to almost black. "You said you wouldn't post any private moments between us. You swore—"

"I didn't post this." I cover my mouth. "It's from the boat. The livestream. It was running when I went over the side, but I didn't think about it catching us in the aftermath of everything."

The next post is a still shot of us: Hudson cradling my body with his. I keep scrolling; there he is doing the sign-off, and right next to his handsome face is my blanket-clad ass.

"Why do all these other people have your photos?"

"They must've taken screenshots, and now they're tagging me in their posts, so it's flooding my feed."

"I understand all those words, but not in this context," he grumbles. Running his hand through his hair, he frowns at me. "Explain it like I'm five."

"Um, people took pictures of the video, then added my name so more people will see them, including me."

Hudson scowls as I close the app and take his hands in mine. "Hey, talk to me."

"I told you I had worries about being on camera and this," he gestures between us. "And now, this moment—a fucking private moment that should've been only ours—is online for strangers. I don't like all those people talking about us." He rises from the bed, pacing back and forth in the tight space between the mattress and the couch.

"You're the one who said I'm too concerned with what people think of me. What are you really upset about?"

"There's a difference between someone critiquing my business based on merit and people widely speculating about and having access to my private life. And how is this good for my business? Wasn't that the arrangement? How is someone having video of me kissing you helping?" His voice is hard. "It makes me look unprofessional and could hurt my reputation. I warned you about that before—" He trails off.

Ice grips my heart at the implications of his words. Does he already regret what we did last night? Is he done with this?

Rather than let the ice spread, I fight back with fire. "Before what? Before *you* kissed *me* after saying no more? Before you looked me in the eye and said we would happen?" I blink back tears. "It was an accident. I didn't do this on purpose. What? You think I threw myself overboard in a bid for attention?"

When he doesn't immediately tell me no, I slump over as if struck. Then I sit up, lifting my chin. I put on my most professional voice and will all the ice in my chest to my eyes. "As far as how this helps you? Are you fucking serious? Guess what, Bear? Half a million people know who you are and are looking you up right now. And do you know what they'll find?"

He doesn't answer me.

I rise from the bed, striding toward him, the sheet hanging behind me like a bedraggled toga. "They'll find a brave man who jumped in the water to save a woman. A sensitive man comforting a scared woman and a considerate man wrapping a cold, wet woman in a dry blanket. And all these things lead them to Peak Adventures, boosting your reputation, not hurting it."

I cross my arms and glare at him. "So the only thing left for you to be upset or ashamed of is kissing me or thinking I did this on purpose."

"Are you done?" His snarled question catches me off guard, and I give him a slight nod. The next thing I know, powerful arms are around me, and I'm being picked up. My legs automatically wrap around his waist, fastening myself to him.

"That's not what I said or meant, and you damn well know it. It's not about being ashamed of you. It's about all those strangers seeing us kissing on the job." Hudson runs his nose down my face, and his voice softens. "Hear me. Understand me. I don't regret this. You. Us. I want you." He punctuates his words by rolling his hips so his hard cock presses into the growing heat between my legs. "I would just fucking prefer that whatever is happening between the two of us be without all the bullshit that's a part of the Blakely Bradshaw show." He waves one hand in the air toward my now discarded phone.

I unhook my legs and slide down his body until my feet touch the ground. Then I put space between us. "That's not fair, Hudson. It's not like I came here expecting to find someone I could see myself—" I stop and take a breath. "Someone like you. But you're right. What's out there now isn't what you signed up for. It was an accident, but that doesn't change anything." I drop my head, staring at his chest as I mumble, "*We* don't even know about us, not really. This is brand new."

Stifling a small, unexpected sob, I turn my back on him. "I'm sorry you got caught up in all this, and I understand if you want to end it."

The room blurs as Hudson grips me, spinning me to face him. He uses his thumb and index finger to guide my chin upward, forcing our eyes to meet. "No. This isn't ending. I told you to hear me, you stubborn thing. I don't regret us." He brushes his fingers against my jaw and down my neck, gently squeezing it. "How could I? I wasn't expecting last night, but I'm not done. Not by a long shot."

My eyes flutter as he strokes my skin. He presses his lips against mine and hugs me close.

"What now?"

Sighing, I hide my face in his chest. "Now, I need to call

Kirk back. He'll have advice." I stand on my tippy toes and give Hudson a quick kiss. "Could you make me a coffee? It's my turn to apologize, but I need to put on some clothes before I call him."

"Yeah." Hudson kisses the top of my head and pads to the kitchen. I drink in the expanse of his back and how it tapers at his waist, and the way his sleep pants cling to his ass. Then, with a sigh, I layer on the armor I brought with me from the city.

Hair tamed, face fixed, clothes on, I straighten from where I sit on the couch as Kirk's face fills the video screen.

"It's massive, huh? There are clips all over. You two are trending on multiple platforms. And no wonder. A dramatic accident, that was you falling into the water, a big heroic rescue—Hudson dragging you back into the boat. The caretaking, him embracing you and wrapping you in a blanket. And, of course, the peak moment when you kissed. People are losing their minds over it."

At my silence, the smile falls off Kirk's face. "What's wrong?"

"Hudson has some... concerns about how this looks from a professional side."

"Tell him not to worry. All the comments about him are positive."

"And what about me?" I ask, quirking a single eyebrow at my manager.

Kirk shrugs. "You know how it is, Blakely. There's some bitterness out there. But you can't take it personally."

"I didn't go comment diving. What are you seeing?"

He winces.

The grimace on his face tells me everything. These are going to hurt. I open an app, randomly pick a post, and read the comments out loud. They range from absurd to cruel.

"I bet her management company paid for her to go there and get laid. Lord knows she needs it. Remember when Ryan dumped her?"

"Y'all are stupid af if you think any of this is real. Blakely Bradshaw is playing everyone."

"I bet she planned that entire scene. #clickbait #pathetic"

"AI. Never happened. Ur suckers."

"No way a man like that wants a spoiled bitch like her."

"She's been trying this natural face crap. Girl needs makeup. Hudson, if you see this, I'm single."

"Maybe we'll get lucky, and she'll fall off a cliff while out there."

I rub the heels of my hands over my eyes. The comments are part of the job, but it doesn't make it easier. What a fucking couple of days it's been.

"You'd never ask me to send you to a cabin in the woods if you wanted an all-expenses paid sex getaway."

When I look up, Kirk winks. Blinking back tears, I grant him a small smile.

"Blakely, you'll come out of this fine, and so will he. I'd wager Peak Adventures' DMs and messages are blowing up right now and will be for months. And your numbers are growing every day."

"So, do you have any advice?"

"Well, you have two options. Option one is to go on as if nothing happened. Option two is to lean into it."

"Lean into it?"

"Give them what they want. Glimpses of the two of you together and watching you grow closer. Don't focus on the hate; there's a lot of positive out there. So, share more of these moments. If nothing else, it will mean massive numbers."

I frown at him and shake my head. "No. Hudson wants what happens between us to stay private, and I—" I suck in a breath. "I agree with him." Holding my hands up, I say, "I know. I usually splash everything all over my socials, but this is different, Kirk. I won't do that to him. He didn't ask for this. I came out here to learn survival skills, and that's what I want to focus on."

Pausing, I glance behind me—Hudson is puttering around the kitchen—and whisper, "I really like him. Don't smile at me like that."

"You like him? Like the way you like dogs and maple donuts?"

"No. I like him in the *every-time-I see-him-I-think-about-kissing-him-and-it's-way-too-soon-to-be-this-invested* kind of way."

Kirk's grin grows. "And how does he feel about you?"

"We're still feeling each other out, but..." Large, warm hands settle on my shoulders, stopping my words. *Shit.*

His baritone voice has my heart jumping in my throat. "We'll do the second option. We'll lean in."

I crane my head to look at him. "How much of the conversation did you hear?"

"All of it."

Heat blooms over my cheeks. "All of it?" I squeak.

"Yep. You're super loud."

Kirk laughs. "He's not wrong, BB."

My lower lip juts out. "I was whispering!" They both snort, which only fuels my pouting. Ugh. I inhale for a four-count, then say, "Hudson, this is the exact opposite of what you want."

"I'm reconsidering."

"Why?"

Without caring that Kirk is watching, Hudson lowers his mouth to mine. I lose myself in the kiss with my handsome outdoorsman. It isn't until we pick up steam that Kirk clears his throat, reminding us we aren't alone.

Kirk's smile could rival the Cheshire Cat's with the way it's stretched across his face. "You asked for my advice?" At my nod, he says, "Don't blow it."

I smash the End button. "Thanks, that's super helpful," I mutter to myself. I miss the days when you could slam a phone down. Now, it just means you risk breaking your screen. I settle for tossing it to the far side of the couch. Slumping back into the cushions, I put pressure on my temples, fighting off a burgeoning headache.

The couch shifts as Hudson drops next to me, lacing our hands together. I rest my head against his shoulder. "Are you sure about this?"

"What?"

"Going public. Officially. If you think today was a circus... I don't want you doing this because of our fight."

Hudson brings my hand to his mouth, rubbing my knuckles against his lips. "I'm not."

Laughing, I roll my eyes. "Well, that settles it."

"Am I still nervous about putting that much of myself on display? Yeah. But it's part of the package. So, I'm willing to try." He sighs. "If it gets to be too much, we'll talk."

I'm not sure what to say. For Hudson, that was practically a soliloquy.

Nudging my knee with his, Hudson says, "So, you like me, huh?"

I groan. "Shit, you really did hear everything."

"I'm telling you, you're loud. Very loud. The first thing I thought when I met you was loud. Now answer the question."

"I thought the first thing you thought when you met me was how much you wanted to fuck my ti—"

"Blakely."

"Yes, I like you. Happy, you insufferable jerk? I wanted to sleep with you the minute I saw you. Who wouldn't? Have you seen you?" I gesture up and down his body. "But I didn't expect to actually like you so much, especially since you're such an asshole."

"I like you too, Spitfire." Then he smirks. "I never imagined I'd be so interested in a spoiled, bratty social media princess."

Before I can snap at him for calling me a princess, he pulls me into a knee-weakening kiss.

I part my lips, loving the feel of his tongue against mine. It's bizarre, the high I get from little things like kissing him. Is this what it's supposed to be like?

Breaking the kiss, I rub my cheek against his beard and sigh. "Food?"

"Yes, but only if I'm cooking."

"Duh." My chest is tight from a combination of worry about Hudson, lingering aches from falling into the lake, and hurtful comments. "Are we... are you okay?"

"Yes."

"You're sure you're okay with sharing more about us online?"

"Yes."

"Can I get a little more here? You're so damn taciturn."

Hudson pulls my hands to his mouth. His voice is serious. "Yep."

This man.

An impish smile flits across my face, along with a wave of energy. "I'm assuming you're saving all your words for another of those *important* times. Let's see if I can coax a few from you." My mouth meets his in a searing kiss. In the heat of that kiss, for a moment, I see a glimpse of forever with this rough, grumpy country boy. A version of forever I swore I'd never want, but suddenly seems so appealing.

I break away, dipping my tongue into the hollow of his neck, thankful for the built-in distraction of his solid body. My lips traverse his torso, planting a litany of gossamer-light kisses, licks, and strokes over his skin until my fingers and teeth graze along the edge of his joggers.

After the intensity of yesterday and the ugliness online today, I need him. The taste he gave me last night isn't enough.

"Blakely, what are you doing?" He hisses as I slip my hand into his pants, palming his cock and nuzzling my nose against him.

"Nothing."

"That doesn't feel like nothing. It feels fucking amazing, but you better not be doing this as some sort of apology." Hudson tugs my hair, lifting my head.

"No, this is what I want, what I've wanted for a long time."

It's true. Is it also a fabulous distraction from everything in my head? Yes. But it doesn't take away from how I want him.

"Lift your hips."

"And you call me bossy." He grumps but does as I command, and I slowly tug his pants down—ghosting my fingers over his thighs, tickling the back of his knees, squeezing his calves, and caressing his ankles. With every touch, his cock twitches for me.

"Are you aching for me, Bear?"

He swallows but doesn't answer.

I kiss and lick my way back up his legs, then settle between the cradle of his hips. I take a moment to rest my cheek against his thigh, enjoying the smell of his skin, the tickle of the coarse dark hair on his legs, the quiver of his firm muscles.

Gazing up, I hover close enough that he can feel my breath but not my lips. Just out of reach. I plan on enjoying this. Savoring him. I move lower. The warm air from my mouth fans over his balls, and I dart my tongue out, lapping at the soft, salty skin.

"Oh, shit."

"Is that okay?"

"Fuck yes." The muscles in his cheek clench. "Do it again."

In response to that, I suck a little harder and cradle this delicate part of him in my palm. I tease him, drawing out his pleasure and anticipation. When I'm happy with how much he's straining, I place chaste kisses from root to tip, then lap the droplets of precum that blossom on his flared head. A moan—a needy, pleading moan—fills the air.

A thrill of power and pleasure pulses through me. "Mmmm, those noises are so good, Bear." I swirl my tongue around his crown before spreading his legs wide and nipping and sucking at the skin of his inner thighs. "Do you want my mouth on you?"

"Yes."

"Yes, what?"

"Yes, I want your delicious mouth on me."

As soon as he says it, I envelop as much of him as I can. The hiss he makes sends jolts of lust and heat through my body. Humming and purring, I hollow my cheeks and sweep my tongue along the underside of his cock, tracing the thick vein that runs along his length.

Hudson thrusts against my face with a curse. "Fuck Blakely, just like that."

My fingers roam his body. When I rub them over the sensitive place behind his balls, he thrusts upward, his cock sinking deeper. I swallow around him. Doing everything I can to coax out those panty-dropping moans.

Pulling back, I track the way Hudson's eyes are glued to my swollen lips, the thin line of spit threading from my mouth to his cockhead. I run my tongue over his slit before sucking lightly, then taking him deeper. Twisting my wrist, my hand and lips meet and then separate over and over. Looking up from between his legs, I relish the way his face contorts in desire.

Lust and wanting cloud my mind as another moan, this one more desperate than before, slips from his lips. Hudson's hands tangle in my hair, and he tugs on me. I shake him off, and he relents, digging his fingers into the sheets. He lets out a stream of curses as I fight my gag reflex to pull him as far into my throat as I can. I furiously pump the last bit of him I can't swallow. He bucks against my face, and I love it.

The fingers of my free hand slip between my legs, and I put pressure on my clit in a steady rhythm. My hips rock in tandem with my head as I hollow my cheeks and suck. His pleasure drives mine higher, and it isn't long before I'm coming, my whimpers vibrating around his cock.

"I'm gonna, fuck—" Before he can complete his sentence, hot cum spills down my throat. "Blakely…" Hudson trails off, at a loss for words. Instead, he curls his fingers in my hair, petting me.

Kissing a path to his stomach, I rest my ear on his chest, and savor his heavy breathing, the frenzied thundering of his heart. I did this; I brought this rugged, powerful man to the edge and shoved him over. I sigh in contentment as Hudson winds strands of my hair around his fingers.

Suddenly, I find myself pinned beneath my outdoorsman's weighty mass. He captures my lips, our tongues entangling, stealing my breath and thoughts. Then, with a devilish glint in his eye, he kisses a winding path down my body.

"What are you doing?"

"My turn now," he growls against my throat. Lower and lower, he moves until his nose is at eye-level with my clit. Glittering green eyes and a tussle of brown hair are the last things I see before losing myself in waves of euphoria.

DAY THIRTEEN

I'm on the porch, bleary-eyed. The nightmares I avoided the night of the lake incident caught me last night. I was trapped in the dark water, but word bubbles floated all around me, calling me a failure, a fake, and worse.

Hudson chased my bad dream away as quickly as I made a sound—my very own knight slaying my dragons. But even with his warm, steady breath on my neck, his strong arms around me, I couldn't fall back asleep.

But the show must go on.

"Good morning, BBs. Today I'm on the front porch of my cozy cabin extra early this morning. Shout-out to my new favorite coffee shop, The Bee and The Bean. This is a Trail Creek staple; luckily, Hudson has bags of their delicious pecan roast on hand!" Pausing, I take a big sip of my coffee. "Also, thank you for the outpouring of concern and for checking in on me after I fell into the lake. I'm doing great! Now, on to the real reason you're tuning in before the sun is up. Let's take a moment to address some of the rumors, stories, and speculation about Hudson and me. It's important for you to understand that Hudson is a very reserved person."

Next to me, Hudson mumbles loud enough for the phone to pick up. "What Blakely is trying to say is we're together. It isn't anyone's business, and you're all too interested in us for reasons I can't understand." I stare at him, mouth agape.

"Uhhh, yes..." I clear my throat before putting my best smile back on. "BBs, don't listen to him; I think he needs a little pecan coffee, too!" I giggle, pointedly ignoring the glare Hudson shoots my way. "While the focus of my livestreams will continue to be the Trail Creek wilderness and the things Hudson teaches me, we're willing to share a little more of our relationship with you as well." I lean in, a serious look on my face. "I'd like to be clear, despite what some of the comments or posts from others have implied, we didn't plan this, and it isn't fake or for show."

Hudson snorts. "It sure as shit wasn't planned. You infuriate me most days."

I elbow him in the ribs, then kiss him on the cheek. Turning my attention to the camera, I say, "So I have another treat for you early birds. You get to watch a gorgeous New Mexico sunrise. I'll be going live again in forty-five minutes; make sure you tune back in then!"

With that, I sign off and let out a breath. "That wasn't terrible. You were nicer than I expected."

"I even let you kiss me on the cheek. I went above and beyond."

"I'll have to thank you properly when we get back from our hike." Lust laces my voice, and I steal a kiss from his perfect lips.

"How do you plan on thanking me?"

"First, I'll nibble your ear, just enough to make you squirm." I mimic my words as I speak, taking his earlobe in my teeth and giving it a tug. "Then I'll kiss your jaw and lick your Adam's apple."

Hudson groans as my tongue teases his throat. An electric pulse fills my body any time I make him moan. My fingers slip under his shirt. "Next, I'll strum my fingers up and down your ribs and stomach, playful little touches that make goosebumps rise on your skin."

"No more." Hudson grabs my hands and sucks in a ragged breath. "If you don't stop now, we'll miss the sunrise."

"Fine. But we'll pick this up later." I brush my lips against his ear. "That's a promise."

hudson

DAY FIFTEEN

I'm jolted awake by a whimper. Blakely jerks in her sleep, pained noises disturbing the early morning peace.

"Blakely, wake up. It's a dream." I brush the hair from her face and feather kisses over her forehead and cheeks.

"Bear?"

"Yeah, Spitfire. I'm here." I spoon my body around hers, pressing as much skin to skin as I can. "Want to talk?"

"Not yet. Can you hold me?"

"Always, baby. Always."

It isn't long before she drifts back to sleep, the stress on her face melting away. I stay awake, studying her, soaking in as much of her as I can. Eventually, light filters in through the windows, and the thin rays highlight her delicate features. I like this version of her, the makeup-free, less flawless, but no less perfect version.

During her live a couple of mornings ago, she giggled and swooned over the sunrise. I can't help but compare that to our second early morning hike, the one she kept for herself. She was so different in those two moments. I wish she'd trust herself, her true self. Let the people who follow her see that other side of her—the softer, real side she shows me.

She lets out a light snore, and I chuckle. Even in her sleep, she has to make noise. So damn loud.

When you're alone with someone, day in and out, it warps things. I've had every meal, every shower, every shit with Blakely feet away. In that sense, two weeks is more like two months. So it's hard to believe I've only known her for fifteen days. And even harder to believe I only have fifteen days left with her.

I brush my thumb over her lips, and she stirs but doesn't wake. "You're maddeningly beautiful. You know that, though, don't you? Got me doing things I swore I'd never do again, and I don't just mean your damn socials." I bury my nose in her hair and inhale.

With a sigh, I leave her to sleep and decide to take a quick shower. I step into the old-fashioned clawfoot tub, yank the shower curtain closed, and adjust the tap until the water runs warm. As it streams over me, memories of last night flash in my mind—Blakely beneath me, hair splayed out on the pillows, face flushed, lips parted in pleasure. Using my soapy hand, I grip my cock. That woman. The effect she has on me is ridiculous. I move my fist up and down, twisting at the head and squeezing.

I'm falling into a steady rhythm when the shower curtain opens and a naked Blakely stands before me. "Let me help you with that, Bear." She smiles and steps into the large tub behind me.

I groan, watching her slender fingers reach around my waist and glide over my cock. "Did you just wake up?"

"I might've been awake when you were saying nice things about me in bed this morning."

"You little sneak." I spin and capture her lips in mine.

She draws back, her hand still ghosting over my cock. "I'm very naughty. What are you going to do about it?"

"Blakely, you've had—"

She pulls my hand to her ass and places it against her skin. "I need to be punished."

I worry she's using this as a bandaid, but how do I say no when my Spitfire wants to play? Nibbling on her jaw, as my other hand glides up her body to settle on her throat, I murmur, "Are you sure you want this?"

"Don't make me ask again, Hudson."

Giving her neck a gentle squeeze, I say, "Lean over and grab the edge of the tub. Brace yourself. Do you understand?"

A rosy hue creeps up her cheeks, and she nods at me.

As she turns away, I stop her. "If you want this to end, what do you say?"

"Stop or red."

"Atta girl."

She jumps when I lightly smack her ass. "I wasn't ready!"

"Consider that a warmup."

Blakely bends at the waist and grasps the edges of the bathtub, offering me an incredibly tempting view. I adjust the spray of the water to keep us from getting cold, turning back just in time to catch her wiggling her heart-shaped ass. Such a brat.

I walk my fingers down her spine, loving how she arches into my touch. When I reach her ass, I palm it, give it a gentle squeeze. A firm slap cracks over the sound of the shower. Blakely makes a noise, something between a moan and a yelp, and rocks toward me.

"How do you feel?" I ask as I trace small, soothing circles over the pink mark.

She swallows. "I haven't learned my lesson yet."

Smirking, I repeat my actions: palm, squeeze, spank. Another moan fills the room and Blakely's hips jerk. *Soothe, palm, squeeze, spank.*

Then again. And again. Until she's panting.

"And now?" Her ass glows a rosy red.

"M-make it an even ten," she stutters.

God, she's perfect. *Soothe. Palm. Squeeze. Spank.*

The knuckles of her hands are white from the vice-like grip she has on the side of the tub, and her legs tremble. Dropping to my knees behind her, I sweep my lips over her tender skin. Goosebumps erupt on her flesh, and she lets out a strangled whine and pushes back towards me, seeking more. I oblige her, my tongue grazing her pussy while my fingers skim between her thighs.

"Always so eager," I whisper as I stand over her. Holding her hips, my cock brushes against her wet heat. I tease along her slit until I bump against her clit, and it takes all my willpower not to bury myself in her right then.

When I step back, my body aches to respond to the desperate groan Blakely makes at the loss of contact. Being with her is like being drunk in the best way: all heady buzz, pleasant warmth, and loss of inhibition.

I grab the adjustable shower head and tug it toward us, spraying her back with the warm water. Then I fiddle with the heat, dropping it by a few degrees, before positioning the spray over the mark I left on her ass.

I drizzle the cooling water against her skin for a moment more until the red fades to pink, and then I change the temperature back to normal. Blakely's arms shake. Her muscles and joints must burn from the exertion of staying bent over for so long, but she holds firm.

Strong. Stubborn. Spirited.

There's a reason I call her Spitfire.

"Lay on your back and spread your legs."

Blakely does as I direct without question, though she quietly moans as she moves. Her quick compliance fuels the depth of my want for her. It's not that I have to have control to get off, but the trust it takes for someone to let you lead them to their pleasure is a feeling you can't replicate. I don't doubt things would be fucking amazing without any kind of play, but this adds another layer for me. And given the look on her face, it does for Blakely, too.

She rests her head against the basin of the bathtub and splays her legs over the sides. My gaze fixates on the way she's spread before me. I stroke myself, committing this moment to memory—her desire-filled eyes, her open mouth, her panting chest, her small patch of curls, her silken lips. Fucking perfection. I hold the shower head and position it so the stream hits her on that sweet button between her legs, making her squirm.

"Stop moving."

She freezes and gazes up at me, hungry eyes burning for me, for her release. Fuck, I'd give her the moon if she asked.

"Only good girls get to move. Naughty girls have to stay still until their punishment is over. Understand?"

She licks her lips and nods. "Yes, I understand." Her voice is breathy, and her muscles constrict as the water pulses over her clit and core.

Locking the shower head back into its holder, I kneel between her splayed legs. I seize her hips and hoist her towards my mouth before placing a kiss on her pubic bone and running my nose down her folds. Nothing but a feather-light caress.

She wriggles, but I give her thigh a sharp nip before tightening my grip. "I said no moving."

"I don't think I can hold still."

"Oh, you can. If you want to come, you'll stay still until I tell you to move."

"Ye-yes, sir."

Fuck. The sir. Gritting my teeth, I groan. Sliding one arm beneath her ass to steady her, I move my free hand until I can slip a finger into her pussy. The way she bites her lip, fighting to keep from bucking against my hand, has me praising her.

"So perfect, Blakely. Look at you. All sass and sex and sweetness." On the last word, I lick around her clit, my tongue lapping up every drop she gives me.

Deeper, I search inside her, hunting for that little spot that will make her break. I want to leave her shattered. To be the one who wrecks her and the one who gathers all those fragments and puts her back together.

She squeezes her eyes shut and makes noises that would have neighbors calling the cops. Good thing we don't have any out here.

It's time to up the ante. I lift her higher, teasing her clit before closing my lips around the sensitive bundle of nerves and sucking.

"Hudson, I..."

Lifting my head, I grin. "I know, but you're still being punished, remember?" My tongue delves into her pussy, searching out the wetness building there. Her thighs twitch, and her walls tighten, so I pull back, removing my fingers and mouth from her altogether.

"No! Hudson! Please, please!"

"Have you learned your lesson, naughty girl? No more tricking me?"

"Yes! Fuck! I've learned my lesson. Please make me come!"

At her pleading, I lower my mouth to her pussy, licking and loving her. Two fingers plunge into her warmth, curling in a come hither motion. I love the way she feels, the way she tastes, the fucking delicious noises she makes while at my mercy. I raise my head long enough to give her permission to move.

She clasps my head, fingers clutching my hair, legs coming off the sides of the tub and locking around my neck. She bucks towards my mouth, urging my fingers and tongue to go deeper inside her.

It's one of the things I adore most about her. She's no passive bystander waiting for satisfaction. No, she knows what she wants. And now, released from our game, she tells me what she needs.

"Harder, yes! Right there!"

All the built-up tension in her body explodes in my mouth, and I work her through her climax, prolonging her release as I continue to suck and roll her clit. She shudders and wails, writhing and mewling as she comes down from the high of her orgasm. Ignoring my screaming knees, I pry her thighs from the sides of my head and lift her, guiding her onto my aching cock.

Everything about this moment—the lingering taste of her on my tongue, the pulse of her cunt around my cock, the weight of her in my lap, the press of her skin against mine—overwhelms me.

My head falls back at the sensation of her hot pussy clenching around me. She rocks her hips, pulling me deeper and deeper until we're flush and as close as two people can be. Her eyes lock on mine, and a fresh round of longing crashes over me as she drops a hand between us, chasing another climax.

She's a goddess, water running in rivulets along her skin,

face flushed in delight, hair plastered to her head in dripping tendrils. I can't tear my eyes away from her. Each undulation of her shapely body sends shivers through me.

She comes on my cock. The intense surge of her orgasm and the contraction of her innermost muscles sends me over moments later. Her head falls onto my shoulder, and her breath, ragged and gasping, tickles my skin. We sit, clinging to each other under the falling water, mini spasms rippling through our still-joined bodies.

"If I'd known it would be like this, I'd have kissed you the moment we met." *Instead of wasting all those days fighting the pull between us.*

She purrs out a laugh. "Who says I'd have let you?"

I press my mouth to her temple and ease my cock out of her before getting us both to our feet. Blakely falls forward, her legs weak, so I hold her against my body, encouraging her to lean on me for support. Without speaking, I grab her shampoo, the same damn shampoo we fought over not so long ago, and squirt a dollop into my hands. I massage her scalp, loving how she melts into my touch. When I finish, she mirrors my actions, scrubbing my head and hair. I hum, amazed at this different kind of closeness, somehow more intimate than anything else we've done.

As the last of the suds rinse away, Blakely wraps me in her arms, drawing me forward so my forehead rests against hers. "That was amazing, Bear. I can't believe I'm here with you."

"You're amazing." I take her chin and lift her face towards mine. "Before that goes to your head, get out of the shower, and let's start our day." I turn off the water, wrap her in a towel, and give her ass a slight swat.

"Ouch! That still stings from earlier!" She rubs her cheek and pouts at me.

"Go get dressed, and I'll make coffee. You're no good to me

without it." She shoots me a withering glare, and I burst out laughing. Shit, I'm addicted to pleasing and teasing her.

Once we're dressed, we set out. The hike is a fair distance down the mountain, but it's picturesque, with the green of the pines mixing with the golds of the birch and aspen trees. Sunshine dapples the ground through the leaves, and Blakely's fingers twine with mine. I'm fucking happy.

I stop when we reach a thicket of Piñon pines, chokecherries, and other shrubs. It's all a part of attempting to teach Blakely how to recognize safe and poisonous plants.

"I'm doing a quick live spot. In or out?"

"No kissing."

"I'll keep my mouth to myself, I promise. But what about groping?" She squeezes my bicep, trailing her fingers over the muscle.

"No groping either... at least not where the camera can see."

Blakely hugs and kisses me, her tongue exploring the depths of my mouth.

I break the kiss with a swear. "Fuck, if you don't stop that, you won't be doing your livestream."

She brushes a finger against her lips and smiles. Then cracks her neck and rolls her shoulders, flipping that switch that transforms her into *Blakely Bradshaw*.

"Good morning, BBs! I hope you enjoyed the sunrise hike we took you on yesterday. If you couldn't join us, you can check out my recent posts. It's truly an amazing sight! I've been here with Hudson for fifteen days and—I'm really excited about this—today, he's teaching me about foraging. Pretty cool, right?"

Turning to me, she asks, "What plants can we find around here?" Then she pans her camera toward the surrounding trees.

"This time of year, you can forage for chokecherries, elderberries, currants, Piñon pine nuts, rose hips, dandelion greens, and purslane. Mushrooms are another option, but you have to be extra cautious when dealing with them. I wouldn't recommend it until you're more comfortable foraging."

Blakely stares at me like I'm speaking another language—or the way I stare at her when she talks about insights and analytics.

"And I can find all these things here?" She gestures around us, talking to me, but into the camera.

"We'll have to hike a bit to find everything I mentioned."

She nods, then goes into a long-winded advertisement for her hiking boots—the blister-giving ones we finally broke in. Shaking my head, I wander towards a cluster of chokecherries. The product placement, the fake enthusiasm. I don't get it. She was two seconds away from throwing those boots at my head two weeks ago.

I agreed to lean in, but seeing how easily she swaps between the woman I care for and this other person gives me pause. Is this thing between us any different? Or am I just another pair of hiking boots to her?

The hurt in Blakely's eyes when she thought I was ashamed of our relationship was real. The way she kisses me is fucking real, too. I run one hand down my face. I need to get myself together.

"What are these?" Blakely startles me, and she laughs when I jerk. "Sorry, Bear. I thought you had super hearing."

"Situational awareness, and normally I do." *But being around you makes me an idiot.*

"So, what are these pretty berries?"

"Chokecherries."

She makes big eyes at her phone. "That's an ominous name."

"They're mostly used in jams or jellies. You can eat them raw, but—"

Before I can warn her, she's popped one into her mouth.

"That's disgusting!" Her lips curl up, and she guzzles water. I bet she'd scrape her tongue if she weren't on camera.

I press my lips in an attempt to hide my grin. "They're very tart."

"Show me something else," she grumbles.

We walk further down the mountain, Blakely chatting to her followers the whole time. When I come to a stop, she runs into my back. I sigh and look to the sky. One day, I'll get her head out of that phone.

I guide her toward a wide shrub. "These are elderberries. You can use them in syrups, wines, and jellies."

"Wine?" Blakely wiggles her eyebrows at me and then grins at the camera. "Did you hear that, BBs? Wild wine! Right here at your fingertips."

"Not exactly," I mutter. "You have to be careful."

I'm trying to clarify when she says, "Hudson, one of our viewers—shout out to SmileyMiley—wants to know: do any of these plants have medicinal properties?"

She thrusts the phone into my face, and I freeze. All I manage to do is nod. This is way easier when I pretend it's just her I'm talking to.

Blakely elbows me in the ribs and mouths, *"Say something."*

"Yes."

The soft slap of her hand hitting her forehead cues me to say more.

"Um, elderberries have immune-boosting properties. There's an old local legend about them."

"Oh?" Her turquoise eyes glitter. "Tell me, please."

"It's a long story..."

"BBs, send hearts if you want to hear this!" The screen fills with floating hearts, clouding out the reflection of my bemused face.

Guess it's story time.

"When we first moved here, my mom learned everything she could about Trail Creek and the surrounding areas, including the local tales. Her favorites are the one about two stars you can wish on and the one about how a man saved his entire village."

Blakely drops onto a small stump and drags me to the ground beside her. "We love a hero."

I can't believe I'm telling this story to thousands of strangers online. If Bo and Gray find out about this, I'll never live it down. But then I look at Blakely and her excitement, and dammit, I want her to keep looking at me like I'm something special.

My ears burn, and I frown at the camera. "Um, I may not get all the details right."

Blakely beams at me, her dazzling smile the only carrot I need.

"There once lived a village of warriors. They built their home in the foothills of the mountains and thanked the gods for granting them such a perfect place to live."

My eyes cut to the phone. How many people are watching this? Shit. Can't think about that.

My voice shakes, but I push on. "Because the land was so fertile, the air and water so clean, others tried to take it away.

So, as a gift for their thanks and devotion, the gods granted the villagers the ability to transform with the full moon."

"Like werewolves?"

"Yes, but more powerful and dangerous. Over time, the people stopped needing to transform to access their strength. They'd become incredibly strong. So strong they rivaled the gods. The many attacks they'd fought off led to them becoming not only fierce fighters but also clever and cunning."

I swipe my sweaty palms on my jeans before forging ahead. "As time passed, the village thrived, each generation growing stronger and smarter than the one before. At the peak of their prosperity, the elders claimed they would one day surpass the gods in strength and wisdom. Of course, this made the gods angry and jealous. The gods, afraid of being conquered, sent a plague that struck down half the village."

Blakely's murmured, "Oh no," tugs a half smile to my lips.

"Despite their abilities, knowledge, and might, nothing the villagers did helped those infected. They tried every herb, every remedy. The leader's wife was among the sick, and each day, his heart ached at her pain. He knew they couldn't go on with so many ill and growing worse, so one chilly evening, he left. His mission: to journey to the peak of the highest mountain, where the gods lived, and do whatever was necessary to lift the curse and heal his people."

I glance at Blakely. She's hanging on every word, eyeing me like I'm the honey on a sea-salt croissant. Her phone is still in her hand, but she's focused on me. Some of the tension in my stomach loosens.

Taking a deep breath, I go on. "There was no path up the mountain, and the trek was treacherous. The leader encountered fierce animals, unrelenting weather, and traps meant to keep him from reaching the peak. Finally, after days of travel, he reached the apex of the tallest mountain and the lair of the gods. They were so impressed by his devotion and drive that they made him a deal—his people's extraordinary strength and powers in exchange for the ability to heal everyone who was sick."

Even though I was an adult when we moved to Trail Creek, my mom made sure I knew the local legends for my future children. Something I always rolled my eyes about. But right now, with Blakely listening to me weave this tale, it's not so farfetched to imagine whispering this to a beautiful daughter with green eyes, honey-blonde waves, and freckles on her cheeks.

"Though the leader impressed the gods, they still feared him, which is why they made him an offer he couldn't refuse. He agreed without hesitation. Without regret, he traded away his birthright—his supernatural strength. And in return, they gave him a single seed."

"One? How's that—"

"Shh, let me finish." I squeeze her thigh and leave my hand there, out of view of the camera. I may be telling this story where everyone can hear, but they aren't stealing any more private moments from us.

"The leader ran to his village as quickly as he could and planted the seed, tending the small bush that sprang up overnight. Tirelessly, he watched it grow until it bore branches and branches of berries."

"Did it heal them?" she asks.

"For days, they watched the berries turn a deep purple and ripen. Meanwhile, the sick faded away to almost nothing. During this time, the leader, holding his wife's limp hand, realized they couldn't wait any longer. Gathering as many healthy villagers as he could, he called them to harvest the berries and cook them down into a syrup to ensure they'd have enough for everyone."

Blakely's hand finds mine, and she laces our fingers together. I glance at the phone and power through to the end. Can't leave my girl wanting.

"From home to home, they traveled, giving the healing syrup to those in need, until finally, he arrived at his house. His wife was all but gone, so weak she couldn't even open her mouth to drink from the cup that held the medicine. In his desperation, he poured the syrup into his mouth and then, pressing his lips to hers, passed the power of the fruit to her through his kiss."

"Hudson, did it heal her?"

I cut my eyes to her watery ones and give her a small smile. "Yes, impatient. It healed her, and they lived many happy years together, settling the town of Trail Creek and spreading the healing power of elderberries, too."

"What a beautiful story," she whispers. She leans toward me, her mouth open, ready to kiss me, the live all but forgotten.

Hating myself for not taking the kiss she's offering, I clear my throat. "Blakely?"

"Huh?" She blinks, then blushes and scrambles to her feet, positioning her phone to capture her flushed face. "BBs, did you hear that story? Are your hearts as full as mine right now? I. Am. Swooning. What a tale! And what a plant."

Like a loyal dog, I trot after her, watching as she zooms in on the berries and slips the glossy leaves between her fingers. She chats a little longer, then signs off. As soon as she ends the live, her legs are around my waist, and her mouth is on mine.

I almost topple over from the force but manage to keep us standing. Tightening my hands on her hips, I take control of the kiss, driving my tongue between her lips. She rocks her hips, and I have the urge to pin her to the ground and take her on a bed of fallen pine needles. But I settle for pressing her curvy body to mine and running my hands over her.

Blakely and I lose ourselves here in the forest, kissing, grinding, licking until I have to stop. I'm not hiking back to the cabin in pants soaked in cum.

When I lower her to the ground, she sways, her eyes still closed, lips bee stung and so fuckable. Fifteen more days with her is nowhere near enough.

I rest my chin on the top of her head. "Drink some more water. We've got a ways to go."

She cocks her head to the side. "Really?"

"Yep."

With a smile and a roll of her eyes, Blakely picks up her things and puts her phone away in her pack. Once we're rehydrated, I lead us down the mountain.

"While we walk, tell me what you see that could help you navigate back here alone."

"What do you mean?"

"Directions have been a challenge for you. So I thought we'd try your location-based idea."

Her pretty eyes narrow. And I'm ready for her to rain hellfire down on me, but she surprises me by blowing a huff of air out of her nose and shrugging. "Give me an example of what you're talking about."

"See those trees?"

"Hudson, there are four billion trees." Blakely waves her hands, gesturing in a circle.

I roll my eyes and grab her flailing hands, guiding the tips of her fingers where I want her to look. "Those two are wound around each other. It's easy to remember and identify and can help you place your location."

She studies the entwined trees and, with a grin, nudges me. "Did you point those trees out to help me navigate or because you're secretly a hopeless romantic? Because after that story, I'm leaning towards you being a big, mushy romantic."

"You're ridiculous," I say as I pull her into my arms and kiss the side of her neck.

"Yeah, ridiculously amazing. Okay, show me how to find more wild food."

Some days, I wonder what it'd be like if Blakely was here without the strings. Would this be our life? Hiking in the forest, foraging for food, sitting on the porch swing until the night comes alive?

She snaps a selfie of us—for her use only—and I remember that without those strings, I never would've met her. A dart of ice zaps my heart. I might've gone my entire life without this dazzling, exhausting, wonderful, annoying woman.

I hook an arm around her waist as we hike together, Blakely pointing out her markers along the way. Most of them are absurd. A rock that looks like a high heel, a faded warning sign, a stump that would make a great seat, a super cute bush —her words, not mine—and a tree that's "probably haunted." So long as it works for her, that's all that matters.

It's also cute as fuck. And I'm a smitten bastard.

What the hell am I going to do when she's gone?

CHAPTER EIGHTEEN

DAY SIXTEEN

I wake, curled up in the bed. Our bed. How quickly I've come to think of it that way without question. Hudson must've carried me in after I fell asleep on the porch. We spent hours out there last night talking.

Well, I talked. He grunted when appropriate.

I opened up to him about the nightmares, the mix of the lake and ugliness from my socials. It helped. Last night's dream was much more interesting.

My neck tingles with the heat of Hudson's stare. With a stretch, I roll onto my side, and sure enough, he's awake and watching me.

"Good morning, creeper."

He gathers my hands in his and presses a chaste kiss against my knuckles. "Mornin'."

"You didn't deny it."

Hudson raises one dark eyebrow. "What?"

"That you're a creeper. It's fine. I like that in a partner."

Grinning, I rub the tip of my cold nose against his chest and dig my icy toes into the meat of his thigh.

"How can you be so damn cold all the time?" He complains but pulls me closer.

Ignoring him, I say, "I had a dream about the Trail Creek settlers last night."

"Better than the nightmares."

I nod and wriggle until I'm in his lap. "I was in the bed dying, but instead of wilting away, I grew angrier every day my husband was gone. And when you—" *Shit.* Maybe he didn't catch that. "When he finally showed up with the fruit, I smashed it in his face."

Hudson snorts. "Sounds exactly like you."

A mischievous smile tugs at my lips, and I lean forward, giving his collarbone a nibble. "After I shoved the fruit in his face, I had to clean it off. I couldn't leave him all messy." I kiss and suck along the length of Hudson's neck.

"So you dream of me?"

I freeze; I knew it was too much to hope he would miss that. "The man in my dream did look a lot like you. Only more handsome."

"Brat." He shudders as I slowly roll my hips and grind against him.

"Aw, don't be mean. Open your mouth for me. Let me show you what happened next." I lick along the seam of his full lips, and when he opens, I suck his tongue, relishing the groan that escapes his throat.

My hips rock against his, building that exquisite tingle between my legs with each roll. But before we can go any further, my phone buzzes.

Hudson grunts in annoyance and buries his face in the crook of my neck. "I hate that fucking thing."

"I have to take this. It's Kirk."

Hudson doesn't answer; he just slides out from under me. I frown at his retreating back, then huff and fling myself back into the pillows before stabbing the answer button.

"What."

"Good morning to you, too, BB."

"Sorry. You have terrible timing."

Kirk gives me an apologetic grin. "I would have waited for you to call me, but the hubs surprised me with a few days away, and apparently, we're leaving in an hour."

Marcus hollers in the background, telling Kirk to say hi to me and to hurry the hell up. I grin. These two are couple goals.

"He's forbidding me from working while on vacation." With a roll of his eyes, Kirk continues. "I didn't want you to think I ghosted you."

"You'd never!"

"Of course, I wouldn't. Everyone knows you're my favorite. How are you?"

"I'm good. I promise." I'm surprised to find I mean it. You won't catch me on the lake anytime soon, and I'm avoiding comments, but each day that passes brings a new sense of peace.

He smiles, then slips into work mode. "What's on the agenda for the next few days?"

"I'm not sure. Hudson plans things, but I don't find out until he springs them on me."

"Okay, keep up what you've been doing." He shifts. "You have two weeks to go, but I've already taken care of the arrangements for your pickup and departure from Trail Creek. When I get back from Seattle, we can talk specifics."

And just like that, Kirk punctures my rising happiness balloon. Pain, sharp and jagged, tears through my stomach and up into my chest at the thought of being without my Bear. Two weeks. Travel plans. Going back.

The fake friends. My lonely apartment. No Hudson.

I sit, silent and unblinking, until the weight shifts on the bed. "She's learning how to shoot a bow and arrow."

Grasping the distraction Hudson tossed my way, I ask, "I am?"

"Yep. Gotta make sure you learn as many skills as possible before you," he pauses, a series of emotions flickering over his face, "leave."

Frustration. Sadness. Wanting. I know because they're mirrored on my own.

Kirk studies me through the camera. "BB?"

Forcing a smile, I chirp. "Yeah, sorry. I'm so jealous of you and Marcus. Have fun!" With a wave and an air kiss, I end the call.

The shift in the mood is noticeable. Hudson stares up at the ceiling, his brows knitted together, lost in thought. My throat stings. I need to touch him. Scooting closer, I rest my cheek on his chest, tracing the veins in his forearm. A rumbly sigh reverberates beneath my ear, and I smile. I love how Hudson reacts to my touch—even from glancing grazes like walking my fingers over his skin.

And it's the same for me. The heat of those pine-green eyes sends shivers down my spine, increases my heart rate, and makes me wet. I wonder, not for the first time, how someone I've known for sixteen days—and liked for less—can make me feel this way. My stomach aches at the idea of going back to Austin. I don't want to think about the car coming for me in two weeks. About the choices I have to make. About what I'll be giving up.

Instead, I turn my face into Hudson's broad chest, inhaling his earthy scent and pretending I don't have any worries. "So, shooting a bow, huh?"

"Yep." His heavy hand settles on my head, stroking my hair.

"Not at anything, though, right?"

"Stationary targets."

"I think I can handle that."

We linger a little longer before Hudson gently shifts me and gets off the bed. "We leave in ten."

On my side of the cabin, or at least where all my clothes, shoes, and assorted bric-à-brac lie, I search for something to wear. But my mind wanders, and I call to Hudson. "What's Trail Creek like?"

He pokes his head out of the bathroom, toothbrush in his mouth. "Huh?"

"Trail Creek. How big is it?"

"Um, around nineteen hundred people live here year round."

So around the same size as Hawthorn. I scowl at my clothes as if they've offended me.

"But it triples in the winter and summer thanks to vacationers. Why?" Hudson leans against the door, the toothbrush gone.

"Just curious." I slip a sweatshirt over my head and attempt to pad past him. He stops me, his thumb brushing my cheek.

"What's in your head?"

"Thinking of all the arrows I'm going to let fly," I lie. I'm not about to tell him the thought of living in a town this small freaks me the fuck out or that I asked because, for a second there, I let myself pretend I could stay.

I shake my head and smile. Now's not the time. I offer him my hand. "Ready?"

He studies me, nods, and laces our fingers together.

Pushing all thoughts of leaving and Austin out of my head, I let Hudson lead me on today's adventure.

"Hey there, BBs! Can you believe my adventure in Trail Creek is halfway over? It's day sixteen, which means Hudson and I are down to two weeks together. We've seen your questions about what we have planned for after, but we aren't ready to share yet."

Hudson grunts from off-camera, and I glance at him. I know how much he dislikes the "Blakely Show" despite agreeing to be a part of it. The more time I spend with him, the more my social media persona feels like the mask he accused me of hiding behind. A mask that stifles and suffocates me more each day.

While I wasn't exactly happy before Hudson, at least the job was simple. Giggle, be quippy, say something outrageous. Now, it feels like work, like precious moments away from getting to know him, being with him. Like the thing that's going to take me away from him.

I remember how belligerent and defiant I'd been when he first called me out about my behavior on camera. How I'd claimed there was no difference in my off-screen and on-screen personalities. But in my heart, I knew he was right all along.

The reflection I saw in the mirror today wasn't one I hated even as I examined each tiny wrinkle around my eyes and scrutinized my untamed waves. Could I be this person always? This woman who wears makeup when and because she wants to, doesn't care if her hair is perfectly smooth, isn't afraid of what everyone else thinks. Is there room for Blake Lee Shaw in Blakely Bradshaw's world?

Clearing my throat, I pack all the heavy away. "What I mean is Hudson and I haven't discussed what we'll do when our time here ends. We're still learning about each other, and it's too soon for us to make a long-term decision. But let's not focus on that. Why, you may ask? Because today I'm shooting a freaking bow and arrow! How badass is that?" I flex my arms for the camera. "Hudson assures me I'll be able to hit a bullseye when he's done teaching me. You've got to love a sexy man with confidence!" I wink into the camera and wiggle my eyebrows suggestively.

Hudson leans against his Jeep, looking every bit the forest god he is. The morning sun casts him in a golden halo, caramel hints glimmering in his hair and beard. I'm taken over by the urge to run my fingers through, and I fight to stop from running to him. His dark green eyes scan me as if he's seen me from the inside out—which, to be fair, he has.

Heat pools in my stomach as memories of our lovemaking crash over me.

A smug look flits across his face, and he mouths, "*Say something,*" throwing the words I've said to him so many times back at me.

"Sorry, BBs, I spaced out for a moment." I giggle into the lens. "I was staring at Hudson!" I turn the camera on my cabin mate before holding it up to put myself in frame. "Who can blame me, though?"

Behind me, Hudson grunts before narrowing his eyes at me. "It'll cement my reputation as the best when I show Blakely how to shoot an arrow accurately."

Closing the gap between us, I grin. "Alright, BBs! I'm taking a quick break to set up the camera so you can watch as I become an expert markswoman!"

Next to me, Hudson snorts. Rude.

We're in an open space, tall pines ringing around us. Sunlight peaks through the boughs of the trees, and there's a chill in the air. November is nearly here. While I set up my tripod and the shotgun mic, Hudson grabs two bows and a quiver of arrows.

"Wait, I need to check the framing," I holler, not wanting to miss his first shot.

Taking stock of the targets on the far side of the clearing, I check that everything is in view. Then I do a quick audio test, and it's time to go live.

"Hey, BBs! Welcome back. Hudson is going to give us a quick demonstration. Who's ready?" Hearts float over the screen, and I grin. For all my ups and downs about social media, I can't deny the buzz I get when things are going well. Maybe someday I'll be enough on my own...

Nope. Already decided I'm not traveling down that twisty road today.

"Blakely?" Hudson is watching me, his brow creasing with concern.

"Do your thing, Bear."

At my prodding, Hudson sheds his flannel, leaving him in a tight white tee. He smoothly draws an arrow and holds it to the string. There's a soft *twang* followed by a solid *thunk,* and there in the center of the target is the arrow.

So. Stinking. Sexy.

He does it again; this time, I focus on the ripple of muscles in his back and the tension in his arms. My only exposure to archery is from my crush on Robin Hood—the cartoon fox version—but I'm quickly gaining a new appreciation.

I don't bother checking my phone. People are watching. Hudson Brooks is magnetic. An outdoor master. And seeing him here—all powerful thighs, broad chest, dark hair blowing in the breeze—is like having a religious experience. Consider me a convert.

Whew. Okay. I can totally do this. Shaking out my arms and legs, I grab the spare bow.

"Do you want—"

"I've got this, Bear," I say with a grin, snagging an arrow from the quiver.

I *so* do not have it.

To start, I can't get the arrow on the bowstring. It keeps falling off. It takes three attempts and a stomped foot before I discover the little slit on the bottom of the non-pointy end of the arrow.

With my bow strung, I'm ready to wow him. The first arrow lands approximately two feet away from me. The second ends up behind me. And the third stops inches from Hudson's foot, where he stands next to my phone.

"Careful, Spitfire."

I duck my head and grab another arrow. "I need practice."

"Practice? I think you need learning."

"Isn't that what you're here for?" My temper flares, and I snap sharper than I mean.

Hudson narrows his eyes and crosses his arms. In a terrible impression, he throws my words back at me. "I've got this, Bear."

Glaring right back, I stare for what feels like a lifetime. "Ugh! Fine. I need your help."

For a second, I think he's going to ignore me, but then a slow smile—one that rivals the sun—breaks out on his face. "Let's start from the beginning. Stance, your feet should be shoulder width apart and ninety degrees to the target. Think of a T-shape." As he speaks, he positions my body, his large hands clutching my hips to angle me just so.

"Then use the nock to settle the arrow on the string. It should fit snugly there to keep it from falling out."

"Yeah, I figured that out," I grumble.

Disregarding my attitude, Hudson goes on, "Next is your grip; you want it to be relaxed. You're holding it too tight." He wrenches my hips against his and into my ear, whispers, "I know you have excellent grip control."

I jerk my head at his words, eyes darting toward my phone.

Using his index finger and thumb, Hudson guides my chin toward the targets. Then he once again brushes his mouth to my ear. "Now, let's talk about finger position. Any thoughts on that?" One hand creeps from my hip to my inner thigh, and I shudder against him.

A small whimper escapes me. "Hudson, we're on camera."

"We aren't. I ended it."

"What?"

"This is for us." His fingers inch closer to the growing wetness between my legs.

"Hudson, you can't turn off the live!"

"I couldn't stand here watching you and not touch. You're so fucking gorgeous. These sexy waves blowing in the wind, your cheeks pink, and your eyes alive. Plus, your tight little ass in these leggings." He groans, and his hand skims over my pussy; the heat of his touch seeps through the thin material.

I give an involuntary shudder, and my hips press forward. Seeking. "I need to d-do the live. And I'll n-never learn like this," I whimper, trying to grind against his palm.

He nips my ear and sighs. "You win. I'll behave." With a huff, he stalks to my phone and brings it to me.

What's gotten into him? Is Kirk's reminder about our looming deadline weighing on him, too? Fourteen days has never seemed like so little time.

Fixing my smile and fidgeting in my wet panties, I sign back on. "Sorry, BBs. Technical difficulties! But we're back."

I jog the phone over to the tripod, then hustle to Hudson.

He clears his throat and directs me loud enough for the microphone to hear. "Position your fingers on the string, letting the tip rest in the 'V' of your thumb and index finger. Then place your index, middle, and ring fingers below it." He takes the time to turn me towards the lens so those following the livestream can view the position of my hands.

"Now you're ready to draw. Bring your elbow to the corner of your mouth. Don't clench the arrow. Pull the string using your back muscles, not your arms."

He runs his fingertips over the nape of my neck, and I accidentally let go. This arrow flies further than the others but still falls far short of the target.

"Try again." He helps me restring and reset my placement. "Breathe. Relax."

Those two words conjure up a variety of scenarios in my dirty mind, and I fumble my hold.

"Focus, Blakely." His whiskey-soaked voice curls in my ear.

I get back into position, and this time, when he tells me to take a deep breath and stare down the arrow, focusing on the target, I do.

"Now, release."

It soars through the air, narrowly missing the target.

"Shake it off. You're getting closer."

Hudson corrects my stance and adjusts my grip. He guides my elbow higher and says, "Breathe, focus, release."

The arrow lands on the target with a *thud*. It isn't a bullseye, but it's a hit. I drop the bow, jumping and squealing in excitement.

"BBs! Did you see that? I hit the target!" Sprinting toward

the camera, I pick it up and race across the clearing to get a close-up of my arrow wedged into the target. "I'm going to practice more, so keep your eyes peeled for photos later today."

Once the livestream ends, I launch myself into Hudson's arms. "I did it! I hit the target," I squeal as I pepper kisses over his cheeks and lips.

"You sure did. Proud of you." A playful glint lights up his eyes. "Now, where were we in our lesson?"

During our "hands-on" lesson, I came. Twice. We spent hours shooting, and I even hit the center target—something I bragged about on the entire ride to the cabin.

Now, I'm on the ground between Hudson's legs while his large, calloused hands work out the aches in my arms, shoulders, and back. I used muscles I didn't know I had today, and my body is not happy about it.

As Hudson kneads a tough knot in my upper back, I sip a glass of whiskey, my throat burning as the alcohol slides down, spreading its heat. The fire crackles, filling the cabin with warmth and comfortable background noise. Goddammit. I could get used to this life.

But no matter how many hands-on lessons Hudson gives me, I can't keep pretending time isn't real.

DAY SEVENTEEN

I wake the next morning—after another nightmare-free night —fingers itching to shoot again. Can I tie a good knot yet? No.

Can I tell my north from my east yet? Nope. Can I build a fire using wood scraps and brush? Not even close.

But I can shoot a motherfucking arrow. Okay, that makes me sound like more of a badass than I am, but still, I'm proud of myself. This is one of the only things Hudson has taught me that I haven't messed up. I guess I didn't do anything terrible during our foraging trip except eat that disgusting chokecherry raw. But everything else, even fishing—*especially fishing*—has been a disaster.

"What's on your mind?" Hudson's deep voice startles me.

How am I supposed to go back to sleeping alone? Who's going to care about me? What will I do when I'm sitting in my apartment surrounded by people but more lonely than before? What happens if I stay?

But of course, I don't say any of that. Instead, I snuggle into his arms and bury my nose in the crook of his neck. He smells so good. Like fresh air and pine trees and something spicy. "Can we shoot again?"

"How are your muscles?"

I stretch, rubbing against him like a cat. "Not bad, actually. Your fingers are magic in more ways than one."

"And," he swallows, "how are you feeling about what Kirk said? About having your trip back to Austin planned."

"Like I don't want to talk about it." I lift my head, resting my chin on his stomach. "You?"

He grunts. "Same."

Avoidance, table for two. It's a weird web we've woven for ourselves. I'm drawn to Hudson, to his grumpy personality that protects a gentle heart. To his adorable freckles that soften his rugged beauty. To the safety of his hold and the heat of his touch. But the massive clock counting down above our heads reminds me this can never be more than a fling.

Fling. I wrinkle my nose and mentally toss that word away.

Hudson Brooks is no fling. He's a deep well you fall into and hope you never find your way out of.

Thick fingers wind in my hair. "We have to talk, eventually."

"Eventually," I agree. Then I blow a raspberry above his happy trail and scramble off the bed before he can retaliate by tickling me. "But for now, let's go shoot some targets."

We arrive back in the clearing from yesterday, and Hudson staggers the distance of two of the targets while I stretch.

"Do you remember your steps?"

"Yes, Hudson, it was twenty-four hours ago," I sniff, pouting at him.

"Considering what a disaster your first attempt was…"

Glaring, I spin, grab the bow, and notch the arrow. Then I repeat the mantra he taught me: "Breathe, focus, release."

The arrow flies from my bow and hits the target with a solid thud. I make my best *told you so* face.

"Before you get too proud, can you hit it twice?"

I toss my hair. "Of course I can. Just watch."

Again, I go through all the steps, checking my position and body angle. The arrow flies in a perfect line and distance, hitting the target.

"In your smug, adorable face!" I dance around, arms over my head.

Hudson rolls his eyes. "Yes, you're practically the goddess of the hunt."

"Hmmm… I like that comparison." I wink and stand with my feet wide, hands on my hips. "Will you worship me as befitting a goddess?"

With a snort, he says, "String up your next shot. You're hitting the target, but the goal is the center."

"Mind how you speak to me, mortal."

I'm going through my steps when Hudson jogs by and

smacks me on the ass, the firm clap of his palm making me jolt. My body automatically turns, following his.

And I release the arrow.

It's like slow motion. The arrow leaves the bow, cutting through the short distance between us. I scream as the broadhead nicks Hudson's arm, ripping his flannel shirt and leaving a thin rivulet of blood.

Holy fucking shit. I shot him.

"Hudson! Are you okay?" I drop my bow and rush to him.

He stares at me. Is he in shock? My eyes dart around the clearing. Can I get us home from here? Which way is fucking north? Did he teach me about plants that can staunch wounds? Crap. I can't remember anything.

Then I hear Hudson's loud, rumbly laugh. "Spitfire, you shot me."

"I didn't shoot you! Well, I did, but not on purpose! You spanked me, and I... are you okay?"

"I'm fine. It's just a scrape." He rotates his arm, inspecting the wound, and grins. "'Tis but a flesh wound."

He must not feel too bad if he's making Monty Python references, but still. I. Shot. Him.

As close as he was, it could have been much, much worse. What would I do if something happened to him?

Wrapping my arms around his shoulders, I cringe when he winces. "I'm sorry. So sorry."

"Blakely."

My eyes blur as blood wells on his bicep. I did that to him. I hurt him. And I'm going to be trapped out here because I can't learn the things he's trying to teach me. How can I be so bad at all this?

"Blakely! Stop." Hudson hugs me tight. "Breathe."

I match the rhythm of my chest to his until my heart isn't pounding in my throat.

"Shit, baby. You look worse than me, and I'm the one who was attacked."

"That's not funny! I hurt you."

"No, you didn't. And it was my fault. I shouldn't have spanked you." He frowns. "I'm thirty-five, and I've been doing expeditions professionally for close to fifteen years, but in the last seventeen days, I've made more mistakes than ever."

Does he mean me? Am I the mistake?

His arms tighten. "Mistakes like flirting with you while you have a sharp object in your hand. I swear, I turn into a complete idiot around you."

Resting my head over his heart, I murmur, "Not a *complete* idiot. Just a partial one."

He chuckles, then lifts my chin so our eyes meet. "That's a wrap on shooting for today."

A laugh bubbles from the back of my throat. "Agreed." Slipping from his arms, I gather all our supplies and load them into the back of the Jeep. Then I hold out my hand. "Give me the keys."

"No."

"Hudson, you're in no shape to drive."

He laughs like I've cracked a fantastic joke but stops when he sees my hand is out, waiting.

"Blakely, this isn't any worse than a hangnail."

"You got shot. By me. The least I can do is drive us back."

"If you drive like you shoot, I'll take my chances behind the wheel."

"Stop being so stubborn, and hand over the damn keys!"

My infuriating, gorgeous outdoorsman gives me a panty-melting smirk. "I sure do like your bossy side, you beautiful brat."

Our mouths crash, mine frantic, his dominating. The kiss is

us. Messy, combative, hot, raw. We don't break apart until my lips tingle and my mind is a haze of lust.

It isn't until we're halfway home that I realize I'm in the passenger seat. This man has a powerful hold on me, and I have no idea what I'm going to do when our time together ends.

hudson

I stand under the soothing stream of the shower, letting it ease the ache in my arm. It doesn't do shit for the one in my gut, though. Kirk's call and Blakely's reluctance to talk about it carved out an uncomfortable hollow.

But when we do talk, what can I say? *Blakely, even though you frustrate me beyond belief, I could see myself falling in love with you. It's been less than a month, but why don't you give up your life of luxury and stay here with me in my cabin in the woods? All those things we don't know about each other? No biggie. We'll figure it out.*

Sounds like a great conversation. One sure to go my way.

I lather her delicate, floral shampoo in my hair. It's worth her yelling at me to have her scent on my skin. Despite my prodding, she didn't say much after we returned to the cabin, just showered and ate before curling up in the recliner near the fire. She's upset, but I can't tell if it's with me or for me.

The whole arrow debacle was my fault. I swear, she short-circuits my brain. I'm making rookie mistakes left and right.

Still, I'll spend the rest of my life as the village idiot if it means she'll stay.

Can I see a future with Blakely? Fuck yes, I can. The two of us sitting on the swing, looking out over our land every night for the next fifty years. Making love, fucking, teasing, sparring. Babies. Grandbabies.

My stomach churns. It's a pipe dream. The doomsday clock started ticking the moment I met her, and it won't stop until this thing we're building is left in tatters. Despite knowing that, I don't have it in me to regret a second of my time with her.

She came into my life like a goddamn wrecking ball—a sassy, bratty, beautiful force of nature. How the fuck do I go back to being alone, working day in, day out, living for everyone but myself?

Sighing, I turn off the water, grab the towel I set nearby, and open the shower curtain.

And holy shit. All my worries about what comes on day thirty-one fly from my mind. Because standing before me is my Spitfire, clad in a white lacy bra, stockings, and a matching pair of cheeky panties. My cock rises to half-mast at the sight.

With a saucy smile, she straightens the tiny paper nurse's hat pinned to her hair. "Nurse Blakely reporting for duty."

"Where'd you get that?" I ask, eyeing the red cross she's drawn in Sharpie.

She clears her throat and taps her foot. "I said, Nurse Blakely reporting for duty, Mr. Brooks."

I arch an eyebrow. "Mr. Brooks?"

"Yes, I'm your personal nurse during your stay here at Hidden Pines Hospital. The first thing we have to do is get you in bed."

Blakely grabs my hand and tugs me forward. I follow her, curious how far she's planning on taking her little role-play game. She stops at the head of the bed and bends over, making a show of fluffing my pillows and pulling the covers back. Then, she unwraps the towel from my waist, pats the mattress, and gestures for me to lie down.

I do as she directs. "What next?"

"I have to bandage the wound." She grabs a shiny pink bandaid from the bedside table and carefully places it on my arm. "How's that feel, Mr. Brooks?"

"It feels like a bandaid."

Her eyes narrow into thin slits. "I was planning on checking your muscle control by having you," she pauses and leans forward, using her elbows to push up her beautiful tits, "squeeze a few things. But if you aren't taking your treatment seriously…"

Well, shit. Half-mast just became fully raised.

Stifling my laughter, I eye the bounty of cleavage just out of my reach. "No. I am. I am." If my baby wants to play, then I'm gonna fucking play.

She nuzzles her tits against my lips, and I close my eyes, the silky press of the lace cool against my skin. After a few more teasing brushes, she pulls away.

"Hmm, I think you're ready for stage two of your treatment plan." She kisses my forehead and, with a hip-swaying sashay, makes her way through the cabin to her disaster zone. I watch her dig through one of her suitcases until she finds a small black drawstring bag.

In a flash, she's at the bedside with a bottle of clear liquid and a slim, purple vibrator in hand.

"This is exactly what you need to take your mind off your injury and get you back on your feet, you poor sweet man."

"Yes. I'm horribly injured. Please treat me, Nurse Blakely." I say, voice deadpan.

She twists my nipple before handing me the toy and dripping lube onto it. "Make sure you cover it completely."

"Where's this going, baby?"

"It's Nurse. And you'll see." Blakely's eyes lock on mine as she slowly peels off her white lace panties. Placing one foot on the bed, she takes the bottle, adds a drop to her index and middle fingers, and reaches between her legs before spreading her pink lips. She gives me an impish smile, and her eyes sparkle with mischief. "Go ahead. Slip it in."

I take a moment to appreciate the splendor before me. Her cunt quivers from the weight of my eyes.

"Go on," she whispers. "Have to check your depth perception."

I work the toy in and out of her pussy until it's nestled inside her. She lowers her leg and shifts her hips as if adjusting the vibrator. Fuck, she's so hot.

Her voice is breathy. "Now, I'm giving you the remote. We must ensure you have full function in your fingers, so I'll need you to press those buttons."

This wonderfully wicked woman. I'd let her shoot me with ten more arrows if this is what it leads to.

Eyeing the remote in my hand, I press one button. A faint buzzing fills the air, and Blakely's corresponding gasp and wriggle bring a smile to my lips.

She kisses the bridge of my nose, grabs the bottle, and climbs onto the bed, arranging herself in my lap. I capture her lips with mine and press a random button on the remote, loving it when she twitches. Her soft lips graze over my bearded jaw, my lips, and neck. She kisses and licks her way down my chest.

The lower she gets, the higher I turn up the vibrations on the toy. Her wiggles and moans are my rewards.

She widens my legs, nipping the soft skin, then positions

herself so her pussy is right above my thigh. I give the remote another push.

Blakely whines, her head falling, squirming at the new pattern pulsing inside her. "It seems your cognitive functions are at the appropriate levels."

Sassy little shit.

"Now it's time to test your reaction response rate."

She steals the air from my lungs when she envelopes the length of my cock in her mouth, swirling her tongue around the base, coating it in her spit. Her sultry gaze fastens on mine as she bobs her head up and down. Then she pulls off, undoes her bra, rubs lube over her chest, and my mind explodes.

If I wasn't already in this woman's thrall, I am now. She plumps her full tits together and nestles my cock there. I watch, jaw dropped like I'm trying to catch flies, as my cock disappears into the snug, slippery warmth of her cleavage. Each time the head appears, she darts her tongue out to lap at it.

Blakely Bradshaw is a motherfucking vision. Her ocean eyes hold mine, the little paper hat now askew on her head. I hit another button on the remote, and my smirk turns into a growl when she grinds her hot pussy against my leg.

"You're so goddamn gorgeous with my cock sliding in between those perfect titties."

Two more firm strokes, then she shifts and lowers her mouth to take me deep. The sounds of her mouth working me mixes with the quiet buzzing of the toy, her mewls, and my groans.

"Rub your pussy on me until you come while you choke on my cock."

Like the good girl she sometimes is, she rides my leg until she falls over the edge, sucking me deeper when she gasps as she comes. This is some sort of divine torture.

With a strangled grunt, I say, "Enough, Blakely."

Dropping me with a pop, she looks up. Face flushed, lips puffy. "You can finish in my mouth. Or on my tits. Or anywhere else you want."

"Goddamn, baby. Get up here, so I can taste you."

She climbs up my body before turning her back to me, her hips at eye level.

"Fuck yeah, I can work with this." I reach out and palm her ass, squeezing a cheek.

"Maybe you should test your other reflexes."

I flex my fingers and give her ass a swat. But as I reach between her legs to tug the toy from her pussy, she passes the bottle of lube to me.

"How else might you test your dexterity, Mr. Brooks?"

Her warm tongue twirls around the crown of my cock and laps at the slit. I can't wrap my head around Blakely's words. Is she saying what I think she is?

"To be clear, baby, you want me to—" When she grazes her teeth down my shaft, I lose my words and hiss as I will myself not to fuck her face.

"Test your abilities. Show me you have mastery over your fingers and mouth. But don't take the toy out." She grins at me over her shoulder, and I swear I half-come just from the desire on her face.

To keep from spilling too soon, I focus on her. I jerk her hips, drawing her closer to my face. Then I spread her open and explore, kissing and licking the outer rim of her tight pucker, all but losing my goddamn mind at the feral sounds she makes. I wrap my arms around her lower back, keeping her from wriggling out of reach, and redouble my efforts, wanting to send her crashing into pleasure like a star falling from the sky.

It's a downright intimate and vulnerable thing to trust a

partner with every part of your body, and Blakely is giving it all to me.

"Fuck!" she cries, her head coming up from my lap at the sensation of my tongue teasing and swirling between her cheeks.

"You like that, Spitfire? Like my tongue and mouth on your pretty little asshole?"

"Oh god... it's Nurse," she whimpers before dropping her head and taking my cock into her hot mouth.

Fingers dig into my thighs, and I'll wear those crescent moon marks with pride. I'm doing this to her. I'm wrecking her.

Releasing her from the bear hug I have on her hips, I coat my middle and ring fingers in lube and trace them around her asshole. Blakely's entire body flushes a beautiful shade of pink as I press the pad of my middle finger into her tight hole. "Relax, baby. Breathe."

She giggles around my cock before raising her head. "The last time you told me to relax and breathe, I shot you with an arrow."

My barked laugh echoes in the cabin. Her mouth is going to be my undoing for so many reasons. Refocusing, I slip my finger past the first ring of muscle, my other hand caressing the twin dimples on her lower back. One finger in, I use my thumb to add pressure on her clit, rubbing small circles. Then I press in my ring finger, stretching her slightly as I slowly pump in and out.

We lose ourselves in satisfying the other. Blakely licking and sucking my cock, caressing my balls. Meanwhile, I work her clit; the vibrator rumbles inside her, and my fingers and tongue explore her ass. The only sounds are our collective moans. The only goal, pleasure.

Together, we fall apart. Together, we meld into something new.

Blakely collapses on me—her skin, slick and sticky with sweat, glistens. I shush her when she whimpers as I ease the toy out of her, mindful of her oversensitive pussy.

"I'm gonna take care of you, baby." At my core, I'm a caretaker. My brothers. The business. And now Blakely.

I bundle my precious cargo into my arms and run a bath. When the water's just right, I set her in the tub. While she soaks, I wash my face and hands and brush my teeth. Then I swap out the sheets, making sure everything is ready for us to crawl into bed.

Post bath, Blakely all but floats to the mattress, sleep creeping into her eyes the moment her head touches the pillow. In the dark of the cabin, she lies in my arms, her supple body melting into mine while I play with her hair.

"Hudson?"

"Yeah?"

"I'm sorry I shot you."

"I'm not."

She snort-laughs before burying her face in my side.

God, I'm so fucking gone for this woman.

DAY EIGHTEEN

Blakely's snores fill the otherwise silent cabin. I hug her sleeping form, and she curls into my body, tucking her face against my chest without waking.

The past few days have been taxing. Between the lake incident, as Blakely refers to it, the post blowing up online, and the exertion of shooting, we're both exhausted. We crashed right after our playtime last night, and neither of us stirred.

Every night Blakely goes without a nightmare about

falling into the water—she refuses to say she almost drowned, stubborn little shit—the better I feel about things. I've kept a close eye on her, but she's masking a lot with the heat between us.

Fuck. I am, too.

Ever since our conversation about my family and her questions about what I thought my life would be, I've been wondering. Am I pushing so hard at Peak Adventures because I want it or because of expectations?

I absentmindedly curl my fingers in her hair. I appreciate her perspective, but I don't agree with her. Dad's methods were hard-assed, but for better or worse, they forged me into the man I am today. I wouldn't be the guide, the brother, the man I am without my experiences.

Plus, I love my job. Parts of it, anyway. Bookkeeping and spreadsheets and all that bullshit can fuck off. But doing this, what I've been doing with Blakely, that part fuels me. Teaching her basics, showing her how to forage, watching her hit the target—those things give me purpose.

I can't see doing anything else with my life, but the idea of a Blakely-shaped hole in it makes me wonder if I could be happy in a city like Austin.

My lip curls at the thought. All those people. All that noise. No peace. No stars. No thanks.

And what would I do? My skills are fucking niche. I could lead guided hunts, but it wouldn't be the same as working at Peak Adventures with my brothers.

How long before my bitterness over being trapped in a smoggy, loud urban sprawl with a bunch of city types snips the threads Blakely and I twined together?

No, I belong in Trail Creek, and something deep inside me says Blakely does, too.

But it's time I live beyond being my brothers' keepers or

the steward of my parents' business. And fuck do I wish it could start with keeping this woman here with me.

It's later than I ever stay in bed, but I don't wake Blakely. Instead, I focus on the steady rise and fall of her chest, the way her legs tangle with mine, how her small fists clench the sheets, the tickle of her breath against my skin. I've spent the last six years in an empty bed. When I date, it's never like this. There's no sharing a bed for more than a night. How quickly this has become my new normal.

I groan before returning my attention to her, smelling her hair and running my palm over the small of her back in tender strokes. She stirs in my arms, and my fingers travel lower, grazing against the swell of her ass, before drifting to rest on her hip. Her skin is so smooth, so touchable. I love the contrast of it to the rough calluses of my hands.

"Morning," she yawns, stretching her limbs. I follow her movements, appreciating the arch of her spine and the sigh she makes as her muscles pull taut. She holds the stretch longer than needed, lifting her chest higher into the air and letting out a soft moan. Unable to resist the sight before me, I pounce, securing her body beneath mine.

"Mornin'." I pepper kisses over her collarbone. "Sleep alright?"

"I did. What time is it?"

"Eight forty-five."

"Did I ruin your plans for the day? I must've been sleepier than I thought," she asks, combing her fingers through my bed head.

"Nope."

Blakely pushes at my chest, so I roll over, giving her breathing room. But not too much. I can't physically bear not to touch her. I casually drag one hand over her exposed stomach before settling it on her ribcage. The lazy circles I draw on her skin raise goosebumps, and she squirms closer.

"So—" There's a halting croak in her voice as she speaks. "You said Trail Creek is small?"

"Yep."

"Are the people nice?" she asks, nibbling her lip.

I prop myself up on an elbow, trying to puzzle out what's going on in her head. There's a soft blush on her cheeks and visible tension in her brow.

"Yeah, I mean, there are assholes like anywhere—Jacob Ashford springs to mind; that guy's a massive tool—but for the most part, it's a friendly town. Why?"

Her noncommittal hum and shrug won't work.

"Blakely, what's going on?" My eyes narrow. There's more to her question than she's letting on.

With a sigh, she says, "I grew up in a town the same size as Trail Creek. And honestly? It was awful. People gossiped and knew all my business, but when I needed them…"

"Hey, finish that thought." I brush my lips against her temple.

She stiffens like she's preparing for a blow. What the fuck is she about to tell me?

"I've never told anyone the whole story. Not even Kirk. He knows the gist, but that's all."

I save her lip from being gnawed by her teeth. "Go on, baby."

"People knew I didn't have enough food or clean clothes. They knew my mom disappeared for days at a time, leaving me on my own. Knew the men she brought around were scumbags. And no one did anything. Except judge me."

Anger bubbles in my gut. What is wrong with people? She admitted she grew up poor and didn't have a relationship with her parents, but shit. This is straight-up neglect.

Tears well in her eyes, turning them the color of the ocean after a storm. "I told you I left home at seventeen because of a fallout with my mom?"

"Yeah."

"It was April of my senior year. I was getting ready for school one morning. Mom was on day three of a bender, but her current live-in, Wayne, was home."

My instincts drive me, and suddenly, Blakely is in my lap, her head pressed to my chest. If it's something universe-shattering, I need my hands on her. Need to keep her safe.

"He tried to kiss me. Thankfully, it wasn't more than that."

I exhale.

"But it was enough. I kneed him in the balls, ran out of the trailer straight to school, and told the counselor what happened."

A surge of pride prickles in my chest. "Good for you."

She presses her nose to my neck and breathes me in. If it comforts her, she can stay this way forever.

With a humorless laugh, she says, "Instead of helping me or calling the cops or anything, she said it was my fault for walking around in such distracting clothes. You know, Bible Belt, sins of the flesh bullshit."

"What the fuck?"

"By the time I got home from school, the rumor mill was already abuzz and everything I owned was in my car. I tried to talk to my mom, but the trailer door was locked. I sat on the rotted, sagging porch steps—the same ones I'd spent so many nights on, wishing on stars—listening to my mom yell at me through the thin walls. Wayne told her I attacked him, and when I tried to explain what happened, she accused me of being jealous and trying to steal him from her."

The urge to smash something rides me hard. The wood pile will be replenished by the end of the day. That much is sure.

"I tried to find somewhere to stay, but it wasn't like I had many friends. Thanks to the counselor, Wayne, and my mom, it was already all over town that I'd tried to kiss my mom's boyfriend, gotten mad when he turned me down, and hurt him in retaliation. I left that night. Drove for hours, anything to get out of west Texas and away from Hawthorne."

"You were seventeen. No one came looking for you?"

She shakes her head. "I didn't have a cell phone or a bank account. My whole existence could fit in the backseat of a used Chevy Metro."

"Where'd you go?"

"Austin." A grin tugs at her lips. "Everyone in Hawthorne used to talk about Austin like it was this den of depravity, so I hightailed it there. The bright lights and endless city sounds were so different. I loved it. I mean, I hated it too, but at that point, it seemed about as far away from Hawthorne as I could get."

I shelter her in the warmth of my larger body. "What happened when you got there?"

"I got lucky. I'd been sleeping in my car. Shit, Hudson, you're crushing me."

It doesn't register that I'm squeezing her. But the thought of teenage Blakely alone in Austin, sleeping in her fucking car? A growl thunders in my throat.

Her lips brush against mine, and I let her soothe me because I'm a selfish bastard. It should be me comforting her. She's so much stronger than I ever gave her credit for. She should've punched me in the mouth the first time I called her a princess.

"You done squishing me, Bear?" At my sheepish nod, her dainty fingers smooth the wrinkles from my brow. "An older couple who owned a small brunch place gave me a job waiting tables and washing dishes. The unspoken agreement was I could sleep in the backroom. Before it was a restaurant, it was a home, and they left the shower untouched during the remodel, so like I said, lucky."

I swallow. She's being so open. With her body last night and with her heart and memories now.

"Sylvie and Buster, the couple who owned The SweetStack, helped me get an apartment once I'd saved up some money. Eventually, I had enough to take some adult learning classes. Turns out I have a knack for graphic and web design. I ended up staying on at The SweetStack until I'd build up a steady client base."

She sighs. "I way overshared, didn't I?"

"Nope. I love hearing all about you." Frowning, I say, "I'm so sorry, baby."

"I have some... hangups with small towns."

Under-fucking-standably. "I can't speak for everyone, but most folks in Trail Creek are decent. They'd never stand by and let something like that happen. And even if they did, I sure as shit wouldn't."

Blakely's petal-soft lips skim against the pulse point in my neck, but she doesn't say anything.

"How about we go into town tomorrow? Let you check it out for yourself." This might backfire, but we have twelve days, and I plan to enjoy every minute. The guaranteed time promised to me. If taking her to Trail Creek—a factor I didn't know I was contending with—increases her chances of staying longer, who am I to complain?

"I'm not sure. I'm supposed to stay out here in the wilderness." She weakly gestures around us.

"Kirk's on vacation. And besides, you're a grown-ass woman. You've shown me more than once you do what you want."

This earns me a smile. A small one that barely curves her

lips, but it still has me staring at her like a moonstruck moron. Her lips meet mine in a fleeting kiss. I grunt, partly at the sneak attack and partly at how quickly she ends it.

"And today?" she asks.

Grinning, I say, "Today feels like a hot spring day."

"No knots or navigating?"

"Nope, just relaxing." I scrape my teeth over the sensitive flesh beneath her ear, then gently suck. She moans and tilts her head, giving me the access I crave. "No phones. No worries."

Blakely softens at my touch. "You forgot one thing," she whispers against my lips. "No swimsuits."

blakely

DAY NINETEEN

I sit in Hudson's Jeep, repeatedly laying on the horn. "Hudson, hurry up! I'm ready to go!"

Curled in Hudson's arms this morning, I considered asking him to cancel the day trip into Trail Creek, but he woke up with a smile. Okay, not a smile, but not a full frown, which is practically beaming for him. No way was I ruining his good mood, even if my mischievous side likes him grumpy.

While I wait, only honking the horn every thirty seconds instead of every ten—I'm not a total brat—I pull up my socials and scroll through.

Though Hudson deemed yesterday a phone-free outing, I talked him into taking a picture of me from behind. In it, the tops of my shoulders and my profile are visible, along with the lip of the hot spring and the stunning view it overlooks. It's a beautiful picture.

You always did put on airs.

The comment stops me in my tracks. Not because it's particularly cruel, but because of who it's from—my mother.

I'm not surprised she's crawling out of the woodwork, given the way the fishing post—and each subsequent one—exploded. I bite down so hard my teeth clack together. Wonder how much she'll ask for. It's happened a handful of times since I first gained popularity. If I don't want the world to know about Blake Lee's pitiful existence, all I have to do is pay her off. Mother of the year, right there.

An echo of Brandee Shaw's gaunt face sneers at me, accusing me of being uppity and too good for Hawthorne and her. A dry laugh huffs from my lips. As if wanting clean clothes, hair, and water, or a bug and asshole-free place to sleep is the same as *putting on airs*.

I shouldn't give her my energy. It's something I work on in therapy: not giving the woman who gave birth to me power, not letting her color my present or future. Keeping up the mental and emotional boundaries I've set for myself.

But I'm very much a work in progress.

Multiple message notifications taunt me. My thumb hovers over the little red number. Do I open them knowing there's at least one from her?

Days like this—when the fear of people finding out about my pitiful past, when the stress of maintaining the curated persona and lifestyle and expectations, when the people who should love you turn against you—seem like the perfect time to quit and disappear from the public eye altogether.

My nerves were frayed *before* finding the comment from my mother, thanks to oversharing yesterday and despite hours soaking in the hot spring and making out. Now they're in tatters.

So, I do what I do best. Closing out all my socials and

locking my phone, I paste on a fake grin and hold the horn down until Hudson's grouchy face appears.

"About time," I holler as I lean out the Jeep door.

"What's wrong?"

"What do you mean?" I do my best to keep my expression neutral and my voice nonchalant.

Hudson rests both arms on the Jeep's door frame and stares at me. Deep green eyes bore into my heart, seeing so much more than anyone else.

My gaze drops, but his thumb tilts my chin, refusing to let me look away. "What's with the smile? Tell me."

My mom is back from the trenches of hell, and it only spells drama and trouble. I'm scared shitless to go into town with you and hate it, or worse, love it. "Can we talk about it later?"

I expect him to push me. Demand to know what's got me wearing the facade he's worked to chip away. Instead, he sighs, knocks twice on the roll bar and walks around to the driver's side.

"What took you so long?" I ask, grabbing the chance to change the subject like it's my morning cup of coffee.

"Calm your horses. This is the first time in nineteen days you've been ready first." He skims his fingers along my jaw. "Sure hope you aren't trying to get away from me."

Goosebumps pebble over my skin. *No, I'm looking for reasons to stay.* "I'm just excited to go into town and eat at a restaurant for the first time in three weeks."

"You're insulting my cooking? After that disaster of a meal you made? Maybe you should fend for yourself for a few days and see how you do."

"You wouldn't dare!" Already, our bickering has my spirits up. I bat my lashes. "Plus, seeing a new face wouldn't be the worst thing."

"And now you're complaining about my face?" He gives me

a smile, not a smirk or a lip tilt, but full teeth. Like a wild animal pouncing on prey, I lunge forward. He's so damn sexy. Always. But *especially* when he smiles.

Our mouths connect, my tongue begging for entrance between his lips. The taste of him rushes over me. Mint, a hint of spice, and pure Hudson. I mean for it to be a quick kiss, but I crawl into his lap, all other thoughts, fears, and anxieties melting away.

He's electric. Energy and emotions well in me, fed by his live-wire touch, until Hudson breaks the kiss. The quiet panting of our mingled breaths is the only sound. Hudson presses his forehead to mine. "If we start that, we won't make it into town in time for lunch." A beat passes, as if he's as reluctant as me to separate, then he shifts me to the passenger seat, stretching across me to click my lap belt.

Now that we aren't touching his words register. "We have reservations somewhere?" Hudson shrugs but doesn't answer. Glaring at the side of his head, I ask, "What do you have in store for us, Bear?"

He flicks the end of my nose and throws the Jeep into gear. "You'll see."

I mentally tally the options. Is this a date? Am I meeting someone important to him? Oh god, his parents?

"Is it your parents? Because if it is, I have to change," I jabber as I tug at my fitted long-sleeve tee and jeans.

"I wouldn't spring them on you."

Relief has my shoulders lowering. I'd love to meet the people who molded Hudson into the man he is today, but it's too soon. And I'm absolutely not dressed for a parental first impression.

Crooking a knee under me, I take in the sights I missed on my initial trip out here, soaking in the passing scenery. The pebbled, rutted path—I refuse to call it a road—is steep and narrow, and in some places, the ground seems to drop away, leaving only the tops of trees poking up next to us. I'm kind of glad I couldn't see it that first night. And now I better understand why Hudson rarely takes his eyes off the road.

I record a short video—no narration, no music—just the beautiful and slightly terrifying view. It never hurts to have extra B-roll, and this makes an amazing one.

As we make our way down the mountain, something small darts out from the rocks hidden in the treeline, and I scream and cover my eyes. "Stop!"

The Jeep jerks, the tires losing traction in the rusty dirt, making me scream louder.

"What?" Hudson barks.

"Did we kill it?"

"What?" Hudson repeats as he eases the car close to the side.

"The little furry thing that ran out, did we squish it?"

Large, warm hands settle over mine, pulling them away from my eyes. With a grimace, I meet Hudson's amused smirk. "No, we didn't kill it."

"How do you know?"

"For one, there was no bump. Two, there's nothing dead behind us, and three, he ran into the trees before you scared the crap out of me."

"You saw it?"

Hudson's chuckle lessens the tension in my chest and shoulders. "Yeah, baby, I saw it. Long tail weasel. They're quick little shits."

My head flops against the headrest and I exhale.

The steady purr of the Jeep's engine starts up. "You good?"

"Yeah, sorry." Heat rushes to my cheeks. I may have overreacted a little. Opening up to him about Hawthorne yesterday left me raw and exposed. My freaking mother is back on my chessboard. We're headed into his tiny hometown full of small-town people, and I screamed at him.

There's an awkward silence, Hudson staring straight ahead, me staring at him. Then a familiar weight rests on my thigh.

"Trail Creek has a great bookstore. You read?"

Bless this remarkable man. Hudson Brooks is making small talk because I need it. Nineteen days, and he knows me better than anyone in my life ever has.

After a solid hour in the adorable purple bookstore, Up a Creek Without a Book—seriously, this whole town is an influencer's dream—Hudson drives us to a tiny restaurant.

He frowns at the overflowing parking lot. "Ava's is the best." But he makes no move to get out.

"The best is a good thing, right?"

He nods but still doesn't move.

"So are we going in or..."

A heavy puff of air from his nose is my answer. I press my lips together to hide my grin. I adore his grumpy ass.

"Come on, Bear. You promised me the full Trail Creek experience."

We step into the crowded entry, and I immediately regret coming to town. Two things I did not think through: one, Hudson is a local, so everyone knows him. Two, because he's a local, everyone in town is following me to keep up with him.

The buzzy din drops to a dull roar and the weight of eyes burn doubts into my chest. *Danger! Danger!* I step back and into the firm wall that is Hudson. The sensation of his lips brushing over my ear drives the rising panic away.

"Give it a sec. They'll go back to their business. They've never seen a celebrity before."

I can't help my snort. "I'm hardly a celebrity."

He shrugs. "Close enough around here."

A tiny woman with silver hair cuts through the busy tables. She stops now and then to scold someone, telling them to *mind their own selves.* When she gets to us, she wraps Hudson in a crushing hug, and despite his stiff demeanor, he seems genuinely happy to see her.

"Ava, you got a table for two?"

"You Brooks boys always have a table here." She turns her lovely, laugh-lined face to me. "And for your beautiful lady friend." She pats my arm and guides me through the restaurant.

Doing my best to avoid meeting anyone's gaze, I examine the colorful murals on the walls, the gorgeous southwestern shades, and the tempting scents coming from all sides. Ava seats us in a large booth, and I sneak into the side facing away from the other patrons.

Hudson is right, of course. By the time Ava walked us through the restaurant, no one was paying us any mind, but I'd still rather not wake up to pictures of me stuffing my face.

"So." I clear my throat.

"So." He raises one eyebrow at me.

"The bookstore was amazing. Saul's a trip, though."

"He thinks he's the fucking pope of Trail Creek or something, but he's harmless."

I smile and fiddle with my menu. The older man questioned me about my motives for coming to Trail Creek and if I planned to give the town a positive review. I tried to explain I'm not a travel blogger, but he didn't seem interested in anything other than telling me about how unique Trail Creek is.

"Yeah, he seemed more concerned—"

"We have company." Hudson's words cut mine off, and panic must be visible on my face because he adds, "It's not my parents, and I swear I didn't plan this."

"Nice to see you again, Blakely!" Next to our booth stand two slightly younger versions of Hudson. Bo and Gray.

"How the hell did you two clowns find us? We just sat down." He frowns at his brothers.

Gray crosses his arms. "Mistake number one—"

Hudson groans. "Saul."

"Yep. The gossip train started when our knock-off Taylor Doose spotted you." The youngest Brooks brother winks at me.

There's a low grumble coming from Hudson's side of the booth, but I'm too stuck on Bo's words about the gossip train to worry about anything else.

My therapist and I talk a lot about why I'm okay with being a minor entity online but hate the way small towns function. Together, we've worked through so many of my feelings about it, and I've concluded it's because I can control the narrative of what I put out there when I'm online. And that comments, while hurtful, don't affect my day-to-day life unless I give them power. She says the same is true about real-life gossip, but I like to remind her that real-life gossip did, in fact, impact my day-to-day life. I'm a gem like that.

Bo grins. "Aren't you gonna invite us to join you?"

I fix my face and smile at Hudson. "Yeah, aren't you going to invite your brothers to join us?"

Of course, my perceptive Bear sees through my mask, his eyes searching me over.

"Not yet. Why don't you two go get us some sangria?"

Bo looks like he's ready to argue, but Gray nods and pulls him away.

Hudson's hands settle over mine, his thumbs tracing random patterns over my knuckles. "Talk to me."

"This is exactly like Hawthorne." He doesn't say anything, so I press on. "The way everyone stared when we walked in, that it took two stops for people to call your family. I can't," I swallow, my eyes darting around the restaurant.

The pressure on my hands increases. "What do you think people are saying?"

"I'm not good enough for you. I'm city trash. This is all pretend, a publicity stunt inside a publicity stunt. I'm a highfalutin hustler."

"Highfalutin?" The creases in his brow deepen.

Despite myself, I smile. "Yeah. Highfalutin. As a former Texas boy, I know you've heard it before."

"Sure, but no one but my Memaw and her quilting circle still use that word." Then he gets serious. "Blakely, I'm sorry you're uncomfortable right now. This is what you worried would happen, but my gut says none of those things you're thinking are what's being said."

My counterpoint is on the tip of my tongue when Bo and Gray return.

"What did Saul say to you two?"

Both of Hudson's brothers smile, and Gray answers. "He said it was nice to see our grouch of a brother happy for once, and if Blakely's the one who turned your attitude around, she deserves a seat on the town council. And if we want to see it for ourselves, we better hot-foot it to Ava's. Why?"

A weight falls from my shoulders. It's only one person, but hearing something nice about myself from the town gossip... It's an unfamiliar experience. And like he somehow keeps doing, Hudson reads me, a hint of a smile curling at the corner of his mouth.

"I'm not covering the bill." He waves Ava over and politely requests additional menus.

"Blakely, get the stuffed sopapilla. It'll change your life," Bo says as he attempts to squeeze in next to me.

"What do you think you're doing?" Hudson asks.

Bo looks to his left and right. "Sitting."

"Not next to her, you aren't."

Gray and I watch as the other two bicker until Hudson all but hauls Bo out of the booth and slides in. His arm wraps around my shoulders and he presses a quick kiss to my temple.

"Now that that's settled," Gray snarks, "how about we give Blakely a menu rundown?"

"You said a stuffed sopapilla? Stuffed with what? When I think sopapilla, I think dessert," I say to Bo.

"Ah, that's your closed-minded Texan way of thinking. You need to broaden your culinary horizons."

Hudson snorts. "You order the same thing every time."

"Why mess with perfection?"

A short time later, a massive plate of food sits in front of me. The football sized sopapilla—somehow fluffy and golden despite being smothered in red and green chile sauce—is calling my name. Bo gives me a grin that I'm sure makes him a favorite of the Trail Creek dating pool and watches until I take a bite. A soft moan slips from my lips as the flavors of slow rolling heat, gooey cheese, and spiced meat explode on my tongue.

The coffee, the food, the books. How have they kept this town a secret?

Hudson's hand settles on my thigh, and he whispers, "Those noises are for my ears only, Blakely. Don't make me murder my brothers at Ava's."

I giggle as he shoots daggers at his brothers.

Gray tilts his head. "Still can't believe you convinced this asshole to show his ugly mug online. We've been trying to get him in our videos and posts for a couple of years."

"I bet I know how she did it." Bo winks at me, then yelps. "Fuck, Hudson! That hurt."

The easy back and forth between the brothers has me feeling more and more comfortable. To the point I forget I'm in a small town. Forget I don't belong here.

For a moment, I indulge in the fantasy of what if. What if this could be my future? No more lonely city. No more fake friends and selling a curated version of myself online. Instead, laughter and love surround me. Years pass by, children play at our feet, the cabin grows, making room for a son, a daughter. Sixty falls, sixty springs, a lifetime in our little cabin in the woods.

"Food okay?"

Hudson's voice drags me to the here and now, and I shake my head to disperse the lingering fog of memories that can never be. "Yeah, yeah, good. I, um, need to use the restroom. Please excuse me."

Hudson stands, and I bolt from the booth toward the opposite corner. Stumbling into an empty stall, I sink onto the seat. I have to stop imagining a life with Hudson.

In a desperate act of self-sabotage, I open my socials and go straight to the messages.

And there, as expected, are several from my mother.

Shaw_Babe: Since you're doing so good the least you can do is help your poor mother. Haven't had electricity in the trailer for two weeks.

I scoff. She found access somehow. Three more messages wait, each time-stamped about thirty minutes apart.

Shaw_Babe: Don't ignore me, Blake Lee. I'm your mother. You owe me. I raised you till you were grown, feeding you, clothing you.

Shaw_Babe: Once again you're out here showboating and making the world think you're better than me. You always did. But remember, Blake Lee, you came from nothing and you're still nothing. No amount of expensive clothes will change it. You might've hidden that part of yourself from your city friends and this new man you've snookered, but your mamma knows. Blood always outs.

Shaw_Babe: I need $5000. Send it, or I start posting.

And there it is.

A soft knock on the door has me fumbling my phone and shoving it into my pocket.

"Blakely? You alright?"

I swing the door open and crash into Hudson, needing his arms around me. His grounding scent and warmth. The security he provides.

"Sorry. Needed a minute."

Together, we walk to the booth and slip back in. Bo and Gray have the decency not to ask where I disappeared to or why I was gone so long.

"So, Blakely, what's next for you when you leave here?" Bo has no idea how loaded his question is.

I weigh my words. "Maybe it's being out here," a flutter courses through me when Hudson's grip on my thigh tightens and rises, "but I'm starting to think when this is over, I may take a sabbatical from social media." Hudson's teasing touches falter, and his eyes burn into the side of my head.

"No way. You've gotta be making damn good money. Ouch, fucking hell, Hudson, stop kicking me!"

The first giggle slips out. Maybe it's the offended look on Bo's face, the glower on Hudson's, the bullshit with my mom, the stress of coming into town, the weight of being down to eleven days, but I crack. Laughs, loud, obnoxious, and unrelenting, shake my body until tears stain my cheeks and my sides ache.

All three Brooks men stare at me, matching open-mouthed expressions on their handsome faces. You'd think I grew a second head, but it just makes me cackle harder. The sounds bubble around me, too loud to not be drawing attention, but I can't stop. Before long, Bo and Gray join, and eventually, the infectious giddiness is even too much for Hudson. He laughs out loud. Twice.

Finally, I calm myself enough to steer the conversation away from me and onto the brothers. I want to find out more about them, to know them.

As lunch goes on, I drink in their easy dynamic. They obviously care for one another, enjoy one another, love one another. Even Hudson has a half grin when he thinks no one is paying attention.

Gray shares stories about camping trips gone wrong, including one from when they were young and Hudson forgot to stake the tent. When they got to the campsite, it was upside down and thirty yards away. I learn that Bo accidentally packed butter spray instead of bug spray one trip, and they didn't figure it out until they'd doused themselves in it. And that on one of the few trips their mother joined them on, her hammock ripped, and she landed flat on her back but never dropped her smore.

I listen to it all, absorbing as much as I can. I love hearing about Hudson. I love hearing about his life and his business. I love that these are *his* people, and he's sharing them with me. I lov... really like him.

Hours later, we climb into the Jeep to head home. The cabin. *A place that is more home than anywhere else I've ever lived.*

As I ponder that intrusive little thought, I study Hudson's handsome profile.

"Why are you staring at me?"

Busted. "Can't a girl stare at her boyfriend for no reason?" I freeze at the *bf* word, but when the edges of his lips turn up, a rush of happiness floods my body.

"Did you mean what you said at lunch today? Are you thinking about giving up social media and the influencer life when this is over?"

Do I mean it? "I meant it when I said it."

"But?"

"But..." The headlights flicker over the trees, casting eerie shadows around us. "It's easy to say when things are going wrong."

He glances over at me before focusing back on the road. "Is this about what happened earlier today and at lunch?"

"Yeah." I reach out, holding his hand, and press his palm to my lips. "A year from now, if I ask myself why I quit—if was because it was hard or I was having a bad day, or for... some other reason—I need to be able to answer honestly. And I don't want the answer to be because it was a bad day. If I walk away from my job, Austin, all of it, I need it to be for something better. Something real. Something lasting."

In the dim cabin of the Jeep, an unreadable emotion flashes across his face, but it's gone as quickly as it appeared. Maybe I imagined it.

But it looked a lot like love.

CHAPTER TWENTY-ONE

DAY TWENTY

Blakely stares into space, occasionally mumbling to herself, while I move around the kitchen. She's been off since telling me more about Hawthorne, and despite enjoying her time in Trail Creek, she's keeping something from me. Something heavy.

Last night she shoved her phone under her pillow and curled around me like I could keep whatever shit's chasing her at bay. I did my best to live up to that expectation, and will every day she grants me the chance.

Dropping breakfast in front of her, I say, "Talking to yourself?"

Her eyes widen, and she jumps when the plate hits the wooden table. "Was I?"

"Yep. In your sleep, too. Last night, it was a lot of my name. Which made it hard as hell to get any rest." I lean and kiss her neck. "Even asleep, you're a nuisance."

"You love me. Admit it." As soon as the L-word leaves her lips, she freezes.

She has no idea how close those words are to being the truth.

"I mean it, you love *it*. Me saying your name."

I softly bite where her neck and shoulder meet. "No need for verbal acrobatics."

Blakely lays her head on her arms and groans. "Hudson, what are we going to do?"

As much as I want to push her right now, I've learned enough about Blakely Bradshaw in our twenty days together to know she's stubborn as shit. So, I give her an out. "Practice your survival skills."

The little annoyed huff she makes is so fucking cute. "That's not what I mean, asshole, and you know it."

I lift her chin from where she tries to hide it and kiss her. "I do."

But there is one thing we need to address. Clearing my throat, I say, "I thought about what you said last night. About needing something lasting. Something real." *Fuck, here goes.* "This thing between us, Spitfire, it's fucking real."

Her mouth opens, but I plow ahead, cutting her off.

"But I agree. You shouldn't make choices based on a single bad day or even a handful of good ones." I swallow. "And neither should I."

Her lashes flutter as if fighting off tears. "So what? We just wait and see what happens?"

"For now." Do I wish I could tell her to throw everything she's built away and stay here? Yes. Do I wish she'd come to that conclusion on her own? Fuck yes. Is it way too soon to be thinking of a lifetime with her? Triple goddamn yes.

I hoist her from the chair, loving how her legs automatically wrap around my waist.

"I can live with that. For now." A crooked smile brightens her face, and I can't help but kiss her.

The buzzing of her phone breaks the moment, and I pull away with a groan. The way I wish that fucking phone had landed in the lake...

Blakely squirms in my grip, stretching toward the table. "It's Ki—"

"Kirk, yeah, I know." I'm about ready to chuck *Kirk* into the lake, too. I plop Blakely back into her seat and stomp to the sink.

In her time here, she's taken every video call out in the open, not caring if I hear the conversation. But today, when she answers, she says, "Hey, Kirk. Give me a sec."

My shoulders stiffen, and I crane my neck to catch a glimpse of her.

Without meeting my eyes, she steps away from the table. "I'm taking this on the porch."

I nod and watch her retreat; irritation partners with concern to two-step in my stomach. Washing the few dishes we dirtied takes all of ten seconds, and while I don't mean to stand where I can hear her half of the conversation, it's a small fucking cabin.

Kirk's voice is muffled, but Blakely's so damn loud I have no trouble making out her words. "Why are you calling me? Aren't you on vacation?"

There's a brief pause, and despite knowing better, I step closer.

"I'm fine, Kirk... trying not to worry about her. Instead, I'm focusing on enjoying my time with Hudson."

Hearing her say that she wants to focus on our remaining days together eases some of the curdled milk feeling in my gut.

"Of course," she snaps, and shit, I want to know what he asked her.

"Give me a break. You didn't call to fuss at me about only posting stills. I'll do a livestream soon enough. Is this about checking on me or because you're worried about your bottom line?"

Fuck. Kirk is one of her people. If she's lashing out at him, this is serious. And now that I think of it, she hasn't done a video since our bow and arrow lesson. Even yesterday, outside of some staged photos while we were in town, she didn't have her phone out.

I'm dropping the ball with her. Something big is going on with my girl.

Her voice rings louder, indignation sharpening her words. "You know what's not fair? My mother threatening to drag me through the mud, talking about my childhood, and leaving nonstop messages to get money out of me!"

That's it. I can't sit in here with my thumb up my ass while she's hurting. I plow through the cabin door and slide onto the porch swing next to Blakely like she's motherfucking home plate.

Now that I'm out here with her, I can hear Kirk when he asks, "Do you plan on talking to her?"

Tears trail down her rosy cheeks, but anger sparks in her eyes. "No. You know how I feel about it. I can't believe you expect me to reach out to her."

I scoop her into my lap, hoping the gentle sway and closeness will be a calming balm. Her eyelids flutter, and she buries her nose in the crook between my neck and shoulder. Warm, wet droplets land on my collarbone.

Kirk's face twists in discomfort and sympathy. "You don't have to talk to her. And I'll back you however you decide to handle this."

"Good. Because it's not happening." Her voice is firm,

leaving no room for discussion. With a quiet *goodbye,* she drops the phone.

"What was that about?"

"My mom."

Those two words are the only answer she gives me. Questions buzz in my brain. There's so fucking much we need to talk about. Her mom. The way she assumed the worst about Trail Creek yesterday. What's going on between us. What happens when the countdown clock reaches zero. But my tongue is lead.

This relationship is a roller coaster on broken tracks. But I'll be damned if I don't try to weld the gaps and keep us on this ride for as long as I can.

"I'm taking you on a date."

She lifts her head, eyes glassy with unshed tears, but the beginning of a smile plays on her lips. "A date?"

"Yep."

"Why?"

"Figure it's about time."

That beautiful smile grows. "You've taken me on lots of dates."

I blink twice. "I have?"

"Sure." She pinches my side, and that little action untangles the knot in my chest. "Not traditional ones necessarily, but we've been on sunrise hikes, shopping in Trail Creek, had a picnic at a hot spring." She pauses and wrinkles her nose. "I'm not counting the fishing trip."

I wince, thinking about that disaster, but it also gives me an idea. "Tell you what. You enjoy the day. Relax, read one of your new books, take a long bath. Just be ready to go at six."

She raises an eyebrow at me.

Pressing a quick kiss to her forehead, I move her out of my

lap. "You'll want your boots and waterproof jacket, but other than that, wear what you like."

"What do you have up your sleeve, Bear?"

"You'll find out at six." With that, I leave her pouting on the porch swing. I've got a date to plan and a woman to woo.

"Blakely, you ready?"

She's sitting amongst the exploded debris of her suitcases. Her side of the cabin is always messy, but this is akin to a disaster zone. Shirts, pants, and dresses are scattered and spread from the bed to the wall and everywhere in between.

She jerks when I say her name and shakes the dazed look from her face. "Shit, is it already six?"

"Yep."

A string of curses falls from her mouth, and she throws a pale pink top to the already heaping pile on the floor. "I lost track of time. Sorry. I've been trying to figure out what to wear for hours. It's stupid. I tried on everything I brought. Then, I thought checking my socials would be a good idea, but that was a mistake. Internet trolls always suck, but it's worse when it's your fa..." She cuts off mid-ramble.

My eyes trace over her features, and what I see has my jaw tightening. Her hair is disheveled, and she's wearing cut-off shorts and one of my flannels. And while that combo ranks pretty fucking high on my fantasy list, it's clear it's not intentional. But worst of all? Her eyes are red and puffy, and the tip of her nose is red. "Have you been crying?"

"A little." She waves her hand in the air in a dismissive

motion. "Hormones. Or maybe a high pollen count." When I don't break my stare, she shrugs. "Really, I'm fine now."

She's lying. And even if she isn't, it doesn't diminish my concern. Anything that makes my Spitfire cry is on my shit list.

"Blakely."

"Can we talk tomorrow?"

She used that line with me yesterday, too.

"I want to enjoy tonight with you. Give me five minutes, and I'll be ready. I can't wait to see what you planned."

I can tell the moment she processes the sight of me. My ego gets a firm stroke when her cheeks pinken and her breath hitches.

"Wow." The single word comes out as an awed whisper. "Handsome. How did I miss you coming in?"

My lips quirk into a half smile. She missed me earlier this afternoon, but I keep that secret for now. "I used a camp shower and got dressed on the porch." The tips of my ears burn, and I cough. "Wanted to surprise you."

"You nailed it."

I'm far more dressed up than she's ever seen. My go to are jeans, a flannel, and hiking boots during the day, and joggers or sweatpants in the evening. But tonight, I pulled out all the stops. Or as many stops as I can stand. Bo ran a white button up and the only suit jacket I own out to me. He gave me shit for the first hour he was here, and the group chat with him and Gray has been going off since he left. Fuckers.

But I'll take their harassment for her.

She rises from the floor, drops a kiss on my lips, and smooths a hand over my furrowed brow. "I promise to tell you. Tomorrow."

Blakely takes her time changing clothes. It doesn't bother me that she wasn't ready. Doesn't even surprise me. What *is* bothering me is that she's holding back. But hell, I can't blame her. We haven't put a label on whatever this thing is between us. The clock keeps ticking on her departure. I consider myself lucky she's opened up as much as she has.

With a groan, I run my hands down my face. I'm not buying the bullshit logic I'm selling myself. The truth is, I don't care about anything except wiping those tears away, showing her she's safe, and making her happy. Keeping her.

I'm waiting by the door when I spot her phone. It's a good ten feet away from where she was when I came in, like it got tossed across the cabin. I consider kicking it even further. Maybe it *accidentally* lands in the fireplace. That fucking thing is nothing but trouble.

A pair of slender arms wrap around me, and Blakely kisses the center of my back and runs her fingers along my shoulders. "Alright, Bear. Show me what you've got."

I spin and press my face into her hair, inhaling her sweet floral shampoo. "Can't seem to deny you anything, Spitfire."

In a wordless answer, Blakely crushes her mouth to mine, her tongue slipping between my lips, her hands twisting in the material of my shirt. Her smaller frame molds against me, a perfect fit.

There's nothing like the feel of her.

When she moans around my mouth, I break the kiss, then rest my forehead on hers, waiting for our hearts to slow. "If you kiss me like that again, we'll never make it out of here," I whisper, close enough for our lips to brush with every word.

"Would that be the worst thing?"

Would it? My eyes travel her body, committing each delicate inch of her to the deepest part of my memory. Fuck off, division. So long, state capitals. All my brain matter is for one thing and one thing only: Blakely Bradshaw.

Blakely laughs and pushes me, putting space between us. "Just kidding! Let's go. You got all dressed up for me. I'm not spending the night inside."

I guide her through the door, taking a moment to appreciate her outfit. The hiking boots and leggings are practical, the skin-tight dress, though? That's all her.

Slinging her forgotten waterproof jacket over my shoulder, I lace our fingers together and lead her to the Jeep.

Being the gentleman my parents raised me to be, I open the car door. But in a move that would make my momma blush, I slap Blakely's shapely ass as she climbs in.

"Hey!" I love it when she pouts.

I drive us down the narrow path meant for hiking, not a vehicle, until it's too overgrown to go any further. Still knocked a good twenty minutes off the trip. A glance at Blakely tells me she hasn't figured out where we are.

The sun sets behind the higher mountains as we hike through the forest, following the last third of the worn path toward the lake. The golden hour glow creates a tawny warmth, the lingering light filtering through the leaves.

"Every day out here is better than the one before," Blakely says, a hint of wistfulness threading her words. I squeeze her hand and bid her onward; the forest isn't our destination for the night.

About twenty yards from where the treeline breaks, I stop. "Trust me?"

"Yeah." She answers quickly, but narrows her eyes. "Why?"

"Asking why defeats the purpose of giving me your trust, Spitfire. Now close your eyes."

She snorts. "If you're planning on *White Fanging* me out here, eyes open or closed, I won't be able to navigate back on my own."

"*White Fanging*? I don't even want to know. Now, close your eyes."

Blakely's lower lip juts out, but she does as I ask. Mindful of the brambles and brush, I steer her out of the trees and into the clearing that surrounds Lake Pica.

"Where are we?"

"The lake." At my answer, Blakely stiffens.

"What are we doing here?"

"Shh." I cradle her against my chest. "Can't have you scared of the water. We're making some new memories."

The tiny nod is enough of an *okay* for me.

"Alright, open your eyes."

Blakely's mouth drops, and she takes two steps forward before turning.

"This is... did you do this? Today?"

I survey my handiwork, proud of what I accomplished. Battery-powered lights loop around the bow of my docked boat, and pillows and blankets pad the floor. At the shoreline, a seating area waits with a basket full of food and a crackling fire.

"Bo gave me a hand, but yeah, I did this today." Sweeping her blonde hair to the side, I kiss the sensitive spot beneath her ear and hug her.

"How?"

I chuckle and kiss her in that same spot, loving the goosebumps that spring up on her skin. "The hardest part was sneaking into the cabin to get the wine. But you were in the bath with your earbuds and some sort of alien-looking goo on your face. You're a terrible singer, by the way."

"People tell me I have a lovely voice!" She cranes her neck and gives me her best mean mug.

"Hate to break it to you, but they're liars. You need more

honest people in your life, fewer yes-men." When her pouty face returns, I can't resist sucking her plump lower lip between my teeth. "Come on. Let's eat."

The immediate dilation of her pupils doesn't pass my notice. Into her ear, I whisper, "Real food first."

My bratty baby arches her back and grinds her hips into my cock. "Fine. Feed me." Then, with a loud laugh, she strolls to the fire pit.

"Wait, so you're saying you foraged for this?" Blakely asks, shoveling another bite of the dandelion green salad into her mouth.

"Yep."

Her eyebrows raise. "All of it?"

I glance at her plate. "Most of it." Her glare at my short answers never gets old.

"What's the crunchy bit?"

"Piñon pine nuts. Toasted 'em."

"And the dressing?" She licks her fork, and there's a corresponding twitch in my pants.

The desire to feed her, care for her, show her she's mine pulses through me, impossible to resist. Shifting, I lean forward and draw her into my lap, spearing a bite before gently slipping it between her lips. With each mouthful, I murmur an ingredient. Anticipation grows thick between us, turning our menu discussion into a test of patience.

"Chokecherries." I slide one hand down her throat, letting the weight settle on her pulse point. "Olive oil." I lick the corner of her mouth. "And honey." I push my thumb between her lips, then slowly drag it back out until she releases it with a soft *pop*.

The empty plate falls to the ground, and we're on each other. Hands. Lips. Teeth. I nip at her collarbone before soothing the sting with a sweet kiss. My fingers trace the path my mouth traveled, and Blakely quivers under my attention.

Her mischievous little hands drift south until one skims over the front of my pants. Fuck. The gentle kisses I'm leaving on her neck turn into bruising, open-mouth ones. Need possesses me, and I grip her waist, attempting to bring her closer.

"Fuck, you smell so good." My words are a rasp in her ear.

Blakely pulls back and licks her bottom lip before tugging it between her teeth. "I could have sworn you said my shampoo didn't smell that good."

"I lied." Our mouths meet again, and I swallow her moan. She guides one of my hands to her chest, encouraging me to draw circles around her nipples—the pebbled peaks visible beneath the fabric of her tight dress. With a roll of my hips, I pinch one between my thumb and index finger.

"Hudson." My name is the most delicious whimper I've ever heard, and when she rolls her hips against mine, I count backward from a hundred by sevens to keep from losing it.

At fifty-eight, I give up. With a curse, I yank her dress up to her belly button and thrust upward, the hard line of my cock pressing against the thin barrier of her leggings. This wasn't the plan. But I'm helpless to stop.

It's fumbling and hungry and sloppy, the two of us chasing pleasure. Grinding, touching, kissing our way to the edge. Blakely falls first, her body tensing before melting into a pliant puddle. I follow hot on her heels, leaving a sticky mess that quickly cools in the night air. This woman just made me come in my goddamn pants.

And then Blakely Bradshaw once again blows my mind.

"Unzip," she says as she sinks to her knees before me. I catch her elbow, but she pulls away and shakes her head. "Need to clean you up."

Fucking shit hell. "Blakely, you don't need to—"

"I want to." Her hands undo my belt buckle, the button, and then, achingly slow, each tooth of my zipper. "Lift."

I do as she commands, this gorgeous woman kneeling before me, everything I don't deserve. "You're killing me, baby."

She nuzzles her face against my thigh, then using little licks, she laps up the proof of how much I crave her. I'm too spent to get hard, but it doesn't mean Blakely cradling my cock in her mouth and purring doesn't feel fucking amazing. It isn't until I'm half hard again that she places me back into my underwear and zips up my pants.

Without waiting, I haul her into my arms, forcing her mouth to mine. The mix of her natural taste, a hint of my salty release, and the bittersweet remnants of the chokecherry dressing are a heady combination on her tongue.

Eventually, our kisses slow, the fire dies around us, and the air grows cold. Resting my chin on her head, I say, "It's getting late, and our date isn't over yet."

I douse the embers of the fire and help a shaky Blakely into the boat. Her nerves are apparent with each halting step, and her voice quivers when she asks, "Are we headed somewhere in particular?"

"No, just to open water." A vicious shiver racks her body, so I settle her onto the boat floor, nestled safely in the pillows and blankets. "You aren't getting anywhere near the side of the boat tonight. Trust me."

"I do." She tucks one of the downy comforters under her

legs and watches me in the faint glow of the string lights and the stars overhead.

The water is smooth as glass and inky black, and the early November air has a bite. As soon as I let the motor idle and drop anchor, I sink onto the makeshift pallet and gather my girl in my arms.

Blakely's head rests on my shoulder while she measures her hand against mine as we whisper back and forth. Silly stories from her twenties for her, bragging ones from my teens for me. A seemingly trivial moment that will never fade from my mind.

"Tell me about Paige."

It's a steep departure from the lighthearted tale of the first, last, and only time Buster asked her to use the griddle. But if I want her to open up, I have to do the same. Even if I'd rather eat raw elderberries.

"What do you want to know?"

She rolls so she's lying on me, her chin propped up on my chest. "You said you met when you were getting your MBA and then she moved here?"

"Yeah."

"And you guys dated for three years?"

"Uh-huh." Wonder how long she'll let me get away with non-answers.

"You proposed, and she ran off a month later."

It isn't phrased as a question, so I don't say anything. But neither does Blakely. With a sigh, I give in first.

"It crushed me. I bought a house, was imagining our life. And then one day, she was gone. Leaving behind a hateful voicemail telling me she deserves more than I can give her."

Blakely kisses my chest. "Don't take this the wrong way, but was it totally out of the blue like that? One day here, one day gone?"

Staring up at the sky overhead I say, "No, not out of the blue... For months she's been dropping hints she wasn't happy, then the hints turned into pressuring me to move. It started small—suggestions that we open up another branch of Peak Adventures in Albuquerque. When I said I wasn't interested, the more hateful she got. Complaining about Bo and Gray being around too much, me being willing to settle and having no drive." I sigh. "That's not it, you know? I have drive. I want Peak Adventures to be a business I can leave my own kids someday, but not at the cost of giving up who I am."

Quiet settles over us again, the lapping of water against the boat the only sound until Blakely says, "Her massive loss is my gain."

"Huh?"

She smiles at me. "That woman's an idiot."

A grin tugs at my mouth. "Yeah? I think I'm the idiot."

"Why do you say that?"

I smooth a stray hair behind her ear, then glide my finger down her cheek. "I keep falling for women who are made for more."

"Hudson..."

"Shhh." Rolling so we're side by side, I pull her so she's once again resting her head on my shoulder. "Look up."

"Bear—"

"No more. Now look up at the stars, Spitfire."

Her sweet gasp tells me she's seeing it. The entire reason I brought her back on the water. Above us is a smog and light-free sky. A perfect expanse of darkness with nothing to block out the creamy swirls of the Milky Way.

"This is incredible."

My eyes lock on her face. "It sure is."

Lying here in the bottom of a boat, cheeks flushed from our earlier activities, nose a little chapped from the cold, makeup-free, hair windblown and wild—she's everything. The universe has nothing on her.

She squeezes my arm and points. "Quick! Two shooting stars. Make a wish. One for each of us."

As the eons old light fades, I close my eyes and wish for the one thing I can't have. For her to stay.

blakely

DAY TWENTY-ONE

I spread my arms and legs out, starfishing in the center of the bed. Wait. If I can stretch out, that means I'm alone. Is it wrong I was hoping to wake up with Hudson's mouth between my legs? Ah well. There's always tomorrow.

With a bone-cracking yawn, I force my sleep-laden eyes open. A sliver of pink peaks out above my eyelashes. I half-heartedly swat at it, but when it doesn't disappear, I put in more effort, coming away with a small handwritten note.

That jerk stuck a sticky note on my forehead. Who does that?

Don't think sleeping in is getting you out of talking.
Last night was great.

- Bear

He signed it Bear. My stomach does a flip. I've learned enough about my taciturn cabin mate over the past twenty-one days to know signing it *Bear* is Hudson speak for *"I had a really fucking good time. I love you and want to put babies in your belly."* Maybe it's not a hundred percent accurate translation, but it's pretty damn close.

I clutch the crumpled sticky note tighter.

Hudson Brooks is a man like no other. Strong, capable, and, yeah, grumpy, but it works for him. Beneath the delicious grump is a caretaker. One who goes from barely speaking to whispering things in my ears that make my heart jump into my pussy, all while trying to wrap me up in cotton wool. And I adore all sides of him.

A tingle slithers down my spine, thinking of our date. Despite not ending in sex, it was by far the most intimate date I've ever been on.

The drip of Hudson's sexy voice, his rough hands so gentle on my skin as he caressed my back until I drifted to sleep, carrying me to the Jeep and tucking me into our bed and his arms.

Ten out of ten. And the icing on the cake?

No one else on the planet knows it happened.

I've spent virtually every moment of the past five years living my life online for others to dissect, judge, or applaud. But last night was for the two of us.

I rub the tender ache in my chest. A voice in my head whispers I can have this from now on if I'm brave enough to take a chance.

A louder voice—the insecure, scared part of me—shouts, drowning out the idea of staying with a flood of ugly reality slaps. But the ugliest one isn't even in my head. It's the buzzing of my phone.

Flopping to my side, I glare at the noise. The alerts climb

higher and higher. It's not lost on me that they look like little red flags.

Nope. Not dealing with that. Not until I kiss Hudson, drink some coffee, and talk to my therapist.

I slip on one of Hudson's discarded flannels and a fresh pair of panties before making my way to the kitchen. Small priority reorder: drink some coffee, kiss Hudson, talk to my therapist.

When I open the cupboard to grab a mug, I find a small folded piece of paper. My lips tilt upward as I take in Hudson's messy, scrawled writing.

Knew you'd go hunting for caffeine. I'm cleaning up by the lake. Be back soon.

- Bear

So much for my kiss. Therapy it is.

I sip my coffee, the sweetness of the pecans cutting through the bitter roast. Not as good as when Hudson makes it for me, but it'll do.

Another fortifying sip, and I send off a quick text to Camila.

> Do you have time to meet?

CAMILA
> Yes ma'am. When?

> Now? 😁

CAMILA
> Give me ten.

Ten minutes lets me grab my laptop, top off my coffee, and grab enough blankets to build a small nest on the porch swing. As I'm adjusting the pillow I snagged off the bed behind my back, the familiar face of my therapist takes me in.

"Hi, Blakely." Her appraising eyes flicker over my face. "You look radiant."

The unexpected compliment throws me off. Camila's always kind and polite, but she rarely comments on my looks or anything related to that. What does she see that's different enough that she feels compelled to say something?

"It's good to see you. How have you been?"

Shaking my head, I refocus. "Considering I messaged you before nine a.m. for an emergency session, not great."

She raises her eyebrows, takes a couple of notes, then says, "At our last appointment, we talked about loneliness and the pressures of maintaining your social media persona. How have you been feeling about that lately?"

"The same. Worse? Better? I don't know." I look around the cabin, hunting for something to stare at instead of meeting Camila's penetrating gaze.

"Remember, you don't have to answer if you aren't ready. Give yourself permission to breathe."

I lick my lips and shift. She gives me wait time. I hate wait time. "On one hand, I'm happier out here than I've been in years. And with each day, I find myself less driven to post, obsessing over fewer comments, ignoring my phone altogether."

"And how does that make you feel?"

"Honestly?"

She smiles.

Duh, Blakely, of course, your therapist wants you to be honest. "Freeing."

"How so?"

I lean back against the couch, chewing the inside of my cheek. "Hudson doesn't need the show. The drama. He wants to be with me. And the me out here is a me I like. I don't have to put on a production to start the day. When I talk, he's here. Granted, he doesn't say much, but he's listening. Always. And at night..." I swallow as my skin flushes. "Apart from the physical attraction, it's so nice not being alone."

We spend another forty minutes exploring the current situation with my mother and what I can do to protect my emotional well-being. After talking with Camila, I come to a few decisions. The biggest one being I'm not paying my mother anything—money or attention—and I won't run from her threats. If she continues posting stories from my childhood, I can handle it.

I think.

Ugh. It was easier to be confident within the supportive cocoon of my therapy session. I run a finger over my dark phone screen. Yesterday afternoon, the first post came out. Followed by a slew of new messages.

I'm not delusional. I'm not a celebrity or anyone of importance. My followers finding out I came from nothing isn't something to be ashamed of. If anything, I should be proud of how far I've come.

The likelihood of her "secrets" impacting me financially is low. I didn't do anything illegal. I was poor. I dropped out of high school. And yeah, I changed my name, my face, my hair color, my entire personality...

The familiar stamp of Hudson's boots on the stairs and the creak of the wooden porch are welcome distractions.

Throwing the blankets to the side and dropping my laptop, I run and jump into his arms. My lips find his in an instant, like they've always known him. I close my eyes at his touch, his hands large and warm against my skin.

"I missed you this morning. I had plans."

Hudson pulls his head back, his green eyes full of questions. "You missed me, huh?"

I run my nose down his corded neck, taking in his spicy, woodsy scent.

"And here I left you a note so you wouldn't worry."

"A note? Really? I didn't notice." I nip his full bottom lip. "FYI, I'd rather wake up to find *you* on me. Not a note."

Hudson's fingers tighten their grip on my hips. "I'll keep that in mind." The deep baritone of his gruff voice is like a physical caress. "Also, you aren't wearing any pants."

"Oh? How silly of me."

"You wouldn't be trying to distract me, right?" His breath against my skin has me inching my hips forward and craning my neck to give him better access.

The softness of plush lips, the tickle of long lashes, the barest scrape of a beard. Hudson's journeying mouth turns my words into a moan. "Distract you? F-from what?"

And there's the record scratch moment. In a move that totally kills my growing lady boner, he drops me on the swing —an *oof* slipping through my lips—and says, "From talking about what happened yesterday. And the day before."

The pout is on my face before I can school my features. I promised him, but also, ugh. Hudson's concern and desire to help however he can—even just by listening—shine through in everything he does and says. He's a fixer. It's his nature. And the universe knows I could use some fixing.

Sighing, I say, "Let me post real quick, then we can talk."

"Livestream?"

"No. Not today. I'm posting a selfie. With you."

He snorts.

"Aww, come on, Bear! You've been handling things like a pro lately. Surely you can survive one tiny little selfie?" I give him my best puppy eyes and quivery lip.

Hudson huffs, and I have him. With a grin, I make with the grabby hands, and he squishes in next to me.

I angle the phone, making sure we're both in the frame, along with my coffee mug. Then I snap a handful of pictures. In a quarter of the time I normally spend, I delete the meh ones and select my favorites.

My heartbeat skips, and warmth unfurls inside me, spreading. It's akin to a wonderful post-sex glow, a happy, satisfied tingle. All because in every single picture, Hudson is staring at me. He never once looks at the camera.

"I like this one."

"What do you like about it?"

He nuzzles his nose in my hair. "You. You look happy."

I snare Hudson's lips with mine. If he was anyone else, I might think he was feeding me a line, but that isn't his nature. If he says it, he means it. And damn. He's right.

Yeah, my mom's a walking trash can. My life away from this cabin is pathetically lonely. I have no idea how I'll leave here in nine days.

"I am happy. Happier than I've been in a really, really long time." *Or ever.* I grin. "My handsome boyfriend posed in a selfie with me and let me post it. It's a blue-ribbon day."

"Twice."

"Huh?"

"That's twice now."

My eyebrows crinkle. "Is this some sort of riddle?"

"You called me your boyfriend." My mouth goes dry. I try to figure out how to smooth my faux pas over, but then Hudson settles his chin on my shoulder. "Good."

With that word, the butterflies that have taken up permanent residency in my stomach squash any nerves as they take flight.

"What else do you need to do to the picture so we can talk?"

I fiddle with the settings, tag The Bee and The Bean, and post. No sooner than it goes up do the first reactions trickle in.

Hudson snatches the phone from my hand, his green eyes darkening as he reads the rapidly mounting comments.

"Typical. He's looking at her and she's looking at herself."

"Could she be more vapid?"

"Poor guy doesn't have a clue."

"Hudson deserves better than spoiled trash."

"Have you seen the pics her mom posted!? I'd delete everything and drop off the face of the earth if it was me."

All the happiness bleeds from my body.

"Blakely, what the fuck? Is it always like this?"

I toy with the edge of the blanket and let my gaze wander over the trees lining the clearing. "No. I mean, some of those, yes. But," I cough, trying to hide a sniffle, "things have been worse the past couple of days."

"Why didn't you say something? Was this what upset you before we went to Trail Creek and then again at lunch? Your conversation with Kirk? The afternoon of our date?" His brows furrow, and his jaw tightens.

Shit. "Something happened with my mom a couple of days ago."

He nods, anger lacing his words. "Yeah. I got that."

Guilt courses through me, and I find myself rushing to explain. "It escalated quicker than I expected, but I couldn't ruin our trip into Trail Creek. And at lunch, things were going so well with Bo and Gray that, for a moment, I forgot. Forgot this isn't my real life. When the truth ran me over—that this is just a month-long escape—I needed air."

His eyes harden when I say *month-long escape*. I'm lashing

out, and it's absolutely at the wrong person. But I'm caught in my own bullshit spiral now.

"You found me after I read messages from *her*." I try to take a breath, my words spilling out faster than I can suck in air. "Then Kirk called. When *Brandee* didn't get what she demanded, she posted some unflattering pictures and details of my life. Then, yesterday afternoon, she struck again. And yeah, I should have told you. Talked to you. But all I wanted was to lose myself in you, Hudson. To forget to remember."

"For a month."

I wince, pain crackling through my heart. "I didn't mean it that way. Being here with you..."

Hudson's never held back from manhandling me—in a good way—and right now is no exception. I swear I'm airborne before landing in his lap, nose to nose, where seconds before my back was to his chest.

"Show me."

"I—"

"Show me."

With a weary sigh, I pull up the tagged posts. The first one features my mother: hollow cheeks, limp hair, smug sneer. There's a manic light in her eyes, the only part of her that looks alive.

"All you little puppets following my daughter are idiots. Yeah, my daughter. She's been passing herself off as some city girl. Her real name isn't even Blakely Bradshaw. It's Blake Lee Shaw." Mom laughs, years of smoking, drinking, and who knows what else evident in her voice.

"I guarantee Blake thinks she's better than this guy she met three weeks ago from the sticks. I'm not surprised she's sleeping with him, though. She threw herself at every boyfriend I had. Always acting like her shit didn't stink." Brandee turns from the camera before holding up a grainy image.

My cheeks burn at my mother's hateful, crass words. The picture is me at sixteen. I'm hugging my cute hatchback that I worked two jobs to pay for myself, with a bare foot arched behind me. It may be the only picture of me smiling. I was so proud of that car, even with all the rust stains and lack of air conditioning.

I scour the picture taking in the other details. The things I've changed about myself. No more gap and buck teeth. Or dull brown hair with frizzy curls framing an overly round face. Long gone are the days of ill-fitting jeans—somehow too short and too big—and tops with moth holes in the back.

Brandee's boyfriend at the time, Dutch, took the picture on one of those disposable cameras, and my mom got so mad at him and me she locked us both out of the trailer for three nights. Dutch went to his brother's. I slept in the lobby of a building I cleaned at night.

My eyes cut to Hudson; he glares as he watches my mother malign me. A shudder of revulsion has me fighting back bile at the thought of *ever* sleeping with any of the men she entertained over the years. How much of this does he believe?

"Is there more?" Hudson's voice is tight and quiet.

I nod, wiping away the stray tears. I'm younger in the second picture. Twelve, maybe? Jimmy, the flavor of the month, has his arm over my shoulder and his eyes cut towards my non-existent chest. My arms are crossed, and my teeth clenched. There's no smile or hiding my discomfort, even in a picture over two decades old. The peeling wallpaper and cracked plaster of the trailer are the background to this unwelcome trip down memory lane.

Seeing no sense in keeping the rest from him, I open my DMs. Hudson reads over the messages Brandee sent yesterday and this morning in silence, his jaw tensing.

Hudson's body vibrates, and I can practically feel his energy pulsing around us. He abruptly stops the porch swing, slides me out of his lap, and paces the clearing. A litany of curses falls from his lips. "Goddamn, motherfucking, pathetic excuse for a… what kind of miserable person talks to and about their own fucking child like that?"

I jump from the swing, my steps faltering as I move closer to him. "Hudson, those things aren't true. I mean, yes, I changed my name, but the other stuff?"

He's a gorgeous beast. A moving mass of muscle and barely contained rage. Is his anger for me? Or at me?

My arms stretch, my body desperate for him, for a modicum of the comfort and care he's given me even when he didn't like me. The second his foot lifts in my direction, the anger cooling and morphing, my stilled heart beats again.

Hudson sweeps me up, holding me against him. He kisses away every tear falling from my eyes, tracking any that land on my cheeks.

"You listen to me. Whatever that woman has to say about you means nothing to me. Nothing." The gentle sprinkle of my tears grows into a full-blown downpour. "Hey. Hey baby, none of that. Shhh."

He holds me, his warmth and the gentle rocking of the swing soothing me. His fingers lightly massage my scalp and smooth my hair until, finally, my sobbing stops.

And then, because he really is too fucking perfect, Hudson

smiles into my hair and whispers, "It's nice to meet you, Blake Lee."

DAY TWENTY-TWO

Delicious sensations spread through my body. A tingle at the base of my spine. Toe-curling pleasure radiating from my center. The scrape of teeth, the warmth of a tongue, the downy softness of hair.

Am I dreaming? I fight through my sleep-addled haze, and when I blink my eyes open, I'm greeted by the most glorious sight on earth.

Hudson Brooks, nose deep in my pussy.

"Morning," he mumbles without picking his head up.

My answer is a moan as his tongue glides over my slick soaked sex. He buries his nose between my legs and licks me from hole to clit in long, broad strokes. Powerful hands hold my legs down when I attempt to squeeze them closed.

"Blakely, if you do that, I can't use my fingers."

"I don't even want your fingers."

It's a lie.

"Are you sure? Usually, you want several of them."

God, his mouth. When I don't answer, he huffs out a laugh, the puff of air driving my hips upward and my fingers into the sheets.

"So stubborn." Hudson's exploration of my pussy continues, his tongue delving into me like I'm his favorite ice cream. When his nose nudges my clit, my hips jerk, desperate for more. But he lifts his head, pulling away. "Do you want me to stop and let you sleep?"

I lift myself up on my elbows, lust and something more racing through me. With a grin, I bite my lower lip and flop back onto the bed. "You know the answer."

Hudson kisses the lowest part of my stomach. "Tell me. Sleep or keep going?"

When I don't answer, Hudson licks and sucks my swollen clit like a man on a mission. My cries become strangled when he clamps it gently between his teeth and rolls his tongue, making my clit thrum in protest. "Answer me."

Again, I stay silent. I'm being a brat, but it makes my heart happy.

The crack of his palm on my pussy sends deep-seated need burning through me.

"Answer me."

My hips shift beneath him, small circles as I desperately seek friction. "You're such an asshole." But, of course, I give in. "Keep going. Please, don't stop. And use your fingers."

"Promise not to smother me." He grazes his teeth along my inner thigh. "It'd be the best fucking way to go, but I'd prefer it happen many, many years from now."

"Hudson..."

Ignoring me, he goes back to his licking, sucking, kissing. Then he slips two fingers in, deep and quick. My breath catches in my throat at the sudden fullness. My walls clench around his fingers. Trying to pull them in, trying to push them out. He curls and slowly twists his fingers inside me, and when I thrust against his mouth, he adds a third. My back bows, coming off the bed, and my hands fly to his head, clenching and pulling hard on the soft strands of his hair.

"Fuck me with your fingers."

"Ask me nicely."

"Fuck. Please, Hudson."

His fingers plunge in and out of me; his tongue works the tiny bundle of nerves at the apex of my thighs. He purrs against my clit, and the extra stimulation from his mouth drives me to the edge. Mesmerizing green eyes look up at me with a hunger blazing in the vibrant depths as a wicked tongue lashes against my clit until I'm crying out. My legs shake where they're held, pleasure rolling over me in waves.

He moves one arm, putting pressure on my lower stomach, and I know what's about to happen.

"Drown me, baby."

I explode on his lips and hand. He keeps going, working me through my orgasm. I moan and push his head away, my words coming out slurred as I mumble, "Too much."

He eases his fingers from my trembling pussy and looks at them, then at me, a smug smirk on his face. His beard glistens, and he licks his lips as if trying to gather every ounce of my flavor.

"You said no one ever told you how amazing you taste." He holds his fingers to my lips. "Let me show you how delicious you are."

I nod and open my mouth. Hudson groans as he dips his fingers between my lips, and I suck my release off his drenched digits. As my tongue rolls around his fingers, he strokes himself, and I'm overwhelmed with memories of his cock buried in me, filling me so perfectly.

Hudson pulls his fingers from my mouth and stares down at me. It's like he's cementing this moment in his mind.

Shifting so his cock is near my mouth, he says, "Spit on it."

Can you come from words?

"Go on, baby, spit."

I do as he demands and watch, enraptured. He's gorgeous. Pine-green eyes eaten up with desire. Lips shining with my cum. Veins visible in his neck and forearms as he strokes himself until he spills all over my stomach and chest, marking me.

He massages his cum into my skin, and fuck, there's something so possessive and primal about it. I need to keep this connection going. I can't lose it. Him.

I yank him forward, kissing him, parting my lips so his tongue can slip into my mouth. I lose myself in his touch, the weight of his body against mine, the brush of his beard. All of it.

When I finally pull away, I grin at him. "You didn't have to wake me up this way."

"Wanted to make sure you know I listen when you speak. Plus, making you happy makes me happy." He kisses me. "'Sides, not like it's a hardship." He grins against my arm, moving higher to sneak little kisses into the crook of my elbow. *Why is that so sexy?*

We lay quietly, petting each other like if we stop touching, we'll shatter. At least that's how I feel. This man is under my skin in the best and worst ways.

"So, besides deeply satisfied, how are you?" Hudson asks, his lips pressing against my forehead.

I smile and shrug. "I bet my mother's put up some new posts."

"Can't you block her? Keep her from tagging you?"

"Yeah. But I can't decide if it's worse seeing it or knowing it's out there and *not* seeing it."

Fingers brush over my neck. "Explain."

I nibble my inner cheek, trying to clarify my thoughts. For him. For myself. "On the one hand, ignorance is bliss, right? But on the other, if she puts out something damaging, I won't have the chance to defend myself. Like the disgusting claims I tried to steal her boyfriends." Revulsion makes my stomach clench. "It's scary."

He doesn't say anything, just rubs his hands up and down my back.

"I've worked so hard to put Blake Lee in my past. To make

her disappear. To become Blakely Bradshaw, the antithesis of everything I was growing up."

"For what it's worth, the girl in those photos, she's nothing to be ashamed of. If anything, it makes your mother look worse, which I didn't think was fucking possible." His chest rumbles under my ear with a growl. "That second picture... if I could go back in time and knock the teeth out of that clown's head, I would. But the first picture? The girl in that one was a hard worker who earned her moment of pride. You know the truth of what those pictures represent; don't let her steal it from you."

It's an unreal feeling being seen. Especially when you've spent the vast majority of your life being ignored or hiding. "How'd you get so smart?" I ask, kissing the place over his heart.

"Born this way."

I did it. I made fire.

I stare at the little fire I built—all on my own. Hudson stands feet away, arms crossed over his broad chest, eyes flickering with pride. The way he's looking at me feels nearly as good as the way he woke me up this morning.

"Good job, Spitfire."

I preen under his praise and toss him my phone. "Picture, please! I need to capture this for posterity."

He clears his throat. "You doing a live?"

My jaw drops open. Who would think there'd be a day when Hudson Brooks encourages me to post to my socials?

"Um..." I scrunch my nose.

"Up to you."

There's so much unsaid in those three words. I hear it. I can take back my narrative. Face my fears. Own my history.

Or I can hide in the safety of the cabin.

Squaring my shoulders, I nod and walk Hudson through the steps. I don't bother with the fake smile. If I'm doing this, I'm leaving behind the armor I've always donned.

"Hey, BBs. It's been a few days, and I'll address that, but before, I want to show you what I did."

As the first flood of hearts rolls in, hope flickers in me. Maybe there is a place in my life for the me I'm becoming.

CHAPTER TWENTY-THREE

hudson

I stroke Blakely's hair as whiskey burns my throat, and the flickering fire casts golden shadows on her face. Our conversation yesterday, the orgasms I wrang out of her this morning, and her excitement over making fire left her worn out. She's passed out cold, her head resting in my lap.

While savoring another drink, I watch her breathe. Soak in the fluttering of her eyelashes. When the first soft snore escapes her lips, I smirk. So noisy.

The familiar and incessant buzzing of Blakely's phone draws me away from studying the masterpiece that is her face. Glancing at the screen, the word Hawthorne catches my attention. Gritting my teeth, I ignore the first two calls, but when it vibrates a third time, my patience snaps.

"What?" I answer the phone with a snarl.

"Who the hell is this?" The voice on the other end is slurred and weathered.

Dropping my voice, I slip Blakely's head out of my lap and onto a couch cushion. "Pretty sure you know," I say as I quietly pace in front of the fire. I have no desire to talk to this woman any longer than necessary, but I have a couple of things to get off my chest. And the inclination to put Brandee Shaw in her place for hurting Blakely. "She doesn't want to talk to you."

A rough snort sounds. "What's it matter to you? This is private business."

"So private you put it all over the fucking internet?"

"She owes me." The amount of hate and entitlement in her words has me gripping the phone to the point I worry I'll crack it.

"She doesn't owe you shit. You're her goddamn mother."

A disgusting, wet hacking cough comes over the line. "You've got it bad." Her laugh is cruel and cold, nothing like her daughter's infectious giggle. "She's gonna go back to her make-believe world and leave you behind. Blake is a stuck-up little snob—always thinking she's better than everyone else. What makes you any different?"

Pain aches through my chest. This woman is nothing but lies and deceit and bitterness. But there's a sliver of truth in her words. Blakely ran to a big city as soon as possible and made a life there. She's told me about her concerns with small towns. And we still haven't talked about what happens a week from now.

She's meant for more than living in tiny Trail Creek with a roughneck like me. She has custom shampoo, for fuck's sake.

"Cat got your tongue? Truth hit too close, didn't it?" Another phlegmy laugh makes my skin crawl. "Get what you can from her now, because she'll be gone. Tell her to give me what I want, and she'll never hear from me again."

"I'm blocking this number. You need to stop messaging. Leave Blakely alone." With that, I end the call.

"Hudson? Who are you talking to?"

Shit. I pride myself on a lot of things, and being an honest man is one of them. I'm not lying to her. So I answer truthfully and wait for her wrath. "Brandee."

She sits up; her full lips turn down into an angry frown. "What the hell?"

"She kept calling, and I... I shouldn't have answered."

"No, you shouldn't have." She nibbles on her thumbnail. "What did she say?"

"That what's going on between you two is private, and if you pay her off, she'll disappear."

"What else?"

My chest tightens and I repeat her mother's ugly words. "That you're going to leave me behind." I meet her gaze, and the sadness I see doesn't give our future away. Is she sad because she's leaving, or is it because she wants to stay? "I told her not to call again and blocked her number."

"Hudson."

I sink to my knees before her. "I overstepped."

"Yes. You did."

Burying my face against her stomach, I say, "I just want to keep you safe. To take care of you." The words tumble from my lips. Their admission sounds a lot like *I want to love you.*

She lifts my chin, mimicking a move I've done to her so many times. Her fingers card through my hair, soothing me in a way I don't deserve. Any lingering frustration melts off Blakely's face. With a sigh, she leans over and kisses me on the cheek. "I'm not letting this steal any more time or energy. I want you to promise the same."

"You're not mad?"

"I'm not thrilled, but," she shrugs and rests her forehead on mine, "it came from a good place. From now on, leave me to fight my battles, Bear. Until I ask for help."

"I'd expect nothing less from you, Spitfire." After a moment, I ask, "So, what's your plan?"

Her soft breath fans over my skin. "I'm not sure. Blocking her is probably the right thing to do, for sure on the phone, but like I said, that takes away my ability to defend myself."

Rising to my feet, I pull her into a hug. "You don't have to decide right now. Whatever you do, I'm here."

With a smile, Blakely takes my hand, leading us to our bed. I marvel at the sight of our entwined fingers. Hers, slender, delicate. Mine, rough and wide. So different, but so right.

DAY TWENTY-THREE

"Come on, Princess, keep up."

"Don't call me Princess!"

Chuckling, I keep my steady pace up the narrow, rocky terrain.

"Ugh, how can you be sweet one minute and an asshole the next?"

"I'm always delightful. Now hurry."

From behind me, she yells, "We aren't all goats!"

I bark out a loud laugh. She makes me better with everything she does, including the things that drive me up the wall. I thought I was in love with Paige, but she doesn't hold a goddamn candle to what I feel for Blakely. Everything with her is so much *more*. More exciting. More frustrating. More satisfying. More real.

And it's fucking clear. I never loved anyone before. Not really.

"Why couldn't we bring the ATV up here?"

"Stop whining. You're earning that *princess* nickname right now. Plus, the path is too narrow. Come on."

"I can't! I'm dying."

So dramatic. And heaven help me, so fucking cute.

Dangling a carrot, I say, "If you hurry, I'll give you a

reward." I toss the words over my shoulder, not bothering to look back as I climb higher up the jagged path.

A part of me worries she'll sit down and demand I come back and get her. The memory of the infamous *fuck the fucking sunrise* hike plays in my head. But one thing I've learned? Blakely Bradshaw is treat motivated. My girl likes praise and touch. Two things I'm more than happy to give her. When I hear her distant footsteps quicken, I grin.

"What kind of reward? What makes you think I even want it?"

Turning, I plant my feet and gaze at her. "Oh, you want it."

Like those four words are a fresh battery pack in her vibrator, Blakely scrambles up the path, catching me.

"What's my prize?" she pants, hands on her knees.

"Stand up and you'll see." My words fan over her skin as my fingers walk up her back until they settle on her neck.

Blakely straightens, closes her eyes, and cranes her chin, expecting a kiss and more from me. I brush my lips over hers. "Open your eyes; you're missing it."

The moment she realizes how high we hiked writes itself on her face. Eyes wide, mouth wider. She looks over the cliffside in awe.

From here, I can just make out the clearing that houses the cabin, Lake Pica, and miles and miles of forest. It's one of my favorite places. The sun glitters off the water, lazy clouds float in the sky, and the trees shift in the distance from the mild breeze.

"Wow." Blakely draws in a deep breath as she takes in the scenic panorama.

"I knew you'd like it."

"Yeah, you cocky bastard. I admit it. This is amazing." She cautiously takes a step closer to the edge and peers over.

Every protective cell in my body goes on high alert. We're

two hundred feet from the next ledge. "Careful. I can't fly, so if you go over..."

"You wouldn't dive after me, breaking my fall with your body? Selfish, really." She winks at me and takes one more step towards the brim.

Another shot of adrenaline courses through my system. "Don't joke about it—now step back."

"Yes, Daddy."

A growl tears from my throat, and I grab her hips, pulling her into my chest. "Daddy? Does my little brat need a spanking to remind her to listen?" I tickle her sides until she wriggles out of my arms and collapses onto the ground. Like an apex predator, I pounce, pinning her to the mossy earth.

"Hudson! S-stop!" She gasps between giggles. "I'm sorry! I won't go near the edge again."

"Oh, you think it's not listening that got you here? Try again."

Biting her lip, she grins up at me. "Sorry, *Daddy,* I didn't know that would set you off."

Groaning, I kiss her like I can brand her lips with mine. This beautiful creature. Shit. The way I want to claim her. I pour myself into the kiss, trying to imprint her taste on my lips.

Only when we're both breathless do I pull back and study the woman in my arms. She's a goddess—covered in dirt, moss, and sweat. Her blonde hair is tangled and askew, her lips pink and swollen, her cheeks flushed.

Whether we're bickering, fucking, talking, or cuddling, it all feels so goddamn right. If I were a different sort of man, an impulsive man, I'd ask her to marry me here on this cliff. But I'm not, and I can't risk driving her away, not when we have so little guaranteed time left together.

Blakely squirms beneath me. "Can you let me up?"

"Are you hurt?"

"No, not at all. This is kind of embarrassing, but I need to, um, you know…"

"Piss?"

Horror fills her eyes. "OMG. You did not say that."

"Take a leak?"

She blanches.

"Urinate?"

This time, she laughs. "Yes, Professor Brooks, I need to urinate."

"You have a shitload of choices. We're in a forest, after all." I roll off her and help her to her feet.

"So, just pick a tree? Any tree?"

"That or hold it until we get back."

She bites her lower lip. "That's not an option."

"Tree it is then. Here." I yank my undershirt off and hand it to her. "This shirt needs to be washed, anyway; use it as needed." The horrified look from before returns. "Why the face? It's just a little piss. Unless you'd rather drip dry."

"Give me the shirt." She snatches the tee from my hands and power-hikes toward the trees.

"Hurry back. I still owe you a spanking." She pauses, a visible tremor rocking her body. *Fuck yes.* Then, because I can't resist, I holler, "Don't go too far! And don't get lost!"

Her middle finger salute is the last thing I see before the pines swallow her. Chuckling at her squeamishness, I plop on the ground and take a long sip from my camelback. For all Blakely's tenacity and bravado, especially in sexual situations, she's shy about other bodily functions. Silly.

While I wait, I stretch out, letting the warmth of the overhead sun sink into my bones and chase away the chill in the air. It's in the high forties today, the perfect hiking weather— made better by not being here alone.

Minutes later, the telltale sounds of Blakely returning break the silence. So loud. Always.

"Hudson! I foraged!"

I sit up, a rush of panic slicing through me. "What do you mean?"

"Elderberries! Like the ones from the story!" Her nose wrinkles, and her lips pucker. "They don't taste very good, though. I figured being so dark, they'd be like cherries or grapes. But they're really tart."

"Blakely, how many of these did you eat?"

She pops another berry into her mouth and grimaces. "I don't know, six or seven? Don't worry, I brought enough to share."

"Stop eating them." I rush forward and knock the remaining berries from her hand.

"Hey! Why'd you do that? I thought you'd be proud of me. Foraging is on my wilderness skills checklist! And I remember these from your story. These are the berries they made medicine from."

"Yes, but they have to be cooked, otherwise they're poisonous."

Her eyes double in size. "What do you mean?"

"I mean, eating them raw is dangerous."

"Am I going to die?" she screeches, clutching her throat.

I hug her to me, trying to calm us both. "You aren't dying." Fuck. I run a hand through my hair. "Need to get you to the cabin ASAP. I swear, you have a knack for trouble."

Her fear morphs into anger. "I'm trying! I thought I was doing something good!"

"Hey, I'm not..." I swallow. "It's not your fault, it's mine. But right now, we don't have time for this." Without asking, I scoop her up and rush down the path. And, of course, the stubborn thing fights me.

"You can't carry me the entire way!"

"I sure as shit can."

"The path is too steep, and it took us over an hour to get to the top!"

"Are you doubting my strength and endurance?"

"Seriously?"

I raise an eyebrow.

With a huff, she says, "You're the epitome of strength, endurance, and virility. Now shut up and put me down!"

"Blakely, listen to me. You might feel fine now, but you're gonna be sick. I'm trying to get you home before your body betrays you."

Her body goes rigid in my arms. "How sick?"

"Very."

We make it three-fourths of the way down the mountain before it hits. With a floundering gasp, Blakely jumps from my arms and stumbles a step or two before doubling over. I sigh, bless her heart. She's a mess. My mess.

I cringe at the sound of her violent retching. It's gonna be a long night.

By some miracle, I get her back to the cabin. We stop twice for her to throw up, but we make it.

Every part of me wishes I could take her place. I'd gladly eat my weight in those fucking berries if it meant she wasn't suffering. If I could take away the pain and discomfort. She's in the worst of it now. Her slight frame trembles as she sobs and heaves.

Sinking to the ground, I pet her hair. "I'm so sorry, baby."

"Please go away," she groans, hiding her face in her hands from where she lays curled around the toilet on the bathroom floor.

"No, I'm here to take care of you. Nurse Hudson. Want me to get the hat? I think it's still by our bed."

"That's not funny."

"Okay, but I'm not joking about helping you."

"It's too embarrassing."

"What's embarrassing about it? It's a natural, albeit unfortunate, side effect of being human." I pause, skimming my fingers along her damp skin. "At least it's not coming out the oth—"

"I'm begging you not to finish that sentence." Another spasm rocks her, and she clutches her stomach. Tears fall in furrows down her cheeks. "It hurts. I'm gross. And this is not sexy."

"Are you worried this makes me want you less? You know me better than that. Now, move your hands, and let me wipe your face." She does as I ask, dropping her hands and facing me. I gently wipe her eyes, her cheeks, and the corners of her mouth.

"I'm sorry."

Incredulous at her words, I gape at her. "What on god's green earth are you apologizing for?"

"We only have a week left together, and I'm ruining it."

"Blakely, hear me." I tilt her face upward. "You're not ruining anything. Being here, taking care of you, is where I want to be."

She gives me a wan smile. "Can you help me brush my teeth?"

I kiss her forehead and reach above us, grabbing her toothbrush from the cup on the sink and putting a thin layer of toothpaste on it. Blakely takes the toothbrush, her wrist limp. Steadying her hand, together we brush her teeth. I help her stand as she rinses out her mouth.

"Better?"

"Much," she says before falling against me as her legs give out.

"Let's get you washed up and into bed." I carry Blakely to the clawfoot tub. Holding her while I prep the water, I adjust the temperature so it's not too warm or cold and lower her into the bath.

Blakely sighs when I massage her shoulders. She settles deeper, and I pour handfuls of water over her head.

"Mmmm, that feels nice," she murmurs, her voice heavy with sleep and sickness.

I grab her shampoo and take a sneaky whiff before squirting some into my palms. That signature Blakely smell washes over me. I work the shampoo into her hair, digging my fingers into her scalp as I lather her tresses. Then I rinse the suds away, keeping it from dripping into her eyes. I repeat my actions with her conditioner, finger combing her silky strands.

Fuck, I love her. I consider telling her. If not now, when? But before I can say anything, Blakely begins shaking again. Shit, she's about to puke. Running, I grab a trashcan and get it to her in the nick of time.

The tears stream from her eyes again as her body spasms, the elderberries wreaking havoc. She shivers, so I gather her out of the water and wrap her in a large, fluffy towel. As I dry her, the trembling subsides, but she starts rambling. Gibberish mostly, more apologizing and bemoaning her embarrassment.

Hugging her tight, I lead her to bed and pull the blankets around her. I sweep a lock of hair from her face, her skin already sticky with sweat. Even clammy and pale, she's perfect. I give her a quick peck on the cheek before changing out the trash bag and bringing it next to the bed. She's not out of the woods yet.

I snag a sports drink from the fridge and open her mouth, tipping it between her lips. It's the best I can do to replenish her dehydrated body. "One more sip for me; you can do it." I encourage her, pouring another mouthful down her throat.

Once she takes another small drink, I turn her onto her side and slip into bed, spooning her. I drape my arms and legs over, cocooning my body around hers. It's all I can offer, having failed to keep her safe again.

I wouldn't blame her if she left tomorrow. The lake, the arrow, the blisters, and now this. How can she see me as anything but a fuckup?

Blakely's eyes flutter close, and her breathing steadies. She's almost asleep, but she's still mumbling. Mostly random apologies and thanking me for taking care of her. But before drifting off, she says, "Not your fault."

"What's that, baby?"

"Not your fault. I love you."

I freeze. It's more gibberish. She doesn't mean it and won't remember what she said. Even though I don't deserve it, I bury my face in her hair and whisper the words that've been on my heart for days. "I love you, too, Spitfire. More than you know."

DAY TWENTY-FOUR

The light streaming into the cabin wakes me. With a groan, I sit up and check on Blakely. She had a fitful night, waking every few hours, her body desperate to purge the raw elderberries.

I press my lips to her forehead, grateful to find her skin cool.

She blinks at me, her eyes heavy. "What time is it?"

Reaching out, I caress her silky cheek. "Morning. How do you feel?"

"Better. No nausea or stomach cramps. No brain fog or chills."

"Do you remember anything?" *Like telling me you love me?*

"Just eating the berries, panicking, and puking. All the rest is a blur."

Damn.

I take two deep breaths, a half smile tugging on my lips. "How someone your size can vomit so much, I'm not sure I'll ever understand. But the good news is, you've gone a few hours without throwing up, so I'm guessing the berries worked their way out of your system."

Blakely groans and pulls the blanket over her head, hiding from me.

"Spitfire?"

"What?"

"Why are you under the blanket?"

"Because I'm dying of embarrassment."

I snort and tug at the cover. She digs her fingers in and holds it tight, but I pry it away. When I lean in to kiss her, she ducks out of my reach.

"Can we not? I'm better, but I really need to brush my teeth."

"Of course." My eyebrows rise. "But I'd kiss you anytime."

Blakely stares at me, aghast. "That's disgusting."

"You're so squeamish. I don't care how—to use your word, not mine—disgusting you are. I still want to kiss you."

"That's sweet. Gross. But sweet."

I inch my face closer to hers. "Are you saying you wouldn't kiss me if *I* spent the night vomiting?"

"No!"

"I must care about you more."

"That's not true! Or fair. I don't think not wanting to kiss you right after you throw up is unreasonable. Most people would agree with me. It's a valid, common feeling, not a measure of whether I care about you more or less."

"It seems like the person who cares more would kiss a disgusting person."

"Ugh! Fine! I'd kiss you even after you threw up. Happy?"

I throw my head back, laughing. "Incredibly."

"You're such an asshole, and I still need to brush my teeth."

"Do you want help?"

"Brushing my teeth? Of course not," she snaps. "I'm not a baby."

"I didn't say you were. I'm offering to help like I did last night."

"Well, stop. I'm already embarrassed that I tried to feed you poison berries and threw up all afternoon and night in front of you. I can brush my teeth."

"Then do it."

"I will!" She sits up too fast, and I catch her in time to keep her from hitting the ground.

"Blakely. Let me help you."

A thousand emotions dance on her face. Pride, shame, and eventually resignation. "Okay, you can help me if it means that much to you."

Little brat. "Yes, please."

Together, we make our way to the water closet. I give her some privacy before joining to help wash her face and brush her teeth. Then we walk arm in arm to the bed. Blakely climbs in and lets me tuck the covers around her.

"I'm ready for my kiss now."

Without speaking, I lower my lips to hers, and she sinks into my touch. Too soon, I break away, running my fingers through her hair and staring at her. "Nurse Hudson reporting for duty."

CHAPTER TWENTY-FOUR

DAY TWENTY-FIVE

Kirk blanches when he sees me. "Are you okay? You look rough."

"Gee, just what everyone wants to hear," I snark. And even though I've gotten more comfortable with my natural face, I still run my fingers through my hair, attempting to tame the snarls.

He has the decency to look ashamed. "Sorry. I mean, you don't seem to be feeling well."

"Eating poisonous berries will do that." *A poisonous mother will also take it out of you.*

Kirk's smooth forehead wrinkles and his eyes widen. "What?"

I wave my hand. "I ate a handful of raw elderberries. Pro-tip, they have to be cooked."

"Are you okay? Do I need to get an ambulance out there?"

"I'm fine. Hudson took care of me."

From behind me, Hudson snorts and grumbles. "Never should have happened."

My eyes roll of their own accord. That man carries way too much guilt and responsibility for everyone else's actions. I don't blame him. At all.

"So besides your treatise on how stunning I look, why did you call?"

"Your mother posted again. I wasn't sure if you blocked her or knew."

In a blink, Hudson has my phone in his hand, a snarl on his lips. "Why would you tell her? Are you trying to upset her? Is this some sort of fucking game?"

The blood drains from Kirk's face, and he stammers. "N-no. I'm ch-checking on her."

Hudson huffs and I steal the phone before he says anything else. "Kirk, it's okay. Hudson is... protective. He and my mother spoke a couple of days ago."

"What? Brandee called you? How'd she get your number?" Rationally, I know Kirk would never sell me out to my mother, but his genuine surprise eases an ounce of the tension I'm holding.

"I've been wondering that myself." Before, her attempts at blackmail were through my social platforms, never on my private number. "Maybe someone in the office?"

Kirk pinches his lips together and taps furiously on his tablet. "I'll find out, and when I do, I'll take care of the problem. BB, I'm sorry." A pained expression settles on his face. "I really called to check on you. To see if you knew about the latest post. Not to hurt you. Or make things worse."

"It's okay, Kirk. I'm still deciding how to handle it. It's worse than it's ever been. She's demanding more money, reaching out in new ways, being aggressive in her posts." I swallow the knot in my throat. "Thanks for the heads up. I'll go check it out."

"BB, I'm not sure—"

"No, I need to see it for myself. To make a choice." About so many things.

With an understanding nod, Kirk says, "Let me know if you need me. Legal help. To talk. Whatever."

Hudson's large frame leans against mine, his face crowding into the camera's view. "She's got support here, too, but thanks." He hits the end call button and pulls me into his arms. "You sure about this?"

I twist my fingers in the soft flannel of his shirt, my mind racing through the multitude of possibilities waiting for me. If Kirk felt the need to call, it's not good. But my need for answers outweighs the fear.

On my nod, Hudson shifts me so I'm sitting in his lap, my head cradled against his shoulder. "Open it, baby. I'm here."

As soon as I see the post, I wish I could turn back time. To thirty seconds ago, before I looked. To twenty years ago, before I kept a diary. Or, hell, to thirty-three years ago, before I was born. Any of those will work.

Sadly, time travel is a finicky bitch. What with not existing and all.

My stomach churns, and invisible ants crawl along my skin. It's a video. In it, my mother, looking strung out and haggard, holds a worn spiral notebook. Doodles of hearts, flowers, butterflies, and bees decorate the faded cover.

"This is for all y'all thinking Blakely Bradshaw is so aspirational."

Her savage smile widens as she flips through the pages. Then she reads.

"*I got sent home from school today. The nurse says I need to shower more because there've been complaints from my classmates. Like I don't wish I could bathe regularly. Of course, mom didn't care. She didn't even pick me up. Instead, she told me to find my own way home."* My mother pauses here, glaring into the camera. "Such a spoiled brat. As if I had time to come get her ass from school."

Huffing, she reads more. *"I tried to shower in the trailer, but Floyd is here, and I don't want to chance it."* Her eyes roll. "Uppity little cow. My men never wanted her."

I can't watch anymore—mortification, grief, and the cramps from yesterday churn in my stomach. Muffling a whimper, I dart to the bathroom, my phone clattering onto the wood floor.

Dry heaves wrack my body. Not from the berries. No. This is pure Brandee. I wear myself out between tears and retching. A cool cloth eases my aching eyes and burning cheeks. A rough palm smooths back my hair before nimble fingers work it into a loose braid.

Hudson.

His familiar scent of pine trees, warm earth, and spice calm my frayed nerves. "Look, I'm not telling you what to do. But I mean it when I say these videos and posts—as shitty as they are—don't reflect poorly on you."

A weak snort is my reply. What does he mean they don't reflect poorly on me? I've built an entire brand on a lifestyle and persona of luxury, indulgence, and fun. My followers know me for my beauty and clothing recommendations. Where to find the hottest Austin night spots, how to live the perfect millennial life. Not as the poor girl who was so smelly the school sent her home.

"Spitfire."

How do I spin this? How do I bounce back? Is being out here reinforcing her story?

"Blakely."

Should I go back to Austin and get with Kirk? Try to do damage control showing me back in my usual haunts?

"Blake Lee!" Hudson's voice echoes off the bathroom walls, snapping me from my spiral.

"Don't call me that!" I lash out with my reply before regret washes over me. He didn't mean it as a dig. He's not like Brandee.

A fresh round of tears well in my eyes, but I squeeze them shut before they fall.

"Nope. Open them." I squint one eye at him. "Didn't call you that to hurt you. Just needed your attention. You're spiraling." He scoops me up and carries me to the bed. "It's time for you to decide if you're ashamed of your past or just sad."

"W-what?"

"Are you ashamed of who you were or sad about the life you had to overcome?" When I don't answer, he kisses me, lips featherlight on mine. "You didn't ask, but if you did, my advice would be to face the bad head-on and acknowledge how far you've come. Because, baby, you've come a long fucking way."

"I don't..." I drop my head and kiss his collarbone. "Thank you."

He buries his nose in my hair. "Whatever you decide. I'm here."

For the next five days.

"Whatever you're thinking, stop. When I say I'm here, I mean it. Today, tomorrow, thirty days from now. You have me."

"Hudson, I—" I stop myself from spilling my biggest truth all over him.

"Come on, let's feed you."

I nod, but in my head, I'm screaming, *I love you.*

DAY TWENTY-SIX

Hudson stands with his back to me, pouring coffee into a mug. Then he turns, his eyes dropping to the half-eaten piece of toast at his feet. The toast that may have bounced off the back of his head.

"Need something, Blakely?"

I don't answer. Instead, I cut my eyes to the ceiling, playing innocent.

He eats up the space between us in three long strides. "Are you desperate for my attention?"

Pouting, I bat my lashes at him. "You're ignoring me."

"I stepped away long enough to make a cup of coffee. I made you one, too."

"Ooh, give me, please!" I hold my hands out, fingers wiggling towards him.

"Someone's feeling better."

Nodding, I sip my perfectly made coffee. I'm finally back to a hundred percent. Those fucking berries can suck my theoretical dick. And my mother can go kick rocks.

Hudson and I spent yesterday in the cabin. Him hovering like a mother hen, me trying to convince him to fuck me into the mattress and out of my head.

Sadly, I didn't win.

"Nurse Hudson took excellent care of me." I wink. "Even if he wouldn't fu—"

"Blakely." His gruff voice has a hint of warning in it. I love pushing his buttons.

"Sorry, Daddy."

The tips of his ears turn pink, and he grumbles. "Is *Daddy* a thing now?"

"You like it." I pull him toward me so he's standing between my thighs.

He runs a rough finger over my jaw and makes a noncommittal humming sound before kissing the top of my head.

The comfort Hudson brings settles over me like a warm blanket. Tilting my chin up, I say, "All kidding aside, thank you. No one has ever taken care of me." And it's true. Growing up, I took care of myself, doing the best I could. Sylvie and Buster did a lot, and Kirk does too, but no one, not one person in my life, has ever made me feel as safe and cared for as Hudson does.

The supreme unfairness of this entire situation isn't lost on me. Why couldn't I have met Hudson in Austin? There'd be no fear, no stress because if it didn't work out, I'd still have everything I had before him. Our situation is a pressure cooker in comparison. What if I give up the life I know, only for things to implode a month later? What if I return to Austin and miss out on the love of my life?

"Hey, come back to me." He pulls me to my feet and lifts my chin. When my eyes meet his, he says, "Now that you're recovered, we've got a lot to do."

My eyebrows pull towards my hairline.

"Three days. Camping." He clears his throat. "With your time here about to end," my heart clenches, "I want to see how far you've come."

"What, like a test?" I squeak. Anxiety and inadequacy pulse through my system. Show what I've learned? Three days? My time here ending...

Shaking my head, I inhale and lick my lips. "I, um, made a decision."

Hudson cocks his head. "Oh?"

"About my mom."

His shoulders drop, and my stomach lurches. He thought I meant about us. But Hudson, being Hudson, doesn't say anything. He simply raises an eyebrow at me.

"I'm going to deal with the current posts in a live, and then I'm blocking her."

Hudson stares but doesn't speak.

"I'm also addressing how my past helped make me who I am. And that I'm not," my words falter, belying what I'm saying, "embarrassed of who I was."

"Good for you, baby." He brushes a knuckle against my cheek. "Why don't you knock that out while I load the Jeep."

"Actually..." My teeth tug at my bottom lip. "Would you sit with me? I could use your strength."

Warmth softens his eyes. "Of course, I'll sit with you, baby. But you don't need my strength. You've got plenty of your own."

Lacing our fingers together, I walk to the porch swing. Steadying myself, I launch one of my apps and a livestream. The storm my mother stirred means more people than normal jump on with me.

No shields. No makeup. No fake smile. Just Blake Lee, Blakely, me. I face my audience.

"Hey there, BBs. As you know, a certain relative from my past has been very active over the past few days. Sharing pictures and private moments from my childhood. Her hope in doing this is that I'll pay her to stop. But thanks to advice from a brilliant outdoorsman—" I pan the camera to Hudson, whose lips quirk up in a half smile. Well, it could be a smile if you squint hard and haven't ever seen one. "I'm taking a stand."

With a deep breath, I stare into the camera. "Before I go any further, I want to talk about a couple of things. Yes, I changed my name. Legally, I'm Blakely Bradshaw, and that's who I'm staying. The girl in those pictures, she's gone. Not because I'm ashamed of her but because she had to change. Evolve. Rise from the ashes."

I swallow, clearing my throat and fighting back tears. "The persona I've presented to you for the past five years, she isn't me either. The truth lies somewhere in between the two. I carry Blake Lee's scars and memories, Blakely's wins and experiences. And from those two versions of myself, I'm evolving again.

"Being here, in Trail Creek, has honestly been transformative. I've learned what I'm capable of, who I have the potential to be. What does this mean for me moving forward?" I shrug, and Hudson squeezes my thigh. "Honestly, I'm not sure. There's so much to think about, and I appreciate your continued support. Please don't tag me in posts related to Brandee Shaw. I have to protect my mental health and well-being."

When I sign off, my Bear kisses the hollow beneath my ear. "I'm real fucking proud of you, Spitfire."

I'm proud of myself, too. I don't have all the answers, and I know I'll falter. But today is a step in the right direction. Now, if I could only decide if I should stay or go.

My arms and back ache. Any enthusiasm I may have felt about camping is officially gone. Not that it was particularly high to begin with. I'm not opposed to sleeping in a tent with Hudson, but I'm not jumping at three days without indoor plumbing.

We're hiking back up the steep path towards the cliffside—the scene of berrygate. The trek was hard enough without a twenty-pound backpack.

"Bear, why are you torturing me?"

Hudson snorts and adjusts the larger pack he's carrying. "You'd rather be up here for three days without supplies?"

"No, I'd *rather* you carry all this for me." Am I being a whiny brat? Yes. Do I care? No.

"Tell you what, Princess. I'll carry your pack."

I glare daggers at his back—for the nickname and the trap I smell.

"What's the catch?"

"I'll carry everything, then give you the Brooks treatment and make you earn your items."

I briefly imagine him tripping over a rock. Not enough to hurt him, just enough to knock the smug smirk off his unfairly handsome face. But his footing is as sure as a billy goat's. "No," I huff. "I'm fine."

"Thought so."

Mumbling a string of creative cuss words, I trudge along. It takes another twenty minutes uphill—all we're missing is snow—before we arrive at the cliff. The view is a worthy reward, though. It's later in the day, almost sunset now, and the colors splaying across the sky are breathtaking.

"Why didn't you bring me here on the first day?" Our first sunrise hike—and our second—were much closer to the cabin and not nearly as high up. Huh. Answered my question.

Hudson raises one eyebrow, then steps closer, slinging my pack off my shoulders. "I love this spot." He wraps his arms around me, one resting on my neck, the other on my hip. "Been waiting a long time to share it with someone."

If my knees give out, I don't think I can be held responsible. My words are shaky when I ask, "You never brought anyone else here? Not even Pai—"

"No one. Only you."

Twisting, my lips crash into his in a sloppy kiss. It's all

tongues and teeth and heat. Need and lust and love rush through me, and suddenly, I'm on my back on the spongy, mossy earth. It's déjà vu. The ground beneath me, Hudson's heavy body over me. But he's not tickling me, at least not on the outside. Inside, though, is going batshit crazy.

Hudson kisses my jaw, my throat, along my collarbone, tugging off my top layers as he goes. "I owe you a couple of spankings from the other day for how close you got to the edge of the cliff." His lips travel lower, and he pauses at my chest, taking a nipple into his mouth, sucking the sensitive peak through the lacy material still covering it.

In a flash, I'm on my hands and knees, peering over the cliff, the jagged rock face giving way to the tops of hundred-foot pines below. A tremor of danger prickles at the back of my neck.

"I've got you. You're safe with me."

My core throbs. Who knew I had a caretaker kink?

Large hands unlace my boots and tug them and my thick thermal leggings off. I'm shaking. From the cold? From the heat? Who the hell knows?

I'm left in my pink panties and matching bra and wool socks. This *so* would not pass the fit check.

All thoughts of my remaining clothing fly from my head when Hudson curls over my back and whispers, "If you want me to stop, say so. If not, Daddy's gonna take care of you." When I fervently nod, encouraging him, he nips my earlobe. "Count 'em out, Spitfire."

Hudson hooks a finger in the elastic of my panties and tugs, the soft material slipping down my thighs, stopping above my knees. Then his palm lands on my cheek with a loud smack. Heat and the sweet sting of pain bloom through me.

"I said count, Blakely."

"O-one."

"Good girl." The words slip over me like silk.

The fast crack of skin on skin has me mewling out. "Two!"

"So fucking good. Three more."

I whimper, trying to push into his touch and pull away.

"Nope, can't go forward. Too close to the edge. Which is what got you here in the first place."

"I thought calling you *Dad*—" Spank number three lands, cutting off my tease with a whimper. My pussy clenches around nothing, and my nipples ache. "Th-three."

Four and five come in quick succession, and no sooner than I count them does Hudson soothe away the sting, rubbing soft circles and kissing the warmth blossoming across my ass.

"Fuck. Need to taste you. Do you want that, Blakely? Do you want me to fuck you with my tongue until you're putty in my hands?"

"Yes. Yes, please. Yes." I chant.

Hudson buries his face into my pussy from behind, one arm locking around my thighs. The other snakes between my breasts, pulling the cups of my bra down, and toys with my nipples. He teases me this way, his licks shallow and light, and so not what I need.

Then I'm staring up at the sky, and my sore ass is on the ground. Hudson's green eyes gleam as he plants sweet kisses on my ribcage and dips his tongue in my navel.

Goosebumps stipple my skin when he chuckles before nuzzling his mouth against my pussy. The nip he gives my clit has me clenching as two fingers plunge inside me.

His tongue strokes me—I swear he's spelling his name— until my toes curl. Hudson adds pressure against my lower stomach, having learned it's the fastest way to turn me into a mess, a feat he seems to prize himself on achieving.

As he licks and laps me into ecstasy-fueled oblivion, the fingers inside me twirl and inch deeper. A hot rumbling sensation against my overly sensitive clit makes me cry out.

"*Fuck.*" Hudson moans. Is there anything sexier?

Warm, coiled tension builds, and my muscles tense in anticipation. A third finger slips inside me, curling and curving, searching for that perfect spot, the one designed to bring me to the pinnacle. I wriggle out of my bra and pluck and twist my nipples until they throb.

Each stroke of Hudson's fingers.

"That's right."

Each suck from his mouth.

"Give it to me."

Each rumble from his throat.

"Drench me."

The tension builds until, like a string wound too tight, I snap.

"Show me how much you love my tongue."

Euphoric tidal waves crash over me, and I cry out his name. He's a god—a benevolent, orgasm giving god.

Hudson nibbles my inner thigh, easing the beard burn he left behind, then crawls over me, claiming my lips. His tongue carries the flavor of my climax.

He breaks the kiss and rests his forehead against mine. "I love the way you taste. You have no idea what it does to me, seeing you come undone that way."

I drink in his green eyes and the spray of freckles on the bridge of his nose and across his cheeks. "I love the way you make me come undone."

He nips my bottom lip. "Feeling good?"

"Very." With a saucy grin, I run my fingers through his hair and say, "Thank you, Daddy."

"Oh, I'm gonna fuck the sass right out of you, Spitfire. You have ten seconds to run. When I catch you, and I will, I'll fuck you so hard, you'll forget your name." As he talks, he sheds his flannel and unbuckles his belt.

I don't move, his promise sending my nerves racing and a flood to my pussy.

"Nine, eight, seven—"

Before he gets to six, I shed my tangled panties and make a run for it. The ground is hard, but the bed of fallen pine needles protects my sock-clad feet. I make it a mere three steps into the trees when a growl sounds behind me. I spin and am met with the gorgeous sight of Hudson moving after me, purpose, determination, and deep-seated hunger written on his handsome face.

With a small *eep,* I take off in a sprint, though I know there's no way I'll outrun him. Seconds later, the world spins as the rough bark of a spindly tree bites into my back, stealing my breath. A needy whimper slips from my lips, and I lock my legs around Hudson's waist, loving the sensation of being trapped between his body and the tree.

"Do you know how long I've wanted to chase you through these woods and fuck you like this?" he asks. Urgency, bright and sharp, shines in his eyes as he yanks his jeans down. He brushes his cock between my legs, coating himself in my cum and desire. I'm ready to beg him to stop teasing when he thrusts, stretching and filling me the way I crave.

"You caught me." My words are little more than broken mewls.

"Sure fucking did." He nips my lips and grunts, fingers digging into my ass as I writhe against him. "Goddamn, you're perfect. Soft, wet, and warm. If I spent every day of the rest of my life inside you, it wouldn't be enough."

His molten tongue burns along my skin, where open-mouthed kisses send scorching, sensual pulses to my stomach, back, and base. One hand keeps me anchored between him and the tree. The other grazes my hips, back, and ass, always moving in butterfly-light glances.

The pure pleasure of his touch and the bite from the bark battle, creating a perfect symphony of sensations. "So good. So fucking good, Bear."

"That's right, baby. Love your tight pussy. How your pretty cunt stretches around me, taking me so deep. I'm gonna make you beg me for more. You're gonna forget everything else, except my name."

I focus my attention on our joined bodies. The sounds of our lovemaking. The look on Hudson's face. As he snaps his hips, driving deeper into me, I clench tight, locking and gripping him as though he's my lifeline.

"Say it, Blakely. Say my name."

"Hudson!" I clasp my hands onto his shoulders, using his body to propel myself up and down in rhythm with his thrusts. His hot mouth sucks and nips at my sternum, my tits, my neck. Every upward drive, every kiss, every touch burns through me. Thundering ecstasy drowns me in frothy waters. I'm totally and utterly awash in my release.

Satisfied and spent, I fall forward, my head landing in the crook of Hudson's neck. Pine, spice, sweat, and sex. He smells delicious. His thrusts slow, and with a grunt, he spills inside me. As I try to catch my breath and recover from the high of my climax, tiny spasms continue to erupt through my body while Hudson's pulse pounds in my ears.

Drained, he collapses, sinking to the ground, taking me with him, his cock still deep inside me.

As we lay on the forest floor, Hudson traces patterns into the small of my back, tempering the scratches the tree left. When I shiver, he rises and walks us to the cliff's edge, bodies still entwined. Stretching to snag his flannel, he drapes it over me, surrounding me with his scent and warmth. While the last rays of golden hour light dance over us, my fingers stroke his hair.

Maybe camping isn't so bad.

hudson

DAY TWENTY-SEVEN

Camping is a part of who I am. Every key memory from my childhood is camping-related, and as I'm learning, those experiences color who I am as an adult more than I thought.

But camping with Blakely? That's a trial in motherfucking patience. Bo had more camping common sense at seven than she does in her thirties. It's not for lack of trying, though. She's come a long way over the last twenty-seven days and is doing her best, but damn, her skills are rough.

After she recovered from being fucked into oblivion—and a tree—I tasked her with setting up our tent for the night. She's been practicing knots for close to a month, but the entire thing looked like shoelaces. Bunny ears and wide floppy loops. She was supposed to secure downed branches to help build a windbreak but ended up with loosely tied fire kindling and a lean-to instead of a sturdy shelter.

It took me half an hour to undo her work and another one to set the campsite up correctly.

I'm gonna have to show her more about knots in a hands-on way. Make her appreciate their beauty. My dick jumps at the idea of Blakely bound in rope, intricate knots biting into her skin. Her hands bound to my headboard or behind her back.

Fuck. Now that would be a sight.

The crackle of the fire and Blakely's off-key singing shake me out of my fantasy. I watch, a smirk on my face, as she slides a marshmallow onto a skewer and holds it over the fire.

Knowing what's coming, I pierce multiple marshmallows onto my stick.

"You're gonna burn it."

"There's no right or wrong way to toast a marshmallow," she huffs.

"Considering yours is melting into the fire, I'm gonna have to disagree."

She pulls her skewer from the flames, frowning at the charred ruins. The glassy sheen of tears has me on high alert.

"I can't even toast a marshmallow. How am I so bad at everything?"

My stomach rolls, guilt churning, since I thought the same thing. Shit, I'm an asshole. And I can't handle it when my girl cries. "You built the fire tonight."

"I can do one whole thing off your mile-long survival skill list. Hurray, me."

"Building the fire means you also figured out how to create potable water."

A small smile pulls at her mouth. "That's true. I did."

Giving her a soft kiss, I say, "And you proved mastery of first aid a while ago."

Her laugh relaxes the pangs in my stomach. She scoots her camp chair closer to mine while burning more marshmallows beyond edible. She's happy, so I don't mention the other skills —like navigation.

Motherfucking navigation. I lost her for over two hours today when I sent her on a fifteen-minute circular path alone.

And after the elderberry incident, I didn't ask her to forage.

Overall, if I rate my city girl on her skills, she's getting a D-minus. And yeah, I'm curving up for sleeping with the teacher.

Blakely eyes my toasted marshmallows, pouting. Heaven fucking help me, it's so damn cute. Her plump bottom lip juts out, begging me to nip it. So, like a chump, I trade my skewer for her lump of charcoal.

"I'll share, Bear." She takes a bite and offers me a nibble from between her lips.

I take her up on it, my teeth grazing her lips as I pull away. When she extends a sticky hand, I lick the sugary remains from the pad of her thumb, biting hard enough to make her shudder.

She snags my lips in a deep kiss, dropping the skewer to the ground. Who the fuck needs marshmallows, anyway?

The idiot inside me wants to tell her she could eventually be an outdoor expert, and we could have two thousand nights of campfires and marshmallows. All she has to do is stay. Instead, I guide her into my lap and tilt her head. My hands brush over her face as I gaze at her. Slowly, I lower my mouth to hers, lips barely touching, a glancing caress. Then another. Tender, chaste, but longer than the first. I hold my mouth a hair's breadth above hers, breathing in her air, not ready to let go of this moment, of her. "Spitfire, I..."

The crash of thunder jolts us. One drop of rain. Then a second and third.

Frowning, I glance up. Heavy, rain-laden clouds hide the stars that were peaking through the branches.

November weather is usually calmer than this. Typically

storms peter out around August, but our fucking luck. Tugging Blakely to her feet, I say, "Get in the tent."

The wind picks up, whipping around us. Before she moves, the sky bursts open, rain pelting down like tiny bullets. Shit.

"Blakely! The tent!" My bark is louder than the scream of the storm.

With wide eyes, Blakely shakes her head. "I can help!"

My protective side demands she go inside, but she's a stubborn shit. So I point to the chairs. "Collapse those and rake the coals." She nods and gets to work despite the water dousing her.

While she does that, I check the latches. I'm not upset about redoing those knots now. I'd never forgive myself if something happened to our shelter during a storm. Once I'm sure we're tethered, I crawl in and join her.

"What a way to end the evening!" Blakely laughs as she unzips her jacket and yanks off her rain-soaked boots.

"We're safe. I won't let anything happen to you." I go through my mental checklist: the tent lines are secure, the windbreak is tight, and the waterproof tarp is double-knotted.

"Of course you won't." She says it like it's as obvious as water being wet.

Damn, if her certainty in me doesn't make me feel like more. Taller. Bigger. Smarter. I'm Superman.

A brilliant flash of lightning illuminates her face, and while she's shivering, her cheeks are rosy from running around, and her hair hangs in riotous waves around her head. *Fucking gorgeous.* A man possessed, I move forward and pull her flush against my body before claiming her mouth.

My tongue delves between her lips, a hint of fruit, wine, and sugar lingering there. Her flavor overwhelms me, and when she curls her body against mine, deepening the kiss, I shift so my knee goes between her thighs. Blakely rocks against me, her desire as evident as mine. We trip over the edge of another rule I broke for her—an air mattress.

She goes to lie down, but I grab her. "Nope. Not yet. You didn't listen to me out there."

Her chin lifts, and her shoulders go back. "You needed my help."

I bite my lower lip. "Sure did. But now I need you to listen."

Pulling her in, my hands grip her hips, and I kiss the spot beneath her ear. "We're about to put this mattress to use, baby. Fucked you against a tree yesterday, gonna fuck you in the rain tonight." She squirms, clenching her thighs, and I chuckle. "But only if you can be a good girl and listen."

"Tell me what you want me to do, Bear." That fucking nickname. I love the way it sounds on her lips.

I slip off my wet clothes, leaving them in a messy pile at the mouth of the tent. Then I sink onto the air mattress, stroking myself. "Undress for me."

Blakely locks her eyes on mine as she peels off her clothes. She stands before me, clad in a pair of pale blue panties and a matching lace-covered bra. An ugly voice dredges up resentment. *She has twenty-plus sets of matching underwear. She doesn't belong out here with me.*

Growling to drown out the rain and my inner critic, I say, "Keep going. All of it."

Reaching behind her back, she unclasps the hooks on her bra and flings it away from her body, letting her full breasts spill into the open air. Then she hooks her thumbs into the waistband of her panties, inching them down her legs.

"Now that you have me bare, Bear, what do you want? Tell me." It's my own private show, Blakely's beautiful body highlighted by the dim glow of the lantern and the occasional flashes of lightning.

My voice comes out husky. "Put your fingers in your mouth, get them nice and wet, then use them to touch those gorgeous tits."

"Touch them? Like this?" She sweeps her slim fingers over her pink nipples, all the blood in my body speeding south when they stiffen into peaks.

"Tug them. Twist them." She loves the pain-pleasure line, and, again, she does as I ask, tugging and pinching the supple skin and sensitive tips of her breasts, a whimper slipping from her mouth. Can't believe this woman is with me.

A sudden crack and thunderous boom shake the tent, but Mother Nature won't drown me out. Louder, I give another command. "Move your hands lower. Glide them down your stomach, across your hips, in between your thighs, but don't touch yourself. Not yet."

As her hands move, so do mine. My speed matches hers, smooth slide for firm stroke.

"Slip two of your fingers inside your perfect pussy. Tell me how it feels."

Blakely parts her curls before pushing her index and middle fingers inside. Her head falls back, and a wanton noise fills the tent as she dips in and out of her cunt. "It feels good, but not as good as you."

I palm my cock. "Are you wet, Blakely? Tell me."

"Yes, I'm dripping. But I wish it was your thick fingers inside me."

"Are you close to coming?"

"Yes, I'm getting cl-close. You w-watching..."

"Stop," I breathe the word, barely audible over the pouring rain, but she complies with a whine. "Good girl."

Surges of lightning illuminate her flushed skin, her peaked nipples, the glisten between her legs. Need overpowers my intent to drag this out, and I crook my finger, beckoning her to me.

The air mattress isn't ideal for what I want to do, but there's no way I can stop. Blakely crawls to me, and fuck if the sight doesn't have precum leaking from my dick. When she gets to me, sitting her wet pussy on my abs, I demand, "Feed me your fingers."

Her pupils blow out, eating up the blue-green iris. Hand shaking, she offers it to me, and I lick her fingers clean, just like I did with the marshmallow earlier.

Rolling, I pin her beneath me and then move back, settling on my knees. "Put your legs on my shoulders." She follows my order without delay—little shit. Only listens when she wants to.

I spread her legs on either side of my head, knees hooked around my neck. Wresting her hips upward, I lift her lower lips to my mouth, relishing her, lapping and laving her cunt, my tongue delving into her before flicking over her sensitive bundle of nerves.

"Goddamn, your pussy is heaven." I release her clit and murmur, "Let me touch you. Give you what you need."

"P-put your fingers in me. I w-want them." I slip two fingers into her cunt and pump my hand. She twitches against my mouth and hand and moans. "More."

"Come on my tongue. You're close. Don't fight it." Two fingers become three, and Blakely arches with a choked sob.

Her orgasm explodes on my tongue as another crash of thunder shakes our small tent. I lick, suck, kiss—a man bewitched by this city siren who blew into my life like the storm raging outside—desperate to gather every drop of her release. I never stop stroking her, curling my fingers, prolonging her orgasm, keeping her quivering in my arms.

When she melts into a boneless puddle, I lower her legs and chastely kiss her stomach. "Get on your hands and knees."

She looks at me through heavy-lidded, lust-filled eyes and clamors to her knees, bouncing on the springy air mattress.

"Need help?" A glare is her reply, and I smirk and hold my hands up in apology.

Finding her balance, she tosses her hair and, grinning over her shoulder, says, "Don't make me wait."

I lay over her back and nibble her ear before kissing the tops of her shoulders and back. Then I line my cock up with her gorgeous pussy and thrust. I sink deep, my body flush against hers.

"Fuck, you feel so good. So tight and warm, always ready for me."

"More, Hudson, please."

I groan, her heavy pants and purrs for me to take her harder threaten to dissolve my control. Gritting my teeth, I pump my hips, driving deeper. She matches the punishing pace I set, pushing back against me time and time again.

My teeth nip her ears, jaw, neck, shoulders, anywhere I can reach. Blakely claws at the mattress, at the canvas walls, searching for purchase, but the tent can't give her the support she needs. So, I cradle her back to my chest and wrap my fingers around her throat, applying light pressure. My other arm snakes down her body, my thumb rubbing her clit as I pound into her.

Every flash of lightning, every roll of thunder is matched by a stroke, a touch, a kiss, a bite.

"You look so pretty with my hand around your neck, moaning for me. Give me all those noises. You love the way I fuck you."

A desperate keen falls from her lips, followed by a cry of my name. "Hudson! I'm so close. I n-need…"

Everything about this woman is fucking perfect. "What do you need? Tell me, and I'll give it to you."

"Deeper, h-harder."

Her pulse flutters under my palm as I give her throat one last squeeze before guiding her cheek to the bed. Snagging a pillow, I slip it under her so she'll have extra friction and plant one foot on the ground. With her ass higher and positioned for better leverage, I fuck her like tomorrow may never come. I clutch her hips, my fingertips digging into her flesh, holding her as if I can keep her from leaving me.

My balls tingle, and warmth spreads through me. Another couple of—

Pop!

We freeze. Before giggles—hers—and groans—mine—fill the air. "Not stopping. Too close." The mattress deflates beneath us, but it does nothing to stop me in my pursuit of pleasing her. "Need your pussy to strangle my cock and drain it dry."

I deliver a sharp slap to her ass, loving the pink blossoming there. She clenches around me, so fucking tight.

"Fuck that pillow, baby. Rub your sweet little clit against it."

Blakely humps the pillow, hungry mewls and desperate whimpers spurring me on—faster, harder. Her walls clasp around me, that familiar, exquisite tightening. We're both so close.

"Come for me, now." I punctuate my command with two more quick spankings.

The sounds of her pleasure drown out the rumbling thunder and bring me over the edge with her, and I fill her. Every nerve in my body sings her praises. Every bit of me lives for her.

Blakely collapses beneath me, my softening cock slipping

out of her as the lower half of her body sinks into the ruined mattress. She's a glorious mess, her breathing ragged.

I roll us, cradling Blakely to my body. I'll be damned if she's sleeping on the fucking ground. My fingers walk up and down her spine, and my lips kiss her damp skin. The salty-sweet taste tingles on my lips. "You okay?"

"Mhmmm."

"Need to clean you up."

"Too sleepy." Her voice is thick with contentment, and she snuggles into my arms.

I shift her, ignoring her little protest. Digging through our bags, I find the package of wipes and use one to clean the mess between her legs. I'd rather push it all back in...

Minutes later, Blakely's soft breath brushes against my bare chest. Masculine pride roars through me. I fucked my girl into oblivion. Brushing the hair from her face, I fist my cock, adjusting us so I can slip back inside her, not ready to lose the heat of her pussy. The feel of her around me.

I'm an idiot, but I'm not stupid, and I'm going to drink my fill of her while I can.

DAY TWENTY-EIGHT

The ambient sounds of wildlife moving in the dark stir me from sleep. My movement wakes Blakely, so I stroke her back, kiss the top of her head, and pull a sex-strewn blanket over us. My only goal is making her as comfortable as possible.

My dick twitches where it's buried inside her. She's wearing me like a glove, and it's goddamn exquisite.

"Shh, baby. It's early. Go back to sleep."

"Bear?"

"Yeah, Spitfire?"

"I love camping with you." She buries her face in my neck, her eyelashes fluttering against my skin.

Something warm swells in my chest, radiating outward like the glow of the sun. I pull her closer. "I love camping with you, too. Even if you're terrible at it." Slim fingers pinch my nipple.

"Rude."

Hours later, I wake to soft puffs of air against my chest, soft hair tickling my nose, soft curves under my hand, and the hard ache of the ground against my back.

I ease out of her, the desire to rub one out and mark her with my cum only outweighed by the need to take care of her. So I pile the blankets around her so she's safely nestled. A pouty frown clouds her face—a brat even in her sleep.

My brat.

"You'll be fine without me, baby," I whisper to her sleeping form. With the words comes a stirring of something ugly inside me. I don't want her to be fine without me.

Shit. I tug on my jeans and throw my flannel over my chest, not bothering to button it. Yanking my boots on, I crawl out of the tent, in need of a stretch and a piss.

The campsite fared better than I expected. Downed branches lay near the tent, but we didn't lose anything. I get to work, doing what I can to find tinder. I rake the coals, moving the dryer ones to the top, and once the fire is going, I set about prepping breakfast.

Two days. She's leaving me in two days. Even though we both know Trail Creek, being away from that influencer bull-shit, is better for her. While I don't agree with her choices, I have grown to understand them. There's a reason for the persona, for the mask, but goddamn, she's so much more without it.

The weight of it looms, heavy, hanging over me. I just met her, and now the universe is ripping her away.

The loud *zip* of the tent precedes Blakely's stumbling footsteps. She ambles towards the trees to take care of business before joining me by the fire. While she uses some of the water I boiled to rinse her hands and brush her teeth, I study her.

Her mussed hair, sleepy eyes, and, best of all, the large hickey on her collar. *Mine.* The possessive roar reverberates through me.

"Did you make this?" Her eyebrows rise as she takes in the fresh coffee and frittata.

I grunt, letting her know I cooked it all. Who else would've?

"You're such a fucking catch, Hudson Brooks." She stretches on her tiptoes and kisses me. As my tongue seeks hers, she pulls away and plops onto one of the camping chairs. "So, are you making a plate for me, or is this a self-serve situation?"

I let out a rough laugh. So goddamn sassy. If she were standing, I'd swat her ass. But like the whipped fool I am, I divvy up a slice of the eggy casserole and drop it on her lap. This pain in the ass, this thorn in my side, is the best thing to ever happen to me.

And then I fuck it all up by saying, "Stay."

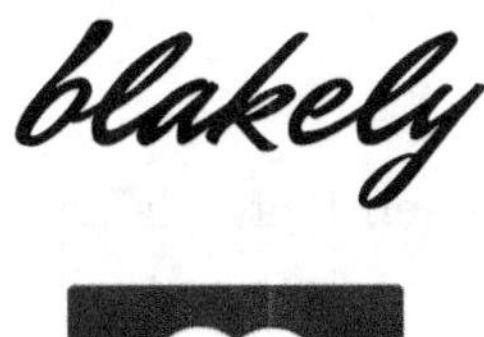

CHAPTER TWENTY-SIX

"Stay."

My heart aches at the word. I've spent years building a new persona for myself. With hundreds of thousands of followers, my social media empire has been my escape, my rebirth. I've transformed myself from the poor, unloved, small-town girl into a confident, glamorous influencer, living a life others only dream of.

Except the truth of how hollow that life is has become increasingly apparent, and it's thanks to Hudson.

He's not a man you have a fleeting romance with—he's a forever man.

I tense, my shoulders drawing up to my ears. Standing, I knock over my plate and coffee. "I, um, I need to use the restroom." Then, like a rabbit, I bolt. Each step toward the dense thicket of trees has my heart pounding, my chest tightening. Once I'm a safe distance away, I bend over, holding my head between my knees, fighting for air and composure.

The ground rises to meet me, and I'm on my ass in the wet

dirt and leaves. With shaky hands, I find my phone and dial the only person I can.

"BB! I'm going to see you in two days. Do you miss me so much you can't wait?"

"Kirk."

My voice breaks when I say his name, and he glances up. "Blakely? What's wrong? Is it Brandee? Are you hurt?"

"No. Not Brandee. Am I hurt?" I pause. "Yes, but it's my doing."

"What do you mean?"

"I mean, he asked me to stay."

Kirk's eyes widen. "He asked you to—"

"Stay, but that's the Hudson version of please move in with me."

"What did you say?"

I blanch. "I told him I had to use the bathroom."

Kirk winces in solidarity. "So he says stay, and you run for the trees?"

"Pretty much." I flop onto my back, not carrying if I'm lying in muck and mud. "What do I do?"

"Do you love him?"

I don't have to think about it. Yes.

Hudson with his adorable freckles on his rugged face. Hudson, grumpy and glaring while taking care of me. Teaching me. Seeing me, flaws and all—and returning for more. The lack of loneliness. The safe space to figure out who I might be. The nights spent in his arms, being loved by him, loving him.

"Yes, I love him," I say, looking around as if speaking my feelings out loud might change them.

"Then, and I know this may sound like a wild idea, why don't you stay?"

If I wasn't already on my back, Kirk's words would put me there.

"Don't look so shocked, BB. Do you remember what I said when I left you there?"

At my nose wrinkle, he presses on. "I said this was going to be life-changing, and I hope it brings you whatever you're searching for." He sighs. "And forgive me for making assumptions, but he's it."

"Kirk, I can't. My job. My life. It's all in Austin."

He fixes his eyes on me, discerning and knowing. "BB, what life?" At my wobbly lip, he softens his words. "What are you giving up? Fake friends like Mia—or worse, Ryan—who are with you for photo opportunities and brand collaborations. Nights spent in your apartment analyzing analytics, prepping posts, and responding to faceless comments. The occasional crashed holiday with Marcus and me."

My eyes fill with tears, and I bite my lip, trying to fight the worry away.

"Hey, we adore having you, and you are welcome with us. There's no question, but you only come because you're lonely. Who do you have for yourself, BB?"

I want to argue that I have people. Buster. Sylvie. Except Buster and Sylvie have been saying they're ready to move closer to their kids and grandkids for years. Are they staying because of me? Am I holding them back? Because they know the truth. Without them. Without Marcus and Kirk, I'm truly alone.

"I'm scared." My eyes close as I whisper. The very real fears of change, failure, giving up what I've created—and ending up trapped in a small town of judgmental people— swirl in my stomach. What if things between Hudson and me crash like every other relationship I've ever had? My own mother couldn't stand me. What are the odds Hudson will want me a decade, a year, even a month from now? Or worse, what if he loves me like I think he could, and it's still not enough? That I'm so fundamentally broken, I can't be happy.

Right alongside those are the fears of giving Hudson up and losing the potential future we could build together. A wonderful life so unlike my childhood, I almost can't picture it.

An existence where I'm loved and wanted. Always.

"I'll support you, whatever you choose, but you need to weigh it out. What's it worth? The money, the status, versus the chance for a complete life. I love you, BB. And your staying won't change that. You won't lose me; you won't lose Sylvie or Buster. But what will you gain?"

The call drops, but I don't move from my sprawled spot on the forest floor. It isn't until I hear Hudson, his footsteps so familiar to my ears, that I stir. Two large hands slide under my armpits, pulling me to sitting, then slip under my shirt, tracing patterns and soothing circles on my skin.

"You okay, baby?"

"No." Tears burn my eyes before spilling down my cheeks. I turn into his touch, burying my face in his chest. It's too much to think about—the idea of staying, everything Kirk said, the crushing weight of reality—so I snuggle into his arms and let the welcome comfort of his scent and warmth soothe me.

"Shhh. Breathe." One of Hudson's hands settles on my chest, applying pressure and forcing me out of my head. "It's time for us to go back home."

Without waiting for an answer, he gathers me into his arms and cradles me close. I don't argue about being too heavy or the trek being too long. I drape my arms around his neck and let the tears fall.

In a desperate attempt to lighten the mood I ruined, I say, "I'm so tired of crying. At this rate, I'll end up like a cornhusk doll."

Hudson grunts. Which I take to mean *you're hilarious, Blakely.*

When we get to the cabin, Hudson carries me straight to the bathtub, never letting me go, even as he fiddles with the temperature. He adds my bath oils, salts, all the things I use. Only when he goes to remove his clothes does his grip loosen.

Giving him a small smile, my chest quivering as I try to steady my breathing, I undress. But even that moment apart, not touching, is too much. Desperation takes control, and I grab his hand, needing his skin on mine to ground me.

Hudson climbs into the oversized tub first, then helps me step in, guiding me between his legs. He draws my back to his chest, hugging me to his body. We stay this way, not talking, just touching each other, cuddling together in the warm water.

Eventually, Hudson shifts and sweeps my hair to the side, his lips pressing to the sensitive spot below my ear. "Tell me what happened."

I shake my head. "Not yet."

He sighs, but then says, "Alright. How about I wash your hair?"

God, this man.

Grabbing his hand, I bring it to my lips, kissing his knuckles, his joints, the tips of his fingers. The hint of his smile against my neck has me quivering. "Yes, please."

With purposeful movements, Hudson undoes the twin braids running around the back of my head and shakes my hair loose. It falls in waves around my shoulders, and I groan when he tangles his hands in the strands, fingers digging into my scalp.

He reaches around me and grabs my shampoo. Nipping my ear, he says, "Remember when I used your shampoo, and you lost your shit? And saw me naked."

The heat of his chuckle against my neck has lust slithering through me and my pulse beating between my legs. But I can't dull the pain with sex. Well, I can, but it won't make the problem disappear.

I scoot down and hook my ankles over the lip of the tub, floating between his knees in the deep water. Once my hair is wet, Hudson helps me sit and lathers the shampoo into my tresses. His fingers massage my scalp and nape of my neck.

He cups water in his hands, rinses the suds, and then repeats his actions, finger-combing conditioner through my hair, working away the tangles and snarls. When he goes to rinse the conditioner, I stop him.

Rising to my knees, I twist so I'm straddling him. "My turn."

Hudson nods and leans back against the tub, gripping my hips as I lean over him, dripping water on his head. "What are you going to do about all your gear?"

His closed eyes flutter open. "Hmm? Oh, the campsite shit? It's fine. You're more important."

My heart seizes. "What if you came with me to Austin?"

Hudson stiffens. It feels like hours pass before he speaks. "Blakely, I can't. I can't be happy there. And I have obligations."

"Obligations." I huff out a mirthless laugh.

He grabs my hands and pulls me closer. "Yes, obligations. To my brothers. My parents. My business. The town."

"And what about me?"

I want to scream. Even with this man who is my person, I don't make the list. Will there ever be anyone who—

"You mean more than everything, so don't let that shit twist in your head." Hudson grips my hips. "But it's not practical. And I'm sorry for that."

Another damn wave of tears falls against his cheeks and lips. "I'm sorry, too."

"There are other ways—"

I cut him off with a shh. Do we need to talk? Yes. But it hurts too much. So we stay quiet, holding each other until the bathwater turns cold.

DAY TWENTY-NINE

I blink open my swollen eyes, hoping I imagined the entire ill-fated end of our camping trip and bath from the night before. But the dull ache behind my eyes and heart tells me it's all too real.

Hudson coming with me is a pipe dream. He has a life here, a far more fulfilling one than what I have in Austin. If I'm too scared to give up that sham, I can't be mad that he won't give up the idyllic world he has here.

One day.

Tomorrow, I go back to Austin. Back to my picture-perfect apartment. Loud parties. Louder people. An empty, lonely existence. And away from him.

The awful throbbing in my chest grows, and my lungs threaten to seize. Doing my best to fight the impending panic, I run my fingers through Hudson's hair. Then, I trace the outline of his handsome features, memorizing the shape of his lips, the universe of freckles, the lines of his nose, and the arch of his brow.

It's funny—not funny, haha, but funny strange—how he can simultaneously be the cause and solution to my pain.

Warm green eyes open at my touch. "Morning."

"Good morning." I brush my lips against his.

Before I can deepen the kiss, Hudson stills me, taking my

arms in his large, rough hands. "About last night and tomorrow—we need to talk."

"I don't want to talk."

"There's no more time." Hudson sighs and drapes himself over me, his head burying into the curve of my neck. "We have to talk. About us. About tomorrow—"

"No." I need one last day of happy memories. "Let tomorrow be the day the real world comes knocking. Today is for us." My throat is thick. "Please."

Hudson sighs, but cups my cheek and presses his forehead to mine. "Why can't I deny you anything? You say please, and I lose all sense."

I pull him down, loving the weight of his body. He always holds his full weight back. Even so, the heft of his solid frame comforts me. He's like a living weighted blanket. I wrap my legs around his hips and press as much of myself to him as I can, drinking in his outdoorsy scent, the warmth of his skin, the scrape of his beard, the feel of his corded, finely honed body.

"Is this how you want to spend the day? In bed? Because I'm okay with that," he whispers against my neck, his teeth grazing against my skin.

"For now, yes. I want to hold you, for you to hold me."

"What else do you want?" he asks as he kisses my collarbone.

What do I want? More time. Him. To love him and to have no doubts about staying here. To take a chance.

But rather than the truth, I say, "Your arms around me while the sun sets over the lake." *One last perfect memory with you.*

hudson

As the sun sets, I think about our first time hiking this same path, that disastrous first day where Blakely had a fit over sore, aching feet. Feet I rubbed and soothed without even thinking of why I was doing it. Already captivated by her. Then I think about the second hike, the sunrise she didn't film, the one that will always belong to us no matter what else happens.

And then, her asking me to come with her plays in my mind. I asked her to stay, and she countered. But I can't leave. I can't. I'll never be happy in Austin, but if she gives it a chance, Blakely can be happy here. Maybe that makes me a pompous, delusional asshole, but she belongs in Trail Creek. She belongs with me.

More frustrating than all of it, though, is her refusal to talk. To make a decision. She pushed it off, and I let her.

I hold her—watching her watch the sky change. There will never be a sunset or sunrise, a star-strewn sky, that holds a candle to Blakely. New shades dance across her skin, bright orange fading to hot pink and burning to rich violet. I'm struck once again by her beauty. My body reacts on instinct, lips sweeping over the sensitive spot behind her ear, along her jaw, down her shoulders. Blakely's fingers lace with mine, pulling my arms around her waist. When the final bits of gold disappear I help her to her feet, and we return to the place we've shared and made a home for the past month.

The moment she burst into my black-and-white world, a beautiful, bratty, pretend princess, Blakely changed me. She brought color and joy and things I didn't know I was missing. But I never thought I'd long for her to stay or of how empty my life will be without her loud, frustrating, life-altering presence.

How did this happen? How did I fall head over heels for a woman like Blakely Bradshaw? A woman never meant to be mine. But the thought of her leaving makes me want to tie her to our bed with knots so intricate she can't break free. I draw her closer, her breath hitching as I brush my hands up her back and down her sides.

"It's your last night. Tomorrow you leave. No more tiny one-room cabin for you, Princess. Unless—"

She silences my attempt at bringing up the looming threat of tomorrow, pressing her fingers to my lips. The shudder she gives when I nip at the pads makes my dick twitch. But when she stays quiet, I frown—willing her to say something. Anything.

Kissing her knuckles, I pull her hand away. "I've tried to figure out how to make you stop talking for the last month, and now you go silent on me?"

"Don't call me Princess."

There she is—my Spitfire.

She unbuttons my shirt. Her lips travel from my neck to my collarbone, before stopping over my heart. Can she hear my desire, my love, with every beat? It's ridiculous, the effect this woman has on me.

Her hands travel lower, skimming my thighs with the tips

of her fingers. When she ghosts over my cock, I stop her. It's my turn. I take my time. I want her scent, her flavor, her touch burned in my brain.

But more than that, I want her to be mine. Forever.

"Stay," I mumble against her neck between open mouth kisses.

"It's not fair to say that while your hands and lips are on my body, Bear." She deflects my attempt to talk about tomorrow, and instead, pulls me to our bed. The place where I've come to know her inside and out over the last month.

I can't wait another second. My hunger for her overwhelms me, and I crush my lips to hers in a bruising kiss. I swallow her moans, my tongue coiling with hers. Breathlessly, I pull away before blazing a path down her jaw to her neck, the rough edges of my teeth scraping against her skin, eliciting shudders from her body.

My mouth moves lower, down her sternum, nipping at the skin between the valley of her breasts before taking one of those perfect pink nipples and working it with my tongue and teeth until she's arching up from the bed. I know the signs of her body, how much is too much. I have a motherfucking PhD in Blakely Bradshaw.

"Fuck me, Blakely, you have the best tits." Cupping her breasts reverently in my rough hands, I push them together before nuzzling my face against her hard nipples, worshiping her body as befitting a goddess.

I push a knee between her legs, teasing her before pulling away. "So eager. We have all night. Need you to be patient."

Like a petulant child, she shakes her head and pouts. "My bratty Blakely, you better watch that lip, or someone's gonna bite it."

At my words, she pushes her bottom lip out further and stomps her foot into the mattress for good measure. Oh, she's getting a spanking. I nip her plump lip and give her inner thigh a sharp slap.

"Hudson. I need you."

"And I told you to be patient. If you're a bad girl, I'll keep you right on the edge, aching to come, dripping and desperate until the sun comes up."

Her panted pleas for more drive me lower. She's writhing and mewling as I nibble the back of her knees and my fingers creep up her thighs. When my fingers ghost over her pulsing pussy, she bucks her hips.

With a smirk, I pin her to the bed, locking her beneath me. A piece of me longs to draw this out, to make her beg, but another part wants nothing more than to give in. To spend the night buried in her, tasting her, fucking her, pleasing her until we're both too tired to worry about what dawn will bring.

"I plan on savoring you. Especially if this is our last night together." The pain of that thought tempers my lust briefly before it comes roaring back.

"Please, Bear. I need you." The power she has over me should be disturbing. There's still so much we don't know about each other, but there'll never be another for me.

"Open your legs, Spitfire. I promise I'll give you what you want. Let me take care of you."

One finger turns to two, stroking the heat between her legs, stroking the craving within me. More. I need more. To watch her come undone with my fingers and my mouth. To relish her flavor on my tongue. To savor her delicate scent. To feel her—the throb and quiver of her cunt around my fingers. The coat of juicy slick on her thighs as she grows wetter and wetter. With a groan from me and a choked sob of my name from her, two fingers become three.

My hunger: ravenous. My thirst: unsated. "I'd bathe in this

pussy forever if you let me. You gonna make a mess, baby? Give me a shower?"

"Hudson, wh-when you say things like that. Oh, fuck me. Pl-please keep going."

"Moan for me, Blakely. Give me those noises."

She falls, and I feast while fighting to keep from coming against the blanket. Her cries curl in my ears, but I continue caressing her insides, lapping at her pink pussy, only stopping when she whimpers *no more*. I'm aching to sink my cock into her, for her to come again, to gorge myself on her ecstasy, but she swirls her finger in the air. With a hungry growl, I flip us, guiding her spread legs over my hips.

She's a queen on her throne, staring down at me. Everything about Blakely calls to me. Like a dying man to water, I'm in her thrall.

"Fuck. You are a thing of wonder. I need to be in you. Now."

My greed for her overtakes me, and in one fluid snap of my hips, I'm seated inside her. Every inch of me buried.

"God, Hudson, you feel so good." Her whimper has me swelling inside her.

"You were made for me, Blakely. This hungry pussy is where I belong. I have to stuff my dirty girl. Isn't that right? Your greedy cunt needs my cock."

"Y-yes!"

"Tell me. Say you need my cock."

"I need it!"

I slam her down as I thrust upward. "I said, say you need my cock. Word for word, Blakely. Say your greedy cunt needs my cock." Fuck, I have to hear her say it.

"My greedy c-cunt needs your cock. Give it to me, Bear!"

Fucking hell. She tightens around my cock, her hips rocking frantically. Her walls tighten around me, pulling me somehow even deeper.

I brush my thumbs over her nipples before my hands wander lower, going to her hips and guiding our connection. My eyes fasten on where our bodies join, watching Blakely ride me. I need to cement this moment in my mind.

Goddamn, I love the way her skin flushes, the way her wild, tousled hair falls, framing her gorgeous face. I close my eyes, focusing all my other senses on her. The indescribable pressure of her wet cunt gripping my cock. The refrain of her breathy moans. The smell of sweat, of sex, raw and unbridled. When I open my eyes, it's to Blakely staring at me, passion, desire, and something deeper written in her gaze.

Overcome with the desire to touch more of her, I sit up, capturing her earlobe between my teeth before burying my head into her neck—my breathing ragged. Fingers claw my back and shoulders, and I'll wear those marks with pride. I snake my hand between our bodies, my fingers dropping to her clit, knowing my touch will bring her to the edge.

I starve without her pleasure. Only her pussy clenching around my cock, the heated rush of her release spilling onto my thighs, the wanton cry of my name from her lips can sate me. It's a banquet—a bounty.

But then her tears spill onto my shoulders, and the drive to comfort her takes over.

"Fuck, Blakely, are you okay?" My hands go to her hips, guiding her to stop and easing my frantic thrusts.

"Yes, don't stop."

I hate myself, but I don't argue with her. *Fuck.* I'm so damn close. She squeezes her pussy muscles and moves her body in tandem with my faltering rhythm, even as tears land on me in salty splats. All it takes is one more powerful clench around my cock, and I spill myself inside her.

"What happened?" I ask. Concern she's hurt has me

searching her over. When I don't see any physical signs besides the tears, I wipe them away.

"I-I'm embarrassed." She tries to turn away, but I tighten my grip on her chin and tilt her head so her eyes fix on mine.

"What do you mean? After all we've been through and learned about each other? We've seen each other in ways neither of us expected." My voice drops. "I've touched every inch of you, licked every inch of you. Seen you vom—"

She gives me a death glare, and I smirk. "Why are you embarrassed?"

"*Iloveyou.*" Her eyes close, as if that can make her disappear.

She loves me. She loves *me*. This isn't a sleep-and-sick-induced confession. No. This is her declaring it.

"Open your fucking gorgeous ocean eyes and look at me. I love you too, you beautifully infuriating creature."

With her admission, those three words, I find myself hard again, hungry again. When she falls forward, her lips crashing into mine, I roll us and bury myself in her. This is no frantic fuck. This is slow, purposeful. Each thrust deeper than the one before. My goal? To fill her completely. To meld my soul to hers.

This time is different for more reasons than I can count.

When I come, I whisper how much I love her in her ear and hold her, not ready to pull out, to lose the physical connection or the emotional one. We lay like that, bodies locked together, sweat, breath, and cum mixing until finally, I press my forehead to hers and repeat my single plea. "Stay."

"Hudson, I…"

At the welling of tears, I hold her tighter. I inhale, filling my lungs. She's the sweetest scent I've ever known, and tonight has been just about perfect. The sunset, making love to her, telling her I love her. But it's still not enough.

This conversation has been haunting us for weeks. And here it is. There are no more tomorrows. No more hiding from the truth. No more running. There's only now. Yet, I can't bring myself to continue despite my insistence on our need to talk. Not tonight. Not after she admitted she loves me.

She's everything I never expected to find. A partner to share my life, to love, whose strength and spirit keep me from being so alone. With her, I can just be. Grumpy, direct. Content with my lot in life. She sees me and loves me.

Though I'm reluctant to let her go, I slip out of bed, grabbing a washcloth to clean her up. Then I gather a few blankets, and we make our way to the porch. She loves me; I love her. The choice should be easy. Right?

She curls up in my arms as though she's always known them. I stroke her hair, let my fingers walk the curves of her body, and hold her.

Can I give up my life here? My family, my business, Trail Creek? Can I leave my home of the last fifteen years and go with her on a new adventure? I've answered that question with myself time and time again, but fuck if the idea of being with her doesn't have me asking it again.

Or can she? Can she give up the city, money, bright lights, and bustle and be happy with me? Am I enough? Old doubts resurface.

"Rest." My lips brush against her ear.

She deserves more. More than me. More than Trail Creek. But I'm a selfish bastard. And I can promise she'll never find someone who loves her more.

Neither of us speaks; the only noises in the air are the rustling of trees and our breathing. Eventually, with a content sigh of my name, Blakely relaxes, the heavy tow of sleep too much for her to resist.

I stay awake hoping I can somehow will the earth to slow

its spin for a night—however, time marches on, heedless of my plea. With a sigh, I let my head fall back on the swing. There's no point in sitting on the porch all night. No. I'll spend tonight in our bed, tangled in her glorious grasp.

Carefully, I pick her up and carry her inside, laying her on the bed we've shared for a month. I slip my fingers into her silky hair, smirking as I think about how she pouted and shouted her way into the bed after our first night. How our days were full of bickering, but somehow, each morning, we woke wrapped around each other. How she somehow wormed her way into every aspect of my life. This infuriating, petulant, wondrous woman.

And though it pains me, shatters me, I know. Deep down, I've always known what the morning will bring.

CHAPTER TWENTY-EIGHT

DAY THIRTY

Like I knew it would, the sun rises on day thirty, and me with it. I don't move. Instead, I lay still, my eyes fixed on the exposed beams overhead. The weight of my choice weighs on my head and my heart.

God, I love him. I can't believe how much, but it's only been thirty days. Is a month long enough to leave everything behind for someone I'm still getting to know? Even if I stay, I have an entire life back in Austin to shore up. An apartment to sell, my job... okay, so not an *entire* life.

I've been out of pocket for close to thirty days and not one faux friend has reached out to ask how I am. The blaring silence of the people waiting for me in Austin says it all.

Why am I such a chicken? Why can't I be as brave as I was at seventeen? I started over once. I can do it again. Right?

As quietly as I can, I creep to the front porch, grabbing the antique quilt from the back of the couch on my way. The blanket smells like Hudson. Like the cabin. Wrapping myself up so I'm cozy, I launch the app where I have the most followers.

Several people sent me DMs with screenshots of Brandee's latest posts. My nostrils flare in annoyance. Clearly, my asking once isn't enough. I mass delete them, not bothering to read or reply.

Out of habit, I fix on my fakest smile, but as the countdown for my camera finishes, I drop it. No more faking it.

"Hey, BBs. I wish I had another month, or," swallowing, I look up, trying to blink tears away, "year out here, but today is my last day in Trail Creek." My voice catches in my throat, and I have to stop until I can compose myself. "This has been the most amazing experience of my entire life. Yes, Hudson plays a key role in that." I let out a tiny laugh. "But beyond him, I've learned so much about myself and what I can do. I've learned I can build a fire. I can identify berries and found out the hard way that, in many cases, you need to cook them before you eat them." Hearts are flowing in, more than I expected, given the early time. I was kind of banking on there being a small turnout.

"I learned how to shoot a bow and arrow. Gained a new appreciation for my GPS and discovered there are four thousand different knots, and they all have their own purpose." My smile is real—no need to fake it now. "But more than that, I learned about who I am. Turns out I don't need the glam squad —not that I don't love them!" I blow a kiss and wink into the lens. "Turns out, I also like my thirty-three-year-old face without all the contouring, highlighting, and over lining. I'm stronger than I knew. More capable than I ever expected."

Looking into the camera, I clear my throat. "The person you think you know isn't who I want to be. Some may think this is in reaction to my mother, but it isn't. It's because of my time out here."

I pan the camera around the clearing as the first rays of the sunrise filter through the trees. "On a serious note, please do not send me any pictures or information about Brandee Shaw. This is a line I can't compromise on." Sighing, I wipe away a tear. "BBs, I hope you book a trip out here. It's amazing. The entire experience with Peak Adventures, with Hudson, has been truly life-changing."

The rising pinks, oranges, and yellows wash over me as I end the live. A cough from the door tells me I'm no longer alone. I glance at Hudson and find him watching me in return. Today's the day I break my heart.

Hudson joins me on the porch swing, and the first words out of his mouth aren't *morning, I love you*, or even *want coffee*. No. They're, "Don't go." As if he's heard my stream and expects my answer.

Turning, I lay my forehead on his chest, arms slipping around him. "How much of that did you hear?"

"Enough to know you decided."

"Hudson, I have to."

He sits up, pulling away from me. "When?"

"When do I need to leave?"

"No, when did you decide? How long have you known you'd be leaving, no matter what I say?"

"J-just now. I—" I take a deep breath. "I love you."

"But?" Hurt and confusion flicker across his face.

"But I can't."

With a grunt, Hudson stops the swing, his feet dragging against the porch before leading him to the cabin door and leaving my hands empty and reaching. "Pack your bags. We leave in twenty."

A thousand knives to the heart couldn't hurt more than his cold, detached words. It's my fault. I did this to us.

He doesn't speak while I pack, but he does make me a

coffee. For a second, when he's handing it to me—and our fingers brush, and our eyes meet—I think he'll say something, but he doesn't.

I want to yell. To pout. To throw things and demand he do the same. Force him to give me anything besides the chilly indifference.

So I press.

"Is this an apology coffee?" Nothing. "You could at least help me pack." Crickets. "Have you seen my pink lace panties? They're missing. They look like these, but pink." I flash my hip and the red lace there. Zilch.

This isn't my Bear. This is the man I met on day one.

Twenty minutes later, I'm hauling my haphazardly packed suitcases out to the Jeep. Hudson follows behind me, his hands in his pockets. He watches me try—and fail—to hoist the biggest bag into the cargo space. One of those work-rough hands—hands that have traced every inch of me—settles over mine, and a flight of birds takes off in my stomach. But all he does is guide me out of the way and jerk his head to the small suitcase.

Together, we load them. Together, we climb in the Jeep. Together, we are silent.

So many times, I start to say *turn around* or *let's go back,* but then the fear takes over, and the words die on my tongue. Eventually, I give up, resigning myself to a silent trip to Trail Creek and an ugly ending to a beautiful month.

We're making slow time, like the universe is colluding to keep us together—as if I don't already regret my decision. The

Jeep creeps down the not-a-road. The recent rain and cool night temperatures have turned the steep, narrow ruts and grooves into a muddy, slippery mess. We pass a handful of downed branches, limbs, and one actual tree. Which means an already difficult journey is now even more so. Like always, Hudson is vigilant, his eyes scanning the area, his speed steady.

The mood in the car, however, is fraught and charged. With each passing mile, the tension builds—a powder keg waiting for a spark.

Forty minutes in, everything explodes.

Out of nowhere, Hudson slams on the brake and throws the Jeep into park. His hand clamps onto my thigh, squeezing. It's as if my leg is a tether, and if he lets go, we'll both shatter. Desperation laces his tone as he says the first words he's spoken since telling me to pack my bags. "Why Blakely? Why can't you stay? What's waiting for you back in Austin?"

Tears sting my eyes. "I can't walk away from my life. I can't give up everything I've worked for."

"Why are you fighting this so hard?"

"It's my life."

In an echo of Kirk's words, Hudson snarls, "What fucking life?"

"It's lonely and fake, but it's mine. I built it! All on my own. I came from nothing and turned myself into someone, and now I'm supposed to go back to being no one? A tiny dot in an even tinier town?"

"You were never no one. You were a scared little girl then, and you still are. And how do you handle what scares you? You run. You hide. You're scared of us. Scared that we could be fucking fantastic, and you don't know how to stay and face it."

"Yeah, everything about this conversation screams *fantastic.*"

"Admit it, Blakely. You hate Austin, and you hate your job. Staying here means people to help you deal with your mother, a community around you, but it also means no more masks. And you're scared shitless to talk about it."

"A community? Hudson, I know what small towns are like. They'd sooner turn on you than help you."

"Trail Creek is different."

I scoff. "This isn't a Hallmark movie where the small town is magic."

The tendons in his neck strain, rigid and tense. "You want to say it's not magic? That's fine. But it sure as shit changed you. And up to today, I'd have said for the better." He yanks on the gearshift, and we're on the move again. Moving toward Trail Creek. Toward me leaving.

"You don't get to decide I'm bad because you don't like that I'm leaving." My voice grows haughty, slipping back into my Blakely Bradshaw persona with surprising ease.

"I don't get to decide anything." His voice is flat. Distant. Done.

"That's not fair. I asked you to come with me and you refuse, but I'm the one being unreasonable?"

"Yes."

In a cartoon, this is the point where steam would be coming out of my nose. The one-word answers. The non explanations. "You can't accuse me of running from the conversation when you do the same damn thing!"

His shoulders stiffen, and he tilts his chin toward me; it's such a small movement that if my eyes weren't locked on him, I would've missed it. "I'm not running. I've made it clear how I feel."

"When?" I gesture wildly. "You said stay. I said go. You said no. Where's the clarity?"

The long, frustrated breath he lets out is my only answer.

My hand trembles as I caress his bearded jaw, but he turns out of my touch. "Hudson, look at me."

When he gives me his attention, there's a turmoil of emotions written in the furrow of his brow, the strain in his shoulders, the way his hands clench my leg and the steering wheel. Anger. Hurt. Confusion. Love. I see it all and know it's reflected on my face.

Without thinking, I lean forward and kiss him, despite knowing it's dangerous. I want to erase all the pain. Comfort him, pour my love into him. The Jeep swerves, and with a muttered *fuck,* Hudson breaks the kiss, jerking away as he straightens the wheel.

"Goddammit, Blakely," he swears, eyes locking on the road. "You kiss me like that, but you're still leaving! What the fuck am I supposed to think? Maybe I was right; this was all a ploy from the beginning. A fucking fairytale to boost your numbers. Maybe that vapid on-air girl was the real you all along, and the woman I fell in love with was the mask."

His harsh words slice me, but I get it—it's easier to lash out than to face reality, and I respond in kind, wielding my words like a whip. "And maybe the man I fell in love with was an asshole all along, and the one who said he could see beyond my mask was the liar."

"Fuck, Blakely. I'm sorry. I—" He shakes his head, cutting off his apology. Then he presses his lips into a thin line. "Are you so afraid to admit that being here is where you belong that you're gonna give it up? Give us up?"

"You don't get to do that. Be mean then try to turn this around on me."

"That's not—"

I cut him off before he can say anything else. Words pour from me like my mouth is a broken spigot. "Of course, I'm afraid. How can I not be? I already started over once before.

With nothing. Do you know how hard that is? No, of course, you don't. You've had your parents and brothers every step of the way. You have no idea what it's like."

"Don't you fucking get it? It wouldn't be that way this time. You wouldn't be alone. You'd have me. Why can't you see that?"

Everything is spiraling. This isn't how our last day together was supposed to go.

"If I'm scared, so are you. You could come with me to Austin, but you won't because you're scared you'll find out your brothers don't need you. That the business can run without you." I'm escalating things, and for a man like Hudson, these are fighting words. "How many times did you call them Hudson? Text them just to check in."

The knuckles on his hand gripping the steering wheel turn white. His voice is hard. "I'm not afraid. I have obl—"

"Obligations? To what? To your parents? To your brothers? You're thirty-five years old. They're twenty-nine and thirty-three, not seven and eleven. Your brothers can take care of themselves. They don't need you to save them. Think of what you want for once!"

He slams his hand on the dashboard so hard I worry the airbag will deploy. "I am thinking of what I want! I fucking want you! Can't you see that? For you to stay here with me where you fucking belong! So we can build a goddamn life together!" He roars the words, and for a moment, there's nothing but pure silence between us. Mine shocked. His seething.

Hudson's frustration-filled eyes flick to mine for just a moment. Less than a second. But that's all it takes. Without warning, the world shifts. Hudson's arm shoots out, bracing me, and he's yelling my name. Tires screech and a rumble sounds like the earth is collapsing around us. Everything twists.

Turns.

Spins.

A blur of green, brown, and gold. Crunching metal. Snapping branches. Breaking glass.

Searing pain. Two loud *pops*.

And then nothing.

I blink my eyes open, but the world looks wrong. Off. Tilted.

Shit.

Why does everything hurt? A steady throbbing radiates from my right shoulder to my left hip. There's white dust all over my clothes. Mud and an acrid chemical scent fill my nose, along with the coppery tinge of blood.

What the hell happened?

Then, like a nightmare unfolding, I remember. The fight. A flicker of tawny fur darting across the road from the treeline. Hudson yelling my name. His arm holding me in place as the Jeep spins. His arm falling away. The crunch of metal crumpling as it battles rocks and trees. Blissful silence.

Wait. His arm falling away.

With a shaky hand, I swipe at my eyes, trying to figure out what I'm seeing. Out my window are trees. Towering trees. And a hint of sky.

The shattered windshield fractures and distorts everything in front of me, like looking through a kaleidoscope of mud and underbrush.

And to my left is...

A whimper slips from my mouth. Hudson lays slumped over in his seat, his leg bent at an awkward angle. I've spent thirty days with this man; he's not into yoga.

"H-Hudson?" No answer.

I cough, doing my best to dispel the itchy powder coating my throat and lungs. "Hudson!" My voice is scratchy. Louder than before, but he doesn't respond.

"Shit. Shit. Shit." I mutter over and over, the word morphing into a frantic mantra as I reach for him. Or try to. I'm trapped, my seatbelt doing its job—to the point of pain— holding tight across my torso. The pressure on my shoulder and chest makes getting air almost impossible. Although, that could be the impending panic attack.

"Shit. Shit. Shit. Shit. Think, Blakely. Think."

My hands flit around me until I get my brain online enough to pat my seat in a desperate search for my phone. But it's gone.

I force myself to inhale for four and exhale for five, then five and six, then six and seven. Once I'm no longer seeing spots, I unlatch my seatbelt. Which—*duh, dumbass*—means I crash into an unconscious Hudson.

"Shit. Sorry, Bear." He doesn't move or react to my weight pressing against him, including against his *it-should-not-be-facing-that-direction* leg. "Why am I talking? You can't hear me. Right? If this is some last day of wilderness training hazing, it's not funny. Or the silent treatment because of our fight?"

Panic sinks its claws deeper, dread slithering in alongside it. *I have no idea where we are. My phone is missing in action. I'm sitting on top of an injured Hudson. Shit, shit, shit.*

Snaking a finger under his chin, I press against the pulse point in his neck. "Don't you dare be—" my whimper cuts off my words. I can't. I can't.

But then, there's a soft *blub* under my thumb. Then another. "Thank fuck." I press a kiss to his temple. "I was going to be so mad at you if you left me here." Brushing dark hair out of his eyes, I whisper, "Dying is no way to win a fight, you asshole."

When he doesn't answer, I crawl into the trunk space, sitting with my suitcases. I take a moment to scream and cry. I rage at the universe, the cosmos, the ether, a variety of deities. Myself. Hudson. No one is spared during my tirade.

And then I get to work.

I check Hudson's pulse again—more for myself than anything else. Feeling the steady thump calms my own thready heart. Bracing myself between our seats, I dig in the glove box and thank the stars Hudson is who he is. The emergency kit hidden away helps move the task of *me* getting Hudson out of the Jeep and somewhere safe from outright impossible to merely implausible.

Choking back the urge to curl up next to my Bear and cry—again—I steel my nerves. Carefully, I pop the passenger door open, relieved when it stays, rather than swinging back and bashing me in the head. With our exit point ready, I take three deep breaths.

Closing my eyes, I release Hudson's seat belt latch. The only positive about the Jeep lying on his side is that he doesn't shift. Stabilizing myself as best I can, I slide my arms under his and maneuver him out from behind the wheel.

"Fucking hell, Hudson, you weigh a ton," I grunt as I try and fail to move him. Another handful of futile tugs and the dread I'm battling morphs into full-blown panic.

Why did this happen? I can't leave him here alone. Not when he's not awake. But I'm not strong enough to rescue us. Hudson is the strong one. Physically. Emotionally.

He's the one who has the skills to get us home safely. The one who always knows what to do.

The one who wanted to talk things out and begged me to stay.

I'm the screw-up. The one no one sees or wants, who has to hide who I am for people to like me. The one too scared to stay when it's all I want. A useless mess.

My mother's alcohol and time-ravaged face flashes in my mind. Her sneer. Her taunts. Ignoring me unless she can embarrass me or belittle me. Her attempts to weasel and con her way back into the new life I made for myself.

All my failures.

I can't navigate. I can't tie a knot. I can't take care of myself. How the hell am I supposed to save us?

Hudson stirs and lets out a soft moan. The quiet noise stops the runaway mine train of intrusive thoughts in their tracks. It's the first sound he's made since screaming my name while the Jeep crumpled around us. The pain lacing through that single sound has me fighting off a matching sob.

I have to be strong. For him. For myself. Be the Blakely, the Blake Lee, he sees and loves. Because he does. Love me. See me.

Throwing my shoulders back and lifting my chin—in the best approximation of a power pose I can do while squatting in a tipped-over Jeep—I manifest safety. Success.

Delulu is the solulu, right?

"I'm Blakely Bradshaw. I'm not a spoiled princess. I'm a self-made one. And that means I can do hard things. Hudson believes it, and it's time I stop letting him down." My pep talk gives me a boost, and in some *mother-lifting-a-car-off-her-kid* moment, I haul his hefty ass out the door. Except I'm me, which means he tumbles out the side and onto the wet earth below.

"Ohmyfuckinggod."

The fall isn't far, but it doesn't stop the alarm bells shrieking in my head, reminding me of things like spinal injuries and traumatic brain injury and a thousand other things I'm not remotely equipped to handle. I scramble out the Jeep door with all the grace of a drunk elephant, landing on my knees amongst the slippery pine needles.

Crawling to where he lays, I make him as comfortable as I can. He groans when I straighten his bent leg, but his eyes flutter open. "Blakely." My name comes out a gruff croak.

"Bear, you scared the shit out of me. If you weren't hurt, I'd smack you," I say as I pepper his face with gentle kisses.

"Are you okay?" He slurs his words, and his pupils are giant, but at least he's awake and talking. Of course, the first thing he's worried about is me. Not his injuries. Me. Because that's who Hudson is.

Almost losing him—the possibility of losing him still—chills my heart. My fingers tremble with the need to touch him. To prove to my lizard brain he's here. I skim my lips over his, a buss of a kiss. "A few bumps and bruises, terrified beyond belief, and relieved you're awake." As I speak, flashes of pain twist his handsome features. There's a large bruise forming on his forehead and his leg... even though I straightened it, it's not lying right.

His normally golden skin is pale, and sweat beads on his hairline. I don't know much about shock, but if I was betting, I'd say he's close to it. But Hudson, being Hudson, raises his hand to cradle my cheek. "Never forgive myself if something happens to you. I'm so fucking sorry."

"Why are you apologizing?"

"My fault." His lids lower, and his hand drops away.

Shit.

"Hudson, stay awake. Please, Bear, I need you to stay with me."

He doesn't respond, so I pat his cheek. When that doesn't work, the pat gains a little more force. It works, and his eyes lock onto mine.

Everything in me wants to crawl into his arms and let him comfort me, but this time, I have to be the comforter. The caretaker.

Smoothing his hair, I murmur, "First, this isn't your fault. It was an accident. Your arm kept my head from smashing into the dashboard. Hear me?"

His eyes crinkle. The Hudson to human translator I've picked up over the past month tells me this is his way of saying he hears me.

"Second, does anything else hurt? Third, tell me what to do." The last is a plea. I need him to stay awake long enough to get us out of here.

A smirk tugs at his lips before twisting into a grimace. "Knew you could follow orders." His nostrils flare, and the war he's waging against showing me how hurt he is plays on his face. "Splint. Stretcher. Cabin." He grits out each word.

Cabin. There's no way I can get us to the cabin. Even with Hudson at a hundred percent, I couldn't navigate us back. But that's future Blakely's problem. Now Blakely has enough on her plate.

Hudson's hand searches for mine. I lace our fingers together and bring them to my lips. "I'm going to take care of you, Bear."

My mouth is dry, and my chest aches as I run through the massive list of things he's taught—or tried to teach—me over the last thirty days: the first aid lessons, the basics of securing a campsite, and surviving overnight in the wild.

Fuck.

I climb back into the Jeep, snagging the emergency kit and my suitcases. After a lot of shoving and cussing, I get them out.

I dig through one bag, then another, searching for painkillers. It's over-the-counter stuff, but anything is better than nothing. Grabbing all the leggings and long-sleeved shirts I brought, and a flannel I stole from Hudson, I hurry back to him.

I'm only gone a couple of minutes, but even in that small amount of time, he's worse. Struggling to stay awake. His breathing sawing in and out. He never answered my question about being hurt anywhere else.

I drop next to him, supplies in hand. "Open your eyes. I have some medicine for you."

Carefully, I help him sit up, once again thankful for Hudson's preparedness. Cracking open the bottle of water, I do my best to pour water into his mouth, followed by several of the painkillers. "I know you're sleepy, but please, stay with me. I need you. Okay?"

The nod is almost imperceptible, but it's there.

"I have a knife and rope. What else do I need?"

"Branches."

I tip a little more water into his mouth and chase it with a kiss. "Don't go anywhere."

He huffs out a brittle laugh, but I've never heard a more beautiful sound. I pop two of the ibuprofen before draping the flannel over him and using my softest leggings to create a makeshift pillow. With one last kiss, I go branch hunting.

The good news about crashing the Jeep where we did is that branches abound. I collect a variety. Small brittle ones that will make good kindling, medium-sized ones I can use to fortify the fire, and large sturdy ones to help brace his leg and make a shelter.

It takes several trips back and forth until I have a sizable pile. Each time I come back to the Jeep, I talk to Hudson. He responds, though his words are getting progressively slower and garbled.

"Bear, walk me through this. We need to get your leg set."

Hudson's hands tremble, and his freckles stand out in stark contrast to the pallid pallor of his skin. Fighting for each word, he says, "Use the knife." He pauses, his breathing labored. "Cut my pants from the ankle up."

I do as he directs, careful not to cut him or myself. I brace myself for blood and bone, but blessedly, it's only bruised and swollen.

Swallowing, I look at him. "What next?"

But he doesn't answer.

"No, Bear. Don't fall asleep."

He grunts and grumbles. "Branch. Tie. You can do—"

His words fade, and the fears I held at bay while he was awake come roaring back. No amount of love taps or shaking rouses him, but he is breathing easier, so I convince myself rest is what he needs.

Grabbing two branches, I set them on either side of his leg. Surely, I can figure this out. "I have to attach the sticks to you somehow. Right?" I crane my head so I can see his face, but there's no guidance there. "I'm taking your silence as a yes."

Using the knife and my teeth—Dr. Holly would have my head on a platter if she knew, but a seriously injured boyfriend trumps orthodontia—I take one of my shirts and cut and rip it into thin strips. I save the rope in case I have to tow him out of here.

I frown at Hudson's sleeping form. I refuse to think of him as being unconscious. "You said stretcher and cabin, but that isn't happening. Here's the new plan. You better be listening." I lean closer, hoping if I'm bratty enough, he'll wake up and spank me. When he doesn't stir, I sigh. "I'm going to splint your leg; then I'll build a shelter and a fire and find some food. You sleep a little longer, but when I'm done with everything, you're going to wake up and be okay. You hear me, Bear?"

In my thirty-three years, I've had my share of bad. A mother who cared more about drinking and men than me. A mother who withheld love. A moth—okay, a whole heaping pile of Brandee. Dropping out of high school. Being forced out of my hometown as a teen. Never knowing my dad. String after string of fake friends and lovers who saw me as a tool rather than a person.

But all of that—every bad memory, every hungry night, every collected hurt—pales to the idea of losing Hudson.

My throat is thick. "You h-have to be okay." A series of strangled sobs burst free. "I love you. I w-want to stay with you and b-build a life together. So you c-can't leave me now." Tears drip from my eyes to his cheeks, rolling into his beard, little salty shimmers. I drop a kiss to his forehead, wipe my snotty nose with my sleeve, and haul myself to my feet. I have tasks to complete.

Hudson is a man prepared for all kinds of scenarios. It's like he sat down and thought, *Hmmm, what might happen? Oh, I know. Blakely and I will head into town, get in a massive fight, nearly hit a deer, and I'll be rendered useless. Better make sure she can't kill us.*

The tarp, flint and steel, and additional cordage tucked away in the cargo hold make my to-do list so much easier. My foraging skills lead me to a cache of beef jerky and granola bars, which beats poisonous berries every day of the week.

It takes a handful of hours, a fair amount of swearing, a few crying breaks, and more sweat than I care to admit, but I get everything done.

"Is the shelter a little janky? Yep. Are my knots looser than they should be? Of course. Did I yell at you more than once while trying to drag your ass onto the tarp? You bet," I prattle at Hudson, not expecting an answer. But my voice echoing off the spindly aspens and pines towering around me is better than the suffocating silence.

"I also built a rock ring and a fire like a boss. Layered my clothes on the tarp to make us a semi-comfortable nest and used an obnoxiously bright dress I didn't wear to create a marker on the road. This way, on the off chance anyone is looking for us, we'll be easier to spot."

Hudson mumbles something and tries to turn onto his side.

I scoot next to him and cradle his shoulders so he can't move. "Hey, no complaining. While this may not be your level of skill, I did the damn thing. We aren't dying on my watch."

He makes another pained sound, and I smother a matching one. I lift his shirt, careful not to jostle him. What I see has my eyes cutting to the sky as I fight off another round of tears. His ribs are black and purple, centralized around his right side. He's been asleep too long. My bruised body begs for rest, but I can't fall asleep. Not while he's passed out. Because if something happens—

Bile climbs in my throat, but I force it and my rising panic down. It won't do either of us any good. He's breathing, he's stable. We have heat. We have shelter. We're going to make it.

Snuggling closer to Hudson, I run my fingers over his stomach and chest, trace his handsome face, count every freckle. When the sun sets, I whisper my plans for our future so his dreams will be sweet, while demanding the universe watch over us.

Hudson Brooks is my second second chance, and I'll be damned if I let anything take him away.

CHAPTER THIRTY

DAY THIRTY-ONE

Pain shoots from my leg through my rib cage and into my head. *What the fuck happened?* On the cusp of my memory are awful sounds: brakes squealing, metal crunching, and Blakely's screams.

With every ounce of persistence, determination, and bull-headedness I possess, I will my weighted eyes open.

The sun shines early morning light around me, all mellow golds and burnt oranges. I'm surprisingly comfortable, given the entire right side of my body feels like my Jeep crashed down a bank and into a tree. There's a pile of clothing beneath me and, below that, a tarp. Random clothes and the emergency blanket I keep in the cargo space cover me. As my eyes adjust to the light, I notice the makeshift lean-to built using the bottom of the Jeep as a wall. Smoke drifts over me from the banked ashes of a fire.

Fucking hell. She did this. I was less than useless, and my city siren kept us sheltered and warm overnight on her own. If

I hadn't already planned on worshiping Blakely like the badass goddess she is, this would cement it.

The deity in question sleeps curled up beside me, her head in the crook of my left shoulder, her nose pressed into my armpit. So fucking cute. God, I love her. She makes a sweet snuffling sound and rubs her face against me.

I want to pull her closer. Sniff her hair. Kiss her forehead, but I can't move. My leg screams, and my ribs burn. The pain in my head is a dull throb, so that's a win. A dry chuckle bubbles up—some win.

Gently shaking her, I say the one word that means more than any other. "Blakely."

Her eyes flutter before squeezing shut. Even on a good morning, Blakely struggles to wake before nine, but given the amount of work she did yesterday, the adrenaline drop, and her own injuries, she must be exhausted.

"Come on, Spitfire, I need you." Speaking is like tearing my throat with sandpaper, but I force the words out. I need her to be okay. For her to be here and whole. To confirm I didn't lose her. That I still have a chance to keep her.

She grumbles and frowns, the lips I've kissed a hundred times pouting. Then awareness hits her, and she shoots up. "Shit! Shit. Shit!"

Her voice is like a river running over rocks, leaves rustling in the wind, and the coyotes singing. Magic. Perfect. Home.

Even if she's cussing like a sailor.

There's dirt on her cheeks and her hair is an untamed mass of waves around her head. She's the most beautiful thing I've ever seen.

Then I spot the purple spreading across her chest from the neckline of her tank top under her open layers. My eyes trace what my hands can't. "I'm so fucking sorry."

Blakely smooths my furrowed brow. "Don't worry about me, Bear. I'm fine."

Her lips brush against mine, and while my instincts are to sink into the kiss, the pain rises, and I have to break away.

With a worried look, she gets up and goes to the fire, poking and tending it until it flickers to life. The temperature is dropping. You can smell the cold coming. Another night out here won't be pleasant.

My leg throbs at the thought. Forcing myself into a leaning position, I look down for the first time. Blakely did a damn fine job splinting my leg, bracing it between two branches, and fastening it with strips of soft cloth.

"It's one of my shirts."

"Huh?"

"The binding. I didn't want to waste the rope." She nibbles on her bottom lip, her nerves evident.

I nod. "Smart. Good choice."

"Really?"

A smirk worms its way onto my lips despite the fire spreading through my body. "Hell yeah. You did so fucking good."

Pink colors her cheeks. I love that this has her blushing. The same woman who let me lick her perfect asshole is turning red because I told her she did a good job on a splint made from aspen branches.

The praise I long to heap on her is on the tip of my tongue. To tell her how much I believe in her. How fucking strong she is. How she's it for me. All I manage is, "Blakely, I love you."

"I love you, too. So much. The idea of leaving—"

"Hudson! Blakely!"

A familiar voice sounds in the distance. Blakely and I lock eyes, whatever she's about to say gone as we hear our names shouted again.

"Blakely Bradshaw! Hudson Brooks!"

I crook a finger until she's face to face with me. "We'll finish this conversation once we're safe and checked over. Agree?"

She nods and kisses me.

Shutting my eyes, I fight the needles in my throat and holler, "Bo!"

Blakely claws her way up the incline toward the road as she shouts, "Bo! Gray! We're here!"

They volley back and forth until their words drop, replaced by two heavy sets of stamping feet I'd know anywhere—my brothers.

Bo gets to me first, concern and worry etched on his face. "Shit, man, we've been searching for you and Blakely for hours. Started around four this morning. The Austin guy lost his ever-loving mind when you didn't turn up at the office, and he couldn't get ahold of her."

Gray joins my youngest brother, his eyes surveying the situation. "Yeah, and then you didn't answer either, and we figured shit had gone off the rails."

I can hear more people moving toward us. The crunching leaves and slap of hiking boots against the wet ground grow louder as a group of close to twenty people pour into the area around the Jeep.

"You were all looking for us?" Disbelief laces Blakely's words.

No sooner than she speaks does Lynn Davis engulf her in a motherly hug, pulling a dry sweater over her head and fussing over her. The rest of the Davis family—Scott, Charli, Waverly, and Clairy, Bond and his wife Tuesday—hover around Blakely, too. Clairy follows after her mother, wrapping my girl in a tight hug, whispering something to her. Blakely's eyes are like saucers in her face as person after person comes by to check on her. Griff Anderson, Dane Mendoza, Saul, Ava and her kids, and so many others from town. All out here for us.

Because this is who Trail Creek is—good people who do good things.

I watch as Blakely excuses herself from the group, making her way to my side. "They were all looking for us." She repeats the words from earlier.

"Yeah, baby. They were."

"All morning. Even before the sun was up."

I don't say anything, just let her detangle this in her mind. Let her see how the people here aren't like the ones from Hawthorne, who turned their backs on her when she needed them. Instead, they show up. This is one giant step forward in rebuilding her trust in others, and if I can convince her to stay, the town will prove it to her.

More people arrive, each kitted to spend the day searching for us. Tears glisten in Blakely's eyes, but she stays quiet. I wish I could read her mind right now. I'm about to ask her what she's thinking when a fresh onslaught of pain rockets through me, and there's no hiding it.

"You look like shit." Bo lets out a loud whistle as he studies our setup. "You're losing your touch, Hudson. This shelter won't last another night."

Blakely arches one eyebrow and stares at Bo, but doesn't say anything. Bo keeps digging the hole he doesn't even know he's in, one stupid shovel full at a time. "EMTs are here. Need 'em?"

Before I can answer, Blakely snaps. "Yes, he needs them." To the arriving paramedics, she says, "His leg is broken; I think his ribs are too. They're at least bruised. And I'm pretty sure he has a concussion."

My brothers stare at Blakely, mouths wide enough to catch

flies. "He's that hurt?" Gray asks, taking over the digging for Bo.

"Why the hell else wouldn't I be standing?" Silently, I tag on, *moron*. A soft *fuck* slips out as the EMTs work to transfer me from the ground to the stretcher.

Gray has the good sense to look embarrassed. Two red spots sit high on his cheeks. "I figured..." He cuts off and tips his head at Blakely.

If I wasn't about to pass out from the pain, I'd be laughing. Blakely stands, turning the full force of her frustration on my middle sibling.

"You figured what? That I was the problem? I was the one hurt and keeping us from being able to get to town? Well, shows what you know. I did this." She waves a hand, the chipped pink polish not slowing her down. "Now get your head out of your butt and help them get your brother up that hill!"

One of the paramedics tries to wrangle Blakely long enough to take her blood pressure, but she squirms away, refusing to separate from me. She puts her hands on her hips, the picture of the willful, headstrong woman I love. "I'm riding with him."

I don't mention there's only one ambulance. "They need to check you out, too."

She snorts and glares. "I'm not worried about me. What are we waiting for?" To Pippa, the sweet woman who works as an EMT and part-time at The Bee and The Bean, Blakely says, "You can check me over after you get him loaded." With that, she picks her way to the road, giving waves and thank yous to everyone she meets on her way.

A smile stretches Bo's lips. "Marry her. Whatever it takes, man. Marry her."

The haze of the meds the EMTs pump into my veins takes hold, and my last coherent thought is, *I sure as shit plan on it.*

DAY THIRTY-TWO

The air around me is stale, sterile. But something sweet lingers on the edge of it. Something Floral. Soft.

A scent I would recognize anywhere.

Blakely.

"Morning, Bear." Her breath fans over my cheek, and the slight weight of her body grounds me. She reaches up to cradle my face, but I snag her hand, mindful of the wires and IVs decorating my skin. Bringing it to my lips, I kiss her knuckles before running my nose over the delicate skin of her wrist. Each deep breath fills my senses, drowning out the antiseptic hospital air.

"Morning."

"How do you feel?"

I grunt and try to adjust the pillow behind me before the ache of the movement reminds me why that's a shitty idea. Blakely shifts off the side of the bed and helps fix it.

"Hate that I need help with everything."

The smile that lights up her face temporarily eases my grumpy mood. "Let me take care of you for a change. It won't be forever. Before long, you'll be back as the undisputed HCIC."

I raise an eyebrow. "HCIC?"

"Head Caretaker In Charge."

My snort makes my ribs ache, but I hide my grimace. They had me in and out of surgery within a couple of hours after getting us to the hospital, and aside from the time I was under, Blakely and I haven't been apart. She sweet-talked the on-duty nurse into letting her stay in my room overnight and ended up sleeping in my arms—where she belongs. Between her and the pain meds, I slept like a goddamn baby.

Blakely stretches out next to me, cuddling as close as possible. My lips find their way to the crown of her head. "How about you?"

"I'm fine. Like I've told you every time you've asked since you woke up. Bruised and sore, but nothing's broken, and there's no internal damage."

Have I asked three or four or five times? Yes. Fucking sue me. The nurse comes in and out, only threatening me twice when I give her one-word answers. With morning rounds done and visitor hours not quite starting, I have the opening I've been waiting for.

"Yesterday, before Bo and Gray showed up, you said something about leaving." I'm bracing myself for her to run, to ask me if it can wait. Or worse, to say she's been waiting for an all-clear to leave.

She tilts her head back. "Is this your way of asking what I was going to say?"

I roll my eyes and nod.

"If you weren't a day out of surgery, I'd pinch your nipple."

"Don't threaten me with a good time, baby."

Her giggle is like a caress on my soul. How will I live without it if she leaves?

"Hudson, look at me." The ocean in her eyes is full of warmth and love. And something else. Hope maybe? "Coming so close to losing you gave me perspective on things. You asked me to stay, and I told you I couldn't. But that was a lie. I could. I can. Fear was holding me back, but the idea of being without you, not seeing your grumpy ass every day, is the scariest thing I can think of."

"You're staying?"

A wrinkle forms between Blakely's brows. "I'll repeat it

because you recently suffered a head injury. I'm staying. You're stuck with me, Bear."

"What about your apartment? Your job?"

Blakely kisses me, sweet and searching. When she breaks it, she whispers, her lips still touching mine. "Are you trying to talk me out of staying? After everything? I mean, you wrecked your Jeep to keep me here."

I chuff out a breath. "If anything, the accident was your plan. What with kissing me and all."

"Nope. The kiss came well before the crash. It was clearly a ploy to strand us so I couldn't go back to Austin." There's no bite to her words, only the familiar teasing tone I love. The playful bickering. The way she presses and pushes me. Her. "Kirk and I talked while you were in surgery and recovery."

"About what?"

Just as Blakely opens her mouth to answer, the man in question knocks on the door. "Hey, you two. How are you feeling?"

Blakely untangles herself from me to hug him. "I was telling Hudson about our plans."

Kirk nods. "Good. I've already had multiple offers from sponsors for the new direction your socials are taking. And a local realtor sublet the apartment for the remainder of your lease, so you're good to go. Moving company is hired." He pauses and glances at me. "One little thing, though, I didn't have an address to give them."

I'm a smart man. Blakely makes me an idiot, but away from her, I'm smart. Maybe it's the pain medicine pumping into my veins, the lingering effect of the concussion I suffered, or exhaustion, but I'm not following.

"Don't think too hard, Bear. You're still concussed."

"Yeah, Bear. Don't sprain your brain." Bo walks in with a

shit-eating grin. Behind him is Gray, his arms full of stuffed animals and mylar balloons.

"Not really into little pink teddy bears," I grumble.

"Bold of you to assume they're for you." Another voice joins the fray. "They're actually for the beautiful young woman who saved your life." My mother pushes both Bo and Gray out of her way, coming over to my bed and cradling my chin in her hand. "How are you?"

The freckles on her face match mine, and her eyes are warm as she studies me, watching for any hint of a lie.

"I'm good. Pain is manageable. Hoping they'll send me home tomorrow."

My father steps into the overcrowded room, his large frame eating up any leftover space. "Son." He nods at me, then leans against a wall out of the way.

"King, get your butt over here and hug your son." My mother scolds him before extending a hand to Blakely, who retreats to the far side of my bed with each arriving member of my family. "Blakely? Right? King and I just got into town this morning. We've been in Victoria for the past few weeks and flew out as soon as Bo called us."

"She doesn't need our life story, Lisse."

Instead of being upset at my father's blunt tone, Blakely rolls her lips to hide a smile. Leaning closer to me, she whispers, "So that's where you get it."

I frown and grunt, proving her point.

"I'm Lisse Brooks, and this big lug is King. It's so nice to meet you, sweetheart. We've been watching you all month long, and the two of you—" Mom dabs at her eyes. "You're so fucking cute."

The shock of my mother dropping an F-bomb breaks any lingering tension, and soon, she and Blakely are chatting like old friends. My dad watches us from the wall with a soft smile.

When my eyes droop, my nurse shoos everyone but Blakely out. Despite not doing anything, I'm tired as hell. I'm over this shit.

Blakely dims the lights and snuggles close. "So we didn't finish our conversation. Again. It's becoming our thing, huh?"

"Nope."

She raises both brows. "Care to elaborate."

"We aren't gonna be that couple. We're gonna talk."

"Are you including yourself in this?"

"Smartass." I nip her bottom lip. "Yes."

With a laugh, she smiles. "Okay, Toastmaster, let's hear it."

Shit. I clear my throat. "You finish, then I'll go."

"Uh-huh." Her plump lips press against mine. "So, an address. I don't have one anymore. Know anyone in Trail Creek looking for a roomie?"

"Kirk was serious? You gave up your apartment in Austin?"

"Sure did. And mapped out a new direction for my channels. I'm currently on hiatus, but it's going to be big. I don't know if you know this, but it turns out I'm not too bad at this wilderness stuff."

My lips pull into a smile. "Yeah, when push came to shove, you were a badass."

"I figure there are probably a lot of women like me. Who may never be up to spending a month alone in the forest but would still like to learn the basics from someone who speaks their language." She pauses. "But it all depends on you."

"Me?"

"I'll need to learn more if I'm going to teach others. Plus, I really need somewhere to live."

I bark out a laugh that rattles my bruised ribs, but it's worth it. "I know of a little place."

"Oh?"

"Yeah. Became available recently. Previous tenants were only there a month."

She nods sagely. "Because it was a secluded sex-torture cabin?"

"No. I mean there was sex, but no torture, unless you count the roommate who never stopped making noises. Even in her sleep. She talked and snored and snuffed."

"That sounds like a blatant exaggeration. If there was any torture, I bet it was at the hands of a know-it-all grumpass."

Despite the dull ache in my side and leg, I pull Blakely's mouth to mine in the kiss I've been dying to give her since the fight in the Jeep. One that holds every promise I plan to keep. Every tomorrow. Every fight and makeup. Every beautiful failure and miraculous high. I don't pull away until I'm certain she understands the message. Until I can find the same promise in her kiss.

"Did you find your phone?"

Her eyes widen. "I can't believe you're asking. I figure you'd be thrilled at the possibility it was lost forever."

I make a *hmph* sound.

"Bo found it. It's in bad shape, but it still works." She unlocks it and hands it to me. The screen is shattered, but I only need it to send a text.

I'm slow and clumsy, and it takes forever to type out the message. When I'm done, I toss the damned thing on the floor. It served its purpose.

"Who were you texting?" she asks.

"Just sending Kirk your new address."

"Yeah?"

"Yep." I tuck a stray hair behind her ear and give her one more soft kiss. "Looks like you'll be roughing it with me from now on, Spitfire."

"I wouldn't have it any other way, Bear."

epilogue

DAY ONE THOUSAND FOUR HUNDRED NINETY-ONE

"Okay, BB's! That's it for today. Thank you for liking, sharing, and subscribing! We'll see you in two weeks, where I'll talk more about how you can sign up for our spring Princess Package." I wave my daughter's chubby hand at the camera before blowing it a kiss.

Hudson, Kirk, and Marcus watch from the porch as I make my way inside. Willow totters on wobbly toddler legs, doing her best to beat me. She reaches her dad, and he scoops her up, blowing raspberries on her tummy and neck. Adorable peals of laughter sound around us.

"Great live, BB. Your sponsored post with that new hiking boot company is bringing in massive clicks and sales." Kirk grins as he gives me a quick update. I'm much less invested in the business side of my socials these days. Now, I post what I want when I want, take sponsorships from companies I want, and spend way less time online. It's glorious.

He clears his throat, "So, Brandee?"

I shake my head and sigh. Four years of flat-out ignoring the woman, and she still rears her hateful head now and then in an attempt to get money from me. My petty side thinks of making a donation in her name to the Hawthorne food bank, but that would mean engaging. So I'll make the donation anyway and never tell her.

Hudson's arm wraps around my waist, pulling me close. "We sent a cease and desist notice. If she violates it, we'll go from there."

"Are you guys sure you're up to Willow-sitting overnight?"

Kirk rolls his eyes. "Yes. Besides, King and Lisse pick her up on Wednesday, so it's only two nights. And she's excited to stay with her favorite uncles." He tickles Willow's tummy. "Isn't that right?"

"Don't let Bo and Gray hear you say that. Those are fighting words." Hudson's lips tilt in a half-smile.

"They get to be her favorites all the time. Let me have this." My manager, and friend, steals my daughter away, he and Marcus closing rank around her, cooing and heaping her with love.

Already, her little life is so different from mine. She'll never know what it's like to be hungry, dirty, unloved thanks —in no small part—to the amazing community around us. Kirk and Marcus, Bo, Gray, and the people of Trail Creek continually prove how much they love and support my family. Me.

"Okay, Lolo, have fun with Uncle Kirk and Uncle Marcus. I love you." I kiss Willow's honey-blonde curls as Hudson carries her tiny suitcase to the car.

The practical SUV bounces down the road, heading to Kirk and Marcus' vacation home, a few streets from where we live in the Davis Designs built Piñon Hills neighborhood. Once they're out of sight, I power walk inside and up the stairs to our lofted bedroom.

I have delicious plans for my gorgeous husband, but first, I have to pack. Then he and I are heading to our cabin for four kid-free days. Willow will be two next month, and while Hudson and I find plenty of opportunities to connect, this is our first time staying away from her for multiple days.

And I am here for it.

"We leave in ten," Hudson barks from the living room.

I look at my empty bag, and like he knows, he adds, "I mean it, Spitfire. I'm leaving your cute ass here if you aren't packed and ready."

Rolling my eyes, I stick my tongue out even though he can't see me. Some things never change.

But so many other things do. The framed pictures decorating our bedroom are a testament to that. I pick up one from our wedding, me with flowers in my hair and Hudson with a jaw-cracking smile on his face.

I toss in everything I need for a couple of days at the cabin. Aside from some soft, warm clothes, I'm bringing some specialty items. A naughty thrill slinks down my spine when I spy them. Toying with my lower lip, I decide it's time to get things going. I'm setting the tone for our getaway now. I'm banking on the entire drive being nothing but foreplay, and that starts with giving Hudson a sneak peek of what awaits him.

I slip off my oversized sweater and pull down the cups on my lavender bra. My nipples pebble when they meet the cool air. Perfect. Using my elbows, I plump my breasts together and angle the camera to capture the tops and rosy tips.

With a smile, I hit send.

From downstairs, I hear a muttered swear. Fighting back a giggle fit, I fire off another text.

A moment later, my phone buzzes. I bite my lip, imagining what he sent. Letting the anticipation build. My finger hovers over the screen. I wouldn't mind a chest pic. Maybe an ass shot? If he's feeling feisty, a dick pic? As much as Hudson's grown and mellowed when it comes to being on camera, there are some things he still balks at. He'll sext with the best of them, but my phone remains sadly selfie dick pic free. The ones I have, I had to take myself. Rude really.

Then I open the message.

What the hell? There's no sexy photo. Nope. Instead, there's a close-up of a pile of my clothes.

BEAR

Yanking up my bra and jerking my shirt on, I stomp down the stairs to the living room. "You're such an asshole!"

Hudson smirks and shrugs. "It's the dirtiest thing I could think of."

"This is not the kind of dirty I wanted, and you know it."

He steps into my space, fingers slipping under the bottom of my sweater, brushing against my stomach. "Love when you shiver for me, baby. And don't worry, we've got the next four days all to ourselves. You won't need a picture to remind you of what's yours."

His lips flirt with mine until I part them, inviting his tongue to tangle with mine. A hungry moan pulls from my throat, and I lace my arms around him. One of his hands goes to my hip, squeezing until he breaks away.

"If you kiss me like that, we won't make it to the cabin."

Pants thread my words. "You should fuck me on the floor before we go."

He spins me around, holding me tight to his chest before nipping my ear lobe. "I'm gonna fuck you all over our cabin, Blakely. The floor, the bed, the shower, the kitchen table, the countertops, against every wall. You're gonna have muscles that ache like you ran a goddamn marathon and my cum in places you didn't think you could when I'm done with you." I clench my thighs together, his filthy promise curling around me.

Then, with a quick swat to my ass, he sends me back to our room to finish packing.

Asshole.

"You're staring."

I glare at the side of his head. "How do you always know?"

"Situational awareness." He turns his head and winks. "Plus, you can't keep your eyes off me."

He's not wrong. I've spent most of the drive imagining all the dirty things Hudson and I will get up to. Each one a stream of lust, all joining together to rush over me. Damn this man and the desire he fuels in me. Without saying a word, I reach my hand out and skim my fingers against his lap.

"What are you doing?"

"Pull over, Hudson."

"Pull over? Do you need to pee? We're ten minutes away."

"No! Really? *That's* what you think I want?" I sputter.

"If you don't need to pee, what could you possibly want—" His words die in his throat as I palm his cock through his pants, a thrill thrumming through me as he hardens at my touch. "Blakely." He lets out a warning growl.

I unbuckle my seat belt and perch on my knees before lowering my head to rub my nose against his growing bulge and laying chaste kisses against his upper thighs. "Do you want me?"

"Yes." He grits the word out between clenched teeth and gently tangles his fingers into my hair. "Yes, I fucking want you."

"Then either do your best to keep us on the road or find somewhere to pull over."

In a flash, he steers the vehicle off the unpaved road and throws it into park. I unzip his pants, and he lifts his hips enough for me to tug them past his knees. Shifting slightly, I arrange myself over the passenger seat and Hudson's thigh. Then, with a mischievous smile, I kiss the tip of his cock before running my tongue down the length. As I work him with my mouth, Hudson's fingers play with my hair while his other hand skims over my back and ass.

"Not that I am complaining, but what brought this on?" he asks, his breathing picking up speed as I reach between his legs to cup his balls.

"I'm thinking about the first time we made this drive, how far we've come, and how I'm so in love with you. It just made me happy, and then I was picturing us, our bodies locked together, your mouth on my neck, your hands on my back... and I decided I can't wait. I have to have a taste." I wink before lowering my mouth back to his cock, swirling my tongue around his plump head, relishing his groan and the way his thighs shake beneath me.

I try to grind against the gearshift, but the angle's wrong, and I can't get the friction I'm searching for. Hudson reads my need and jerks my leggings down, his fingers gliding over my ass before dipping into my wet heat and then tracing back up.

Over and over. Never deep enough to get me off, but the sensation is delicious. And will be repaid in kind.

He bucks against my face and swears, but before I can undo him, he pulls back. "I need inside you." Lust and love seep into his words. I crawl into his lap, brushing my pussy against his rock-hard dick and crushing my lips to his in an air-stealing kiss. Rolling my hips against his cock, I grind down as Hudson grips my ass in his large hands. He gulps, his head falling back against the headrest as I lick his Adam's apple and nibble on his neck.

I love driving this man to the edge.

Like I'm moving in slow motion, I lower myself onto his cock at a painstaking pace until he fills me to the hilt. He goes to move his hips, but I lift, easing him out of my pussy. "I want to play, Bear, but I'm in charge. Are you up for it?"

His grip on my hips tightens, and his green eyes flash. I run my tongue along his neck, impatiently awaiting his answer. It's a rare treat when my grumpy outdoorsman gives me complete control, but it's so fun when he does.

"Yes." He breathes the word against my lips.

"Then you better get us the hell home," I say as I take him back inside me.

With a snarl, Hudson throws the Jeep into drive, and we take off. A little quicker than he normally drives, but still cautious—despite my being impaled on his dick.

I suck on his neck hard enough to leave a mark, but when he tries to thrust up, I scold him. "Uh-uh, naughty boy. I'm keeping my cock warm. You and it have a lot to do when we get to the cabin. But no one's coming until then."

"Fucking hell, Spitfire, you're killing me." The steering wheel groans and I know his knuckles are white with pressure. Seven minutes of bumpy road and excruciatingly glorious teasing later, we make it.

Hudson all but jumps from the Jeep, me still wrapped around him like a koala.

"I need my bag." He lets out a pained moan at my declaration.

As I unhook my legs from his hips—and his dick from my pussy—he tries to hold me in place, a scowl on his face. Years of knowing and loving Hudson Brooks, and I've never seen him pout. Get mad, get annoyed, storm off, sure. But pout? That's my thing. But here, in this moment, he's full-on, bratty-lip pouting.

I nip his plump bottom lip and raise an eyebrow at him. "You clearly need some reminders about who's in charge, Bear. Put me down." When he releases me, I stroke his cock, wet from my pussy. "Now, be a good boy. Take off your clothes, and wait for me on the bed."

For a second, I think he's going to call it. The rules are firm. If anyone says *red,* everything ends, my Bear just yanks up his pants, huffs out a breath and stomps inside.

Such a grump. I love it.

When I open the cabin door, Hudson's waiting for me. He's on his back, one arm behind his head, while the other strokes his thick cock. The urge to let those thighs crush me and ask for more floods my mind and my panties. God, he's sex on a platter. Four years have done nothing to dampen my need for him. Forty years won't. Because when it comes to him, I'm an addict. I crave Hudson Brooks.

With a grin, I drop my bag and dig until I find the green jute rope.

Hudson's eyes narrow. "What do you have planned?"

"A demonstration of how far my knot-tying skills have come."

"What else do you have in that bag?"

"An assortment of items one might need to survive in the

wilderness. If you're good, I'll show you. Now," I smile at him, "are you up for this?"

I can see the wheels in his mind turning, emotions flickering across his handsome face. Eventually, he smirks. "Do your worst."

"Oh, this is going to be fun. Hold your hands up to the headboard."

Hudson does as directed, and I slink onto the bed and up his body. "I'm going to tie your wrists to the headboard. If you want me to let you go, say stop or red."

He nods and situates himself. "I'm comfortable." He raises an eyebrow. "Tell me what kind of knots you're using."

"Oh, you dirty talker." I kiss the side of his neck, making sure to hit the same spot from earlier. I want that mark visible for days. In a husky voice, I say, "I'm starting with a single column." As I talk, I wrap the forest green rope around one wrist. In between steps, I kiss up and down his arm, murmuring how much I love him into the crook of his elbow and kissing his unbound wrist before repeating everything.

Hudson lifts his arms, and I loop the rope through the wooden slats of the headboard. As a reward, I grind against him as I work, punctuating my words with moans as I find friction. "Then finishing with a double half hitch."

The sight of my big, burly Bear bound before me sends another aching wave of need through me.

"Fuck, baby, you're so goddamn sexy. What are you gonna do with me now that I can't go anywhere?"

"Nothing you won't like, I promise." I rise from the bed and make my way to the kitchen. The heat of Hudson's eyes burns into my back, so I make a show of it. Swinging my hips, stretching up on my toes to get a glass, and slowly bending over as I fill it with ice.

"Why do you need ice?"

"You are full of questions tonight, aren't you?"

He grunts but doesn't respond.

"Relax, Hudson. I'm going to take good care of you." I pop an ice cube in my mouth before crawling between his legs. Starting just above his knees, I kiss my way upward until I get to his inner thigh. Taking my time, I nip and suck closer and closer. Then I snake my tongue out and trace the vein that runs along the underside of his ruddy cock. "Mmm, you taste like us."

"Yeah?" he asks with a husky moan.

I smile and kiss higher, exploring his body. I'm enjoying myself—thoroughly. When I reach his chest, I snag a piece of ice from the cup and run it over his nipples before chasing the cold away with my warm kisses. The small gasps he makes at the dueling sensations send a screaming surge of desire to my core. I drag ice down his stomach, enjoying how his muscles flex beneath me until it melts away. Before going any lower, I pop another ice cube between my lips. Then, with a coy grin, I suck him into my mouth.

He sucks in a gasp of air at the change of temperature, and a pool of moisture builds between my legs at the sound. The soft scrape of rope against wood tells me he's fighting to bring his hands to my head.

"Fuck, Blakely." He groans as I swirl my tongue around his dick, the remnants of the ice cube melting in my mouth and dripping down the length of him. "God, your mouth. So fucking good."

I take him deeper, delightfully obscene slurping noises filling the air in our cabin. Hudson bucks his hips, thrusting against my mouth, a string of curses and praises pouring from his lips.

"I fucking love you. Your sassy mouth swallowing my cock."

Opening my throat, I take as much of him as I can, gagging myself before relaxing and taking even more.

"Just like that. You're doing so good. Let me feel your throat around me."

I slide my hand between his legs and gave his balls a gentle tug and a squeeze. The headboard scrapes. There will be scuff marks on the wall in the morning.

"I'm so close, baby."

Oh, I know.

Hollowing my cheeks, I focus on the velvety softness over his hard cock. The salty, earthy flavor of his skin. The way he moans my name and jerks, his climax spilling down my throat. There's something so powerful about being on my knees. I'm not here because he commands it. I'm here because I want it, and when I'm on my knees, he still worships me.

With a demure wipe of my mouth, I crawl forward and kneel above my husband's face. I'm soaking wet. Aching. And ready to sit on my throne.

I torture us both, hovering mere millimeters above his mouth. His tongue snakes out to lap me, but as he skims my lips, I raise myself out of his reach. A rough growl emanates from the depths of his chest.

"You want to taste me, Bear?"

"Yes."

"You want me to ride your face?"

"Fuck, yes."

"Ask me nicely."

"Can I taste you?"

"Ask me." I tease my lower lips against his mouth, then pull away. "To ride your face. And say please."

"Goddammit," he murmurs from between gritted teeth. "Blakely Brooks, please ride my fucking face until you're squirting down my throat."

Heat sets all my nerves alight. I'm a throbbing, needy mess. But I'm still in charge. It just happens we want the same thing. With a sigh of relief, I lower myself, zero concern about smothering him. Hudson's made it clear: if I don't sit, he will quit.

Hudson's tongue delves into my pussy, licking at me as though he's a man dying of thirst in the desert who stumbled into a watery oasis. His tongue flicks over my clit, and I grind against his face, circling my hips as he sucks, licks, and pleasures me. Through my lust-filled haze, I recognize the telltale sound of creaking wood as he strains against his restraints. It's incredible, the way this man shows his love. Hudson knows what I like, the places to suck, nip, and lick for ultimate satisfaction. It isn't long before *I'm* gripping the headboard to steady myself as the first waves surge through me. He hums and rolls his tongue, and that's it. I'm out. My orgasm charges through my body and onto his lips. I throw my head back as I pant his name.

I crumple, my limbs like putty, melting into the bed next to him as we both catch our breath. I smooth his hair and gently trace his face before undoing the knots and massaging his wrists, forearms, and shoulders.

"Change of plans?"

"Yep. I need your hands on me."

He raises one eyebrow.

"I want you on top of me, in me." I want our bodies locked together, his lips on my skin.

Hudson chuckles. "You're in charge." With that, he pounces forward, forcing me back and pinning my body beneath his. He kisses me, his tongue twisting with mine, the taste of myself fresh on his lips. I moan around his mouth; I love when he kisses me after making me come that way.

"Next time, I'll tie you up, but I'm going to knot you from

shoulder to thighs. You look so beautiful when you're bound for me," he mutters, his lips burning a trail down my neck.

"Yes." I take his hands, leading them over the peaks and valleys of my body. His calloused touch electrifies my senses, and when he adds his mouth to the mix, snagging a nipple in his teeth, I can't help but writhe beneath him. He teases me for a moment more before breaking away and moving to kneel between my legs, splaying me out wide. He sits on his heels, his eyes tracing me before locking onto my center.

"Do you have any idea how you look, spread open like this?"

"Do you like it?" I ask, my voice raspy and low.

"Yes, you're the most beautiful woman I've ever seen." Hudson takes one of my legs and brings it to his shoulder, kissing my ankle. The other he wraps around his hip. Then, without another word, he plunges into me. My eyes close, and I mewl in delight as Hudson pounds into me. His teeth graze my ankle, and his fingers dig into my calf and thigh. "It feels so fucking good when you take my cock like the goddess you are."

A strangled plea slips from my lips. A hedonistic battle cry for *more, harder.*

He obeys my command, placing his hands on my hips, pulling me against him, relentless in his goal of bringing us both pleasure. Fuck, he's handsome. A living god. His muscles flex, his eyes close, and his jaw tenses as he pounds into me. I bring my hand to my clit, tracing circles around the sensitive bundle of nerves.

"Please."

Hudson's eyes snap open, and he bats my hand away, his thumb applying the steady pressure I need. All the while, he never breaks his thunderous pace. His glittering green eyes fasten on mine, and the intimacy of the moment proves to be my undoing. A lifetime flashes in those eyes—my lifetime with him.

I scream his name, and my pussy clenches around his cock. My entire body trembles, goosebumps erupt on my flesh, but he continues thrusting into me, working me through my orgasm. A moment later, he pants my name, and the thick, hot burst of his cum rushes into me.

Hudson collapses on top of me, our bodies still joined, my pussy pulsing around his cock. His weight is like my favorite weighted blanket, settling deep in my bones. I kiss his forehead; the salty-sweet sweat he worked up during our lovemaking tingles on my tongue. Content, spent, and limp, I tangle my fingers in his hair, massaging his scalp as he lies on top of me, panting.

"I love you, Bear. So much."

"Not as much as I love you, Spitfire."

I pinch his nipple. "That's not true."

Hudson makes a *hmm* sound as he slips out of bed. He sends me off to pee while he lights the fire. Once I'm done, he carries me back to our bed. Then he pushes his soft cock between my legs. He loves to sleep like this, buried inside me, especially after we've fucked hard. So many nights, I fall asleep this way, only to be woken by him gently fucking me or his face and fingers buried in my pussy, showing me how much he loves me.

It's not so bad being Mrs. Blakely Brooks.

Despite being as close as two people can get, I snuggle deeper into his arms. "Remember the first day we met?"

He snorts. "Like I could ever forget."

"You were such an ass."

"You were such a brat." His lips brush over my skin. "Still are. But I wouldn't change it for anything."

"You swore up and down you wouldn't give me any special treatment."

"And you had me breaking all my rules on day one. Should've known then you'd own every part of me."

"You really should've."

The sun has long set, and the sounds of the forest at night and the popping of the fire mix to form a soothing lullaby. This is our life—a wonderful existence I never expected. All because of my beautiful outdoorsman and a little cabin in the woods.

The End

dick-tionary

If you want to skip straight to the spicy parts, or if you want to avoid them entirely, here are the chapters that contain explicit sex. Some of these are small scenes, some are long and detailed. Take care of your needs!

Chapter 1: v/p scene between MCs
Chapter 7: solo masturbation scene
Chapter 12: solo masturbation scene
Chapter 15: v/p scene between MCs
Chapter 16: oral scene between MCs
Chapter 17: v/p scene between MCs, includes light spanking
Chapter 19: 69, toy usage, light anal play
Chapter 21: dry humping to completion
Chapter 22: oral scene
Chapter 24: v/p scene between MCs, includes light spanking
Chapter 25: v/p scene between MCs
Chapter 27: v/p scene between MCs
Epilogue: v/p scene between MCs, includes light rope play

acknowledgments

J and A thank you for making friendship bracelets, counting stickers, and keeping me fed.

Ellie, you are an amazing author and CP, and I am so thankful we stumbled into each other's orbits. Your writing is like a warm blanket on a chilly night.

Taylor thank you for being fresh eyes and support as I brought this story to life.

Tiff thank you for the cookies, the love, and for being a real life cheerleader for my books.

A huge massive thank you to the talented ladies in *The Smuttering,* who listened to me doubt myself and talked me out of deleting everything too many times to count. Thank you for making me laugh, providing visual treats, and being there when I need you. I am so thankful y'all let me tag along.

To my betas: Thank you for your thoughts, feedback, and emoji reactions. You helped make this book better!

My amazing ARC readers, I so appreciate you sharing your thoughts about Roughing It out in the world.

To Flying Pig and Luna Literacy: Thank you for helping get word about Roughing It out there to new readers.

Finally, to all of you reading this now, THANK YOU. From the bottom of my heart, I hope you love the story, the characters, and the way they love each other.

also by albany archer

Keep This Between Us (Davis Designs Book 1)

www.ingramcontent.com/pod-product-compliance
Lightning Source LLC
Chambersburg PA
CBHW070307310726
48976CB00005B/1609